THE DARK HEROINE

DINNER WITH A VAMPIRE

Abigail Gibbs was born and raised in deepest, darkest Devon. She is currently studying for a BA in English at the University of Oxford and considers herself a professional student, as the real world is yet to catch up with her. Her greatest fear is blood and she is a great advocate of vegetarianism, which logically led to the writing of her first novel, *Dinner With A Vampire*. At age fifteen, she began posting serially online under the pseudonym Canse12, and after three years in the Internet limelight, set her sights towards total world domination. She splits her time between her studies, stories and family, and uses coffee to survive all three.

ABIGAIL GIBBS

THE DARK HEROINE

DINNER WITH A VAMPIRE

HARPER
Voyager

HarperVoyager
An imprint of HarperCollins*Publishers*
77–85 Fulham Palace Road,
Hammersmith, London W6 8JB

www.harpercollins.co.uk

A Paperback Original 2012
1

A catalogue record for this book
is available from the British Library

ISBN: 978 0 00 750367 4

This novel is entirely a work of fiction.
The names, characters and incidents portrayed in it are
the work of the author's imagination. Any resemblance to
actual persons, living or dead, events or localities is
entirely coincidental.

Set in Meridien by Palimpsest Book Production Limited,
Falkirk, Stirlingshire

Printed and bound in Great Britain by
Clays Ltd, St Ives plc

MIX
Paper from
responsible sources
FSC **FSC C007454**
www.fsc.org

FSC™ is a non-profit international organisation established to promote
the responsible management of the world's forests. Products carrying the
FSC label are independently certified to assure consumers that they come
from forests that are managed to meet the social, economic and
ecological needs of present and future generations,
and other controlled sources.

Find out more about HarperCollins and the environment at
www.harpercollins.co.uk/green

For wattpad.com.
To the team for providing a place to share.
To each and every member who read, voted, nagged
and criticized. You shaped this story.

To Joanne and Terran, and lastly, to Soraya. You reached out to
a child across the world and gave her the encouragement she
needed. You started this journey.

O Rose, thou art sick!
The invisible worm
That flies in the night,
In the howling storm,

Has found out thy bed
Of crimson joy:
And his dark secret love
Does thy life destroy.

– The Sick Rose, William Blake

ONE

Violet

Trafalgar Square is probably not the best place to stand at one o'clock in the morning. In fact, it is probably not the best place to be if you are alone at any time of the night.

The shadow of Nelson's Column in Trafalgar Square loomed above as I shivered, the cool air of the July night rushing between the buildings. I shuddered again, pulling my coat tightly around myself, seriously beginning to regret wearing a skimpy black dress – my choice of wardrobe for the evening. *The sacrifices I make for a good night out.*

Jumping as a pigeon fluttered down beside my feet, I scanned the empty streets for any sign of my friends. So much for getting a 'late night snack'. The sushi bar was only a two-minute walk away; twenty minutes had passed. I rolled my eyes, in no doubt that some guys were in their knickers by now. *Good for them. Why would they have to worry about little old Violet Lee?*

I walked towards the benches, sheltered by the sparse and gloomy canopy of trees. I sighed as I rubbed my hands across my knees to try to get the blood flowing, bitterly regretting the decision to wait behind.

Taking one last glance around the square, I pulled out my mobile, hitting speed dial. It continued to ring until, eventually, the voicemail cut in.

'Hi, this is Ruby. I can't answer right now, so leave a message after the tone. Lovage!'

I groaned in frustration as the tone beeped. 'Ruby, where the hell are you? If you're with that guy, I swear I'll kill you! It's bloody freezing out here! As soon as you get this, call back.'

I ended the call, slipping the phone back into the inside pocket of my coat, knowing that my efforts were likely to be in vain as she probably wouldn't listen to the message for days. Rubbing my hands together and drawing my knees up to my chest in a bid to keep warm, I debated whether I should just get a cab home. But if Ruby did turn up, I'd be in trouble. Resigning myself to a long wait, I laid my head on my knees in the quiet, watching the orange haze that coated the city of London.

Opposite, late-night drinkers disappeared into a side-alley, stumbling along until their raucous laughter was lost in the darkness. A few minutes later, a red double-decker bus with the words 'Visit the National Gallery' splashed across its side appeared from behind the very attraction it was advertising. It followed the road around the square before disappearing amidst the maze of Victorian buildings that dominated the city centre. As it left, the dull hum of far-away London traffic seemed to fade away into silence with it.

I wondered which of the two boys we had met tonight had struck lucky with Ruby. I felt a pang of regret, wishing I could be as carefree and, well, *loose* as she was. But I couldn't. Not after Joel.

More minutes passed and I began to feel uneasy. Nobody had drunkenly stumbled through for a while and the cold night air was descending like a blanket around my exposed legs. I glanced about for a taxi but the roads were empty and the square deserted, save for the light skimming over the surface of the water in the two fountains either side of the central column.

I pulled my phone back out, thinking I could call my father and ask him to pick me up, when something flickered in the corner of my eye. Almost dropping my phone I jerked up, heart in my mouth, scanning the square for any sign of movement.

Nothing. I shook my head, the panic waning. *It was probably just a pigeon*, I assured myself. I began to dial my home number, the cold numbing my fingers, though I glanced up every few seconds, willing my breathing to slow.

But no, something *had* moved.

A shadow had flitted across one of the huge fountains, too quick for my eyes to discern a shape. The square, on the other hand, was deserted, save for a few panicked pigeons taking flight. I shook my head, pressing my phone to my ear. The line crackled, ringing feebly and breaking every few seconds.

I tapped my foot impatiently. 'C'mon . . .' I muttered, glancing at the screen. *Full signal.*

My eyes wandered as the number dialled and dialled, lingering on Nelson's Column, towering hundreds of feet in the air. The blazing floodlights that lit up the statue at the very top flickered, like a flame in the breeze. They stilled again, as intense and bright as before.

I shivered, but not from the cold. I prayed someone would answer the phone, but the line crackled and with one last pitiful ring, went dead. I stared at it, wide-eyed, before adrenaline began to rush into my veins and instinct cut in. I slipped off one of my heels as my eyes glued themselves to the column, watching in disbelief as the shadow I had seen just moments before swept across the statue, vanishing from view as quickly as it had come. Fumbling with the last strap, I wrenched the other shoe from my foot and snatched both up in my hands. I started forward. But no sooner had I taken a few steps than I froze, rooted to the spot.

A gang of men, clothed in brown coats and carrying long, sharpened canes were descending the steps. Their grim, weather-beaten faces were dark and heavily scarred, every brow set in an unwavering, determined line. Their heavy footfall rang in my ears, pounding out an uneven march on the paving as they moved ever closer.

Stunned, I shrank back into the shadows, silently crouching behind the bench. Hardly daring to breathe, I tried to make myself as small as possible whilst inching towards the edge of the square.

The man at the head of the group barked something and the men spread out, creating a line as wide as the square, stretching from one fountain to the other. There were easily thirty of them. As one, they came to a halt just in front of the column, only their coats moving as the wind billowed in the fabric behind them.

Not even the trees made a sound. Every one of the men looked straight ahead with unwavering concentration, watching and waiting. I glanced towards the top of the column, but the statue was bathed in light as usual, the only shadows being those cast by the men and the trees that I sheltered under. A few leaves drifted languidly to the ground, settling on the bench beside me.

Then it happened.

The square came alive in a frenzy of movement and out

of nowhere something sprung from behind the trees, soaring high above my head and landing without so much as a stumble on the hard stone, about ten feet away. I blinked, not believing that my eyes had seen a person, but before I could take a second look, whatever it was had disappeared.

Taken as much by surprise as I was, the line of men staggered back a few paces in panic. Those at the very end of the line edged inwards, order only restored as the man I presumed to be the leader raised a hand. From his coat he pulled a silvery baton, one end sharpened to a lethal point. With a flick of his wrist, it became twice as long. He spun the baton a few times, as though admiring the way it glinted when it caught the light. His lips curled into a satisfied smile and he stilled, waiting once more.

The leader was quite young – twenty at the most. Tall and lean, his face was free of scars unlike those around him. His hair, cut short, was bleached so it was almost white, a stark contrast to his leathery coat and tanned skin. His smile widened as his eyes darted towards the figure that had landed so close to me. I drew in a sharp breath, expecting him to spot me, but his attention was whipped away as a man stepped out from around the fountains.

No, *not a man*, but a boy, not much older than I was. His eyes were sunken, skin ashen pale and almost translucent, pulled taut over hollow cheeks. He too was tall, but beneath his tight shirt I could see the rippling trace of muscles. His arms were just as pale but covered in red blotches, as though he had been badly sunburnt. His lips were stained a bright, bloody red, as was his hair, which was spiked and unkempt.

I blinked, and he was gone. I searched the square as others appeared, all with the same pale skin and haggard gaze. They circled the group in the middle, their faces twisted into a mixture of amusement and disgust. They appeared from nowhere, darting from one side to the other at inhuman speed, vanishing and emerging within a second. I rubbed my eyes, convinced that I was just too tired to focus. They couldn't be moving *that* fast.

The boy with the flaming hair appeared again, leaning against the fountain as though standing at the bar. Near him stood a young man with sandy-blond hair who I thought I recognized as the one who had sprung from behind me.

In total there were five of them, casually herding the group of brown-coats into the centre like animals. The tanned men's faces were contorted into a picture of fear and loathing as they broke their ranks, stumbling back a few steps with their stakes lowered. Only the leader remained unmoved, his smile becoming a smirk as he clasped his baton to his side and jerked his head upwards.

Suddenly, a man dropped from the column – all one hundred and sixty-nine feet of it. He plummeted faster and faster towards the ground, surely to his death. But I watched, amazed, as he landed nimbly on the stone, dropping to a crouch in front of the gang's leader.

The square stilled and the leader, for the first time, stirred. 'Kaspar Varn, such a pleasure to see you again,' he said, his voice tinged with an accent I couldn't place.

The man, Kaspar, straightened up, his face blank and unreadable. He was as tall as the leader but his bearing and well-built, muscled stature made the other man seem a lot smaller.

'The pleasure's all mine, Claude,' he answered coolly, his gaze sweeping right to left. He gave a curt nod to the sandy-haired boy and I managed to steal a look at him.

He, like the others, had pallid, slightly sallow skin, devoid of any colour or blush. His dark, almost black hair was streaked with shades of brown and was windswept, his fringe falling across his forehead. If anything, his features were gaunter than any of the others; his face shadowy as though he had not slept for days.

Perhaps he doesn't sleep, a voice in my head muttered. As the thought crossed my mind, he seemed to look past the sandy-haired boy, his brow creasing a fraction. I held my breath, realizing he was looking directly at me. But if he saw me, he chose to pay no attention as he turned back to the leader, his face clearing and becoming impassive again.

'What do you want, Claude? I have no time to waste on you and the Pierre clan,' the darker haired man said, addressing the other.

Claude's smile widened, running a single finger down the sharp edge of his stake. 'Yet you came.'

Kaspar waved his hand dismissively. 'We were hunting anyway; it was no great distance.'

I shuddered. *What is there to hunt in a city?*

Claude chuckled darkly. 'As are we.'

In a flash, he brought the stake up to the other man's chest, thrusting forward. But it never found its mark: Kaspar reached up and brushed it away. It seemed to take no effort; he hardly blinked, but Claude lurched backwards as though a truck had hit him. The stake clattered to the ground, the metallic ring echoing in the silence.

Claude staggered, tripped, then clumsily regained his balance and straightened himself up. His narrow eyes darted towards the stake and then back to the man stood in front of him. His lips curled back into a smile.

'Tell me, Kaspar, how is your mother?'

Out of nowhere, the pale man's hand snatched forward, seizing Claude's throat. Horrified, I watched as his eyes bulged and his feet left the floor, the colour draining from his face. He coughed and spluttered, his feet writhing in midair. His hands grappled with Kaspar's wrists, but he soon began to give up as slowly, agonizingly slowly, he turned purple.

Without warning, the pale man let go. Claude crumpled to the ground, gasping for breath, feverishly rubbing his neck. I breathed a sigh of relief, but the man collapsed on the ground didn't. His whimpers became pleas and his face seemed to show some sort of recognition as he stared up at the maddened face of Kaspar. He shuffled back, squirming and grabbing the hem of a coat one of his men was wearing. The man did not move.

Kaspar's chest was heaving and a deranged, sick expression was twisted onto his face. He lowered his hand, clenching it into a tight fist.

'Do you have any last words, Claude Pierre?' he growled, the menace in his voice barely restrained.

The leader drew in several long, shaky breaths. He wiped away the sweat and tears on his sleeve, bracing himself. 'I hope you and your bloody Kingdom burn in hell.'

Kaspar's lips widened into a smirk. 'Wishful thinking.'

With that, he pounced forward, his head ducking behind Claude's neck. There was a sickening crack.

I gagged. My hands instinctively clapped to my mouth as bile rose in my throat. With it, came fear. Tears leaked from my eyes, but I knew that if I made any noise I would be next.

Self-preservation kicked in as Claude's lifeless body dropped to the stone. I was witness to a murder and I had watched enough of the six o'clock news to know what happened to witnesses who stuck around. *I have to get out of here. I have to tell someone.*

If you ever get out of here, said that same, niggling voice.

I hated to admit it, but it was right: all hell had broken loose.

The pale skins jumped onto the men, a huge, bloody fight breaking out, if you could call it a fight. The men barely had time to use their stakes to defend themselves against these killers: like lambs to the slaughter, their tanned bodies dropped to the floor, blood splattering everywhere.

My stomach clenched and I swallowed hard as I felt burning in my throat. Unable to look away, I watched as Kaspar yanked yet another of the men towards him. My mind told me he must have a weapon; my eyes saw none. Instead, he sank his mouth into the flesh above the man's collar and tore. I caught a glimpse of twisted sinew before the man collapsed to the ground, shrieking. His killer followed him, dropping to one knee and wrapping his lips around the wound, cradling the man in his arms. Drops of blood pooled on the stone beneath them and into the cracks between the paving. My eyes followed it as it seeped outwards, forming a bloody grid, joining with the blood of another man, and another, until my eyes had risen to take in the full carnage they had created.

Every one of the tanned men was dead, or dying, their necks broken or bleeding; several had sunken to the bottom of the fountains, staining the water a grim red. One man near me lay on his back, his head so contorted his ear rested on his shoulder.

Six teenagers had just slaughtered thirty men.

I whimpered on the bench, drawn as far into the shadows as I could possibly get, praying to every deity alive that they wouldn't see me.

'Kaspar, are we going to clean this one up or just leave it?' said the one who stood nearest the fountain, even his fiery red hair dull compared to the water he swirled his fingers through.

'We'll leave it as a little message for any other hunters

who think they can cross us,' he replied. 'Scum,' he added, spitting on the nearest limp body.

His voice had lost its cool and had been replaced with a deep, satisfied sneer, and anger began to override the fear as I watched him carelessly kick the arm of another dying man out of his way, causing him to let out one last meagre moan.

'Jerk,' I breathed.

He froze.

So did I. I held my breath, stomach knotted. *He can't possibly have heard me from across the square. That's just not possible.* But slowly, almost leisurely, he turned so that he faced me.

'Well, what do we have here?' He chuckled darkly, voice carrying, his lips curling into that same cruel smirk.

Instinct worked faster than my mind and before I knew it I had jumped up, sprinting my way across the square. Leaving my heels far behind, my feet thudded against the cold stone as I ran, literally, for my life. The nearest police station wasn't too far, and I would bet on the fact I knew London better than them.

'And where do you think you're going, Girly?'

I inhaled sharply as I crashed into something hard and cold, so cold I sprung back from it instantly. Standing right in front of me was the dark-haired man. I recoiled, eyes darting from the spot he had been stood in before to where he stood now. *That really isn't possible.* I backed away, my hands grabbing at the air behind me as though they expected some magical saviour to appear. He didn't even flinch, as though a girl running into his chest was an everyday occurrence.

'N-nothing. I was just going to . . . err . . .' I stuttered, my eyes cycling between the bodies, the man and the road: my only possible escape route.

'Going to report us?' he questioned. He already knew the answer, but my eyes widened guiltily and he leaned in so close that I could see that his eyes were a vivid shade of emerald. His voice lowered to a whisper. 'I'm afraid you can't do that.'

Close up, I could not help but notice how staggeringly handsome he was. Something deep in the pit of my stomach stirred. I recoiled again, repulsed.

'Like hell, I can't!' I yelled, ducking around him and making another frantic getaway. Running, I glanced behind me. To my astonishment, none of them pursued me. Spurred on I kept going, the tiniest spark of hope striking into life in my heart. I was just metres away from the road when I stole another look over my shoulder.

This time he seemed to give an exasperated sigh and I didn't allow myself to watch any longer, not wanting to slow down. My feet were just about to step out onto the road when I was yanked back, a hand clutching at the collar of my coat. I teetered, fighting for balance whilst also fighting the hand that restrained me. I wrestled, kicking and screaming, but it was no use – he held me with ease.

Turning around with my eyes ablaze and sounding a lot braver than I felt, I screeched out a threat: 'You have ten seconds to get off me, freak, before I kick you so hard in the bollocks that you'll wish you were never born!'

He chuckled again. 'You're a feisty one, aren't you?'

As he laughed, I caught sight of his upper canines, both perfectly white. Perfectly white, and tapered to an unnatural point.

Hunting. Hunters.

Something in my brain registered that this was not normal. Not even close to normal, but just as quickly, rational thought dismissed the conclusion my mind was rapidly forming.

Struggling again, I tried to get close enough to kick him, but his grip tightened on my collar, holding me firmly away.

'You saw all of that.' His words were chillingly cold. It was a statement, not a question, but I answered it anyway.

'What do you think?' I retorted, pouring as much sarcasm into my voice as I could muster.

'I think you're going to have to come with us,' he growled, taking my elbow and beginning to drag me away. I opened my mouth, but he was quicker. He clamped a hand down on my lips. 'Scream and I swear I will kill you.'

And, thrashing and biting, I was dragged away; dragged away from the gruesome bloodbath these pale monsters had created.

TWO

Violet

We flew through the streets, speeding to a sprint as we left the square. Kaspar had a firm grip on my wrist, tugging me along in his wake. His fingernails cut deep into my arm and I felt them tearing open my skin, gouging out considerable amounts of flesh. I winced – it was like falling over and scraping my arm in slow motion – but did not say anything: I would not give him the satisfaction. We weaved from alley to alley, Kaspar at the front, leading us down roads I never knew existed. Already, I could hear the whining sirens of police cars and the side streets were awash with flashing blue lights.

'Bloody police,' Kaspar snarled. 'Wait here,' he ordered. He thrust me forward, straight into the chest of one of the other men. 'Fabian, look after Girly here.'

For the second time that night I hit something rigid. He too was cold and I sprung back like I had been stung, toppling over into the gutter beside the pavement. But I never reached the ground. I looked down at my arm, caught in midair by a hand almost as pale as my own.

'Don't fall,' a soft voice said. I followed the arm up, dazed, to find the smiling face of the boy who had jumped over me in Trafalgar Square, sky-blue eyes twinkling down at me with some sort of amusement. For a brief, ludicrous moment I admired his fair, untidy hair and muscled chest, just visible beneath the unbuttoned collar of his shirt, before my mind caught up and I pulled my hand away, horrified at my thoughts. Unperturbed, however, he carried on.

'I'm Fabian,' he said, holding the same hand back out.

I shrunk away, rubbing my hands and wrists on my coat where his blood-tainted hands had touched me. He frowned, eyeing me as I backed away, his hand left hanging in the air.

'We won't hurt you, you know.'

Four other pairs of eyes watched, tensed and waiting for me to run. But I had given up hope of that. Instead, I was relying on the fact that this Kaspar would be gone long enough for a passing police car to spot us.

'That back there' – he gestured along the street – 'was necessary. I know it doesn't look that way but you have to believe me when I say it needed to be done.'

I stopped. 'Necessary? It's not necessary, it's wrong. Don't patronize me, I'm not a child.'

The words were out of my mouth before I had time to think about anything beyond wanting to buy myself time. My hands tightened around my wrists and I stopped rubbing. They seemed shocked that I had found my voice and Fabian's eyes darted behind me every now and then.

'Then how old are you, one who knows so much about morality?' He cocked his head to one side and I closed my mouth, hesitant about whether to tell them but glad they had ignored the rest of my outburst. 'Well?'

I bit on my lip. 'Seventeen,' I murmured.

'I didn't know seventeen-year old girls wore such short dresses these days.'

Jumping at the sound of a conceited voice behind me, I spun around, my dark hair whipping behind me, heavy fringe settling over my eyes. Kaspar was leaning against a lamppost with his fingers in his pockets and his thumbs sticking out, a grotesque smirk tugging at his lips again. His eyes raked my form and I wrapped the coat tightly around myself to try to cover the flimsy dress.

His smirk widened. 'Blushing really clashes with those purple eyes of yours, Girly.'

I flinched at his reference to my eyes – an odd shade of blue and the reason behind my name. I should have been used to the mockery. Between having freak eyes, a matching name and being a devout vegetarian, I had my work cut out dodging jokes. I opened and closed my mouth several times. But as my eyes naturally averted, his smirk vanished.

'Go!'

The others had already disappeared, swallowed by the darkness of an alley, whilst I was thrown violently sideways, landing behind a line of bins. I looked around, dazed. The only light came from a seedy bar further down the alleyway, tucked between a fire escape and an overflowing skip. Heaving for breath, winded, I began to clamber to my feet, but a hand clamped down on my mouth, the other yanking me fully up as I was half-dragged, half-carried along the alleyway, feet coated in grime from the paving.

Just as we rounded the corner at the end of the alley, blue lights illuminated the brick walls. A drunkard, slumped against the skip, shirked away, moaning loudly and muttering curses even I reddened at. But his groans could not drown out the growing sound of sirens, rising to a crescendo just a few streets away.

'You have to run faster,' Kaspar told me. The panic was absent from his voice but it was written in every other feature of his face. Every face was the same. I recoiled.

'Are you fucking crazy? Why should I run faster for you? You murderer!' The words were pouring from my mouth, unchecked – the adrenalin was back and it was banishing the fear.

His eyes flashed dangerously and for a moment I thought they lost their emerald gleam. 'We're not murderers.' Though he did not raise his voice nor change his tone it still sent shivers running up my spine, making my hairs stand on end.

'Then what are you and why did you kill those men?'

The question hung in the air; nobody offered a reply. Instead, I was pushed onwards, tugged from alley to alley, changing direction as the police cordoned off more and more of the city, working just a road behind us as we fled the centre.

London was coming alive. Every window reflected cyan blue as the protective ring sprawled outwards.

'Come on!' Kaspar hissed, tugging on my sleeve.

'I can't!' I screeched. And I really couldn't. A side stitch clutched at my ribs and my breaths were coming in short, sharp rasps.

'Tough,' he said coolly.

'I can't b-breathe,' I gasped, trying to do exactly that. A few tears leaked from my eyes, which I hastily wiped away. 'I'm going to pass out and die or something!'

'Oh, and what a loss that would be,' he muttered dryly, rolling his eyes.

'I didn't volunteer for this!' I winced, dropping to my knees, wondering why he had gone to the effort of keeping me alive if my death didn't bother him.

'No, you didn't. But you're a part of it now and how I

see it, Girly . . .' He yanked me up by my collar. 'You don't have any choice. Now go.'

I did not move, still rubbing my chest. 'My name is not "Girly"! It's Violet!'

Like a shot he was just inches away from me, forcing me against the wall as his hand wrapped around my neck. A single finger was pressed against my vein, stroking it.

'And I'm the fucking Prince!' he snarled, grip tightening. My eyes widened and I struggled under him but his grip just tightened further. I closed my eyes, not wanting to see his face, so close to mine and reeking of blood. A single image flooded my mind behind my closed eyes: the lifeless body of Claude Pierre, crumpled and bleeding on the stone flag.

'I could snap that pretty neck of yours in two with less effort than it would take for you to squeal,' he whispered in my ear. 'So I suggest that you do what we say, because you can't outrun us and the police won't stop us.'

I didn't know what the hell he meant by 'Prince' but I believed the rest of it. The sincerity in his voice was equal to the malice. I bowed my head, beaten.

'Better,' he murmured. He grabbed my hand and tugged. As I whirled around to follow him, I saw a man sprinting into the end of the street. His dull beige suit looked odd when compared to the narrow streets and sordid bars of the back alleys. His feet slowed and he came to a stop, staring straight at us, his hand shooting up to his head, almost as if in defeat. I inhaled sharply. I knew him. He worked with my father. Or rather he worked *for* my father.

He took a few hesitant steps forward, his eyes resting on me. For a brief moment, I met his gaze, but he averted his eyes and backed away. With a raised hand, he gestured behind him as policemen and -women rounded the corner. Their steps slowed and they came to a halt, watching us with fear burning in their eyes as Kaspar turned, allowing his gaze to roam across the officers, almost daring them. He exhaled and squared his shoulders, pulling me close to his chest. I tried to fight him and yell out for help, but he twisted my arm behind my back, leaving me yelping as though daggers were being thrust into my side where the stitch was. Entwining his arm around my waist, he backed away a few paces, dragging me with him.

He bent down to my ear and snarled. 'Too slow.' Without another word, he swept me up in his arms and flung me over his shoulder. I started to protest, pummelling his back, but he didn't seem to notice as everything became a blur. The buildings were flashing by and when I looked up, the crowd had gone. In fact, we were not even in the same street. My heart sunk. He had been right. They had not chased us. *Why had they not tried to stop us?*

In minutes, we had left the chaos behind. I did not want to know how fast we were moving – all I knew was that it was fast enough to make my head spin. I closed my eyes to keep my head and breathing in check, but just a few seconds later my feet made contact with the ground and I landed in a heap at Kaspar's shoes beside two very expensive-looking cars.

I blinked, convinced I was seeing double. They were identical, from the perfectly polished black of the body to the heavily tinted windows. Even the number plates were similar, except for one letter.

Who the hell are these people? Handsome and brilliantly rich; their fatal flaw was murder. I swallowed as those thoughts faded. I knew enough of London to know the hallmarks of organized crime. *Yet the police didn't stop us.*

The sound of distant sirens broke the quiet of the side-street and somebody behind me picked me up, bundling me into the backseat of the nearest car. He slammed the door and walked around, getting in the other side. I recognized him as the one who shared the same eye colour as Kaspar – emerald. Kaspar and Fabian got in the front of the same car, with Kaspar driving.

'Put your seatbelt on,' ordered the guy sitting next to me. I ignored him, sitting as rigid as a plank, with my arms folded across my chest. He gave an exasperated sigh and reached across, grabbing my belt.

'Freak,' I muttered. The boy chuckled.

'The name is Cain, not 'freak'. I'm his younger brother,' he revealed, nodding in the direction of Kaspar, which explained the uncanny likeness. 'What did you say your name was?'

'Violet. Violet Lee,' I muttered and with that went silent. Gazing out the window I could see yet more police cars pass by. My stomach flipped as I saw a policeman glance over at us. His eyes locked with mine for a brief moment, before he turned away, as if he hadn't seen me at all.

We were leaving the city behind now, already out of the congestion zone. As we started hitting the open roads, I felt the car speed up and I glanced at the speed dial. It was hitting one hundred. I felt a familiar thrill in my stomach, but for once, it wasn't welcome. My head was pounding and throbs of pain were still shooting down my side. I pressed my hands to my ribs and it eased a little, but not much.

I curled up on the seat, drawing my knees up to my chest, leaning my head against the cool window. My eyes were drooping and my body was begging for the release of sleep, but I didn't want to think about what would happen if I allowed myself to drop off. Holding back the tears, I mechanically began analyzing my situation with as much detachment as I could muster.

I had just witnessed the mass murder of thirty men in the centre of London. I had been kidnapped by six fast and strong guys who did not seem to want to kill me – yet. I did not know where the hell I was going, who the hell these people were, and what the hell was going to happen or how long it would take for someone to notice I was missing.

I began to contemplate jumping from the door, but just as a plan had started to form there was a click and the central locking turned on. A dry sob escaped my lips.

Joining the deserted M25, we left the city I loved behind. The scenery gradually changed from city to suburban and eventually to sprawling fields, dotted with the occasional town or village. The signs we passed read Kent and I began to wonder whether they might be heading to the port at Dover to get to France. A glimmer of hope began to ignite in my heart. *There was no way they would get through the port.* But that hope dwindled as we veered not south, but north, towards Rochester.

Another sob escaped and I saw Kaspar glaring into the rear-view mirror. His brother, Cain, placed a hand on my shoulder and I stared at him, wide-eyed. He didn't look like a killer. He looked like a kid.

He smiled. In my mind, I heard a man shrieking.

I shrugged him off and turned into the seat, my hair forming a curtain, shielding me from view. I let my forehead rest against the window. Tears began to fall, unchecked, streaming down the glass and tracing patterns in my breath on the window. Wrapping my arms around my shoulders, I delved into my mind.

I knew what I had left behind. The question was: What was I going to find ahead?

THREE

Violet

An hour stuck in a car with three deranged killers was not my idea of fun. I couldn't sleep, for fear of what might happen. I couldn't talk because Mr Charming-went-out-the-window constantly reminded me that I was at his mercy and should therefore keep my mouth shut. I couldn't even look out the window, because it was too dark, so instead I had to listen to an animated conversation about someone called Amber von Hefner's tits. *Lovely.*

The sun was beginning to rise, and I glanced at my watch: an early birthday present from my father. *My father.* What would he and my mother do when they found out what had happened to me? What about Lily, my little sister? She was just thirteen; she should not have to deal with this.

But more crucial thoughts ran through my head: What would these strange killers do? Hold me to ransom? *'Silence' me?* It didn't even bear thinking about.

Looking back at my watch I realized it was half-past four in the morning and approaching sunrise, the first glimmers of light appearing. The fields were falling away, giving way to thick, dense forest. The road was becoming more winding, and fewer and fewer cars were passing by, as all the time we climbed up and up.

The road swept sharply around to the left as we passed through a large gatehouse. Huge, intricate iron-wrought gates were swung open, the Gothic arched windows guarded by gargoyles.

As we passed, I could have sworn I saw several faces peering from the windows, but before I could take a second glance we were again enclosed by the forest. The road continued to weave as the trees began thinning out, sunshine sporadically breaking through the needles of the many pines. A little further on, they gave way to leafy blooms and as the trees fell away, I gasped, hardly able to hold in my astonishment.

Before us, surrounded by a vast expanse of lawn, was a magnificent mansion, so large the forest seemed to quail at its presence. It was a strange mix of architecture: tall Gothic spires jutted up from the pale stone, hundreds upon hundreds of arched windows lining the three floors, whilst an elegant balcony protruded from the centre, resting on four pillars above the entrance. In the distance I could see rows of garages and stables; early morning light danced off lily pads floating on a lake at the foot of the grounds. The whole area was enclosed by trees of every shape and size before they gave way to the pines that made up the forest. Sheltering the mansion behind was a steep hill, also coated in forest.

We swept around the sandy drive, rounding a fountain and stopping outside the impressive entrance.

'So where's the drawbridge?' I breathed to myself. But instead of a drawbridge, wide steps led up to a set of marble double doors, which in turn were covered by the stone balcony.

My door was flung open and somebody grabbed me by the shoulders, yanking me off the seat.

'Get off me!' I snapped. He kept pulling, but I wriggled free and got out myself, despite the gravel that made my toes curl as I crossed it. He shrugged, walking off. Kaspar flicked the car keys at a boy, about my age. My eyes followed him, dressed in a black suit lined with emerald, as he jumped into one of the cars and started it, heading towards the garages.

I tore my eyes away as Kaspar grabbed my wrist and darted up the steps, the other five following behind. The double doors swung inward and my jaw dropped as we entered. A grand staircase circled the wall, made entirely of white marble. It led up to a large balcony and a passage, lit up by torch-like lamps fixed high up on the wall. Directly in front of me were a set of double doors, identical to the ones we had just passed through, but we were headed for a smaller door to my left. We passed a butler, who bowed.

'Your Highnesses. Lords. Sir . . . and Madam,' he added, clearly surprised at my appearance. I eyed him, unsure if what I had heard him just say was correct. He composed himself. 'A guest, Your Highness?'

Kaspar chuckled darkly. 'No, just fun.'

'Very good, Your Highness.'

Your Highness? Kaspar had mentioned before about being a Prince. But Britain had royalty already, unless he was some distant relative of the Queen. But I would know about that if he was. Everyone would know about a royal like *him*.

Kaspar made a vague sound of acknowledgement, before chuckling again. Suddenly, his attention left me and with one hard push, I found myself stumbling through the smaller door into a lavishly decorated living room. The walls were wood-panelled and the carpet a worn deep red; the same torches used in the entrance clung to brackets on the wall between huge oil portraits framed with silver. But the room held all the same modern trappings as any other: a plasma television was mounted on the wall and below it was an array of games consoles; remotes were scattered across a glass coffee table, which the boy with the dark hair and glasses slung his jacket over as he flopped down onto one of the leather sofas.

Kaspar walked over to the windows, where heavy drapes framed the glass, stretching from the high ceiling down to the window seats tucked behind the shutters. He yanked the material across and shut off the light, save for one thin strip that divided the room in two.

'Do you want me to take your coat?' a voice said from behind me and I drew in a sharp breath, startled. Glancing behind me, I saw it was Fabian. I shook my head. 'Sure?' he added, smiling, and I couldn't help but notice that with barely any light in the room, his eyes seemed to be just two pinpricks of brilliant blue framed by shadows, gaunt and hollow. I shirked away but took it off and handed it to him. A small, sympathetic smile crossed his lips and he gestured towards the sofas. I edged towards them, but decided to go no further. Instead, I continued to absorb the room and its occupants. There were six of them in total – Kaspar and his younger brother Cain, the blue-eyed boy Fabian and three others: the one with the flaming hair, another with what looked like fake glasses and the tall blond-haired guy who had pulled me from the car.

All of a sudden, Kaspar sprung forward and reached down into one of the pockets of my coat that Fabian was now holding. He pulled away and I realized that he held my phone.

'I'll keep that,' he said, smirking. He pressed unlock and began searching through.

'Don't!' I said, making a lunge for his hand. He side-stepped me, letting me stumble a few paces forward.

'Why, do you have something to hide?' he sneered. His fingers darted over the keyboard. 'Dirty messages from your boyfriend, perhaps?'

'No!' I dived at him, making a second attempt at grabbing it back. But he held it out of my reach. 'Give it back!' I yelled, jumping, trying to snatch it from his hand. He smirked, holding it higher.

'Who's Joel then?'

I went to grab his wrist but he snatched mine instead and twisted sharply, leaving me screeching. He let go, but I backed away, rubbing my wrists. With a chuckle he began reading, his voice becoming high-pitched and mocking.

'Hey, I was just wondering if we could meet up sometime? Just you and me. We need to talk about what I did. I miss you, babe. Text back, Joel.' He stopped and pouted. 'And aww, look, he even put a kiss at the end.' He was clearly enjoying himself. I scowled at him.

'Touched a nerve, did I?'

'Fuck off,' I muttered under my breath, not intending for him to hear.

'Happily, Girly, happily.'

'Kaspar,' Fabian hissed. He was glaring at Kaspar, his eyebrows lowered and eyes shooting daggers at the other man. They said nothing for a full minute until Kaspar tossed the phone at Fabian, who caught it, slipping it into his pocket. With a shrug, Kaspar leaned against the sofa and drummed his fingers, staring down at me with an amused expression.

'You saw too much and that is a problem for us. So you have a choice, Girly. You can become one of us or we can keep you here, indefinitely.'

I didn't stop to think: my mind was made up before he

had even finished his sentence. 'I'm not a murderer and never will be.'

Kaspar shrugged his shoulders. 'Then you will stay here until you agree to change. And don't get your hopes up of rescue. Nobody human can enter here without us knowing.'

I frowned. 'Human?'

'Yes. Human.' He turned to the others, smirking. 'So much better when they have no idea, don't you think?' There was a general murmur of agreement in all but Fabian.

'No idea about what?' I asked, cautious, glancing from one face to another.

'How old do you think I am?' Kaspar asked.

It seemed irrelevant but I answered, not wanting to shorten his temper. 'About nineteen?'

They turned to each other, chuckling. But this time they seemed to decide on something.

'Wrong. I'm one hundred and ninety-seven.'

I raised my eyebrows. 'Nobody lives that long—'

'My kind lives that long, and longer,' Kaspar interjected. 'Vampires, Girly.'

I shook my head as a chill passed down my spine. *They were mad.* I took a couple of steps back and laughed nervously, partly at the ludicrousness of what he had just said and partly because I was wondering what sort of mind game they were playing, and what response would keep me alive the longest. 'Is this some sick joke?'

Kaspar's smirk vanished. 'Am I laughing?' he answered, parting his mouth and allowing his lips to roll back over his gums. Resting on the plumpness of his bottom lip were two sharpened teeth, inconspicuous enough to pass in the dark, but now, in the light, it was clear as day that they were fangs.

'They're fake,' I said, staring at them. I sounded more defiant than I felt.

'Want to test?' Kaspar replied.

'Vampires don't exist,' I breathed, still shaking my head. 'You're just madmen.'

Before I could say another word, I was pressed up against the wall and Kaspar's lips were brushing against my neck. His chest heaved and I felt his strength, his power, his hunger. His breath did not warm my skin as the breath of any other person would, but chilled it, sending a trail of goose bumps across my shoulders and down my arms. I could feel my heart pounding out an uneven rhythm so frantically that the veins in my wrists pushed against my skin, becoming raised and mottled. Closing my eyes, I felt a gentle pressure as his razor-sharp teeth traced the line of the throbbing vein in my throat before one of his fangs snagged my skin and forced its way down; down between the layers of my skin, peeling one from another. A cry escaped my lips and my eyes flew open, my hands balling into fists, my fingers kneading my palm as I gritted my teeth. I was totally helpless. He was built to kill and I *really* wasn't.

He drew back, his body still pressed against mine, stopping my escape. He looked me straight in the eyes, and my breath caught. They were no longer emerald, but red.

'Listen carefully, Girly. I am not just any vampire. I am vampire royalty and you will do what I want. So be careful what you say, because you never know when I might be hungry.' He pulled away, and backed off. 'Join us or remain here. Your choice.'

I didn't hang around for him to say anything else. Scrabbling behind me, my hand searched for the door handle. I found it and pulled the door open, falling out of the room. I slammed it shut behind me, and leaned against the marble wall of the entrance hall. I doubled over as my breaths become shorter, hands on my knees, mind overloading.

Something warm trickled down my neck and I ran a finger down my skin. Drawing it back, I stared at my now red, moistened finger in horror.

They were not murderers; they were predators.

Something clicked in my mind and adrenalin gushed into my veins and trickled down my neck. I sprinted towards the doors, thanking the heavens the butler had gone.

I had to run, and I had to run now.

Brambles snatched at my skin and my bare feet throbbed in protest as thorns and rotting needles dug into my soles. But I pressed on. I knew it wouldn't be long before they realized I had fled and if they really were what they said they were – *vampires* – then they would know I had sought cover in the forest.

Twenty-four hours ago and I would have laughed at that thought. Vampires were works of fiction meant to frighten children. Vampires were mythical creatures girls drooled over. They weren't meant to be *real*.

Around me, the pines were becoming taller and the gaps between them smaller. The light that did filter down was patchy and tinged with an early morning mist, meaning that as I slowed and looked back, I couldn't see much beyond a few trees, let alone the path I thought I had been following.

How could people not know about their existence? How could six vampires waltz into the middle of London and feed on thirty men?

My throat burned and the dampness wrapping around my toes was almost welcomed. Blood trickled down my scratched legs and sweat mixed with grease to slick my fringe back, the tips sticking together. My dress had ridden up and one of the straps across my shoulder had frayed and was threatening to break.

Vampires. It's ridiculous. Yet . . .

I reached up and touched the spot where Kaspar had bitten me. It no longer bled and only a few flakes of dried blood remained, which I flicked away. But below that was smooth skin. I pressed my whole hand to my throat, feeling around for a wound. I frowned. There was nothing, other than a small indent in my skin where the bite should be.

A twig snapped. I whipped around; searching for the source of the sound, yet everything was still. My breaths became deep and short, my chest rising and falling in time with each one. A breeze trailed across my skin and I toyed with my hair, staring into the gloom.

Run, the voice in my mind whispered. Or perhaps it was just the wind weaving between the trees. *Run*, it repeated. But I stayed put, still peering between the trunks.

The silence was broken as the sound of something crashing through the undergrowth reached my ears. Dark outlines appeared in the mist and the voice in my mind erupted with cries to *run!*

I didn't need telling twice this time.

Fleeing, I glanced behind every few seconds, convinced that hands were grappling at my flesh, though they were not gaining. Yet I could hear them. Leaves rustled and branches groaned; the mist swirled as though something was moving – and moving fast – through it.

My feet carried me deeper into the forest, but I knew I could not keep this up for long. I was gulping down air but my lungs were empty and another side-stitch clung to my ribs. They would catch me and something told me they would not be so merciful this time.

All of a sudden, I broke free from the trees into a large clearing. I flung out my arms, teetering forward on my toes as I came to an abrupt stop. The earth crumbled beneath my feet and I shuffled back, raising my gaze and taking in my surroundings. I was standing on the banks of a small lake, its dark depths shimmering in the morning sun, a low mist clinging to the opposite bank.

An eerie silence descended. There was no crashing, no sound of footsteps, nothing. I took a lengthy look behind, searching the forest for any sign of the killers I was sure were following me.

The quiet was even more unsettling than the noise and I began to edge around, speeding up to a bolt as my hairs stood on end. As I started moving again, the crashing returned, definitely footsteps this time and they were following me around. As I sped up, so did they, and reaching the opposite bank, I realized they were circling on the other side too. I had nowhere to run.

I backed up as far as I dared, waiting, like prey herded into a trap.

Without warning, six figures leapt from amongst the trees, and in fright I scrabbled backwards, forgetting that I stood on the very edge of the bank, and with a shriek, I was sent floundering down into the water.

Before I even hit the surface I felt its chill and saw my skin turn an icy blue. As the water erupted around me, it poured into my still shrieking mouth. I coughed and spluttered, gulping down even more. My legs flailed and searched for the bottom, more resembling an octopus than a human being. Nevertheless, I broke the surface long enough to snatch a breath. But it wasn't long enough to scream as something that felt like seaweed wrapped around my ankle. With one yank, it pulled me back below the surface. Looking down, I realized it was a tentacle wrapped around my leg, and that I was face-to-face with what looked like a giant squid.

I groaned in my mind. *Why can't my life be normal?*

Panicking, I started attacking the tentacle, trying to pry it from my skin but the squid didn't seem to notice and just pulled me deeper. My lungs began to burn and scream for air and I realized there was nothing I could do but give up.

My mind became fuzzy as something white flashed in the corner of my eye. *A white light. How very original.* I vaguely recognized that it was moving and that its blurred outline resembled a body before my eyelids fluttered and then shut.

Kidnapped by a vampire, death by squid. How tragic.

FOUR

Kaspar

'Violet! Wake the hell up!' Fabian said, bending over her limp body and slapping her cheek. He raised his hand to hit her again when her eyes flew open, water spewing from her mouth. I caught sight of the fleshy roof of her mouth and her teeth, fangless. Fabian sprung back, yanking his hand away. But I stepped forward, finishing the job for him. My hand came into contact with her skin with a satisfying crack and her cheek became a bloody red.

Fabian turned to me, his eyes becoming black. *Kaspar,* he growled in my mind.

I shrugged, pushing my dripping fringe from my forehead. 'Just making sure,' I replied, aloud. Her dress had become sheer and my eyes roamed over her body, wondering what I had done to have such a good specimen cross my path. Fabian pulled his jacket off and slung it around her shoulders as she sat up, his consciousness lingering around the edge of mine.

But she didn't miss my gaze either. 'Oh, Kaspar, my hero,' she said between gasps of air, her voice thick with sarcasm.

'And yes, you are the damsel in distress,' I answered, equally sarcastic, pulling my soaking T-shirt up and over my head.

'That's all the thanks you're getting, so I suggest you take it,' she muttered, clearly thinking I wouldn't notice her stealing a glance at my chest. I ignored her, shouting to Cain and the others to start heading back. Two of us should be able to handle a half-drowned human girl, even if she was a little feisty.

Fabian offered her a hand and she got to her feet, only to drop again, her eyes – such an unusual colour for a human – becoming unfocused. Fabian caught her and I stepped forward, sighing, resigned to the fact I would have to carry her. Her eyes slid back into focus and back out again as she squirmed and buried herself deeper in Fabian's arms.

'You take her,' I said to him, figuring she would be less likely to kick up a fuss. He whispered a few words in her ear and picked her up. Sure enough, she was good as gold. I raised an eyebrow at him and he winked, his hand wrapping around the back of her bare knee. I turned away, stepping into the shadow of the trees.

Behind, I heard her question him about the squid. His reply was vague as he glossed over the details of where it had come from and who had given it to us.

Around us, the mist was lifting and the main grounds came back into view. I extended my mind, curious, and touched upon hers. Right away I was hit with a barrage of emotions, the first being fear and the second anger. Images of the water and her phobia of swimming blurred with those of Trafalgar Square, which floated again and again to the forefront of her mind like a stuck record player. Snapshots of her friends and family passed through too and one of an ageing man in his fifties caught my attention. I focused on it and then recoiled from her mind like I had been slapped.

I stopped and whipped around. 'Girly, what is your surname?'

'Lee,' she said. 'I already told—'

'Who is your father?' I demanded.

'He's a very powerful man,' she retorted.

'Quit with the damsel stuff, it really doesn't suit you,' I growled. 'And besides, I would bet my inheritance that my daddy could beat the crap out of your daddy. But what is his name? What does he do?'

She raised her chin, triumphant. 'Michael Lee and he is the Secretary of State for Defence.'

I exchanged a glance with Fabian who looked as though he might drop her.

'Shit,' I said.

'You've done it this time, Kaspar,' Fabian groaned in my direction, his eyes changing to become colourless, matching my own and betraying his worry. The girl stared openly; as soon as I met her gaze she looked away and I was glad that despite her sharp tongue, I retained power over her. 'The King won't like this,' he added.

No, of course he won't. Neither will the council. I said nothing and surged back towards the mansion, Fabian following at a slight distance as he fussed over her, adjusting her body in his arms so he wouldn't hurt her.

The run allowed time for panic to set in. I was already on thin ground with the council, where a no-confidence vote against my position as heir was only ever a misdemeanour away. Bringing the daughter of a man so high up in government into our world, therefore breaching multiple treaties, was definitely in the sin category.

Why didn't I just kill her?

When Fabian caught up I immediately grabbed her wrist and dragged her up the steps. She winced and trod lightly,

and I briefly took in her battered feet. With a resig
I tugged harder.

'What are you doing?' she demanded, digging her h
in despite the obvious discomfort.

'Getting out of this mess,' I responded, relieved to see my
sister, Lyla, waiting at the bottom of the staircase inside.

'Do you think you could get out of this without slicing
my wrist up?'

My stride was shorter than usual as I faltered slightly,
struck by a sudden admiration at the ease with which she
accepted our existence, mixed with irritation at her boldness.
This girl just does not give up.

Lyla – more irritating than any sopping wet human girl
could ever be – worked her features into a scowl, which was
particularly effective on her usually doll-like face. She took
Violet's wrist without a word to her, instead focusing on me.

'You really screwed up this time, little brother,' she growled.
Violet stared up at the other woman – who was almost a
head taller and considerably slimmer – with utter awe. Lyla
ignored it. She knew the effect she had on both sexes. *Have
fun with your fucking human war,* she finished in my mind,
sweeping upstairs with Michael Lee's daughter in tow.

I wasn't concerned about any war. I was highly unlikely
to survive to see it, with the King's wrath progressing across
the entrance hall.

Fabian dropped to his knees in a very low bow, screwing
his eyes shut and crossing his fingers at his sides. 'Your Majesty.'

I straightened and clasped my hands behind my back,
looking at anything but the hollow grey eyes piercing me.
Pleading ignorance of her namesake wasn't going to work,
and so I accepted the brewing storm with as much enthusiasm
as I could muster. 'Good morning, father. I brought breakfast.'

FIVE

Violet

'Here,' said the girl who introduced herself as Lyla. She smiled as we stopped by an open door about halfway down the corridor. She stepped through. I hesitated but, after a moment, followed her.

The room was huge. The wooden floor gleamed, although a large black rug covered most of it; on that rug a mahogany four-poster bed stood, deep indigo drapes falling to the floor. Black and purple voiles hung around French doors, boxed in by iron railings on the outside. Beside them were several arched windows with ledges just large enough to sit on.

I soaked it all in as Lyla began bustling about, pointing out different things, although I was only half-listening. 'That's the wardrobe – walk-in – over there. We'll get you some stuff, but until then, you can have some of my clothes. I mean, you can't be *that* much bigger than me. The bathroom is just across the hall.' She frowned. 'We thought you probably shouldn't have an en-suite, but there's a washbasin if you need it in the wardrobe,' she added, brightening. She smiled again, but it faded as she turned back to me. 'Don't say much, do you?'

I stared at her. *If she thinks I'm going to start having a friendly chat, she has another thing coming.* Especially as I was beginning to feel quite sick: I wasn't sure I had coughed up all of the water I had swallowed in the lake.

She shifted. 'Well, you should get out of that dress, so I'll leave you.' She began to back away and then stopped. 'I'll get the servants to bring some food up to you too. You're a veggie, right?' she asked. My eyes widened even more. *How can she know that?*

I didn't reply and after a while of just standing there, she headed towards the door. But just before she left, I spoke.

'You don't seem like a murderer,' I blurted.

She laughed, like an adult who laughs at a child asking a stupid question. 'That's because I'm not.' With that, she closed the door and left.

As soon as she had gone I dashed towards the wardrobe, diving in and finding the basin in a small room within the wardrobe, which was as large as my bedroom at home. I leaned over it, gagging a few times and wishing I could just throw up so the horrible lurching in my stomach would go away. Eventually, I did.

Splashing my face with water, I sipped a few drops from my cupped hand, holding them beneath the cold tap. My eyes never left the mirror but all I could see was Claude Pierre falling to the paving, dead, over and over again.

You shouldn't dwell on that, the voice in my head said. *Focus on your own survival.*

It had a point and I wrenched my gaze away from the mirror, walking back into the wardrobe. A full change of clothing had been laid out for me and I flung it on, glad to take off the soaking and torn dress. The jeans were a little tight around the hips, digging into my skin and it took some effort to pull the T-shirt down over my breasts. But they were dry, so they would do.

When I went back out, a tray had been left on the bedside cabinet. On it was a plate of sandwiches cut into minute triangles, a rectangle of paper and a glass of water, which I drained in one swig. Picking up the paper, I left the sandwiches untouched. I unfolded it, revealing a note written in a sprawling and almost illegible script.

Violet,

You are free to roam the house whenever you please, but do not *go into the grounds. If you come across my father, curtsey and address him as 'Your Majesty'. I will do what I can if you need anything – just ask the servants to call me.*
    H.R.H Lyla

P.S. Murderers kill for pleasure. Vampires kill to survive.

I read it through twice more before crushing it into a ball and throwing it into the corner of the room. 'Screw you,' I muttered, walking over to the French doors. I tried the handle, fiddling about for a minute. It was locked. *I guess they're not taking any chances. Not that I would come out too healthy dropping from the first floor anyway.*

I leaned my head against the cool window, smashing my palms against the glass, frustrated, feeling the huge barricades I had thrown up around myself beginning to crumble. I knew I could not be strong much longer and my eyes stung as tears started to prick them.

The hope I had maintained dissolved, replaced with an increasing sense of frustration as I realized I had no control of the situation.

I walked back and pulled the huge silken blanket from the bed, wrapping it around my shoulders as I curled up on the ledge of one of the windows, listening to the gentle tapping on the window as rain started to fall. It lulled me in my exhausted state. After a while, the drizzle became great sheets that battered the grounds, which in the sunlight had looked lavish, but just looked bleak and hostile now; or maybe that was because I now knew what stalked those grounds.

How cliché, I thought as the first claps of thunder sounded, shaking the window. A storm. I closed my eyes, holding the tears in as somewhere deep within the mansion a clock struck nine times.

I will not cry over a bunch of messed-up murderers. Never.

SIX

The rain still pummelled the glass when I woke up. It was dark outside and the blanket that I had pulled from the bed had slipped off my shoulders, piling in a heap on the floor. A few drops of water slid down my cheek as I prised it away from the window-pane, which I had steamed up with my breath. My hand wandered to my neck. *Vampires.* It was all completely crazy.

Yet you can't deny it, the voice said and I shook my head, trying to mask it with other thoughts.

A few drops of rain plummeted from the top of the window outside. I blinked. *Drip, drip, drip.* Behind my closed eyelids, I could see a stained body lying on the pavement.

No, I can't deny it. I don't want to deny it. If I do, that would mean a human had done that *to another human. Vampires are monsters. Monsters do horrible things. Humans don't.*

The clock beside me read 5 o'clock in the morning. I rubbed my eyes, realizing this was the earliest I had been up in years and that it must be the next day, August 1st.

One day. One day would be long enough for the police to find witnesses, set up a search party and start to find me. There was so much evidence. The friends I was with. My heels. The man who worked for my father had even seen me. Yet he had done nothing.

An uneasy feeling crept through my chest. What if he had known about vampires? Had he kept away because he knew he would put his own life at risk? It wasn't too far a stretch to assume that people within the government would know about vampires – someone must know about them. *If he knew and he didn't do anything, does that mean they won't come after me?* I didn't want to think about it. My father would come find me. My father wouldn't abandon me, not even to vampires.

Or would he? said the voice in my head.

I glimpsed Lyla's note, on the carpet. Picking it up, I read it through once more. She had mentioned being free to roam the house and I was desperate for a wash to get rid of the grime on my feet.

I dropped the note and darted towards the door, stuffing one of the sandwiches – dry and stale now – into my mouth. Pressing my ear flat to the door, I listened. It seemed to be silent outside, but the door was wooden and probably thick so that didn't mean much. I took a deep breath and opened it, to find the corridor empty. A little way down on the opposite wall there was a door, which must lead to the bathroom that Lyla had mentioned. Opposite that, on the same wall as 'my' room, there was a set of double doors. They were panelled and would have blended in with the wall if they were not set back a little into an alcove. Two gas lamps hung on brackets, one either side, although they were not on, leaving the corridor to be lit by the natural light that was beginning to stream in from the window at the other end of the corridor. I edged down, tensed and ready to spring back into my room if I needed to.

Nobody came and I began to relax, allowing my hand to wrap around the knob of one of the doors. It was smooth and warmed at the touch like glass, although it had the same appearance as the marble downstairs. I placed my other hand on its twin and turned. The one on the left glided around and clicked with no effort, but the one on the right was stiff and would not turn. The left door swung open a fraction. I stared at it. *Should I?* The temptation was strong but curiosity really would get the cat killed this time.

Just as I started to shut the door again I heard footsteps coming from the stairs. My heart hammered and I jerked forward, bursting through the doors. Shutting it with as little noise as possible, I kept hold of the handle to stop it from turning and clicking shut.

I waited, petrified, and only when everything went silent again did I allow myself to take in the room. It was huge – much bigger than the one I had slept in. All the walls were wood-panelled, and an all-black, wrought-iron four-poster dominated the one side and a fireplace the other. Above the mantle, which was strewn with magazines, there hung a painting of a man and a woman. The man resembled Kaspar, although he looked older. I took a guess that it was his father in his younger days. The woman beside him must be his wife, Kaspar's mother, judging by the hand of the man placed on her bare shoulder. She sat upon a stool, her emerald dress hugging a curvaceous figure, dark chestnut curls tumbling down to her waist, which was so tiny it must have been encased in a corset. Her eyes were wide and bright, full of the same colour and sheen as her dress. But what really caught my gaze was her skin: whilst her husband's was pale and papery, her skin had a tinge of olive in it, although the sunken sockets of her eyes were encircled by deep purple rings – she was without doubt a vampire.

I trod as softly as I could around the bed, almost tripping over a guitar that poked out from under the bedstead. A breeze stirred my ankles and, as I neared the fireplace, the black drapes that hung around the open French doors moved. A feeling of unease crept up my arms. *Doors are left open when someone is not far away.* The lamps dotted about the room had been left on too, although first light was beginning to filter through the trees and across the grounds.

Forcing myself to be calm, I reached up on my tiptoes and ran a finger across the canvas of the painting. It was thick with dust and as I wiped it off it floated away in clouds, smelling heavily of musk mixed with that of expensive cologne, which already hung in the air. I waved my hands in front of me, coughing and spluttering. *I can see – or rather smell – why they left the doors open.* I grabbed one of the magazines to try waft the dust away, but took one look at what was on the cover, blushed, and dropped it, realizing just who this room must belong to.

'Crap,' I breathed, backing away towards the door. I didn't bother to check whether anyone was outside as I practically fell out of one door and through another into the bathroom. It slammed behind me and I was relieved to find it had a chunky bolt for a lock, which I slid across.

Turning, I was once again struck by the grandeur. The whole room was almost entirely made out of red marble, even the bath. The shower was of the same larger-than-it-needs-to-be proportions and would fit three and still leave room to move. It was spotless too: there wasn't an old toothbrush or squeezed-to-death tube of toothpaste in sight.

I fiddled about with the shower dials for a while, confused by the settings until water poured from the shower head. I began to strip down, but caught sight of my reflection in the mirror and stopped. I was not a pretty sight.

My hair looked as though electricity had been passed through it and bits of twig clung to the knots. There were countless cuts and grazes dotted about my neck and mud was smeared across my face, mixed in with my smudged make-up. The rest of my body did not look any better. Dried blood caked my arms and my feet were brown and muddy and I realized I must stink. But it was my eyes that looked the most pitiful. They looked old and weary, as though they had seen a hundred years of suffering, not two days.

I shook my head and turned away, disgusted and angry. I continued to strip down and stepped in, letting the water run over my sore muscles.

I got out when the water ceased to feel warm on my skin. I grabbed a towel, dried myself and got dressed, slipping back into the T-shirt and jeans. I wrung as much water as I could out of my hair and darted back to 'my' bedroom, freezing as I noticed somebody had been in and tidied up.

The blanket that I had moved the day before had been spread back out on the bed, the sheets tucked in. The plate of food had been removed and, right on cue, my stomach growled. I ignored it, dropping onto the bed. But it only got worse and I realized I would have to go and search for Lyla to get some more food. She didn't seem that bad, but the prospect still wasn't a great one.

Outside in the corridor, things were still quiet, although I sensed that wasn't because everyone was asleep. I passed the double doors, unnerved at the fact the room must belong to Kaspar. When I reached the top of the staircase, I leaned over, thinking I could ask the butler where Lyla was. Just as I did, Fabian emerged from the downstairs corridor. I jumped, trying to scamper back into the shadows but he spotted me and smiled.

'Morning,' he said cheerfully, stopping. I didn't reply but eased back towards the banisters, eyeing him with caution. 'Hungry?' he asked. The mention of food set my stomach off growling again and he chuckled. 'Guess so. Come on, I'll find you something.' He gestured for me to follow him and started walking towards the living-room door. When I didn't follow him, he paused, smiling again. 'I'm not going to do anything to you. I promise.'

He looked sincere enough and I scrambled down the stairs until I caught up with him. He opened the door and led me across the living room and through another door. It was like stepping through a time portal. Whereas the main entrance hall didn't look as though it had changed in hundreds of years, the passage we walked down was thoroughly modern and, as we entered the kitchen, I was hit by an array of stainless steel and glass counters, cabinets and tables, although the floor was made of the same marble as the entrance.

Fabian rounded the breakfast bar and began searching through the cupboards. 'Do you like toast?' he asked, his head popping up above the counter. I nodded, hoisting myself up onto a stool. 'Toast it is then,' he said, dropping a couple of slices of brown bread into a toaster. I watched him as he pulled a plate from another cupboard, fascinated by his fluid movements. He met my gaze.

'Hey, I know I'm inhumanly hot, but you don't have to stare.' A huge grin appeared on his face and he winked.

I blushed a tomato red and my eyes hit the floor before bouncing back up to him. 'I wasn't staring.'

He put his hands in the air. 'Sure,' he chuckled. 'Good to see you talking though. You don't strike me as the shy type.'

He's right, I thought. *I'm not usually shy, but then again, I'm not usually being held captive by vampires.*

I continued to watch him as he pulled the door of the fridge open and took the butter out. Before he closed it again, I caught a glimpse of several tall bottles containing a red liquid that didn't look like wine. I shuddered.

'I'm sorry I can't do anything nicer than toast, but we only keep snacks in here,' he nattered, spreading the butter on the bread, which was burnt around the crust. 'The servants usually cook downstairs when we actually want food and not blood.'

He slid the plate towards me, took one look at my face and then spoke again. 'Okay, you have questions.'

I nodded, biting on my lower lip. 'Can I ask anything?'

For a second, a flicker of doubt crossed his face, but it soon disappeared. 'Of course,' he replied. I didn't speak for another minute or two as I rehearsed what I wanted to say in my head. He said nothing, pouring a glass of juice and pushing that in my direction too.

'It's real, all of this, isn't it?'

He placed his elbows on the counter and rested his chin in his hands, watching me with as much fascination as I had watched him. 'Yes. Why?'

'I don't want to believe any of this, but I do. I've seen too much not to.' I tugged on a strand of hair, picking out patterns in the marble floor.

"How many have you killed?'

'I'm not sure I should tell you that,' he murmured.

'How many?' I repeated.

'Hundreds, thousands, maybe . . . I lost count,' he said. I felt my eyes widen and I leaned away from him. *That many?* He shook his head. 'Don't look at me like that, that is a pretty good track record considering I am two hundred-and-one.' The calm blue of his eyes dissolved and became black.

'What about the others?' I managed to whisper, my voice hoarse as I fought back the horror.

'Kaspar, thousands, and Cain, around thirty, but only because he isn't full-fledged yet. I'm not sure about the others.'

My fingers gripped the edge of the steel counter, warming the spot they touched. 'Can't you drink donor stuff?'

'We could.'

'But you choose to kill people instead.'

'No,' he hissed and I was taken aback at his sudden change of tone. 'We choose to *drink* from humans. We don't set out to kill them.'

'Oh, I see,' I breathed. 'Was that the plan when you killed all those men in Trafalgar Square? Because it didn't look like you were just dropping by for a pint to me.'

His eyebrows lowered. 'That was different.'

'Was it?'

He didn't answer and I went back to my toast. Aware that he was watching me, I lowered my head and hid behind my hair, which was drying and twisting into ringlets. It chilled me that he could talk of the people he had killed as though they were just numbers and not people with loved ones and hopes and dreams. It chilled me even more that he wanted my approval. But they were his prey and it was probably easier for him to think like that.

'I know you think that we're murderers, Violet. And I know you would do anything right now to get out of here, but maybe, for your own sake, it would be better if you hold judgement until you know us better.'

I didn't move my gaze away from the plate, afraid he might see my eyebrows arching in disbelief. *I'm not going to get to know you any better,* I thought. *I'm not going to hang around for long enough.*

Don't be so sure, the voice in my head chuckled. It wasn't my mind imagining someone chuckling, but the actual sound, bouncing off my skull. I heard Fabian say something and I blinked a few times, coming back to my senses.

'What does full-fledged mean?'

He walked around the counter and pulled up a stool beside me. I shifted my stool back. 'Changing the subject, are we?' His eyes had returned to blue and a watery sheen coated them, making them twinkle in the light that slipped through the small windows high up the walls. 'A fully-fledged vampire is an adult vampire.'

Seeing my confused face, he smiled. 'A vampire born into vampirism – yes, most vampires are born and not turned,' he added, interrupting himself. 'A born vampire ages normally until he or she is eighteen. As in each year, they look a year older. They are not fully grown yet, so they are slightly weaker and not as thirsty. Cain is sixteen, so he won't be full-fledged for another two years. Get it?'

I flicked a crumb across the plate. 'Sort of. But what happens when a vampire reaches eighteen?'

I went to flick another crumb, but the plate tipped and fell off the edge of the counter. I cringed, waiting for it to smash. But the sound never came as Fabian reached down and snatched it from midair. Unfazed, he placed it back on the counter, brushing the remaining crumbs onto the floor.

'We get faster and stronger,' he said in a low voice, watching me watching him, my mouth ajar. *He had moved so fast; so effortlessly.* 'And we start to age, but very slowly. Centuries pass and it doesn't put a year on us.'

'So vampires aren't immortal?' I asked, feeling a slight spark of interest.

'Theoretically, no. But it's such a slow process, we practically are. The oldest vampire in the Kingdom is hundreds of thousands of years old and he is still going strong.'

'Wow,' I breathed. I couldn't even grasp being that old. A thousand questions popped into my mind, as I buried the initial repulsion. 'Can you go out in sunlight?'

'Yes, but we're at risk of getting really bad sunburn. So pushing me outside won't kill me if you are thinking about it,' he said, pulling funny faces and making it look as though he was melting. 'And if you are thinking of bumping me off, feeding me garlic bread will just make my breath smell; buying me a necklace with a cross on it will just make me look religious and giving me a shower in holy water will make me smell rather pleasant.'

I snorted into my drink at his mockery. 'How do you kill a vampire then?'

'You can push a stake through his heart and break his neck or break and bite his neck or suck him dry,' he explained, a wicked look in his eyes. 'The remains are often burnt, although you don't have to do that.'

'Brutal. Can you turn into a bat?'

His lips quivered and I could tell he was trying not to laugh. 'No.'

'Can you cross running water?'

'Yes.'

'Can you enter a house uninvited?'

'No.'

'Why?'

'Because that would be rude. And to answer your next question, the only way a human can become a vampire is if they have their blood drained by a vampire whilst they also drink the vampire's blood and yes, our eyes change colour according to mood.'

I crossed my arms over my chest, shifting away again. 'How did you know I was going to ask that?'

He tapped his temple with a finger and grinned, his cheeks becoming round and puffed. 'Psychic.'

I raised an eyebrow. 'Are you being serious?'

'Yes, and we're telepathic too, but not with humans,' he stated in a matter-of-fact way. 'And I'll let you in on a trade secret. As long as you are here, lock everything private in your mind in boxes and just focus on one thing if someone tries to get in your mind. I know, it sounds crazy, but you will stop smiling when you realize there are some here who won't respect your privacy.'

I sobered. 'Like Kaspar?'

'Perhaps.' He shrugged, spinning around in the seat to look over his shoulder. 'Speaking of . . .'

Kaspar appeared beside the fridge and in the time it took to blink, the dark-haired boy with the glasses had dropped onto a stool beside me and spread the newspaper he had tucked beneath his arm out on the counter. He started to read, peering over the top of his glasses.

More vampires were not far behind. The ease that I had begun to settle into with just Fabian around disappeared along with the warmth of the room.

'Morning, I told you my clothes would fit,' Lyla said brightly in my direction. 'And I hear that this rude bunch have not introduced themselves,' she chirped. 'That's Charlie,' she nodded her head towards the fair-haired boy who nodded his head in reply. 'That's Felix.' The boy with the flaming-red hair waved. 'And that is Declan.' The last boy looked up from his newspaper.

'Pleasure, I'm sure,' he said in a thick Irish accent – so thick I had trouble working out what he was saying.

'You know my idiot brothers.' She pinched Cain's cheeks

and he shoved her away, groaning in embarrassment. 'And Fabian, of course.' Her mouth curled a little and she sat down on the other side of him as one of the red bottles and several glasses were passed around.

'Kaspar,' muttered Declan in a dark undertone as he turned a page of his paper over. 'You should see this.'

Kaspar darted over and Declan wordlessly slid the paper across so he could read. I shuffled my stool across a few inches and looked over his shoulder. My eyes bulged.

Dominating a double-page spread was an aerial photograph of Trafalgar Square, cordoned off, and for the most part, shielded from public view by large white tents. The photo was black-and-white, but areas of the paving were dark where pools of blood had gathered. Printed in large, bold font above it was the headline LONDON'S BLOODBATH: MASS MURDER IN TRAFALGAR SQUARE.

I realized I had stood up and I gripped the breakfast bar, fighting to stay on my feet.

In the early hours of yesterday morning, London awoke to one of the worst mass murders in centuries, after thirty victims, all male, were found lying dead in Trafalgar Square.

The Metropolitan Police cordoned off the scene at approximately 3 a.m. on July 31st. The victims were pronounced dead upon arrival at the scene. All thirty, as yet unidentified, were found with broken necks and serious flesh wounds, also to the neck. Nine had also been found to be drained of their blood, sparking controversy among the public.

John Charles, head of the Metropolitan Police, said, 'We are deeply shocked by this horrific incident, and we are determined to bring these evil and very dangerous killers to justice. We have forensic teams working at the scene, but we are appealing to witnesses who may have been in the area between the hours of midnight and 2 a.m. on July 31st to please come forward.'

Miss Ruby Jones, who discovered the scene, was unable to comment and is being treated for shock at the Chelsea and Westminster Hospital.

A pair of high-heeled shoes have also been found and are being treated as evidence, although insiders have reported they may belong to a young woman, believed to have been at the scene during the incident. It is feared that she may have been taken by the murderer[s], although confirmation is yet to be released.

This gruesome murder is being compared to the infamous 'Kent Bloodsucker' incident, where three young women were found dead near Tunbridge Wells two and a half years ago. All three had broken necks and had been drained of their blood.

Any witnesses are being urged by the Met. Police to either visit a local police station or call a special hotline on 05603 826111. All identities remain anonymous.

For further images, turn to page 9. For opinions, turn to page 23.

By Phillip Bashford.

I lifted the corner of the page, wanting to turn to the pictures, but Declan laid a hand on the print, holding it down so firmly that as I tried to lift it, it tore down the middle. I let go and he folded it up, leaving the sport page face-up. I tasted salt on my lips and realized I was crying.

It was sickening. But I was crying because Ruby had found the scene. She wasn't as strong as me.

I looked up and saw Kaspar standing behind me, holding a glass of blood in his hand. I rounded on him. 'Why did you do it?'

His brow lowered and small creases appeared around the corners of his eyes as he narrowed them, surveying me. 'You wouldn't understand,' he murmured, his lips barely moving.

'Wouldn't I?' I challenged, taking a step closer.

'No.' His lips parted even further and he looked as though he wanted to say something else, but chose not to. The room was silent, other than the sound of my heavy, irregular breathing.

'Those men had families!'

'So do we,' he muttered.

I shook my head. 'You're sick,' I spat, placing two hands on the shirt stretched over his chest. I shoved, pouring every emotion into the thought of hurting him. To my complete surprise he took a step back. It wasn't a stumble: I hadn't forced him to move. He just let me push him back without a word. 'Sick,' I repeated.

I pushed past him and fled the room, tears flowing unchecked now. The thought of those men, lying in a pool of their own blood kept bouncing around my mind, making my stomach turn. I ran upstairs to the bathroom and it was my turn to be sick.

SEVEN

Kaspar

'Feisty,' Felix muttered. He switched to his mind, musing on one thought. *Maybe it would have been easier to just kill her?*

No, it wouldn't have been easier. I let the thought fill my head, before throwing up walls around my mind, wanting the others out. I needed to think, privately.

Something about the look on the girl's face had disturbed me; made me step back when she pushed me. It was a feeling I thought I remembered, but couldn't grasp.

'He means it would have been better for her if she didn't have to deal with us,' Declan clarified. I felt him pushing against my mental barriers and I lowered them slightly. *Your reasons for taking her were selfish, Kaspar, despite what you might tell the King.*

And so what if they were? Then your selfishness has got the Kingdom in trouble. He opened the paper back up, turning to an article about the rising costs of defence. Blocking his mind to everyone but me, he pointed to the headline. *Michael Lee: taking the hard line on defence. He will want his daughter back.*

And you know he has been looking for an excuse to drive us out since they won the election. This is exactly the ammunition he needs. He wouldn't dare do anything. He's too scared. I drained the rest of the blood, enjoying the warmth that came with freshness. Declan's exasperation came across in waves, but he didn't say any more on it. He knew that a lecture from father was enough for one day.

'I talked with her. She is scared and angry, but she's curious too,' Fabian said, participating in a conversation I hadn't been listening to.

'You answered her questions?' Lyla asked with a poor attempt at offhandedness.

Fabian nodded and Declan peered from over his news-paper again. 'That is only because she is still clinging to hope. Once she realizes she is stuck here, that will go.' He returned to the paper, apparently satisfied with his doom-and-gloom prediction. 'And when I'm right, I will happily say, "I told you so",' he added, rustling the paper. Cain glanced in my direction and I knew my eyes must have dropped through to black.

Yes, I didn't kill her! I roared to myself as way of reply to their disapproving expressions. But not because I wanted her as a toy, though I would happily let them continue thinking that. I didn't know why I had taken her. I didn't know why I had saved her – why I had done it personally, and not let Fabian, always the nice guy, play saviour.

No, it wouldn't have been easier to kill her, I thought, continuing on from Felix's earlier statement. *Because I suspect this particular human would have weighed on my conscience.*

EIGHT

Violet

I didn't know where my legs were taking me. I lost myself in the maze of corridors, my awe increasing with every turn. It wasn't a welcoming place – there were few windows and most of the light came from gas lamps fashioned to look like torches or the occasional spotlight, which would highlight an alcove containing an expensive-looking painting or vase – but it was certainly grand. There was wood panelling everywhere and the floor was so clean I could see an outline of my reflection on the polish. It was cold too and if I lingered for too long on one spot, it felt as though I was standing on a pile of snow in only my socks. The few windows I did come across I fiddled with, trying to open them, but every single one was locked or too stiff to lift; the one I did manage to open was several floors up and positioned on a completely smooth wall, high enough to rule out jumping.

I found another set of stairs and climbed them. The upper floors seemed to be deserted, adding to the eeriness. I found empty room after empty room and there were only a handful of windows on the whole floor, it seemed – but from those few I could just about see over the tree-tops to the sea, a thin blue strip sandwiched between the green of the trees and the silvery lining of the sky.

Suddenly, the wood panelling ended and I found myself in a whitewashed corridor, lit with bright, artificial light – a stark contrast to the rest of the mansion.

'Excuse me, miss, but are you okay?' I jerked my head up, startled at the new voice. 'Sorry, miss, didn't mean to scare you,' the voice said, thick with a cockney accent. It came from a young girl, not much older than I was by the looks of her. She was dressed in a plain black dress and a maid's cap. Her face was round and plump, her mousy-blonde hair framing rosy cheeks. She would be quite stunning, if it was not for the lines of hard work that adorned her face.

'Don't worry, I'm fine,' I replied, trying to smile and failing.

'You must be the human the Varns took from London. Violet, isn't it?' I nodded. 'I'm Annie,' she said, smiling, revealing two small fangs.

I eyed them, my eyes sliding down to her dress. 'Do you work here?'

'I'm one of the servants,' she replied. 'Are you sure you're all right?' she added.

I shrugged. 'Lost, I guess.'

'Well, I can help with that.' She smiled and picked up the bucket and mop beside her feet. 'Take the servant's stairs. They are at the end of here.' She pointed in the opposite direction from where I had come. 'Go three floors down and follow the main corridor and it will bring you to the entrance hall.' With one last smile, she hurried off before I could even thank her.

Sure enough, at the end of the corridor there were a set of narrow spiralling steps, which twisted around and around

a column until they opened out into a wide hallway, which
in turn had smaller passages branching from it.

I stopped, staring down its length. The emptiness of the place
left me feeling very alone and very vulnerable, as the scale
of the situation hit me again. At the end of the corridor,
blending with the darkness, I could see a man crumpling to
the ground, rubbing his neck and scrambling away from me.

I shook my head, smacking my palm against the panelled
wall.

'Shit,' I breathed, as I realized a tiny trickle of blood was
flowing from my raw knuckle. I quickly wiped it away, not
wanting to attract any unwanted attention.

'Father says you shouldn't swear. It's unladylike,' said a
quiet voice from below me. I looked down to see a little girl
with the widest, most emerald-green eyes. Her long blonde
hair fell in tight ringlets around her face and she had perfect
features, right down to her button nose. She looked to be
about four.

'Who are you?' I asked, taking a couple of steps back.

'I am Princess Thyme,' she sung, twirling around, making
her pink frilly dress whip around after her. She smiled,
revealing two pinpricks for fangs. *A kid vampire.* 'And you
are Violet, and Kaspar brought you from London.' It was a
statement, not a question. I said nothing, astounded at the
sureness she had of her words.

After a minute, I recovered my voice. 'You're Kaspar's
little sister?' I asked, bending down to her level.

'And Cain's and Lyla's and Jag's and Sky's,' she chimed,
doing another pirouette.

'Who are Jag and Sky?'

'They are my big, big brothers. They are really old,' she
stated with pride. 'I like them better because they are fun
when they come and visit from Romania.' She pouted,

looking down at the ground. 'All the others are mean when I ask to play games.' Her bottom lip quivered and I panicked at her complete change of mood.

'Hey, don't get upset.'

Her little eyes filled with hope, and she looked up at me. 'You'll play a game with me, won't you?' She tightened her grip around my hand. 'Will you carry me?' She didn't wait for me to answer, but took a few steps back and made a running leap – I only just caught her in my arms. Realizing I didn't have much choice, I complied and followed her directions down the corridor.

'Do you have a sister?' Thyme asked, twiddling with my hair.

'I have a little sister,' I answered. 'She's thirteen.'

'What's her name?' she asked with vague interest, more preoccupied with my hair.

'Lily,' I answered.

'That's a pretty name. Do you have a brother?' she carried on.

'I did. But he died,' I mumbled.

'That's sad,' she replied.

'Yeah, it is,' I breathed.

'Do you have a mummy and daddy?' I turned my head and saw her cute little face twisted with something I couldn't read and she tugged a strand of my hair, making me wince.

'Yes, I do.' I stopped myself, wondering why I was volunteering so much to a little girl. My eyes misted over and a sick feeling clutched at my throat. *Homesickness.* 'What about you? Do you have a mummy?'

'Mummy can't be here at the moment,' she said with a blunt tone far beyond her years. 'My daddy is always too busy to play with me. He is *always* in a bad mood.'

We fell into silence for a while. She started playing with my hair again, twisting it around her finger.

'You're really pretty.'

'Thanks,' I said, unsure how to take the compliment. 'You're really cute,' I replied.

'I know.' She gave a little sigh. 'I wish I had a sister like you. You are nicer than Lyla and much nicer than those horrible girls Kaspar keeps bringing home,' she muttered darkly, again sounding far older than she must be.

'Girls?' I asked, trying not to seem too interested.

'His friends. But they always stay for the night and they are really mean to me,' she blabbered.

It didn't take much brainpower to work out what these 'friends' were here for. Again, she seemed content to play with my hair until I felt a cold breeze on the back of my neck and I almost dropped her.

'What the heck are you doing?' I screeched as she ran her teeth up and down my neck. She pulled away, giving me a toothy grin.

'I'm not going to bite you, silly!' She giggled. 'I'm smelling you.'

'Well, don't do it. It's not very nice.' I replied, trying to keep my cool whilst eyeing her with suspicion.

We wandered through the corridors until she finally pointed out a door, telling me it was her playroom. We went in and she soon had her dolls lined up, ready to attend a tea party. She kept me captive for what seemed like hours, although it can't have been much more than one.

'Thyme, I think I had better go back now,' I announced at last, setting aside my imaginary cake and tea. Her eyes became round and a sheen coated them, but she gave in when I remained firm.

'Okay,' she said in a wistful tone. Taking a hold of my

hand, we headed off again. She led the way as I had no idea where we were until we broke out into the light of the entrance hall. We crossed and were just passing the staircase when Kaspar appeared from behind the banisters.

'Thyme! Why aren't you with your nanny?' he barked. I froze. Thyme wiggled out of my grip, scurrying behind me and peeking out from behind my leg.

'Give her a break, she was looking after me,' I explained, trying to dislodge her from my jeans.

His face went from blank to furious in less than a second and I saw his eyes become black. 'Thyme, go to your room. I need to have a word with your friend here.' His voice echoed across the hall and Thyme disappeared in a flash. Although his tone remained steady, there was a steeliness to it that made me regret opening my mouth. I knew he meant business when he grabbed my shoulder and pulled me through one of the grand doors that mirrored the entrance.

Wow, talk about a ballroom. The door we had just entered through was raised on a balcony overlooking a huge room, at least the size of several tennis courts put together. The walls were made of white marble flecked with gold and the huge pillars that were embedded within the walls were coated in gold leaf. The floor was wooden and so well varnished it resembled liquid more than anything else. At either end there were two arched, cathedral-style windows and to the left a throne had been set upon a slightly raised platform. But what really caught my eye was the chandelier dangling precariously from the ceiling. Hanging from a central ring, tiny baskets woven from glass cupped thousands of black candles, all unlit. As Kaspar shut the door behind us, a gust of air whipped through the air and stirred the glass. A few of the baskets jostled each other and they were so delicate that I half-expected them to break. Instead, they chimed and continued to ring long after the baskets had stopped moving, chased by the echo of the door closing.

'How dare you tell me how to treat my own sister?' He only needed to whisper as his voice travelled across the empty room. 'You know nothing of my family! Nothing!' he hissed, as he clenched and unclenched his fist.

'I know enough.'

He narrowed his eyes and the dark circles below them became even darker and the area between his nose and the corner of his eyes became shadowy too. He stared and something began to feel out of place in my mind. I searched through, feeling restless all of a sudden. I thought he might say something, but he just kept staring and as the bugging sensation increased, it hit me. *He is in my mind.*

I realized he could see every memory and struggled to focus on one thing. Thoughts seemed to slip through my grasp like water and, giving up, I settled on the word jerk. I screamed it in my head and pretty quickly, I felt him withdraw.

'Jerk? I suppose Fabian told you how to guard your mind. Pity.' He placed a hand on the wall beside my head and I went to sidestep away, but he placed his other hand on the other side of my head, trapping me. 'No. You know nothing of my family.' His body pressed up against mine and my nose wrinkled in disgust as I tried to fold into the wall, away from him. He bent to my ear and spoke. 'Do you fear me, Violet Lee? Do you know what I could do to you?'

I could smell blood on his breath, copper and iron, mixed in with the heavy musk of cologne that smelt identical to the one that hung in the air of the bedroom with the painting.

'I know what you can do.' The tip of my tongue ran over my lips and I could taste salt. 'But I'm not scared of you.'

He hummed a low, disbelieving note, which I could feel rumbling in his chest, pressed to mine. 'Do you lust for me, Violet?' He might have said something else, his voice was so low, but there was no mistaking that smirk as he drew away to enjoy my reaction, allowing his lips to brush my ear, sending shivers down my spine.

I forced myself to keep my voice steady. 'No.'

'Then why is your heart beating at twice the rate it should be?' I bit my lip, realizing he was right. It was pounding against my ribs like there was no tomorrow. 'And why are you flushing?' My cheeks were hot like I had stood in the sun for hours. 'And why,' he said, roughly grabbing one of my wrists and pulling it up to my eye level, 'are your palms sweaty?' I didn't want to look, but I stole a glance. Right again. I averted my eyes.

He hummed again, satisfied this time. 'Humans. You hide nothing.' I watched him out of the corner of my eye as he let go of my wrist and ran a hand through his hair, pushing his fringe back, which just flopped right back into place. 'Don't be ashamed of it though, Girly. I'm royalty, I'm rich and I'm damned good looking. I'm designed to be attractive to humans. But you're resisting.' He narrowed his eyes. 'Why is that?'

Oh, where to begin? 'Because you are a bloodsucker and a murderer. And a jerk. The list goes on.' My body might betray me, but I wasn't truly attracted to him: I was repulsed.

His head snapped up, and his eyes, a dark, forest green around his large pupils, met mine. 'Is that so? Well I will get to you, Violet Lee,' he lingered on my name, drawing his sentence out. 'You will give in to me; I will make sure of it.'

'No. You really won't get me.' I made to move to the side, away from him, but he placed his hands either side of my

head again, dragging his nails down the wood, making a
horrendous screeching sound, like chalk on a blackboard. He
ran his hands all the way down, until they reached my waist.
His hands moved around to my back, pulling me into him,
and he began to close his fist around my waist, pinching the
skin just below my ribs.

'Get off me! You have whores for this!' I shrieked. His
eyes found mine in an instant and I saw recognition in them.

His irises became as black as his pupils. They lost all shade
and tone – they were black, just black. 'You will pay for that
one, Girly,' he said, his voice trembling.

In one swift movement, he had brushed away the hair
from my neck and pushed my head away. In the corner of
my eye, I could see him lowering his jaw to my neck and
I began to duck away. But he grabbed a fistful of my hair
and tugged. I yelped, seeing him bare his fangs as he forced
me onto my tiptoes.

'Don't!' I begged, cowering away from him.

'I will teach you to fear me,' he growled, taking no notice
of my pleas for mercy. 'And I will make you regret the day
you ever stood in Trafalgar Square.' With his taunting words,
I felt pain as his fangs pierced my skin. They drove deep
into my flesh, ripping my skin. I cried out in pain, unable
to stop curses spewing from my mouth as stars flickered in
front of my eyes. But every time a word formed my jaw
moved and the skin on my neck stretched taut over his
fangs, releasing a dribble of something warm, which trickled
down to the round collar of my T-shirt.

He extracted his fangs and his tongue chased the drip,
leaving a trail of saliva. He sucked at it, his lips forming
words against my skin. 'Sweet,' I thought he said.

He rubbed his thumb across the material of my collar and
brought his eyes up to meet mine once more, but my eyes

flicked to his lips, which I saw were coated in blood. *My blood.*

I felt weak and my knees began to buckle. Only the force of him pushing me into the door kept me upright. 'The Princes of this Kingdom *always* get what they want,' he breathed and drew away from me, leaving me to crumple to the floor, pale and sickened. He watched me slide to the ground and, unable to bear the smirk on his lips, I buried my head in my arms, drawing my knees close to my chest.

'Keep denying me and you could make your time here very unpleasant. And believe me, Violet Lee: your time here shall be long.'

With that, the door slammed, leaving me whimpering on the floor, very quickly learning how to fear him.

NINE

Violet

'How about this?' Lyla jabbered, pulling clothes down from the racks of her gigantic wardrobe and passing them into the arms of a waiting maid – Annie. 'Seems like your style.'

She held up a black skirt – more like a belt – and pressed it against her stomach, modelling it. It was short, to say the least.

'I think the dress I was wearing the other day was a one-off.'

She hummed with an obvious tone of disbelief and added the skirt to the growing pile in Annie's arms. I shifted, uncomfortable, leaning up against one of the mirrors. 'Listen, Lyla, you really don't have to lend me all this, I—'

She cut me off. 'Violet, you might think we are all murderers, but we have a basic standard of hygiene here and that includes changing your underwear. So while you're here, you play by our rules.' She shot a warning look in my general direction and I closed my mouth. There was nothing I could say to that.

My thoughts wandered as she continued to pick out clothes for me, insisting they were cast-offs she never wore. The scene with Kaspar yesterday preoccupied my mind as it kept playing itself over and over like a stuck record, tormenting me. I hadn't told anyone about it. I didn't plan to. Not out of consideration for him, but for the sake of avoiding even further humiliation. It felt private.

'Earth to Violet,' an exasperated voice called. 'I said try them on. You're bigger than me and I want to know they fit.' She pushed me into the washroom and one by one, Annie handed the outfits through.

When I emerged, she was draining a glass of something red that smelt faintly of alcohol. 'All good?' she asked, turning to me as I walked out. I nodded. 'Vodka and blood,' she explained, noticing that I was eyeing the drink. 'Enough of that and that's about as close as a vampire can get to sleep.' She drained the last few drops and handed Annie the glass. 'Fetch me another one. I've got a blasted head-ache.' Annie curtsied with the faintest trace of a disgruntled expression, but Lyla didn't seem to notice the rudeness in her words.

I began to pick up the clothes when she piped up again. 'If you ask me, it would be far easier just to buy you more clothes – I mean, you're going to be here a while – but Kaspar doesn't seem to think you're worth it.' My hands balled into fists around the handful of clothes I was carrying. 'No offence, of course,' she added, watching me.

It wasn't Kaspar's lack of concern that bothered me, (although I was keen to avoid the subject of him) but the assumption that I was hanging around. I nodded, trying to look unbothered.

'So vampires can get headaches? You're not immune to all that?'

She laughed. 'God, no. We can get headaches, stomach aches, sore throats, that type of thing, but not anything serious or complicated. And not any STDs, luckily for the likes of my brother. Still, vigilance at all times. Use condoms and all that.' I blushed at her reference, trying not to think too much about it. She walked into her bedroom and I made for the door, clothes in hand.

'Hey, no rush,' she said, smiling. 'I get bored of just having the guys around. Female company wouldn't go amiss.' She patted the cream sofa in the corner of the room and, after hesitating, I joined her, letting the pile rest on my lap. After a moment of awkward silence, I spoke.

'Do the others live here?'

'Fabian and Felix and the rest of them? Yes. This is their second home,' she answered.

'Why?' I probed.

'Oh, they like to go hunting together, kick slayer butt, that sort of thing. Passes the time.'

'Right,' I replied, pretending that her answer sounded normal. More questions bugged my racing mind, but I knew better than to ask them. I had to be tactful with those questions if I wanted to remain alive.

Back in the relative privacy of my own room, I curled up on the ledge beside the window. It was raining again – what little sun we would get for the year had been and gone in June. My eyes began to droop, and I walked over to the bed. I couldn't be bothered to change, so I just slipped off my shoes and swung under the covers. I hadn't even shut my eyes, however, when there was a loud bang, which sounded as though it came from the walls itself.

There was a second bang and I sat bolt upright. I stared in fear across the dim room; I was sure it was coming from the opposite wall, and therefore, the walk-in wardrobe. My fingers tightened over the sheets.

But there was no other sound and I plucked up the courage to slip out of bed and investigate. Taking a deep breath, I pulled the door open and dove for the light switch in one move, not wanting to look up until there was light. Yet there was nothing there and my hammering heart calmed a little. Glad of the carpeted floor as it cushioned my steps, I crept forward, until . . . bang!

I jumped back, startled as I realized it sounded like a door slamming, or heavy furniture being pushed across the floor in the next room – Kaspar's room. With it, came a voice and my cheeks flushed so bright that I would put a tomato to shame.

'Oh, Kaspar,' someone giggled. A woman. 'You're so dirty.'

I back-pedalled out of the wardrobe, followed all the way by groans I didn't want to hear. I bounded back into my bed and tried to muffle the sound by smothering myself with a pillow. But it didn't work. I lay awake, my eyes wide like I had placed matchsticks under my lids, pulling out my hair in frustration as I was forced to listen as they went on and on and didn't stop.

TEN

Violet

'Annie!' I screeched, running flat out down the downstairs corridor. 'Annie!' I repeated as I slowed down at the servant's staircase, which spiralled downwards into the bowels of the mansion. At their bottom was a vast network of kitchens, used to cook for the royal family upstairs at formal events. Beyond that were launderettes and small, dim rooms for the servants to sleep in. It was here that I was spending most of my time, away from Kaspar and Fabian and the others. Here, no one took any notice of me, nor lusted for my blood because most of them hated drinking it as much as the idea revolted me – it was here, at Varnley, Annie had told me, that the vampires who never wanted to be vampires came. The vampires turned, not born.

I followed the walls of the unlit kitchens, hearing my footsteps echo off the stone walls and curved ceiling, shaped like a cellar. I knew Annie would have heard me a mile off, and sure enough, she stood at the opposite end, arms folded and her tone a little exasperated.

'You shouldn't be down here this late.'

I brushed her off. 'But I have a favour to ask.'

She nodded her head, the blonde curls that she tried so hard to maintain – a throwback to when she was a teenager in the 1940s, she said – flat and dropping around her ears. Her usual cap and pinafore had gone, but the black dress remained.

'You clean the bedrooms, right?' I asked, biting my lip because I didn't know how she was going to react. She nodded once more. 'Could I help out?'

She gave me a puzzled look. 'Why?'

'I have a little surprise for Kaspar,' I blabbered; keen to get it out as fast as possible.

A sceptic smile grew into an excited grin on her face. 'What are you planning?'

I had not slept a wink in three nights. Every night had been interrupted by various moans and groans. Each morning, a girl would leave. The previous morning, I'm pretty sure it had been two girls. In the end, I resolved to do something. I hadn't expected Annie to agree, but she hated the Prince: he treated the servants like the dirt beneath his feet and worse. But when we reached his door, my resolve began to weaken.

Annie knocked and called in a timid voice through the door. 'Your Highness?' There was no answer. Again she knocked, harder this time. We waited a minute, and there was still no answer. She poked her head in.

'All clear,' she muttered and, entering, quickly began sweeping up.

'Where did you say he kept them?' I said in a hushed tone, afraid he might return at any minute.

'Try the drawers in the bedside table, under the bed, behind the clock and the bathroom cabinet.'

In the back of my mind, I questioned what the hell I was doing, knowing that pushing things too far with Kaspar could get me hurt or killed, yet getting revenge on him for bringing me here, even in the smallest way, was just too tempting.

Besides, they would have hurt you by now if they wanted to, wouldn't they? my voice said, putting into words what I had become more and more sure of over the past few days.

I began dashing about, pulling open drawers; checking under the rugs. Sure enough, in the bathroom cabinet there was a box, three behind the clock and two boxes in the drawers.

I lay down on my stomach and crawled under the bed. I fought the urge to scream as something scuttled in the shadows and disappeared between the skirting boards and floor. But I hit gold: there were boxes and boxes here, all unopened. I gathered them up and piled them on the newly made bed, along with the others. I did one last sweep of the room, checking to see if I had missed any. I hadn't.

I returned back to the bed and began ripping the packaging open, emptying the boxes of their contents. I tipped each upside down and chucked all but one of them into the empty boxes into Annie's rubbish bag and stuffed what had been inside them into my pockets.

'I'll be right back,' I whispered. I slipped out, stopping to check if the coast was clear. I tried to walk casually down to the kitchen, knowing my eyes were shifting from one shadow to the other; sure someone was going to appear. When I reached the kitchen, I headed straight for the fridge and pulled an almost empty bottle of blood from the shelf, pouring the thick 'drink' down the sink. There was a definite sweetness to the smell, although that was overshadowed by the pungent stench of congealing blood. *And they drank this stuff? Rank.*

I left a few drops of blood in the bottom before taking the packets out of my pocket and ripping them half-open. I poked each one into the bottle, before tightly screwing up the lid and shaking it, coating each packet in the sticky liquid. I placed it the back of the fridge and headed back upstairs.

I think I know someone who won't be screwing tonight, my voice said, dripping with glee and interrupting my thoughts. It rung in my head with no tone, no timbre, but it did not belong with my thoughts, so to save my sanity I was going to assume it was my subconscious.

Running back up the stairs two at a time, I bolted back into Kaspar's room to find Annie finishing off and tying a knot in the bag that carried the empty boxes.

'Are you sure he won't just go ahead anyway?' I asked.

'No, 'cause if anything goes wrong, then he's in trouble.'

I nodded and scrawled a note out on a slip of paper I had found on the mantle – *'Always use protection, sucker!'*

I placed it into the one remaining empty condom box and slipped it back into the drawer of his bedside cabinet, before darting back into my room to wait.

It was near midnight when I heard the first giggles and, peeking out from my door, I could see it was the same leggy blonde who had been over a few times. Charity, I think she was called – she was anything but.

About fifteen minutes slipped by before I heard movement and frustrated exclamations followed by a roar as my door was flung open. Kaspar stormed into my room and glared, his eyes a bottomless black.

'Recognize this?' he said between heavy breaths, holding the condom box up, the note scrunched in his hand. I shook my head, trying to focus on that action rather than his eyes, or worse, on Annie, in case he tried to get in my head and read my thoughts.

Charity came in behind him, dishevelled as though she had dressed in a hurry. Her bleached hair stuck out at odd angles and her bright pink lipstick was smudged across the corners of her lips. She glared at me through narrowed eyes. 'What the heck is your problem?' she whined, like a child who had lost her favourite toy.

'No problems. Why, do you have one?' I pulled my most innocent smile, aware that Kaspar looked a little more than angry.

In a blur he had launched himself across the room. He collided with my side to take me with him and I was sent rolling across the bed, coming to a halt when my head hit the bedside cabinet. I let out a scream as he landed on top of me, pinning me to the bed. I winced through gritted teeth as the corner of the cabinet dug into my spine.

'Get off me, you horny git!' I screeched, kicking and flailing, revolted at his closeness.

'Why, am I making you uncomfortable? Maybe I will use you instead!' he snarled, a tormenting smirk twisting his face. His eyes were devoid of any emotion – he meant it. Straddling me with one leg either side of my stomach, he forced me deeper into the mattress, pinning my hands above my head. He began to pull my shirt up and I heard squeals of protest from Charity, which merged with the protests of the mattress as I tried to fight free.

But then he was gone. I raised my head a little to see Fabian and Charlie wrestling him away, gaining quite a few scratches. With the tiniest sigh of relief, I scrabbled back up and pulled my shirt down back over my stomach, blushing and full of more anger than ever.

'What the hell is going on?' Fabian bellowed. He looked

Kaspar and Charity in the eye, as though daring them to lie. 'Are you all right?' he added, glancing in my direction. I nodded, wrapping my arms around my middle without thinking.

'Never mind if she's all right, she stole Kaspar's condoms!' Charity accused, pointing at me.

At that moment, Lyla entered, laughing. 'Tragic,' she muttered, but everyone heard. Kaspar shot her a furious look and shook himself free of Charlie's grasp.

'Is that true, Violet?' Fabian asked, assuming the role of the diplomat. My expression of guilt must have answered his question, because he continued. 'Where are they?'

I shook my head, refusing to answer. A second later, several very powerful, very intrusive minds entered mine and my thoughts became displaced and chaotic. I fought to hide everything, but somehow, the details of my plan slipped through. I could do nothing but hope they hadn't realized a maid had helped.

'Kitchen,' Fabian grunted and Kaspar raced out, followed by Charity. I didn't plan to follow, but Fabian's look of indignation corrected that.

'You idiot,' he scolded. 'Why couldn't you just keep your head down? You're going to make your life here hell.'

I pushed past him as he held the door open for me. 'I don't want a life here,' I muttered. Not waiting to see if he replied, I headed down the stairs and towards the kitchen. *But maybe he's right. Maybe I have gone too far.*

When I got to the kitchen, they were pulling the bottle from the back of the fridge. Fabian tipped it upside down over the sink and a few drops of blood dribbled out. The condoms collected around the neck, ruined.

Charity turned to me, her expression moving from stunned to disappointed to murderous and it was at that point that I knew I was in for it. I turned to run, but she was already flying towards me, razor-sharp pink-acrylic nails bared. Grabbing my shirt she yanked me back and swiped at my face. I felt her nails gouge my skin and howled as she went to take another shot, but came to my senses long enough to throw my full body weight at her. It didn't do much, but it was enough for Charlie and Lyla to grab her.

'You're just a fat jealous cow,' she spat, wiping her eyes and smudging her make-up so she had a grey ring around each eye.

'Excuse me?' I hissed.

'I said, you're a fat jealous cow!'

'I heard what you said,' I jeered back.

She shrugged free from Lyla's grip and straightened her skirt, which had ridden up. 'Whatever. Just keep out of other people's business, will you? Come on, Kaspar.'

'Wow. I didn't know they made bitches and whores rolled into one,' I muttered as she was just about to pass through the door, Kaspar following like an obedient dog. She froze.

'Take that back,' she snarled, her eyes moving from blue to black.

'No,' I said coolly and she let out a cry, lunging for me with her eyes transfixed on my neck. I yelled, trying to throw her off. She scratched me once more, but, before she could do any more, we were being yanked apart – Fabian's strong arms were wrapped around my stomach, as Kaspar pulled Charity away. She wasn't struggling, but she threw insult after insult at me, which I ignored until she struck where it hurt.

'You should have killed her while you had the chance, Kaspar. I know what these human girls are like. They'll come on to anything with legs.'

I surged forward, but Fabian held me firm. 'Don't worry; I wouldn't touch your kind with a bargepole.'

'Yeah, right,' she replied, squirming into Kaspar's arms, stroking the side of his face. Kaspar didn't respond with the same affection, but pulled her closer, in a mechanical fashion. She didn't seem to notice. 'Come on, baby, let's go hunt for humans; I'm sick of animal blood.' She eyed me as she said it, knowing what effect it would have.

'You're sick.' My voice was becoming hoarse. 'Sick parasites.'

Charity didn't notice. She was staring at the door as the King entered. With downturned faces, the vampires bowed and curtsied. Fabian stood straight with difficulty, his arms still clenched around me.

I did nothing, turning away. *Why should I curtsey?*

He turned to Charity first, who extracted herself from Kaspar's grasp and hung her head, managing to throw me a scathing look every few seconds.

'I will remind you, Miss Faunder, that your father's position in the council and court is subject to the actions of both himself and his family.' His deep voice did not waver with anger, but contained a clear menace. 'Go,' he instructed, and she disappeared, not waiting to be told twice.

Then he turned to me and I shrunk, pierced by his grey eyes, so cold they sent a shiver running down my spine. Fabian loosened his grip, realizing I was not going to try anything now. 'You play a dangerous game, Miss Lee. You will end up injured, or worse, if you are not wary of your actions.'

'Better dead than one of you,' I shot back, going to leave, but Fabian caught my arm. It seemed as though the King wasn't finished.

'Your sentiments will change when you have grown

accustomed to our ways, which will happen in time. And time you shall have, Miss Lee, for your father is not foolish. He knows of our power and will not attempt to free you for a considerable length of time, at which point it will be too late.'

My eyes widened. *Does he mean what I think he means?* 'My father doesn't know about vampires.'

Behind the King, Kaspar laughed. It was a cold, hollow laugh, full of mocking. 'Your father is in charge of the defence of this country, Girly. Of course he knows about us. He knows it was us who killed the slayers in Trafalgar Square and he knows it is us who have you.'

The King raised a hand and Kaspar quietened. As he did, his shirt sleeve slipped down, revealing arms scattered with raised, mottled veins.

'No charge will be brought against us, Miss Lee. The case will be quietly closed by the Metropolitan Police once the media interest has died down. The idea that your disappearance is linked to you witnessing the killings will be fastidiously denied by your father, as instructed by my ambassadors, and if your father tries anything rash, such as to reveal our existence to the greater population, you will suffer. Unless you turn to become a vampire, you will remain here so you cannot reveal our existence. If you become a vampire and then reveal our existence to humans, you will suffer as we do.'

My mouth opened and my heart dropped through the pit of my stomach. *They have everything covered*, I realized. 'You can't do that. How can you do that?'

'We are above the law and as I'm sure you can tell, Miss Lee, your situation is rather dire,' the King said, turning to Kaspar. 'Miss Faunder is welcome to stay as long as she likes. Whilst she is here, however, Miss Lee is to be confined to her room.'

I started to protest but the King ignored me and left the room, leaving a smirking Kaspar behind to gloat.

'Is revenge sweet, Girly?'

I scowled at him, and laughing, he left the room. Fabian looked down at me, sympathy shining in his eyes as he led me back to my room.

That night, the groans from the room next door were even louder.

ELEVEN

Violet

It was the morning of August 7th when Fabian came in. One week and the hope I had of getting out had faded. On the bright side, Charity the whore had left.

'There is something on the news about your family. Do you want to come and see it?' he asked after explaining I could leave my room again. I followed him, a small spark of hope reigniting as we entered the living room and I saw my photo – a school photo, of all things – plastered across the screen. Above it was the word 'missing'. The others were gathered around the sofas, watching the screen as the news theme blared and images of various stories flashed up.

The music finished, and the female news anchor on the left looked up from her laptop. 'Violet Lee, daughter of the Secretary of State for Defence, Michael Lee, was today officially reported as missing.' My face popped up once again. 'Miss Lee was last seen on July 31st at around 1 a.m., in the area around Trafalgar Square. Fears have arisen that she may have witnessed the murder of thirty men, dubbed

London's Bloodbath, and been abducted by the murderers. This claim has not been verified by the Metropolitan Police, who are widening their search to include the Greater London area.'

The screen switched to footage of several police officers with sniffer dogs, searching the outskirts of London. My hands gripped the back of the sofa as my knees ceased to feel so solid.

'It has been confirmed that a high-heeled shoe found at the scene of the murder belongs to Miss Lee, although police have dismissed the idea of her being a suspect.' A picture of my shoe in a clear plastic bag appeared behind the male anchor's head. 'Questions have been raised as to why Miss Lee's disappearance was not reported earlier, and today the Secretary of State gave in to public pressure and made a statement.'

My father appeared, clutching my mother's hand. They were sitting behind a table, a rabble of journalists snapping pictures and holding dictaphones. A large picture of me as well as the hotline to call with information scrolled along behind them on a blue screen. I choked a little as I saw them, especially as I saw tears roll down my mother's cheeks. My father's expression was calm; controlled.

'We are working with the police to try and find our daughter, and we would like to thank them for their support,' he said, speaking without wavering, into a micro-phone.

A journalist stood up, calling over the buzz. 'Do you think this may be linked to anti-war protestors, who oppose your decision to send more troops to the Middle East?'

My father shook his head. 'I refuse to comment on policy. This is not the time or place. We just want our daughter back. We miss her.' At this point, my mother broke down into sobs; through them, I could hear her begging for me to come home.

My eyes stung as my own tears formed. I wanted to reach out and touch her. I wanted to comfort her; to tell her I was okay, even though I wasn't; even though I wouldn't come out of this human. Tears rolled down my cheeks. I was frozen to the spot, wanting to stop watching, but unable to tear my eyes from the screen. Fabian placed a hand on the small of my back. I pushed him off.

'Since Michael Lee ascended to the position of shadow defence minister and then took up the role with his party's election three years ago, the family has suffered unparalleled grief. Four years ago, at the age of just seventeen, the Lee's eldest child, Greg Lee, died after taking a heroin overdose. In October of last year, Lillian Lee was diagnosed with leukaemia and is currently undergoing treatment.' The reporter finished and I felt the blood drain from my head. Air stopped reaching my lungs as I forgot to breathe.

'We now have a message from Lillian.'

Lily – my beautiful sister, Lily – came up on the screen. She was lying in a hospital bed, all sorts of wires attached to her wrists. She was paler than the parasites beside me, her arms seeming to have a faint green tinge. Her eyes were sunken and bloodshot and she looked thin and frail, save for her cheeks, which were swollen from the steroids. She was bald, but it didn't matter. She was my beautiful little sister, cancer or not. She looked so ill, but I knew that was from the treatment.

A microphone was placed under her mouth, and she began to rasp her words. I could tell it took effort.

'V-Violet. I know you're out there. T-they'll let you go and come home.' She closed her eyes, a peaceful expression taking over her face.

The screen changed back to the newsroom, and the anchor people, looking awkward, began explaining how to contact the police with information.

Hours later, I was still numb. Numb and cold. I couldn't feel anything: no pain and no hope, no happiness and no fear. Just nothing.

Fabian was holding me and I let my head fall onto his frozen shoulder. His arm snaked around my waist and pulled me into him. I was beyond tears, which I knew he would be glad of: his T-shirt was damp. A thousand and one tissues lay in the bin nearby, and my nose was sore, my eyes red and puffy.

'No more crying, okay? I won't let you cry any more. Your family would want you to be strong, wouldn't they?' Concern etched his angular face, twisting it into beautiful contortions.

I nodded and rubbed my nose; his face lost a little of the worry. I blinked and noticed that the others were surrounding me. The King, Lyla, Kaspar, Cain, Thyme, Charlie, Felix, Declan and two men I didn't recognize. Two beautiful women clung to their sides, a baby in the arms of one, a child clinging to the other hand of the same woman. Both of the men and children all shared the same mesmerizing emerald eyes.

Sky and Jag, I thought. *They have to be, with those eyes.*

The one with the family looked older and I guessed he was Sky – Thyme had said he was the eldest. The beautiful women I could only assume were their partners. Not one of them looked a day older than twenty-five. Once I had taken in the newcomers I lowered my head to stare at my lap, feeling like a fish in a fishbowl.

Kaspar cleared his throat and I looked up to see him holding a phone in his hand, which he offered to me. 'Two minutes, no more.'

I stared at it in disbelief.

'Go on, knock yourself out,' Fabian murmured, a small smile crossing his lips. 'You need it.'

I looked down at the phone, uncertain, not sure of whether I wanted to do this. *What if it made me hurt more?*

Oh, but you want to, don't you? my voice taunted and I knew it was right. I snatched the phone from his hand and hurried from the room, working the stiffness out of my hands as they gripped the phone like a newborn child.

'Remember we can hear every word you say,' Kaspar called as I closed the door of the living room behind me, settling on the staircase. I didn't really listen and dialled my home number, listening to it ring with baited breath. My heart peaked and stayed there as two rings became three, and three became four. I was nervous. I didn't know why.

'Hello?'

My heart fell through my gut and I made a whining sound, and choked out, 'Dad?'

'Violet?' the all too familiar voice replied, astonished.

'Yeah,' I murmured in a feeble voice, words failing me.

There was a crackling down the line as though he was covering the mouthpiece and I thought I heard voices at his end, talking heatedly. Then there was another crackle and he came back, speaking with an unnerving urgency.

'I'm going to assume you're being listened to, so I can't tell you much. I know it's the Varns who have you and I know what they are. It must be a shock to you to discover about all of this and I never intended for you to know about it at all. I know your situation must seem impossible, from what I've heard from these bloodsucker ambassadors.' He spat out the last sentence with such venom, even I was shocked – and I had heard him angry. 'But it's really import- ant you don't give up. Don't turn, whatever they say or do.

Do you understand, Vi?' When I didn't answer because I was trying to absorb his hurried words, he pressed the question: 'Do you? Promise me you won't turn.'

I stared at the marble floor. *Do I understand?*

'I promise,' I murmured. I heard the door open in front of me and glanced up to see Kaspar slipping through. Leaning against the wall, he folded his arms and eyed me. My two minutes were running out. Meanwhile, my father carried on.

'We'll get you out of there, Violet, but it's going to take time and I need to know some things. Have they bitten you or taken any blood at all?'

Kaspar's eyes flickered up and met mine. I hesitated and stared. He stared back.

'No,' I lied. The tiniest crease of surprise appeared on his brow. *Why did I lie?*

'Good,' my father said. 'Make sure they don't try and give you any of their blood whilst taking your blood. That will turn you.'

I shook my head and a few more tears pricked my eyes, which I wiped away, conscious of the fact Kaspar was still frowning at me. 'You can't leave me here, Dad. You can't,' I muttered, jumping as a small sob escaped. 'They kill people!'

I heard him sigh – it wasn't much, but I clung onto it, savouring the sound. 'I have to, Vi, for the moment, anyway. But we won't give up, I have contacts and—'

I cut him off as Kaspar started walking towards me. I clutched at the phone with two hands, as though that might stop him taking it and asked the most burning question I had, realizing it was my last.

'How's Lily? Quickly,' I added, trying to put across the urgency.

He picked up on my panic and didn't hesitate. 'Weak, but

the doctors say she's doing well and should make a recovery by—'

Kaspar whipped the phone away from my ear, pressing it to his own. As if my hands were nailed to it I followed him, refusing to let go until I found I was clutching at thin air: he had flitted back into the living room and rejoined the rest of his family.

The door was slammed in my face before I could follow him and when I tried the handle, it was locked. Falling against it I tried to listen, but heard nothing.

I didn't even get the chance to say goodbye.

TWELVE

Kaspar

'I think that's enough time talking, don't you, Lee?' I spat, closing the door to the living room behind me and shutting Violet out.

'Put her back on, Varn.'

I chuckled, aware that my father was stood back, scrutinising my words. 'I don't think so. We have to talk business.'

The sound of his breathing down the line stopped: I assumed he pulled the phone away from his mouth. In the background, I could hear him discussing what to say, presumably with one of his poisonous advisors who were so determined to make our life difficult as government policy.

'I refuse to speak directly with anyone other than your ambassadors or the King,' Lee eventually replied, coolly.

'Well, you are out of luck then, Lee. I'm heir and any business of my father's is mine too. If you have a problem with that, take it up with my father's advisors. Oh, wait, that's me.'

I imagined the cogs turning in his head. Sky's wife,

Arabella, took both their children, the eldest only two, into her arms and out of the room, muttering something about disliking the politics. She had made her stance on Violet quite clear – she disapproved of the whole thing; so much so, she had initially refused to visit with Sky from Romania.

'Then you will do,' he mocked. *He sounds like the girl.* 'You know of John Pierre, I presume?'

John Pierre? Yes, I know him all right.

'Of course.'

'And I will assume you are aware that it was his son you killed in Trafalgar Square?'

'Clearly.'

'Then I am sure it will not come as a surprise to you to hear that he is not particularly pleased.'

No shit, Sherlock. 'No surprise whatsoever.'

'Men fuelled by revenge are the most dangerous. Watch out, Varn,' Lee snarled.

The whole room stared at me, my father's gaze the most prominent, listening, waiting for my reaction. 'That's not much of a threat, Lee. You are aware that our Kingdom could halve the population of this country in a day, aren't you?

Tick, tick went the human mind. 'You might be a leech, Varn, but somehow I don't think you're cut out for genocide.'

'Perhaps not, but I would happily make a start with your daughter.'

The words had hardly left my mouth when Sky held his hand out for the phone, obviously deciding I had done enough damage. I gave it to him gladly and he continued the conversation, Father diverting his attention to him. Jag sauntered up and nudged me below the ribs.

'Look at you, little brother, talking politics. If I didn't know better, I'd say you have had a personality overhaul.' Then he lowered his voice and turned so he was no longer facing Mary, his girlfriend. 'Nice catch for a human.' He winked at me and left to shower Mary with compliments. *So he hasn't changed in the time he has been away then.*

I slipped from the room, tired of the talk. Girly sat curled on the bottom step, her head buried in her arms. I couldn't hear sobbing, although as she raised her head her eyes were still red and blotched, but gleaming with a hope that changed to an accusing stare once she realized there was no phone in my hand. She scrabbled up and backed into the banister as I passed, her stare following me as I thought I heard her mutter that I was a jerk.

THIRTEEN

Violet

Hours merged into days, every day as insignificant as the next, time passing in a blur, nothing standing out.

I spent almost all of my time cooped up in my room, amusing myself as best I could. It had been a week exactly since that short phone call, and it still troubled my thoughts. I had hoped that I would be able to call my family again, but had given up on that. Nobody talked to me, apart from the occasional, brief exchange.

It would be my birthday in thirteen days. I would turn eighteen a hostage. My fingers tightened into a ball as I felt a familiar lurch in my stomach and my throat closed up.

A brisk knock at the door interrupted my thoughts and I quickly wiped my eyes, just in case they looked teary. Without waiting for a reply, the person entered as I was standing up. To my surprise, it was not Fabian, who seemed to be the only one interested in me, but Sky.

He cleared his throat, filling the room with a definite

awkwardness. I shifted from one foot to the other. 'You're wanted downstairs. Now.'

'Why?'

As he left, his gaze glided up and down my body, taking in my attire – a scruffy pair of Lyla's old pyjamas. 'You have two minutes.'

His deliberate avoiding of the question unnerved me, but I was already in the wardrobe when I heard the bedroom door close. I grabbed something a little less inappropriate and changed.

I left the room, wondering what the great urgency was. I had never been requested to be 'seen' in the fifteen days I had been here and Sky had never spoken directly to me.

The eldest Varn child was much older than the other five: a thousand, Fabian said, but he was not the heir to the throne. No, *Kaspar* was heir. Sky was married to Arabella, a few years his junior and they had two daughters. They lived in Romania mostly, as did Jag and Mary; I suspected it was my arrival that had prompted their visit.

The entrance hall was a frenzy of activity when I reached the top of the staircase. It seemed as though most of the household had gathered, all wearing long black cloaks, even tiny Thyme. Servants rushed about, passing various objects around, before hastily bowing and darting off to their next task. I spotted Annie, who gave me the smallest of smiles.

'It's like trying to get an army on the move,' Fabian said, coming up to greet me, grimacing at the bickering of the Varn siblings below. Unlike the others, he wore normal clothes.

'What's going on?' I asked, leaning over the banister.

He grimaced again. 'It's a hunt.' My lips pursed and I swallowed back a gag, realizing why Sky had avoided my question a moment ago.

'A hunt for what?' He shot me a look that said, 'As if you don't know.' I closed my eyes. 'But what do I have to do with that?'

'They're going for the weekend, so I'm staying to keep an eye on you.'

Below, Kaspar and Cain snapped at each other, unbothered by what they were about to do. 'I don't need babysitting. What the hell would I do? It's not as though I could go anywhere.'

He shrugged, heading down the stairs. 'You tell me. But it could be worse. Kaspar could be staying.' He gave me a knowing look.

That is true. I would be an idiot to trust Fabian, but he was a lesser of two evils when compared to Kaspar.

The King strode forward and, as he did so, the butler rushed forward, swinging both of the enormous doors open. He disappeared down them and one by one, the others filtered after him. Kaspar, however, hung back, waiting for Fabian at the base of the stairs. We both descended.

'Don't let her out of your sight.' He jerked his thumb towards me and I dropped my gaze to the floor.

'I am perfectly capable of looking after a human, Kaspar,' Fabian replied testily.

'Perhaps.' He went to leave but I dived forward and grabbed his wrist in a sudden burst of energy as my heart leapt. The floor squealed beneath his boots as he swung back around; his cloak slung away from the loose linen shirt he wore underneath, revealing a coat of arms emblazoned on the breast: a black rose, dripping a drop of blood into a large 'V' below.

'Please, don't kill anyone,' I whispered.

I thought I saw his eyes soften for a moment. But he tore his wrist from my grip like I was no more than a child, which I realized I must be to him. *A child.* He walked down the steps after the others, who were already halfway across the grounds, stopping once he reached the lawns, turning back towards me as I stood watching from the open doorway, inhaling the first fresh air in weeks.

His eyes rose from the floor to meet mine. He held that gaze for a moment, before he pulled the hood of his cloak over his head, casting all into shadow, save for his glistening emerald eyes. His dark figure lingered for a little longer, until he swept around into the sunset that had bathed the world in pale gold. As he reached the other cloaked figures, they all sped up, becoming a dark blur on the landscape, running into the falling sun and on the hunt as they had been the first time I had set eyes upon their kind.

The moon soon replaced the sun and stars dotted the clear night sky, untainted by the orange glow of the built-up areas. Somewhere, a clock chimed, telling me it was getting on towards midnight.

'There's far more to this world than humans think, isn't there?' I asked, turning to face Fabian from my window seat.

His face was framed by the dancing fire, which roared in the hearth. It was eerie, watching the orange flames light up his pale skin, lapping at it as though it longed to burn his unnatural presence away.

'Far more. This is just one royal family of many,' he continued. 'But you don't want to know more. Ignorance is a blessing. Treasure it.'

I nodded. *He's right.*

Unfolding my legs, I slipped off the seat and moved myself to one of the armchairs. He looked up in anticipation, by now used to my quizzing.

'What happened to the Queen?'

I instantly regretted asking, because whatever it was, it had stirred some deep, forgotten emotion in him. He sank back into the chair and his blue eyes flashed to black, and then to grey, where they remained. They were pitiful, lost of all the life they usually contained. If colour could drain from his face, it would.

'I-I'm sorry, I shouldn't have asked,' I stammered. His eyes glazed over and he didn't move. 'Fabian?'

His head snapped up and the greyness in his eyes seemed to melt away, returning to their usual sky blue. His stiff body loosened and he ran a hand down the back of his head.

'I'm sorry, but when you know someone that long . . . you . . .' he trailed off. 'I will tell you on the condition that you never speak a word of it to anyone but me.'

I didn't hesitate. 'I won't say a thing.'

'I will start from the very beginning. It's a long story.'

I shifted a little, trying to make myself as comfortable as possible, never taking my eyes off his saddened face.

'Vampires have been around for millions of years. We lived alongside nature without any conflict and drank the blood of any animal we could lay hands on. If the theory of evolution is indeed correct, then when humans appeared, the vampires first met their match. But we treated them like we did any other – we continued to hunt them and quickly developed a taste for their blood.'

'How can you know this if it was so long ago?' I asked.

'I've already told you, the oldest vampire is, well, *old*,' he answered. 'As I was saying, the early humans eventually learned to fight back, and the vampires realized their mistake. The most powerful vampire family, the Varns, ordered all vampires to go into hiding. They were to try not to kill humans when they fed, and to hunt at night wherever possible. It was a drastic attempt to prevent the destruction of both species.'

I nodded. 'But I don't get what this has to do with the Queen?'

'It will all make sense in a moment. Humanity was growing, and fast. Forced by the humans' relentless fighting, the Varns and a few hundred others fled to Romania. They took advantage of the unsuspecting people of Eastern Europe, unaware of the threat living in their lands. Around the same time, it was discovered that humans could be turned and the Varns' ancestors ordered a mass turning. Thousands became vampires in just one night. Stronger, more confident, they branched out.'

He paused for a breathy sigh, which I realized he hadn't been taking.

'But the old rules still stood and, unseen, the vampires were gradually forgotten, and stories told by fathers to sons turned into myths and legends. But there were always those who never forgot. These are the humans that became the hunters and the slayers, and they vowed to protect humanity. They succeeded somewhat, by driving the Varns from Transylvania about three hundred years ago.'

'King Vladimir, the current king, has ruled for millennia now. But when he was just a Prince, he met a vampire who lived in what is now Spain. She was called Carmen Eztli. Over time, they fell in love and married a century later. The match was perfect and together they ruled for almost ten thousand years and had six children.'

He rested his chin in his hands. 'She was the perfect antidote to the King's pessimism and temper and, in turn, he tamed her sharp tongue. You don't find love like that every day.'

I couldn't help but notice that he kept using 'was', but it seemed as though he was about to explain that.

'Just over three years ago, a new human government came to power. Outwardly, they seemed more sympathetic to our cause, so the Queen, seeing an opportunity, quickly sought the passing of a new treaty to update what had already been signed. The government agreed on the condition that their slayer allies, the Pierre clan, would also sign it.'

He didn't seem to notice me slipping onto the coffee table as I tried to catch his hushed words, which were becoming quieter and quieter.

'The Queen went on a state visit to Romania to open up discussions. She went to the Pierre's ancestral home in Romania, and before she could even . . . they had leapt on her . . .' He was choking up, sobs escaping his lips but no tears falling. 'They leapt on her, and pushed a stake through her heart!'

My hands flew to my mouth and I took in a sharp breath. 'She was murdered?' I didn't know what I had expected, but it wasn't *that*. I felt something wet drop into my lap and, astonished, found tears falling from my own eyes. I glided to his side and hovered beside the arm of the chair, hardly knowing what I was doing.

'I'm so sorry,' I whispered. 'I shouldn't have brought it up.' He wrapped his arms around my waist and rested his head against my stomach. I tensed at the sudden contact but he didn't seem to notice how uncomfortable he was making me.

'It's okay,' he murmured back, 'You couldn't have known. It was two-and-a-half years ago now but for us that feels like yesterday. It ruined us. She was so loved. Thousands went to her funeral.' His sentences were disjointed and clipped, his pain at recounting what had happened clear. 'It was the worst day of my life. So many people cried and,

Violet, vampires don't give up their tears easily. But they did. It was awful. I'm used to people dying, but this . . . this was different. It was like I had lost a part of me, like half my heart had died.'

I nodded, knowing the exact feeling.

'Afterwards, everything changed. Nobody was ever the same. The King moved out of the main bedroom and Kaspar had it instead. He died along with his wife.'

His eyes filled with more remorse; more pain; more regret.

'There were mass killings at that time. Did you ever notice that?'

My eyes went wide. The newspaper article had compared Trafalgar Square to the Kent Bloodsuckers incident, which had happened around that time.

'And Kaspar?' I prompted.

'He took it hard. Harder than the rest of us. He was so close to his mother. But it wasn't just that. Only fourth and seventh children can inherit the throne, and her death means there will never be a seventh child and he is indefinitely heir.'

His eyes flashed a black-grey once more and his hold around me became unbearably tight. I let out a little whine as my ribcage felt like it was being crushed. He loosened his grip, but his fists remained clenched.

'His grief changed him. He isn't the Kaspar I used to consider as good as a brother any more.' He laughed hollowly. 'Sure he was a womanizer even then, but that was nothing compared to now. Now he uses and abuses his power, bedding everything that walks, and he thinks nothing of taking a life . . .' he trailed off, too traumatized to carry on.

Yes, I knew that Kaspar. But somehow, through my loathing, through everything he had done to me, I felt pity.

I knew how he felt. I knew how grief shaped and remoulded your life. I knew how it could make you hate the ones you love with such a passion. I knew how you would do anything just to ease the pain for a single moment.

'I wish, Violet, that you could have seen us all before it happened. You would think of us differently then.'

I said nothing. I couldn't agree. That hate of vampires was embedded deep within me, passed from generation to generation, all the way back to those first humans, who had first learned to fear these powerful creatures.

'And with her died any hope of peace with the humans and the slayers. Now the war is just getting worse.' He squeezed me, as though I wasn't on the opposite side of this so-called conflict. 'It will destroy us, unless you're one of those who believes in the Prophecy.'

I prised myself away and lowered onto the arm of the chair. 'Prophecy?'

'The Prophecy of the Heroines. Some eighth-century crackpot predicted that if nine 'chosen heroines' find each other and learn to work together, they could create a lasting peace between us and humanity. But why leave something so important to fate? Everyone believed that the Queen could do it . . . but now we have to wait for the impossible,' he finished in a bitter undertone.

'But do you know what the worst thing is, Violet?' he asked after a long pause, which included the flexing of his fists. 'It was planned. We had an anonymous tip that someone within your government ordered her murder. We don't know who. But I swear, if I ever find out, I will drain someone they love, so they know what it is like to lose someone. So they can feel that pain too.' He finished, growling, lips rolled back. His eyes were blood red, but flashing to black and back.

I drew back, scared of this side of Fabian I knew of, but had never seen. He looked down at me, his blond hair falling over his livid eyes. Immediately, his expression softened, and his eyes returned to their airy blue.

'I'm sorry, Violet. You don't want to know this,' he murmured softly. He pulled me back to him and I sank onto the arm of the chair, letting the onslaught of information sink in, fitting its way around what I already knew. It made so much sense.

'You need to go to bed,' Fabian's musical voice chimed in my ear. I nodded, my eyes dropping.

I felt him begin to lift me and, in seconds, I was being lowered onto soft sheets. My eyes were just about open when I saw him sweep down. For a moment, panic swept through me, but it faded as his lips, as cold as they would be on a winter's day, brushed my cheek.

'Sweet dreams, Violet.'

I heard a click and the lamps went out. Lazy thoughts drifted in and out of my mind, forming the beginnings of dreams.

My father had entered government just three years ago. He didn't like vampires. My eyes flew open, and I sat bolt upright in bed.

He couldn't have, could he?

It's a coincidence, I told myself firmly. *A coincidence.* Anyone could have ordered her death. Desperate, I placed all thought of it into a box in my mind, locked it and chucked away the key. I would not think of it again.

FOURTEEN

Violet

So much time passed here unnoticed, as if the sands of time seemed to take pleasure in dropping when my back was turned. Before I knew it, the sun had set over the Varns' estate, Varnley, and the moon would be rising, if it were not covered by menacing storm clouds that rolled in over the forest-covered hills. It had started raining earlier, just as it had on my first night here. I gave the weather merit – the rain persisted right through the afternoon and well into the evening and still fell as night drew in.

Just as I changed for bed, the first flashes of lightning illuminated my dark room. Great shadows were cast on the walls, and I watched, almost in awe, as forks were sent rocketing to the ground. Seconds later, great clasps of thunder echoed over the valley. The voiles covering the French doors swayed a little, as the fierce winds found there way through minute cracks in the frame. I slipped into bed, forcing the childhood fear of a storm aside and pulled the sheets tightly around myself, banishing the cold.

I screwed my eyes shut and waited until I fell into an uneasy sleep.

A cloaked figure swept his way through the forest, deep into the parts where rogues ruled. Rogues like himself.

He didn't make a sound as he walked, his movement fluid, graceful as a lark, but stealthy as an eagle and as fast as a falcon. He had been compared to them all and he *enjoyed* that.

The figure knew the path well, so he need not look down. Instead, he focused on the ever-nearing building: his destination. It was an ornate building, but quite insignificant considering what it concealed. It was not large and was built entirely of grey stone – granite, perhaps. The figure did not know, and he did not care.

A breeze blew through from the open door, and eager to be done with his business, the cloaked figure descended the steps inside, taking three at a time, impatient. When he reached the bottom, had he been human, he would have felt the considerable drop in temperature and the chill in the still air.

He bowed his head, not out of respect, but to prevent bumping his head on the low roof, and walked quickly down the long corridor, passing the resting place of charred corpses of long-dead vampires. His footsteps were the only sound in the darkness and even he admitted he had to strain to hear them. He smiled to himself. Not even the rats dared venture down here. His ego swelled, knowing only he had the courage to explore the dark depths of the catacombs.

He came to a room and allowed his eyes to sweep across it until they came to rest on a young girl, tied to the legs of the stone throne that guarded the tombs. Her head drooped and there was no colour in her cheeks. Huge gashes on her neck oozed blood and her clothes were ripped, leaving her almost naked – he could see that her young, once-smooth breasts were covered in small scratches and her stomach looked red and swollen, like she had been punched several times. The frayed rope tied around her wrists had gauged out chunks of skin, and a bone penetrated the skin where her ankle should be.

He looked on, disgusted. The rogues could have at least brought him something a little more *appetising*. He would think her dead if he could not see the pitiful rising and falling of her chest.

He stepped forward. His footsteps echoed in the silence and, startled, the girl raised her head, her eyes searching the gloom and struggling to focus.

'W-who are you?' she croaked.

'Who I am is of no concern to you, but *what* I am is,' he taunted, parting his lips to reveal his two sharpened canines.

Her eyes widened in fear, and she attempted to scrabble back, but the ropes binding her prevented her from doing so. 'Please—'

He cut her off. 'What is your name?'

'S-Sarah.'

He smiled once again, revealing his gleaming fangs. 'Well, Sarah. I have a proposition for you.' He stooped down to her level. 'You and I can have a little bit of fun and you can become like me – once I am done with you of course. Or you can become my dinner and . . . die. Your call.'

Her eyes widened, and tears trickled down her cheek. 'Just kill me. Please,' she sobbed – at least, he thought it was sobbing. It sounded more like the whine of a dog.

The smile dropped from his face. This was not what he wanted. Lust and thirst were pumping through his system, driven by his dead heart, and he wanted to have his way.

He wiped her tears away with his thumb, grimacing as grime coated his fingers. He stroked her cheek, rubbing his thumb in small circles, fighting to keep his calm demeanour.

'Are you sure, Sarah? We could have *so* much fun,' he prompted breathily.

'It hurts too much! Just end it,' she sobbed, her head drooping once more. He knew unconsciousness would soon envelop her, sheltering her from the pain. He would not let her get away that easily. He took hold of her neck with both hands, wrenching her free of the ropes.

'You're lucky that I am a merciful vampire.'

With that, he broke her frail neck, almost snapping her in two. The crack echoed in the stillness as he felt her go limp. So thirsty now, he yanked her neck towards his waiting fangs and began to drink.

Her blood was bitter and nowhere near satisfying, but it would do for now. He picked up the mangled body in his arms and walked outside, tossing the corpse into the dark forest.

A tiny trickle of blood escaped his lips and slid down his chin. He wiped it away, smiling to himself, already wishing for more.

I sat bolt upright in bed and screamed, the horrendous sound echoing off the walls. Cold beads of sweat ran down my forehead and I was shivering, gagging for breath between shrieks.

'Violet!' The door burst open to reveal Fabian, wearing a panicked expression. 'Violet, are you okay?' He rushed over to me, untangling me from the mass of sheets that had wrapped around me whilst I slept. Dry sobs tickled my throat and I took several short and shallow breaths, desperate for air, trying to nod my head but failing.

'What's wrong? What happened?' he quizzed, placing an arm around my shoulders.

'I was asleep . . .' I began, confused, my eyes darting about the room, searching for nonexistent answers.

'Was it a dream, Violet?' Fabian cooed, peeling himself away from my sweaty side and looking at me through his soothing blue eyes. I nodded.

'What was it about? Why was it so bad?' he asked as I took deep, shuddering breaths, unsure of whether to tell him. He wouldn't understand. How could he? He never slept; never had dreams; never had nightmares.

'There was a man. And a girl. H-he killed her,' I sobbed, the tickling feeling returning. Bile rose in my throat as I thought of her begging to die and I gagged a couple of times. 'It seemed so real.'

'It was just a nightmare, Violet.' Fabian muttered sternly; unconvincingly. 'But tell me if you have any more, won't you?'

'Only if you promise not to tell anyone that I have nightmares.' It was a strange request, but I didn't want anybody knowing, especially Kaspar.

'You have my word,' Fabian assured, extracting himself from my sheets and getting up to leave. 'Are you okay now?'

I smiled and nodded, and he left my side reluctantly.

But I wasn't okay. Even as my eyes closed and I tried to drift back towards sleep, a far more disturbing thought crossed my mind. If they were real, then an innocent girl had just died and somewhere out in the darkness of the night, a true monster prowled the nearby forest.

FIFTEEN

Violet

I woke up early the next morning, my dream still troubling me. I was groggy and tired, but eager to be awake before the Varns returned. The sun was breaking through the fluffy white clouds and the day had more of a summer feel to it – *finally*. I got ready, and headed out, only to stop dead in my tracks when I reached the top of the stairs. My mouth fell open. The Varns had returned. But they weren't alone. I darted back into the shadows and stared wide-eyed at the opposite wall. *I need to go back and change.*

'I saw you, Girly,' a voice sneered from the bottom of the stairs – Kaspar. All pity that I might have reserved for him after learning of his mother's fate evaporated with his tone of voice and I groaned. 'Don't be rude. Come down.'

Reluctantly, I edged back around the corner of the wall and teetered on the top step, folding my arms around my middle. First to look up was Fabian, who smiled. In a flash, twenty other vampires were staring up at me.

They were mostly men, but there were a few women too,

Charity amongst them, shooting me murderous looks. They were a mix of ages, some looking as young as Kaspar, some looking like they should be lying in a coffin.

There was a wolf-whistle from the bottom of the stairs and I looked down, searching for the source of the sound. Leaning against the bottom step was a man, his tussled blond hair cut short, a little stubble on his chin and his skin an odd pale orange in colour. He looked up casually at me, not bothering to hide the fact that he was staring at my breasts.

'Well, who's this then, Kaspar?' He had an American accent – a complete contrast to the Varns' upper-class British voices.

'Who's the leech?' I muttered, not intending for them to hear, but of course they did.

'The human?' The man's voice filled with glee as he quizzed Kaspar, who nodded. 'Well, come on down then. I'm sure Kaspar won't mind sharing.'

I wasn't going to move but Kaspar's glare made me think otherwise. I didn't have to hang around long until his glare turned into a weapon as his eyes scanned the writing on my – well, *Lyla*'s – T-shirt:

'SORRY, I DON'T DO SPARKLES. BUT I WOULD TAP VAN HELSING ANY DAY!'

'Kitchen. Now,' Kaspar growled. He pointed towards the living-room door and followed me through, rounding on me as soon as we reached the counter.

'What the hell?' He pointed at my T-shirt.

'It's Lyla's!' I protested.

He rested against the countertop and ran a hand down the side of his face. 'That's half the council out there and you had to wear it today! God, you are more trouble than you are worth.'

'Vampires have councils?'

'Plainly; you were just looking at it,' Kaspar retorted. 'Go, just go. But you're to be down for dinner later. Wear something nicer than that.' He gestured at my clothes and motioned for me to leave at the same time.

I gave a disinterested *humph*, and left, climbing the stairs. But as I climbed the hairs on the back of my neck stood up and I was compelled to glance behind me. Someone was watching. Sure enough, a young man in the far corner of the room was studying my back with unwavering concentration. He had long silver hair, tied back, and an extremely angular face, with prominent cheek bones. He was not plain, quite handsome in fact, but there was something that made him repulsive. Perhaps it was his stance, looking up at me through his slit-like eyes, expression cold. Or maybe it was his crimson cloak, the same colour as blood. I turned away and sped up the stairs, taking them two at a time.

I crashed on my bed, thumping the mattress in frustration. Dinner with a vampire. *Joy.*

The clock was nearing six and, reluctantly, I slipped off the bed, sleepy after my afternoon doze. I hadn't meant to fall asleep, but I was paying for the early mornings. Lyla had already laid a short, dark brown dress out, which I changed into, disgruntled by how low the cut of the lace neckline was.

It wasn't long after when there was a knock at the door. Thinking it must be Fabian, I got up to answer. But when I opened it, I did a double-take as I saw who was outside.

It was the vampire from the far corner of the entrance hall. His dark blue eyes were wider now, warmer, and a smile adorned his face. He wore a black suit with a red tie and his long hair was loose.

'Forgive me, Miss Lee, but I have been sent to escort you to dinner,' he said in a smooth voice. I blushed.

'Right.' I nodded, trying to remember what to say. 'Err, just give me two minutes, I'm nearly ready,' I said, backing away and darting back into the wardrobe.

'Of course,' he called after me. I ran back in and scrabbled around, searching out a pair of shoes.

'So who are you?' I called from the wardrobe.

'I am the Honourable Ilta Crimson, second son of Lord Valerian Crimson, the Earl of Wallachia.'

I sprung up as I heard his voice right behind me.

'Do not be scared, Miss Lee. I will not hurt you.' He reached out and took my hands in his. 'I am simply inquisitive about your most intriguing future.' He smiled, a little too nicely, revealing his sharp fangs, which I could have sworn were far longer and pointier than any of the Varns' or their friends' fangs.

At that moment, Fabian appeared in the doorway, surprise then anger covering his face. 'What are you doing here?' he demanded, turning to Ilta. I glanced at our hands, still joined, and wrenched them away.

'I am here because I was sent by the King to escort her to dinner,' said Ilta.

Fabian arched an eyebrow. 'Well, Kaspar sent me, too. Are you all right?' he asked me, shooting me a look as if I should be shaken.

I nodded, 'Lead the way, I guess.'

SIXTEEN

Violet

I walked into the dining room, Ilta leading me, Fabian just behind. Candles flickered in their holders on the walls, bathing the room in a soft light. Red drapes were closed over the windows, and in the centre of the room was an extremely long table, covered with a deep red tablecloth and laid with elaborate cutlery – and just a single plate of the china must have cost the earth.

Ilta led me to the middle of the table, where he pulled out my chair for me. I sat down and in a blink he was opposite me, pulling his own chair out. Other vampires filed in after us, taking their seats. Sat next door to me on the left was the American and to my right was Fabian.

After a few minutes everyone was seated and a dull chatter filled the room. I turned to Fabian. 'Why am I here?' I whispered, trying to keep my voice as low as possible.

'Well, as the council are discussing what to do with you in the morning, they wanted to actually meet you.'

'Why are they discussing me?' I answered in alarm.

'There have been . . . developments.' He twiddled with one of the many knives and, catching my ever-so-slightly horrified expression in the gleaming blade, he placed it down. 'Oh, don't look so worried. You won't be shot of my wonderful company that easily.'

I wasn't worried about *that*. I was worried about the 'developments'.

'What sort of developments?'

'It's worth more than my inheritance to tell you that. Anyway—' He glanced towards the door before hooking an arm under my elbow and hoisting me up onto my feet. 'The show is on the road.'

The door opened and the King entered. Everybody hushed, shifting as they stood, waiting as the chair at the far end of the table was pulled away a fraction and then pushed back in once the King had sat down; only once he was seated did the other thirty guests – including the Varn children – sit down.

I leaned forward, absorbing his presence, noticing that both he and Kaspar wore the same suit, embroidered with the coat of arms. The only real difference between father and son was the arrogant smile that Kaspar wore as he winked at Charity, who giggled, twirling her hair and returning the gesture. As I stared at him, his gaze flickered my way. His smirk widened, but he was distracted as a waiter poured him a glass of blood.

A waiter appeared at my side too, offering me wine. I accepted and he returned within seconds – after only a minute or two, they had filled every glass and they moved to the side of the room, where they retrieved large platters of food. It didn't look very substantial – there were small canapés and tiny bowls of soup, one of which I took, staring down at the assortment of knives, forks and spoons laid out in front of me, unsure of which to use. I glanced to my right for help, but Fabian and Ilta were already engaged in conversation with those sat on their other sides.

'Work from the outside in,' a soft American voice whispered from my left. I looked up, startled to see the vampire I didn't know talking to me.

'Thanks,' I hissed back, taking up the spoon at the very edge. The vampire dipped a spoon into his soup, scooping away from him. I copied his actions, watching how he ate exactly. I grimaced as I took my first mouthful. *Asparagus. Yuck.*

He smiled a little, amused. 'I'm Alex,' he said.

'Violet,' I replied, returning his smile.

'Oh, I know,' he chuckled.

I raised my eyebrows, displeased that everyone knew my name, but he just laughed once more.

'So, tell me, Violet, what do you think of the royal family?' he asked. 'Honestly,' he added.

My face fell. 'They're all right, they haven't done anything to me, but Kaspar is . . .' I trailed off. He looked taken aback. 'What?' I asked.

'Kaspar and I are friends.'

Oops. 'Oh,' I breathed, awkward. 'Well, I guess he is kind of—'

'It's fine, you are entitled to an opinion.' He smiled, but it looked forced. We fell into silence for a while, then Alex began to start talking animatedly to Fabian, across me. *Guess they are friends too. Small world.*

I was saved from my solitary vigil by the arrival of the main meal. The vampires all had steak, cooked so rare that blood still oozed from the tender meat. A plate was placed onto the table in front of me and I was surprised to see something vegetarian-looking, which I poked at with my fork, not too sure about it. The room became quiet for a while, as everyone ate. I watched others eat, and I had to admit, it was really quite weird watching vampires eat human food with knives and forks. *Very civilized.*

'I hear, Violet, that you were accepted at university. Do tell us what you were planning to study?' Ilta asked, his slick voice breaking through the stillness.

'O-oh,' I began with a nervous stutter, aware that most of the vampires were now looking at me, interested. 'I was going to study politics, philosophy and economics actually,' I gushed, knowing it wouldn't go down too well – it was obvious that meant I was going to follow in my father's footsteps.

A black box rattled deep within my mind and I frowned a little, trying to lock away what I suspected about my father.

'Ah, I see,' Ilta replied. I looked at the floor, embarrassed.

'You must be an intelligent student,' Fabian intervened.

'I guess . . .'

'Who are you kidding? Anyone can get into university these days!' Charity cut in with disdain.

Kaspar raised his glass and I was sure I heard him mumble '*you* couldn't, Charity' into it.

'Indeed. Education is no longer simply for the elite,' an old man said. His wispy white hair was tied in a long pony-tail, his beard flicked over his shoulders. He spoke to Charity, but watched me with an increasingly pensive stare.

Fabian noticed the man's stare and shifted. 'Violet, this is Eaglen. He is the vampire I told you about the other night. The old one,' he mouthed. The man, Eaglen, smiled.

'Yes, the old one,' he echoed, finishing off the last drop in his glass, which was hastily refilled. He chuckled and turned away, seemingly satisfied. I arched an eyebrow at Fabian, who shared my puzzled expression.

'He's like that sometimes,' he muttered.

Glasses continued to be filled at the King's order, but as the waiters moved forward, bottles now empty, they paused, staring at me – the next nearest blood source. I saw Alex and Kaspar exchange worried looks and Fabian did the same whilst discretely shuffling his chair closer to mine. Conversation died away and the room rippled into hush.

'Violet, go,' Ilta said, as Fabian pushed my chair back. 'Quickly.'

I didn't need telling twice. I scrabbled out of my chair and backed to the wall, feeling my way across the room, too scared to turn my back on any of them. Every blood-thirsty pair of eyes followed me until I reached the door and fell out, slamming it behind me.

I leaned against the wall of the corridor, breathing heavily. A couple of tears escaped my sore eyes and I wished for nothing more than my bed, at home, where it was safe. A knot of homesickness formed in my stomach once more. At that moment, the door opened and Kaspar slipped out. I wiped the tears away before he noticed I was crying.

'You okay?' he asked, stiffly. I shrugged, trying to act offhand.

'They won't attack you, you know,' he said. I looked up at him disbelievingly. 'If they kill you, there could be an all-out war. Believe it or not, we don't want that,' he replied, glumly.

'This meeting is about me and that is why the council has assembled,' I replied, equally as sullen. He nodded mutely. 'Why now?'

Sighing, he leaned up against the wall beside me. 'Because we have been informed that the slayers have made a truce with a group of rogue vampires. They plan to attack us, take you, and God knows what else.'

'I—'

'Don't bother, no slayer will set foot here,' Kaspar interjected. He stared blankly at the opposite wall, deep in thought.

'Life is so crap sometimes,' I mumbled to myself.

'Tell me about it,' I heard him say, ever so softly. I turned to him, surprised. He felt my gaze and turned too.

'I won't be safe here any more, will I?' In an instant, he was right in front of me, breathing on my neck, his chest rising and falling in time to mine. My heartbeat quickened.

'You were never safe here, Violet Lee.'

He lowered his head to my neck, his hands settling themselves on my hips. I backed as far into the wall as I could, but he just pushed himself further into me. I was shaking and my hands clenched into fists, my body tensing, waiting for the onslaught of pain. I tried pushing him away, but he didn't move – I doubt he even felt me trying to escape. His fangs met my neck, grazing the skin. I whimpered and turned away. He took a deep breath, inhaling my scent. His mouth opened wider and I prepared for the bite.

'Don't. Please.' A single tear rolled down my cheek, as I resorted to begging. 'Kaspar,' I whispered. To my surprise, he pulled away, his eyes opening. Another tear slid down my cheek and he caught it with the back of his thumb, wiping it away.

'I don't understand why you don't get it.' His hand ran down the length of my neck and side, until it came to rest on my hip once more. 'We lust for you and your blood and your body. You want it too. I can see it in your eyes and feel it in your heartbeat.'

My eyes searched for the floor, but I could only see him.

'You don't get that right now I could snap you in half and suck you dry. You don't get that you are food and that we struggle to see you as a living creature. An equal. Because you're not.'

'And you don't get that I am a person with feelings,' I breathed.

He backed away a little, taking his hands off me, searching my face with his eyes. 'No, I don't,' he murmured back. 'You are never safe here, Violet Lee. Remember that. *Never.*'

He turned his back to me and I could hear him breathing; see his hands balling into fists, fighting the urge to bite. He turned back, placing his hands against the wall either side of my head. 'Stay away from Ilta Crimson,' he said, his eyes burning and menace fuelling his words.

'Why?' I asked, surprised at his complete change of tone.

'Because I don't trust him,' he growled.

'You don't trust him?' I mouthed, surprised. 'In case you didn't notice, he wasn't trying to bite my head off back there. He is the least of my worries.'

'Goddamn it, Girly! Why don't you just listen to me? Just trust me!' he yelled back, all softness in his nature gone, disappearing so quickly I flinched and hit the back of my head on the wall.

'Trust you?' I squealed. 'Why would I trust you? You kidnapped me! You constantly try to suck my blood! I'd *much* rather trust Ilta than you!'

'But you don't know him! You don't know what he is capable of!' Kaspar roared back, grabbing my shoulders and shaking me like a ragdoll.

'No. You're right. I don't know him,' I replied, more calmly, taking deep breaths. His hands unsnapped from my shoulders like my skin was made of hot coals. I sidestepped away from him. 'But I'll take the risk, thanks,' I spat.

His face lit up with anger, his eyes turning pure black. I turned and walked away, fuming.

'Where the hell are you going?' he shouted down the corridor after me.

'To my room!' I screamed back, spinning to face him. Our eyes met, and I glared at him for a full minute.

'On your own head be it, Girly. Don't say I didn't warn you,' he snarled.

I turned on my heel and stormed up the hall, towards the stairs. But as I reached the end, I couldn't resist having the last word. I spun around to see Kaspar staring at me, anger still evident in his face.

'You know what, Kaspar? I wish you had just killed me back in London! Just ended it there. Then I wouldn't have to suffer *this*. Why didn't you? Why?' I shrieked, and ran, but not before I caught his expression, which spoke a thousand words.

He didn't know why.

SEVENTEEN

Kaspar

Council meetings really are the best fun one can have, I thought bitterly, staring out the window at freedom. I sat at the far end of the table, hardly listening as my father debated with Ilta Crimson over something or other. His whole family were swindlers. They thought the sun revolved around them, but Ilta was the worst. Quiet, calm and controlled, he was always the charmer. It wasn't hard to see how Girly was fooled by him. He was a snake. He would slither in, hiss at you until you were lulled and then he would rise up and bite you. *Especially* if you were much younger and female.

I suppressed my thoughts as the meeting progressed. My only consolation was the firm grasp on my leg, which came from Charity, who sat next to me. She looked up at me with adoring eyes, batting her eyelids, giving me the occasional seductive wink.

She began stroking the inside of my leg and I shuddered, enjoying the feelings of lust gushing through my system. I shuddered again, as her hand reached for the fly on my trousers.

'Ghost pass over your grave, Kaspar?' Ilta sneered from the other side of the room, false concern in his voice. His dark blue eyes were crinkled with amusement.

I snapped back from my trance. 'No, quite fine, Ilta,' I answered.

My father turned to glare at me. He gave the tiniest shake of his head and I knew he was perfectly aware of the whereabouts of Charity's hand. I discretely slipped one of my own hands under the table and moved hers back down to my knee. She looked up at me for a moment and feigned hurt. But I knew she was faking it. She *always* faked it.

'How do we even know Lee will retaliate with the help of the slayers? Until then, I refuse to even consider a plan of action,' Lamair declared, placing his hands on the table as though that was that.

I sighed. We had been over this twice already.

'My dear Lamair, as I said before, we have reliable sources,' my father said.

Mutterings erupted throughout the room and I resolved to stare at the bookshelves of my father's study, desperate to entertain myself. *I wonder how long it would take to read all of them?*

A while, my voice answered.

I gritted my teeth. *Nobody asked you.*

But you're still talking to me, it sniggered, which always beat me. Voices aren't meant to snigger.

Well, you get used to it after eighteen odd years, I finished and it fell silent. It never had an answer to that one.

'Well then, I say we just kill her. That way all our troubles our over.'

'No, Lamair. That will cause problems with the human government. We have to be diplomatic.'

'Surely—'

A vampire I should probably know the name of cut in on him. 'Forgive me, Your Majesty, but I don't understand why we are risking the Kingdom for the sake of one human girl? She is not worth a fight with the slayers and a possible loss of good relations with the human government, is she?'

There were several calls of 'hear, hear'. I noticed Eaglen was unusually quiet. He leaned on his hands thoughtfully, but almost as soon as I looked at him, he raised his eyes to mine and I turned away.

'This is the daughter of one of the greatest antagonists vampire kind has ever faced. We cannot afford to be rash, for fear of starting something we will long regret,' my father explained. That one crucial fact – who she was, or rather, *who her father was* – still didn't seem to have sunk into their thick skulls. My father turned to Eaglen. 'You acted as one of our ambassadors to the human government most recently. What is your opinion?'

Eaglen sighed. 'The government's and, crucially, the Prime Minister's stance on us is a no intervention policy – in other words, they turn a blind eye. The PM refused to see Ashton or I whilst we were in Westminster, although he sent his assurances that the investigation into the London Bloodbath will be quietly closed, alongside an insistence that he will not be so compliant in the event of a similar incident.' He looked pointedly at me. 'But he is not our problem. Lee is.' He leaned forward and rested his arms on the table, flicking his hair back behind his shoulders. 'Lee cannot make a move yet. He has direct orders from the PM not to do anything to threaten national security – he is afraid that any attempt on our lives will result in retaliation and the consequent loss of innocent life.'

Cain, who had looked just as bored as I was, sat bolt up, a spark of alarm in his voice as he spoke. 'It wouldn't though, would it?'

Father shook his head.

Eaglen continued, pointing in Cain's direction. 'Ah, but we're better off letting them think that, because as long as we do, Lee won't do anything. To disobey that order would end his career.'

'And no job, no power,' I interjected, following his train of thought.

'Exactly, young Prince!' he exclaimed, turning his crooked left forefinger to me. 'We must remember that Lee doesn't just want his daughter back, he wants to bring about our downfall.' That was no secret. Ever since the current government had come to power just over three years ago, Lee had made his intentions towards us quite clear. 'But he is fully aware that bullets and guns won't achieve that. So he needs the hunters and the rogues. But the hunters will not liaise with him unless he has power, influence and money.'

Or access to the taxpayer's money, I thought.

'The Prime Minister's orders are to not intervene unless we make any threat or show of violence. If we do, Lee will be ready.' A blanket of silence descended upon the room and wrapped itself around the table. 'We need to avoid confrontation at all costs. We cannot kill the girl or force her to turn and we cannot threaten Lee or his government, and presumably the hunters, either.'

'So what do we do then?' was Lamair's uneasy question. I was sure it was one almost every person sat in the room shared.

'We do nothing and wait until the girl turns of her own free will,' Father replied. There was a badly hidden gasp of shock. The idea of doing *nothing* was not one anybody in the room had entertained, clearly. But I gawped at my father for a different reason. If he thought Girly was going to turn anytime soon, he had another thing coming.

'Quite agreed,' Eaglen said. 'We carry on as normal and give them no reason to suspect we know of their plans and no reason to attack. Meanwhile, I suggest we keep Miss Lee as sheltered as possible – there is no need for her to know of the other dimensions with all these prophecy rumours circulating among the Sage. A human knowing the strength of our seers and the Prophecy of the Heroines is the last thing we need. I'm sure the inter-dimensional council will agree to that.' He waved his hand dismissively. 'I also propose, Your Majesty, that to ensure her life and her blood are not threatened, you place the King and Crown's Protection over her.'

Father nodded. 'It will be implemented with immediate effect.'

'I think it might be wise not to let her know of that, or about anything to do with her father,' Sky added. 'She strikes me as the sort who would act rashly if she knew. Neither do we want to give her any hope of leaving Varnley. She would never turn if that were the case.'

Finally, some sense!

My father cleared his throat. 'Agreed. Nothing that we spoke of today leaves this room. But for now, this meeting is adjourned until we receive further news.'

I sighed again, exasperated. Chairs scraped and people began to leave the room, bowing and curtseying. Charity skipped off after them, exclaiming excitedly that she was going dress-shopping for the Autumnal Equinox.

'Try and stay focused next time, Kaspar,' my father scolded from the opposite side of the room, where he stood waiting for me to join him. Reluctantly, I walked towards him, waiting for the lecture I would undoubtedly receive.

'Five hours, Father! Five hours and the only thing they could agree on was that Violet should choose to turn. You do know that is not going to happen, don't you?'

'That is where you come in, young Prince,' Eaglen chuckled, limping around the table towards us. I frowned. Eaglen never usually had a limp. He might be old, but he wasn't frail. Yet he had aged over the summer. His hair was whiter and the fine lines that appeared around the corners of his eyes didn't disappear when he stopped laughing. 'And you too, young Earl,' he added, addressing Fabian who was hanging back, waiting for me. He came forward.

'You two interact with her on a daily basis, correct?' my father asked. We nodded.

'Then you are what she sees of our kind. Give her a reason to believe we are not murderers, which is doubtless what she thinks. Convince her that this is a life she could lead,' Eaglen instructed. Fabian nodded, almost eager, but I scowled, sceptic.

'It will take more than that to persuade her to turn.'

Eaglen smiled. 'When she has lost hope of returning home, it will take far less leverage.'

'I won't do it.'

I saw my father's eyes become black. 'You will do it. It's time you took responsibility for your actions—'

'And accept the consequences of my rash escapades. Yeah, I've heard it before. It's getting old,' I snapped, turning on my heel and leaving the room. The door slammed behind me with a satisfying bang. But it opened just as quickly again and Eaglen appeared, limping after me.

'Give it a try,' he said, patting me on the back. 'You might have more in common than you think.'

I arched an eyebrow, but said nothing, walking away before I really did get angry. Yet I couldn't resist one glance back at the aging, but by no means foolish, man, who watched me retreat with a knowing smirk.

What are you playing at, Eaglen? I thought. *What do you know this time?*

EIGHTEEN

Violet

August 28th brought my eighteenth birthday, and with it little reason for cheer. I had kept my mind well-guarded since I made the connection between the Queen's death and my father, so nobody realized I was a year older.

I should have been out partying, enjoying my first legal drink of alcohol; instead I was stuck in a living room full of vampires, because sitting up seemed a better option than running the risk of experiencing yet another dream. They were endless, and I didn't believe Fabian for a single second: they *were* real. The chill I felt every morning told me that.

The fire flickered lazily in the hearth, the warmth burning my legs. The long red-and-black drapes were pulled across the windows and whistling could be heard outside as a faint chime on the wind. The moon was at half, dully lighting the pond at the edge of the grounds.

I walked away from the window where I had been peeking through the curtains, watching as yet more clouds rolled in. I had never known an August like it, weather-wise. Storm after storm seemed to persist in ruining the summer and any thoughts of hot days had been given up long ago. Not that the vampires minded. I collapsed into the squashy armchair by the fire, the only person in the room to realize just how much heat it was throwing out.

I listened as Cain, Charlie, Felix and Declan played poker in the corner, occasional exclamations of 'Cheat!' breaking through the quiet. Lyla lay with her phone on the sofa, her fingers darting over the screen, smiling to herself. Kaspar sat in the darkest corner, aimlessly plucking strings on his guitar and averting his gaze whenever his name was called.

I looked back to the fire, seeking solace from the tongues lapping at the grate. Mesmerized, I gazed at it for a minute before I sensed someone watching me. Fabian, sat in the chair opposite me, stared at me through curious eyes, as though he was trying to decipher something.

'You haven't had a very good birthday, have you?' he asked, keeping his voice low.

'How do you know that?' *My mind was guarded, wasn't it?*

He smiled, his eyes twinkling with mischief. 'Looked you up online.'

I slumped back into the chair, which moulded to my back. 'As you ask, no, I haven't.'

The grin remained. 'I think I might know what will cheer you up.'

I raised an eyebrow. 'It's not dinner, is it?'

He chuckled. 'No, nothing like that. There's a royal ball coming up in a couple of weeks' time. Humans can go if they are invited,' he gushed. I narrowed my eyes, having a sneaking suspicion of where this was going. 'It's good fun and there is dancing and all sorts of music and it will cheer you up; maybe you'll even see a different side to us and the

Kingdom. Anyway, I was wondering if you would maybe like to go? Possibly?' he finished.

I raised an eyebrow again. 'Do you mean go with you?' I asked.

'Well . . . yeah.'

I grimaced. 'Well, I have a very busy schedule of avoiding being sucked dry, so I will have to check my diary. But I can pencil it in, if you like?'

A huge beam spread from ear to ear on his face and he laughed, getting to his feet, pulling me onto mine too. The four boys had stopped playing poker to watch and Lyla peered over her phone, her lips parted a little in surprise. Even Kaspar looked out from his dark corner, studying me with his piercing gaze.

'I would like that . . . I would like . . .' He swept down into a bow and took my hand, planting a kiss on my knuckles. My eyes widened in embarrassment. 'I would like you, Miss Violet Lee, to do I, Lord Fabian Marl Ariani, Earl of Ariani, the honour of accompanying me to the ball? Glass slippers and all?'

There was a pause as I digested his overkill. 'If I must,' I replied, rolling my eyes. His smile became wider and he jumped up. I glanced over at the others, who were all smiling, save for Kaspar and Lyla, whose faces were totally blank.

My heart fluttered for a moment, both in fear, disbelief and a little in excitement. 'There is only one slight problem,' I said.

'What's that?' Fabian asked.

'I don't know how to dance.'

Fabian smirked, his eyes twinkling with mischief once more. 'Oh, we can fix that.'

NINETEEN

Violet

'What do you mean you're going to give me dance lessons?'
I screeched, head whipping around from one vampire to
another.

'It means exactly that. Dance lessons. Would you like me
to spell it out for you?' Kaspar leered.

'I am perfectly capable of spelling it, thank you very much.
I am sure I am far more intelligent than you anyway,' I
replied.

'Sure thing, Girly,' he retorted, laughter curling his lips
into a lopsided smile. 'I have years on you. Now come on,
I don't have all day.' He grabbed me by the elbow and
marched down the corridor. I glanced over my shoulder,
looking for some pity from Fabian and Declan, but both just
shrugged and followed.

We arrived outside the music room and stepping inside I
saw Sky, Jag and Lyla stood beside a jet-black grand piano,
placed at the edge of a square of varnished floor.

'Here, put these on,' Lyla said, throwing a pair of super-high, shocking-red heels at me and, fearing impalement from the stilettos, I let them fall to the ground. I glanced at them and then back at my flat shoes. I caught Lyla's glare, however, and decided it would be best to do as she said. I slipped them on, the thin straps digging into my skin. Straightening up, I glanced at the ground, noting that it was a lot further down than usual.

Sky sat at the piano and Fabian grabbed my hand, pulling me onto the dance floor. I teetered on the spot, grabbing him for balance. I blushed wildly and an apologetic look formed on my face.

'Violet, have you done any dancing before, other than this grounding?' Sky called from the piano, where he sat playing scales up and down the piano, not paying the slightest bit of attention to his hands but never missing a note.

'Grinding,' Kaspar, Fabian and I corrected in unison.

'Well, whatever it is called, it is merely a filthy excuse to procreate in public. Young people these days . . . He trailed off, his voice full of disgust. A stifled snigger escaped my mouth and I saw Fabian's lips twitch. 'I will take that as a no, you have not danced before. Well, Violet, listen carefully. I am an impatient teacher. I will not wait for you to fall over.' I sobered up, smile wiped from my face. 'We will start with the box step for a waltz. Now, stop slouching and imagine there is a box on the floor. You are starting at the bottom left-hand corner. On beat one, step forward to the top left-hand corner . . . yes, like that,' he said as I took a step forward. 'On beat two, step to the top right corner with your right foot and on beat three the left foot follows.' I did as he instructed. 'And yes, bring them together! Good! Now, step back with your right foot and take your left foot back to your original position, the right foot following, and thus, you have completed your box. Good, now, try again . . .'

Over and over I did this, Sky barking orders as the others watched from the sidelines, occasionally correcting a step. After a while, he told me to start rising and falling and whirling, which left my feet in a tangle but once 'Box, remember the box!' had been shouted at me a few times, they seemed to find their way and I was sweeping across the floor without any trouble.

He stopped all of a sudden. 'I think you are ready to try it with a partner, don't you? Fabian, if you will.'

I froze. This was the bit I was scared about. Fabian stepped forward, taking my right hand in his left. He placed my other hand just below his shoulder and his hand snaked around my waist, resting just above my hip. I tensed up as soon as he touched me, afraid of the contact.

'Relax,' he mouthed, eyes full of warmth. As he breathed, I felt his cold breath stirring my hair and I was aware that we were close, very close – so close that I blushed again.

'Now just do what you were practising before, but allow Fabian to guide you,' Sky called, turning back to the piano. The music began to play and we were frozen for a moment, before I felt Fabian gently push me back a step, his feet following mine as he guided me around the room.

'I don't know what you were worrying about,' Fabian said, smiling. 'You look like you were taught in the nursery, just like the rest of us.'

I raised an eyebrow. 'You're just saying that.'

'Really, I'm not,' he retorted, beaming.

'I think we can leave the waltz for now, but there are many more dances for you to learn. Are you familiar with the dances of the late eighteenth century?' Sky asked. We came to an abrupt halt and I wobbled on the spot, relying on Fabian's steady hand to keep me upright. I looked at Sky, dumbfounded and mute. There was a wistful sigh from the corner.

'Ah, the minuet. My forte,' Jag said, coming forward.

Three hours later and I knew more dances than I had eaten hot dinners in my life, from so many eras of time that I felt like I was getting more of a history lesson than a dance lesson.

'Remember, this one is called the *Sauteuse*. Now we must move on to etiquette,' Sky said as I broke hold, relieved at the prospect of a rest: the joints in my elbows had rusted into place, leaving them stiff and sore.

'Etiquette?'

'Yes. Etiquette is as important as the steps of a dance. And stop looking so abashed, it is quite simple really,' Sky snapped, clearly displeased at my tired expression. 'First rule: a lady may never ask a gentleman to dance. She must wait to be asked. No exceptions.'

'How sexist,' I muttered, irritated and desperate to unpeel the shoe straps from the skin on my ankle.

'Yes. It is sexist,' Sky replied. 'Second rule: if you wish to decline a dance, do so politely and timidly. Yes, timidly, Miss Lee, something that is clearly not in your repertoire.'

I had opened my mouth to question it but he beat me to it and was rewarded with a snort of laughter from the corner, where Kaspar stood.

'Now, this is the most important part: curtseying. It is quite simple for you. On account of the fact you are human, you must curtsey to every partner, both before and after the dance. Aristocracy will bow back, royalty will not.'

I scowled. All curtseying and etiquette seemed to be was a humiliating, degrading exercise, designed to remind me of the fact I was human. But when I was about to voice that thought, the smile on Fabian's face stopped me, leaving me tongue-tied. *I can't spoil this for him,* I thought. *Vampire or not.*

'It is also essential that if a member of the royal family app-roaches you, you are especially courteous to them. Understood?'

I nodded. *At this rate, I'll be half-crouched all night.* 'How will I know if someone is royalty? And what if I dance with a human? Do I have to curtsey then?'

'Look for the coat of arms. But I highly doubt you will encounter any humans. They tend to stick with those they are familiar with.'

My heart sunk a fraction. One of the reasons I had agreed to go was to talk to, or at least see another human. To just glance at a set of normal teeth seemed like a dream.

'Lastly, ensure that you are never alone. This is ludicrous enough as it is and such actions will only exacerbate the danger.'

I stared at my feet, scuffing the bottom of Lyla's shoes on the floor. I knew it wasn't safe. But it would be safer at the ball than it would be alone in my room. Seeming satisfied, Sky turned back to the piano.

'Now, there is just time to go through these dances once more. Fabian, if you will . . .'

We ran through every dance once more, the vampires scrutinizing every tiny movement, correcting every minute mistake, until they were finally satisfied.

'Now the waltz. Kaspar, you are our expert, would you lead?' Kaspar stepped forward, but I backed off, wary.

'Why do I have to dance with him?' I asked, eyeing his movements as he swaggered towards me.

'Because I have to ensure you are good enough to dance in a royal court, Girly. *Royal,* Girly, *royal,*' Kaspar drawled in his aggravatingly patronizing voice.

'Kaspar here is quite a dancer, near as accomplished as

our father,' Sky explained, proudly. Reluctantly, I inched closer, my eyes never leaving his, as a more and more devilish smile formed on his lips. But he stopped and waited and took a step back when I came close.

'Do it properly. Curtsey,' he said. I bobbed down, not doing it 'properly', but in the second I took my eyes off him he had darted forward, pulling me towards him. He forced my hand to entwine with his, whilst he placed his other hand a little too firmly on my waist.

'Oh, "accomplished" are we?' I imitated in a low voice so only he could hear. 'Why didn't *you* teach me how to dance then?'

'Watching gives a far better view.' His eyes very deliberately slid down to my chest and his lips cracked into a smirk. 'Nice top.'

I grunted in disgust. The music began playing and a chill passed down my spine. We began whirling, but my feet struggled to find the rhythm, because the piece was slower and darker than any waltz we had previously practised to.

Suddenly, we had broken hold and Kaspar was holding me at arms' length. I panicked and looked at him in alarm.

'Turn!' he snapped. I turned under his arm; as I did, he pulled be back towards him until we were stood chest-to-chest, one of my hands caught in his high in the air, the other wrapped around his back.

'This isn't part of a waltz!' I hissed at him.

'No, it isn't,' he replied, looking down at me through darkening eyes. 'But I like variety. Get used to it.' He twirled me around again and we returned to the hold, gliding around the floor.

'This isn't very gentlemanly of you.' To my surprise, he cracked a smile – and a genuine one at that.

'Very true. But we aren't at a ball, so tough luck.' At that moment, the music began to fade away and we retreated away from one another. I curtsied and Kaspar turned away.

'Well?' a low, raspy voice asked. My heart skipped a beat. The King had appeared from nowhere, standing in the shadows of the room, face hidden in shadow. I curtsied, and Fabian and Declan bowed.

'She'll do,' Kaspar replied. The King nodded, thoughtfully, eyes never leaving me. I turned away, uncomfortable, and I felt his stare on my back for a moment more as everybody left. Lyla paused and I tugged my feet out of her heels, handing them back. When she had gone, I limped over to the piano stool, wincing as I put my flat shoes back on.

Why am I even doing this? Why am I letting myself get close? Everyday the image of the slaughtered hunters faded away and I found myself struggling to remember that these were the same vampires that had ripped them apart . . . these vampires that I had just danced with.

I shivered, chilled to the bone. The cool gloss of the grand piano seemed to mock me, as my pale, frightened reflection stared back. My eyes were even wearier these days, and I sighed. It wasn't just the memory of the London Bloodbath that was fading. So was the hope of getting out of Varnley.

We'll get you out of there, Violet, but it's going to take time . . .

My father's parting words haunted me. I was waiting it out all right. But how much longer could I last?

TWENTY

Violet

'Can I look yet?' I asked, eyes squeezed shut as Lyla guided me towards the mirror.

'No, not yet.' There was a tugging as she teased a loose strand of hair around her finger, before fastening it into a clip. 'Okay, you can look,' she buzzed.

I opened my eyes to see an unfamiliar person staring back, violet eyes ablaze as they widened in shock.

'Is that me?'

Lyla nodded, eyes examining her creation. She waved two of the maids from the room as I looked up and down the length of the mirror, hardly believing that the person staring back was what I had been transformed into.

My dark, black hair was loosely curled, falling just below my shoulders. My fringe and some of the looser curls had been swept back off my forehead, pinned by a tiny rose clip on one side of my head. My skin was all one colour: a pallid, pasty white and I wore barely any make-up, just mascara, eyeliner and a sweep of dark eye shadow. Around my neck was a black lace choker, another ornate rose attached to it. I could feel it pressing into my windpipe, as a steady pulse throbbed against the delicate material.

But it was the dress that was the real transformation. It was a strapless ball gown, violet in colour – no coincidence, obviously. The neckline was heart-shaped, a figure-hugging corset clinging to my waist as thousands of tiny glass beads ran across the bust and the length of one side. The skirt flared from the hip, the material puckered and gathered with yet more beads until it just brushed the ground. I would *kill* to own a dress like it. *Kill.*

I looked once more at my sallow-looking skin. Blush was strictly taboo in the world of vampires, so I wasn't wearing any – it left me looking ill, *but it worked.*

'Here, you will need these,' Lyla said, handing me a pair of crystal-white gloves. I pulled them on and they reached just past my elbows. 'Don't ever take them off,' she instructed, and I nodded, turning to look at her properly for the first time.

Gone was the usual pink tinge from her hair, replaced by an even shade of deep chestnut. It was pinned up, a few loose strands falling around her face. Her dress was emerald and backless, the material falling as low as the hollow in her spine. The rest of the material flowed to the floor, where it pooled in a small train. She wore very little make-up – not that she needed it.

She pulled an emerald sash over her dress, the Varns' coat of arms emblazoned across the material in silver. The one maid who had remained came forward, placing a dainty, not to mention very expensive-looking diamond tiara on Lyla's head, and handing her a pair of white gloves, almost identical to the ones I wore.

'Well, I think I am ready and you certainly are. I must say, you are my most impressive achievement,' she prattled.

'Thanks,' I mumbled sarcastically.

'You could almost pass for a vampire,' she continued, as the maid helped to fasten a silver chain around her neck. I turned back to the mirror. *Do I really look that different? Can I really pass as a vampire?*

The answer was no. I could still see a throbbing vein in my neck; see the natural blush colouring my cheeks; feel my steady heartbeat. I did not have the grace, or the elegance of a vampire and I completely despised everything they stood for. And of course, I knew I would smell most appealingly like a human.

Butterflies tickled the lining of my stomach and a little dread poisoned my mind. I could hear soft sounds of an orchestra playing downstairs and the drumming of many feet moving across a hard, marble floor. Outside, it was a hive of activity as cars pulled up, butlers and valets rushing to attend to the guests. Each time I heard the incoherent voice of someone speaking far below, my stomach would do back flips, making me lurch. Even the clock seemed to taunt me, as the hands crawled towards midnight.

'Who did you say you were going with again?' I asked, anxious to preoccupy my mind.

'My second cousin. Arranged of course. A favour to my aunt,' Lyla explained in a displeased tone, clearly annoyed at her lack of choice in the matter.

'Minger?'

She raised a perfectly shaped eyebrow. 'Have you ever met a vampire who was a minger?' I shook my head. 'Precisely. They don't exist. He just has an infuriatingly big ego. He will have the first and second dance and then disappear. We'll be lucky if they find him tonight.' She scowled, before muttering something incomprehensible under her breath.

'Guessing you wish you could have gone with someone else, huh?' I asked, nonchalantly.

'Yes. And I know *exactly* who I would have gone with,' she pined. Her eyes dulled, but that could just have been a trick of the light, because immediately afterwards, she straightened up and smiled. 'Ready?'

Just then there was a brisk knocking at the door and the maid hurried to answer it.

Fabian strode into the room, wearing a dark tailcoat. His white shirt was well fitted, and hugged his torso until it disappeared behind a royal-blue cummerbund. His fair hair was sleeker and tidier than usual. A triangle of white poked out from his breast pocket and he also wore a pair of white gloves.

'Wow,' he breathed, his eyes taking me in. 'Lyla, you've worked wonders!' I blushed, not sure whether to take that as a compliment or insult.

Her eyes turned a faint shade of pink, and her gaze glided to the floor. 'Oh, it was nothing.' I noticed that neither she nor Fabian credited the maids, who had done most of the work.

She walked over to me and softly pecked me on the cheek, but not before she whispered, 'Take care of him,' in my ear, a single fang tugging at her bottom lip, which quivered. My eyes followed her as she withdrew into her enormous wardrobe, a lump forming in my throat. *How could I have been so stupid?* It was *Fabian* she had wanted to take. That explained her expression when he had asked me to the ball. *But does Fabian know?*

'Time to go.' He smiled, linking my arm with his and leaving me no time to ponder that question. He led me out of the room and down the stairs, where we joined the throng of people moving towards the ballroom. A few heads turned towards me and I flushed, over and over, the blood rushing to my cheeks. Fabian received a few nods from noble-looking men – *vampires* – and I tensed up, stricken.

'Relax,' Fabian murmured in an undertone. 'You're safe, I promise.' I nodded, uncertain, not having the heart to tell him that it was just as much his touch that was causing me to become rigid

Gradually, we moved towards the double doors that led to the ballroom. I vaguely heard Fabian complaining that people should stop loitering in the entrance, but I wasn't really listening. My eyes were set dead straight, at a head of long blonde curls, twisted into a wreath of tumbling red flowers.

Again, we inched a metre or so forward. I was afraid that if we didn't keep moving, my feet would stiffen and refuse to move, or worse, my knees would buckle from under me. I was sure that if I went down, I wouldn't get back up again – the bodice of the dress had been laced so tightly that I had to maintain a completely straight back or face being stabbed by one of the stays.

I found that if I rolled up onto my toes, I could just see the sparkling light of a thousand black candles in the chandelier. The roar of voices in the entrance hall mingled with the muted sound of violins and a choir and the echo of what seemed like thousands of yet more voices.

In one wave, the crowd loosened and those in front of us surged through the double doors and onto the wide balcony where Kaspar had confronted me over Thyme. Fabian, perhaps mistaking it for fear, pulled me closer.

We crossed the threshold into the ballroom and the woman with the blonde curls and her partner veered to the left, descending one of the two sets of steps onto the dance floor. With that, the view of the room opened up.

I gasped.

Hundreds of couples were gathered about the glittering room, the ladies in elegant ball gowns and gentlemen in dress suits. The only source of light came from the chandelier, which threw a pool of light onto the centre of the room. Waiters, dressed in white, weaved about the guests, carrying tall flutes containing a liquid that I'm sure wasn't wine.

Heads turned as we entered the room, eyes of every colour staring curiously up at us.

'Is that her? The human?'

'She doesn't look human . . .'

Voices broke through the low murmur, as more and more people turned to look. But I didn't care. Everywhere I looked there were dark flowing dresses, almost all wearing blood-like crimsons and maroons, blacks and shades of midnight blue and I gripped the banister of the balcony on which we stood with a sort of feverish excitement, breathless as my childish imaginings of fairytale balls were proved true.

Every person in the room looked so dark, so compelling, as the soft light illuminated their haunting, emaciated faces. They were not perfect, like the stories always said: they were not moral enough to be perfect. But they were as damned near as nature could get.

'Violet?' I turned to see Fabian beaming down at me, hand on my arm as he took in my animation.

'It's beautiful,' I whispered.

'Like you,' he whispered back. My smile faltered and my eyes flickered up and down as they struggled to meet his.

'I—'

'Come on,' he said, pulling me by the arm towards the left-hand set of steps. We descended and began to meander through the crowd. Some parted as we came their way with a respectful silence; others turned away in disgust. Fabian was guiding me, and glancing around; a frown appeared on his face. He muttered something that I could not hear and suddenly his expression was clear again. He grabbed my hand, and started pulling me back through the swarm of people again, who buzzed like flies.

'Fabian, where exactly are we going?' I asked, sensing he was leading me somewhere.

'To my parents.'

'*What?*' I exclaimed. My expression must have looked panicked, because he shot me a 'be sensible' glare. I dug my heels in and put up a protest anyway until he gave up.

'Later then,' he warned above the sound of the orchestra on the far side of the room, retuning with the grand piano. Gone was the soft, soothing music. Instead, the violins drew out three long, clashing, spine-chilling notes and launched into the most haunting fanfare I had ever heard.

The marching beat of a huge timpani drum sounded, and the violins followed, notes crisp and unforgiving as deep, resounding horns echoed around the room.

The crowd parted, creating a winding path leading from the grand door to the throne at the far end of the room. The hairs on my neck stood on end, as the bloodcurdling sound of a choir joined in with the strings.

My blood ran cold.

'What's happening?' I muttered in an undertone to Fabian, extremely conscious of the vampires opposite staring at us. Whatever was happening, I didn't like it, as an unwelcome spirit began to take over my flesh, making me shiver, my stomach roll, my legs go weak.

'The Varns are arriving,' was all the reply I got.

A compelling thrill rippled through the crowd as they waited with such electrifying excitement that the room seemed to churn like multicoloured water, swaying as one.

It struck me that most here probably only saw their rulers on very rare occasions, and that this must be such a long-awaited appearance. *And I get to mutter some new curse at the Prince every day. Lucky me.*

A bitter draft worked its way up, stirring my hair and dress, tickling my skin. High above us, the candles spluttered in their holders. The room moved from light to dark to light as the soft autumnal glow of the candles returned.

Run! my voice suddenly cried.

My throat was constricting, my skin crawling as all-consuming, vice-like anticipation took over. I had no will left, no strength to stop this irrational desire; this irrational want to set eyes upon them; them, the predators so well suited to destroying my own kind.

Run from the rose!

My breathing came in short, sharp rasps, not enough oxygen reaching my head. My hand tingled and I felt something cold through the gloves. A gentle pressure. I looked down to see Fabian's white-gloved hand clutching mine, holding onto me as though I might blow away at any second.

'Keep breathing, it will pass in a moment,' he said in nothing more than a whisper. I nodded shakily, vision wavering.

Run before it's too late! Run now!

The music was rising and rising, filling my ears, as it towered to a crescendo, sending my heartbeat spiralling out of control.

Run or face rising to the throne!

The candles completely blew out, a ferocious wind raging through the ballroom, as the great grand doors were flung open. *The Varns.* The King swept down the stairs in the absolute darkness – darkness that turned to a flickering glow as he clicked his fingers. An astonishing crown sat atop his dark hair, made of some metal that looked to be liquid, lithe to his movements as the dark emerald jewels glinted in their silver settings. Set above those jewels, contained in four points made of glass, was a red, flowing liquid.

Run, or become one with their blood.

My breath caught and I gagged, throat tightening. My vision swayed, the room spinning and settling. I clutched at my chest, my ribs feeling as though they were being crushed, constricting around my heart that wasn't beating in any sort of pattern.

The rest of the family followed, and I could see the true extent of the vampire royalty. There were thirty of them, maybe more, all dressed in black or emerald, sash about their shoulders, partners clinging to their arms with down-turned eyes. Kaspar followed directly behind his father, Charity clasping his arm.

A wave rolled across the crowd, as all bowed and curtsied. I did so too once the King reached our quarter, bowing my head low, hand still encased in Fabian's. But my legs began to give way when I went to stand and something sinister, something that was not my own mind erupted inside my head, but booming and thundering.

Throw yourself down, mortal child. You are not worthy. Die before fate catches you. Die, child. Die before it is too late.

My eyelids drooped, my knees gave away, and I was falling to the ground, ready to give in.

Run from his sin!

My eyelids snapped open and I was being pulled up, a comforting hand in mine, a pair of blue eyes staring worriedly down at me.

'Violet?'

I grabbed at my chest with my free hand, clawing away, desperate to release this darkness clutching me, to be free from its strangling hold. Kaspar passed by and his eyes snapped to meet mine. Unease momentarily crossed his face, before his head faced forwards once more. My head thumped. The family reached the dais, filing out into a line facing their subjects. The King carried on to his throne, veering around to face us all.

A clock deep within the halls of the mansion struck midnight. Twelve reverberating booms, each making my blood run to ice.

Time will not be infinite forever, Violet Lee. It's running out.

'Welcome, ladies and gentleman, to Autumnal Equinox.'

Run!

TWENTY-ONE

Violet

The King's gaze locked onto mine and a flicker of doubt creased his face, before he returned to his pensive glare, staring down at his subjects as though they were pawns to be moved on a chessboard. When satisfied, he sat down upon his throne, lazily waving his hand at the waiters, who disappeared to the sidelines.

'Violet! Breathe!'

Stricken, I realized there was no oxygen in my lungs. Panic rose and my chest burnt, pleading for oxygen.

'I can't,' I croaked.

'You can,' Fabian insisted, gripping my shoulders. 'Just concentrate.'

I screwed my eyes shut, focusing on the rise and fall of my ribs. After a minute, the vice around my neck lifted and I took a shuddering breath. The darkness disappeared, coherent thought returning. My vision returned, the room taking on normal shades, untainted by my tunnelling vision. I stayed there, gasping for breath for a minute or so, before I recovered.

'What the hell just happened?' I gasped.

'Don't worry about it. It was nothing,' he murmured back, avoiding meeting my eyes.

'Bullshit!'

'Keep your voice down,' he hissed.

Bitterly, I lowered my voice. 'Just tell me, Fabian! I have a right to know! And you quite clearly knew this was going to happen, so why did you invite me?' I hissed back in an undertone, leaning in closer to him.

He sighed. 'I invited you because I wanted your company and I wanted you to enjoy yourself. I didn't tell you about this because I thought it might scare you off.'

'And "this" is what?' My tone was not as demanding this time. *He wanted me to enjoy myself.*

'The King's crown.' He jerked his thumb towards the throne. 'It contains cursed blood. If a human sees it, they are affected as you were. It was used back in the days when there were human sacrifices. Which is all just symbolic now,' he added, seeing my face, which must have frozen at the thought of 'human sacrifices'.

The voices and the dark might have subsided, but their message had not. *That crown made me want to die.* 'Will it affect me again tonight?'

'No. It only works once.'

By now, the crowd had parted to form a large circle, walled with people. The crown was gone, the King was striding towards the centre of the circle and the enchantment of the ball was fast returning as the candles burnt brighter.

The violins struck up once more, and in the time it takes to blink, the Varns, in all their crowning glory, were stood there, poised to dance. They bowed low, before taking hold.

'Wait until I lead you onto the floor before you move,' Fabian instructed in a low murmur.

The Varns began dancing; gliding around the floor as though they belonged to the music, their steps flawless, perfected by thousands of years of practice. I watched in awe as Kaspar and Charity became one, her surprisingly elegant dress flowing around his ankles as she swirled around, melting into his form. The only clue in the mauve material to her true nature was the long slit running up the side, stopping mid-thigh.

A smile almost cracked on my lips as Kaspar glided past us, looking bored. He had donned regal wear, the tight black military-style jacket fastened with an ornate silver belt. A few medals hung from his breast pocket, underneath an emerald handkerchief tucked inside it. Around him, he wore an emerald sash, much like Lyla's; it was emblazoned with the Royal Crest, proving his purity of blood.

The music rose to a crescendo and I gasped; as one, the Varns wheeled around, completely changing direction. The choir sang, the whole room echoing with their hallowing notes. The candles flickered, again, softly lighting the dancing figures. Any fear or terror had long gone now, forgotten as the majestic scene took over.

A huge grin spread across my face. This is what every girl dreamt of, but would never live.

'It's time.' The music lulled and Fabian matched my grin. I placed my hand on his arm and he escorted me out onto the dance floor. We weaved our way about other couples, as hundreds, if not thousands, of vampires assembled themselves, dodging the now still figures of the Varns. We somehow made it to the centre of the floor, and I looked about to see many familiar faces – Cain poised perfectly still with his young partner, Alex and an unfamiliar girl, Eaglen stood by an ageing lady.

'Curtsey,' Fabian mouthed at me and the room dipped as one.

We took hold, the music lulled and then rose . . .

And we were dancing, whirling, spinning, around the room, interlaced with the other couples, ball gowns whipping around, music rising. I closed my eyes, trying to remember every detail, the scene imprinted on my dark eyelids. My smile faltered, remembering something the King had said many weeks before.

'Your sentiments will change when you have grown accustomed to our ways, which will happen in time. And time you shall have, Miss Lee . . .'

I slowly opened my eyes to see Fabian gazing down at me, a curious lopsided smile playing on his lips. His eyes were the clearest of blues, so clear it put the sky to shame, the deep blue waves of the sea becoming weary as they admitted defeat compared with such a perfect colour.

How cheesy, my voice muttered in a dry tone.

'What are you thinking about?'

'I'm thinking about how amazing this is,' I lied. 'This whole ball. It's just incredible. All these people . . . I feel like Cinderella.' I laughed, unsure of what else to say. To my relief, he chuckled.

'This is nothing. You should see some of the balls later on in the year,' he cooed.

We stopped whirling and the music changed to something more dulcet and melancholy. Within seconds, we were dancing once more, slower this time, and I was forced to concentrate on my steps for a few minutes.

My eyes began to wander, watching the spectacle around me. Lyla glided past, her partner, an extremely attractive teenage-looking vampire, quite clearly staring down at Lyla's chest. He seemed to like what he saw. I flushed red when

I caught her eye. I liked Fabian – as far as vampires went he was one of the nicer ones – but she liked him in a much different way. And Lyla had been nice to me during my time here – I didn't want to mess that up.

The King danced in the centre with an extravagantly beautiful vampire. Her long, light brown hair fell down to her waist, pin straight. Her angular jaw was set in a controlled line, aloof to everything around her, including the King. He too shared that same indifference, hardly glancing at the woman in his arms.

My eyes continued to roam. They settled on Sky and Arabella, who wheeled past us at that moment. They stared deep into each other's eyes, as though they were the only two people in the room. I averted my gaze, uncomfortable. I felt as though I should not intrude on their moment. A tiny pang shot through me.

That's what Fabian and Lyla should have.

I refused Fabian a third dance, claiming thirst and escaping for water.

I stumbled towards the refreshments table, grabbing a glass of water. I downed it, closing my eyes as the cool liquid ran down my parched throat. I didn't dance much after the second dance, preferring to sit near the edge of the wall with my drink, wary of the lustful glances coming my way. At every passing opportunity I would talk to a vampire I knew, clinging to them until they decided to join a dance. Fabian had long disappeared, dancing with almost every young vampire in attendance. But I earned myself considerable attention despite my cowering, not least because every few minutes, Fabian's eyes would search around the room until they rested on me, making sure I was okay.

I would often see Kaspar or Sky looking my way too: brief looks, checking to see if I was still here, still alive; every time I turned, Eaglen or Arabella would have their backs to me, seemingly having an animated conversation, but I knew their full attention was devoted to me. Whenever an unknown vampire approached me, a Varn would miraculously appear, initiating a conversation, sweeping them away in seconds. I spotted a few humans amid the sea of deadened skin, but they too were passed around in their own protective circles, shunning anyone unknown.

A group of choirboys walked out and began singing, hallowed voices echoing around the room. I watched them for a while. They were so young, most not even ten. Their sweet, youthful faces were untainted by the horror of life, their mouths opening to reveal the voices of angels. Tiny fangs were visible and my face fell. *How can something so angelic, be so dangerous?* Those children would grow into monsters and would kill when they were older.

'It is beautiful, is it not, Miss Lee?'

I jumped and promptly wheeled around to see a young vampire standing there, with the deepest blue eyes imaginable and a most dazzling smile.

'Ilta, you scared me,' I flustered, feeling the surge of adrenaline course through my chest.

'I am deeply sorry; I did not mean to startle you.'

I brushed his apology off. 'It's fine, I should have been paying more attention anyway.' I shook my head, turning to look at him. His smile wavered.

'You should not have come here, Miss Lee. You are never safe around vampires; you are intelligent enough to know this, are you not? But I fear you underestimate the danger of this night.'

The voices of the choirboys became shrill and unnaturally

high-pitched, filling every arch of the ceiling. I nodded my head uncertainly.

'To be here, Miss Lee, amongst so many thirsty vampires, many of whom have not eaten in many days due to their long, arduous journeys, well . . . I thought the King would have better sense than that. But no matter, you are safe among some, and I like to consider myself one of them.' He smiled that charming smile and I could not help but feel my heart leap. *Kaspar should take notes.* 'May I ask, Miss Lee, for this dance? And perhaps the one after?' he continued, sweeping down to take my hand, bowing low.

'Of course,' I curtsied.

He took my hand and led me into the large space in the centre, where couples were dancing an extremely slow, ornamental dance. I vaguely recognized it from my lessons, and began turning on the spot, seeing that the other girls were doing the same.

When I returned to hold, he placed a cold hand on my cheek, cradling my head until I faced him once more. I shifted my gaze, uncomfortable with his unmoving stare. I stared at his chest and noticed he was wearing a deep red shirt, and around his neck was an ornate chain, hung with something that looked horribly like a vial of blood.

'Do not be shy, Miss Lee. For I know you find our allure most irresistible; an allure you despise so very much. It is not something to be hated, but accepted as the dire, under-hand ways of nature.'

I nodded glumly, shame washing over me as I realized that was probably the truth.

'No matter. Do not let me upset you. Let us change the subject. I have heard so much about you, dear Violet, but you never ask much of us. Do you not desire to ask me a single question?'

I thought for a moment. 'Where do you come from? Your family, I mean.'

'My family,' he chuckled. 'What an extensive subject you have landed upon. I come from Romania, although my family has residences all over the world, as do most powerful families.' A smirk played on his lips. 'We were one of the few not to flee when the slayers overtook Romania, many centuries ago.' The pride in his voice was unmistakable, though I did not find the feat so impressive. Sky and Jag also lived in that part of the world.

Suddenly, Ilta whirled around, lips rolled back and snarling. 'Oh, Your Highness, forgive me, I thought you were somebody else,' Ilta said, bowing low. There was begrudged politeness in his voice.

'I wish to have this dance with Violet.' Kaspar glowered. Ilta reluctantly let me go.

'Of course, Your Highness.' Stiffly, he bowed again and swept off, disappearing into the whirling crowd.

'What was that for?!' I hissed, shooting daggers at the Prince, whose eyes were cemented to the spot where Ilta had slipped into the crowd. I took a step forward, but he took a step back.

'Curtsey,' he snarled. I lowered myself as little as possible, never letting my eyes leave him. I didn't bother to take his hand as I turned on the spot once more.

'I told you to stay away from him!' he scolded, talking to me like a child.

'I know you did. But I am not a child or a vampire so you have no control or right to tell me what I can and cannot do. I will make my own judgements about people, thank you very much.' I went to leave, but he grabbed my wrist. His nails dug into my skin, as they had done that first night I met him.

'Do not walk away from me. No one refuses the heir to this Kingdom.' He glared at me, the power he clearly knew he possessed radiating in waves as the admiring eyes of the passing women and girls swept over him.

'I do,' I whispered, leaving him and the dance floor behind.

TWENTY-TWO

Kaspar

'I do,' she whispered and with that she was gone. I narrowed my eyes, watching the flash of purple disappear into the crowd.

'Damn it,' I muttered, shoving my hands into the pockets of my trousers. I had never met such an irksome woman, let alone a human one. But I had enough experience of irritable females to know I should let her think she had escaped for the time being.

Instead, I meandered through the crowd, enjoying the attention my title and good looks attracted, until the scent of hairspray started to loiter in the back of my throat, and a flash of bleach-blonde hair caught my eye. Sleeping with Charity was one thing, and dancing with her bearable if I wore steel-capped shoes; spending time with her when I didn't have to, on the other hand, was plain traumatic.

I made a beeline for the alcove in which Fabian and the others were talking, and was far more satisfied to see a head full of dark curls amongst them. That feeling quickly moved to surprise as I realized Violet was comfortably leading the conversation.

'I'm intrigued. How do vampires liven their balls up?' she said in reply to Fabian.

I saw my opportunity and seized it. 'May I ask for the next dance, intrigued one? I can show you how.' I bent down and kissed her knuckles. She flustered and I was pleased to see the shiver travel up my arm; pleased to see her react like any other girl would react in that situation.

She recovered quickly. 'Fine,' she snapped, with a flick of her head. 'But if you dare lecture me, I *will* step on your foot.' She met my gaze as steadily as she would if her threat was not hollow, and I held it. I was not going to alter my view on Ilta Crimson. He was no friend of my family, and I had no doubt that he had contacts with various slayer clans. That wasn't to mention the fact he was a known lecher.

To simply get her to give in and stop being so stubborn, however, I would tell her the sky was green. 'Fine,' I agreed, equally as terse.

She removed her hand from mine and I found Fabian frowning at me. I rolled my eyes with a slight shake of my head, which Violet didn't miss.

'Lyla!' She seized my nearby sister's hand with as much vigour as when I had seized on the chance to steal a dance. 'You dance with Fabian.' She joined their hands and left before they could protest.

I hurried to catch up with her. 'Girly, you little match-maker!'

'You know too?'

'She *is* my sister.'

She seemed somewhat disappointed that she wasn't the only one to know about my sister's obsessive – but very recent

– crush on Fabian, and didn't speak as she curtsied without any prompting and gazed over my shoulder. She broke out into a smile and when I glanced back, it became obvious that the sight of Lyla in Fabian's hold was the source of her happiness. But Fabian was my best and oldest friend, and I knew him well enough to see that he led my sister only in a stiff, mechanical fashion.

'This is a little too risqué for the elders,' I explained as I moved away and circled her, already having missed the more traditional waltz at the beginning. As much as I thought my sister's love of clothes was almost as fanatical as her feelings for Fabian, I couldn't deny that she had done a good job with this waif.

She watched me warily, craning her neck as far as it would go. 'I'm sorry about—'

I cut in before she could finish. 'Sorry about lecturing you and crap.' Her eyes narrowed and I could see in her face exactly what was in mine: *apologies?* I looked away before she could register any surprise in my expression.

Everywhere I looked there were joyous smiles, raucous laughter, and the younger vampires holding one another far closer than what was 'proper'. Hands grazed necks and shoulders; outwardly, it looked innocent, but the looks in their eyes told me it wasn't. And I was about to show Violet exactly why that was.

'Are you ready?' I grinned and placed my hands firmly on her waist, tightening my fingers around the boning of the dress.

'For what?' She looked rightly anxious.

'For this.' The music paused and with that I hoisted her high into the air; she shrieked and her hands automatically sought my shoulders, forcing me to inhale first the perfume dabbed on her wrists, which I recognized as Lyla's, and second a scent that made my throat burn. She might *look* like a vampire for the ball, but she still smelt like dinner.

I lowered her a heartbeat too early and as soon as her court shoes kissed the floor she was telling me off.

'A little bloody warning would be nice next time!' With that she purposefully stepped forward instead of back and jammed her low heel onto my toes.

I let my eyes flicker closed. 'You do realize that didn't hurt me in the slightest?'

'You do realize you're intolerable?'

'The feeling is mutual then.'

I lifted her twice more, and would have done an extra time if she hadn't put up such a loud fuss, cursing vampires under her breath.

'You never learn, do you? You have to be polite to me. I am the Prince. *Prince*. Ring any bells?'

She folded her arms as she curtsied. 'No. And the Prince will receive some courtesy when he is so kind as to show some himself.'

I smirked. 'In your dreams, Girly, in your dreams.' When she started to back away, that smirk only widened and I grabbed her wrist. 'No, you don't get away that easily. You're having a second dance.'

She looked at my hand like it was a manacle, and shook it off in much the same way. 'I have to go,' she muttered with a frown. 'But I'm sure Charity would love a dance.'

In the second I was distracted by the platinum-blonde to my right, the brunette somehow slipped away. Nowhere amongst the crowd was there a purple dress.

My hands found themselves in my pockets again. That was twice in one night she had escaped. *I really am going to have to do something about that.*

TWENTY-THREE

Violet

The truth was, that dance had been a little *too* easy. *Too* comfortable. I shouldn't have enjoyed it. Especially when it was with *him*.

He brought you here. Don't forget that, Violet.

Forced, more like, my voice added and I was inclined to agree.

I stood there for a while, content to be alone with my thoughts. Yet I was interrupted when Fabian stepped into the gloom.

'Where's Kaspar?'

'Where's Lyla?' We spoke in unison, before laughing.

'Kaspar's dancing,' I explained.

'Lyla said she was going to go and get a drink,' he explained. I raised an eyebrow. *Gone to get a drink. Sounds familiar.*

'So you two just had the one dance then?' I probed.

'Yes. She seemed flustered,' he said, clearly puzzled. I almost smiled at his ignorance. *Honestly, men.*

'You really have no idea, do you?'

He shrugged his shoulders.

I couldn't take it. I had to tell him. He had to know. 'Lyla likes you.'

I expected his face to light up, or a smile to curl his lips, or at least to acknowledge what I had said. But he didn't. He just stood there, as the minutes fell away.

'Fabian?'

'This makes things complicated,' he eventually said, sighing and moving further into the darkness.

'How?'

He sighed again and I saw his eyes go slightly black. 'I don't feel the same way about Lyla, if that is what you are thinking.' He looked out towards the ballroom, before turning back to me, his eyes back to their original colour, but brighter, more alive. More stunning. 'You're so young and ignorant. I don't blame you for not realizing sooner. But I know you don't feel the same way, so don't let this change anything. Not one thing, okay?'

My mouth fell open as the realization of what he had just said hit me. *Fabian doesn't like Lyla. He likes me.* I nodded mindlessly, edging around him.

'But maybe, one day, you might feel differently. Maybe when you become one of us—'

'No,' I whispered. 'No, no, no.'

'Violet! Please, listen to me!'

'No,' I breathed. I wouldn't. *Couldn't.*

'I-I'm t-tired, I think I will go to b-bed,' I stuttered, turning on my flimsy heel, fleeing from the room.

'Violet!' I heard him call, but too late, I had passed through the great doors and out into the entrance hall. I walked towards the open marble door, inhaling a deep breath of fresh air. I gazed out at the expansive lawns, knowing it would be so easy just to run right now.

But I wouldn't.

I took another heaving breath. *How can I have been so stupid? It was obvious! So blazingly obvious! Why else would he have invited me to the ball? And all those weeks ago, he had volunteered to stay with me whilst the others hunted. Is this why? And what about the others? Do they know? Kaspar must surely know. But does Lyla know?*

But he doesn't like me. He can't like me. He just thinks he likes me. He doesn't know me, not properly, I reassured myself, and it was true. He only knew the defensive mask that I was using to survive and stay sane here.

My eyes began to droop and I trudged up the stairs towards my room. I felt eyes on my back, as some of the passing vampires left through the entrance hall, but I did not have the energy to care.

I reached the top and took one last look down, remembering the first time I had passed through those great doors, wondering if I would ever make the return journey a human.

Ignorant.

For a moment, I wondered what it would be like to be a vampire. What it would be like to truly leave humanity behind. What it would be like if these were my last few minutes of true human life. Could I leave it all behind?

I blinked and a corner became dark for a moment as one of the gas lamps blew out. Sleepy, I turned away, dismissing it. I walked the last few steps towards my room as a single tear fell down my cheek.

Where is the mask now?

I leaned against the wall beside my door, forcing myself not to cry, taking deep, shaky breaths. I had to become stronger. I had to. I leaned my forehead against the cool wall, breathing becoming more regular, hands pressed up against the wall. Something cold brushed against my neck, tickling me, and my hairs immediately stood on end. It felt like a bitter draft.

Except bitter drafts don't snarl.

I wrenched my whole body around, heart beating at an impossible rate. I clutched at the wall, searching for my door handle.

A figure stepped from the shadows, outlined by the little light that slivered in from downstairs. He was tall and a liquid version of silver seemed to trickle down the side of his face. A red vial glowed around his collar. I breathed a sigh of relief.

'Oh, it's only you, Ilta.'

TWENTY-FOUR

Kaspar

My eyes searched the room, but to no avail. Some faces stared back, others scowled, but nowhere amongst them was there a small girl wrapped in purple.

They're not here. Fuck.

I spotted Fabian and Alex deep in conversation in a dark corner near the door and flitted over, anguish rising. I could sense the tension mounting in my family, as they too shared my worry.

'Fabian.' They both turned to look at me. 'Where's Violet?' I asked urgently.

'She went to bed, about ten minutes ago,' he said, averting his gaze. *So he told her.*

'What? Didn't you go with her? Why aren't you with her?' I demanded, anguish turning to panic.

It could be nothing. It could just be a coincidence.

'Kaspar, what—'

'Ilta Crimson has gone too.'

They looked to each other and then back to me, eyes wide.

'Oh, God,' Fabian breathed.

And with that they darted off in different directions. I paused to gauge the room, before quickly flitting off to join the desperate search. Every Varn and friend of ours was looking up, dread turning their eyes colourless.

With sick guilt, my words from earlier echoed around my brain. *Then on your own head be it, Girly.*

TWENTY-FIVE

Violet

'Ilta, what are you doing here?' I peered closer, as he stood motionless, two paces in front of me. 'Ilta?' I called softly once more.

Still he did not move and I waved a hand in front of his face. He seemed to be caught in some sort of trance, eyes glazed over and unseeing.

'Ilta!' I said, more sharply. Suddenly, his head twitched and I recoiled away from the unnatural contortion. His body stirred and his arm darted out, a blur, snatching my wrist from midair. I gasped. A shiver rippled along the skin of my arm, across my shoulder and towards my hardworking heart, as it refused to slow its rapid beating. His icy skin scolded mine and I tried to wrench it from his tightening grasp, but I did not have the strength.

'*Ilta*?' I struggled once more to pull my arm free, but his grip only became more constricting. I felt the blood drain from my hand and saw it wither and go limp.

'I am sorry, dear Violet, I was not entirely focused. Caught up in my senses, one might say,' he purred, oily and slick as he soaked his lips with his saliva. I heard a faint sniffing and begged for my volatile heart to calm. He paused to look at me and I was forced to look into his eyes. Gone was the dark azure. Instead, they were *red*.

I drew in a sharp breath, eyes round, and took a step back, withdrawing away from his snarling, hissing face. He yanked me closer, using the lock he had on my wrist.

'No, my sweet. You will not go anywhere.' He pulled me up against his chest, before stooping down and placing a hand on the back of my knees, buckling them. I collapsed into his waiting arms. A second later, I felt the chilly air battering my cheeks and knew he was running from Varnley – where, I did not know. I closed my eyes, attempting to stop the tears falling. Only then did it occur to me to scream. And I did. A horrific, dreadful, spine-chilling scream that rang around out into the night.

But it was futile. No one heard and no one came.

Something sharp caught the skin on my cheek, teasing it away from the lower layers it was stitched to. My eyes flung open to see a bramble slash my skin and I winced as blood oozed from the fresh wound. I tried to raise my arm to wipe it away, but found it immobilized. I looked down and saw it was pinned between my hip and Ilta's chest, all feeling gone as I tried to bend my fingers.

'Do you not wish to struggle, sweet child? Do you not wish to be away?' Ilta soothed, leaning over my face. He opened his mouth a little and I saw his sharp fangs, curved, lethal, as they dug into his lower lip. His breath reeked as he opened his mouth wider, a mixture between the stench of rotting flesh and the salty odour of dried blood. My nose wrinkled and I leaned away.

'You're stronger than me, so what would be the point? And get some mouthwash,' I finished, determined to at least fight with words.

'We will see if you feel the same way in a while,' he spat. He leaned down further into my face, and swirling his tongue, licked the blood from my smarting cut. He siphoned every last drop. I could not help but close my eyes as his lips gradually followed my jaw line, until they came to a rest on my neck. He inhaled deeply and I felt him shudder violently. His hand came up to meet his lips and he trailed his fingers slowly across my collar, down to my breasts, inching his fingertips through the crease between them. I gritted my teeth throughout.

He inhaled deeply once more, before shakily exhaling against my skin. 'Fuck! I cannot wait any longer,' he hissed.

Without any further warning, he dropped me, leaving me to land on the hard ground with a sickening crack as my dead arm cushioned my fall beneath my back. I shrieked in pain, the feeling fast returning. I barely had time to register that I vaguely recognized this dense part of the forest, especially the ivy-covered stone building nearby, before Ilta had crouched down to my level.

'Time for some fun, don't you think?'

He roughly grabbed me by my bodice and pulled me up, thrusting me against a nearby tree. The bark shredded my bare back, grating the satin of my dress.

'Don't touch me, you monster!' I shrieked, willing every ounce of courage I had to help form those words.

'Ah, but why would I do that? It is my duty to ensure you die before you ever fulfil your fate.' He chuckled and raised his arms, gesturing around at the forest. 'Look around you, Violet. What do you see? What is there here, other than trees? See reason, my love. You can scream all you like, but you are miles from anyone. You will not be heard. You can run; but I would soon catch you. Or you could just give in to my power and accept that this pitiful life of yours is coming to an end.' He leaned in closer. 'Is that so hard? Think about it, Violet. What do you have to go back to? Your mortal life can never be reclaimed, and your future offers only sacrifice and betrayal. You will have no choice, Violet Lee. What do you have left? What? *Answer me!*'

Tears streamed down my cheeks and I pursed my lips, searching for an answer. I looked to the mossy ground, watching as my silvery tears fell onto the fallen leaves, coated in a thick layer of pine needles. I closed my eyes, before slowly opening them, raising my head to his level.

'Hope is what I have left.'

His slender bloodthirsty eyes narrowed to slits, and he growled. 'No, you don't! You must die before your time comes, child, and I will have my way whilst I do this dimension a great service.' He seized a handful of my hair, and roughly tilted my head to the side. His body drove into mine, pressing me to the tree.

'No! Get off me!' I screeched, scrabbling around with my uninjured arm, trying to push him off. His free hand grabbed that arm and pushed it out of the way, using his long, sharpened nails to restrain me. They pierced the translucent skin on the underside of my wrists and blood began to emerge. Out of the corner of my eye, I saw red and I convulsed, gagging. Ilta's mouth gaped, lips rolling back over his gums.

'No! P-please, no! No!' I begged.

'I have waited too long,' he whispered and he bit down hard upon the tender skin of my neck.

I screeched, the panic-ridden scream escaping my lips as pain, all-consuming pain, shot down from my neck, stopping my heart; freezing my blood; killing my mind.

He began to suck. Unhurriedly, and savouring each mouthful, he drew drop after drop of blood from my failing body. My vision was wavering, darkening to the gloom of the forest. My voice refused to work and my lungs burnt as they were starved of oxygen. My heart spluttered, fighting to pump the decreasing amount of blood around to my vital organs.

As quickly as he had started, he stopped. But my legs went weak and if it were not for the constant pressure of Ilta leaning into me, I would have collapsed to the ground. I sighed in relief, the tiniest, most frugal sigh imaginable, but Ilta still picked up on it.

'No, my sweet. Do not think I am done with you. I am far from done. I just want you to be conscious and alive for this.' He trailed off and cupped a hand around my breast. He traced the neckline of my dress with his nails, before allowing his fingertips to slip underneath the material. His intention was clear.

'No,' I pleaded, shaking my head and body, trying to release his grip. 'No, please!'

'When you are alive to feel the shame, Violet Lee, to feel yourself violated, it makes it far more fun, you see . . .' His head bent down to my ear and he took my lobe between his fang and lower lip, tugging it. 'But do not worry, I will keep going once you are dead.'

'You're sick,' I said in no more than a whisper.

'I know,' he replied and yanked a nail down the material, slashing the dress and my bra. I shrieked again as his nails ran deep into my flesh and he laughed like someone had told a good joke. 'I thank you for telling me, Violet. I do get rather bored of being told how good-natured I am.'

He raised both his hands, baring his nails. He placed them on my collarbone and slowly ran them down the length of my torso, tearing my skin and the dress. Ten long lacerations ran deep over my breasts and each left a streaky trail of blood behind. I gritted my teeth, refusing to wince.

He took a finger and thumb to one of my breasts, fondling them, squeezing the cuts so more blood oozed out, running his tongue across my sore skin. I recoiled from him, but he placed a hand behind my back, tearing the laced corset too.

'Your blood does taste most sweet. Has anyone ever told you that?' he mocked, smiling up at me. I couldn't answer.

All of a sudden, he drew back for a moment. I held my breath against my will, waiting for his next move. He reached out a hand, grabbed my skirt and bunched it up. There was a ripping sound, as he tore that too. He pressed himself into me once more and I felt something hard against my abdomen. Pulling me up straight, he paused to look right into my eyes. All I saw was lust. Burning, flaming lust. Reaching a hand underneath my dress, he ran it up and down my inner thigh until he traced the outline of my knickers. He slowly pulled them aside, and I felt his other hand reaching for the fly of his trousers.

'Get off her!'

Abruptly, his body was ripped away from mine and I crumpled to the ground.

'You will pay for this, Ilta Crimson! You'll burn at the stake, you fucking bastard!'

'On what grounds, Kaspar?' Ilta's voice mocked. 'I am sorry to correct you, but she is a human! I am perfectly within my rights to do with her what I will.'

Kaspar?

'You forget something. She is under the King and Crown's Protection. And on those grounds, drinking her blood without consent is punishable by execution. You should read your law books, Crimson.'

'You lie,' Ilta hissed back.

My eyelids were stitched together, but I forced myself to open them to catch a glimpse of two outlines for a second. But the effort made my heart falter, forgetting to beat for a second.

'Do you want to test that?' I heard Kaspar reply. I heard no more sound, but felt breath on my cheeks and fingers pressed to the vein on my wrist. Beneath them, I could feel my faint pulse. 'You've lost too much blood,' he muttered, and again, I forced my eyes open, catching a peek of his eyes, passing straight through green, dropping to a clear, colourless shade. They ran up and down my form, almost naked, examining my torn flesh. He shrugged his jacket off and placed it around me, before gently lifting me from the ground. Only then did I notice the true pain I was in. A rasping breath scratched my throat and my eyes snapped shut. I shuddered, both from the agony in my arm and the freezing air.

I felt a gentle pressure on my uninjured hand. 'Hold on, Violet. Don't give in.' I could hear his panic. It added to my own.

Cold air assaulted my skin when he sped up; but within a few minutes, he stopped again. Even with my eyes jammed closed, I could tell where we were. The darkness glowed orange and I felt warmth engulf me, the clatter of footsteps below my back. The light became even more intense.

Die, child. Die before it is too late.

The echo of my voice's earlier words resounded in my chest and my heart caught and spluttered. I thought about breathing, but the effort was too much.

'Don't you dare, Girly. You've come too far. Stay with me, Violet . . .'

With the thud of the doors, my heart constricted again, but it was pitiful and trying to force my ribs up and out was too much.

'Open your eyes, Girly! I'm the bloody Prince and I'm telling you, you can't let go!'

My eyelids twitched and I saw a thousand vampiric eyes staring at me, as I lay in the Prince's arms, fading into blackness.

But not before I heard one last colossal roar, as a single word echoed around the mansion from the mouth of the vampire clutching me.

'*Father!*'

TWENTY-SIX

Kaspar

Thousands of vampires stared at Violet as she lay limp in my arms. Immediately, my father's tall, dark figure emerged from the thousands of utterly silent, motionless onlookers, all staring at Violet's desecrated, limp form.

'Get her inside,' he ordered, as soon as his eyes fell on her. I jerked forward and the crowd parted to reveal Galen, the family physician. He jerked his head, motioning for me to place her on the floor as he bunched his jacket up to form a pillow for her head. Seeing her, torn and caked with blood, the expressions of my family became horror-struck. Lyla let out a dry sob.

Galen's amber eyes bore into mine, as though he thought I had done this to her. 'What happened?' he asked in a brusque tone.

'She was attacked,' I growled. A collective snarl washed across the room, and eye after eye turned jet black.

'Who?' Ashton spat, loosening his cummerbund and shrugging his tailcoat off.

'Ilta Crimson. He was going to rape her.'

Hisses of disgust passed around the room, and several vampires walked from the room then and there. There was a commotion too as a small party of trackers assembled, darting from the room. Ashton, an efficient, merciless vampire known for his ability to track, gave me a terse nod as he left the room, leading the others into the grounds.

'For Pete's sake, man, clear the room, will you? Don't you think her dignity has suffered enough?' Galen insisted in an undertone, taking her pulse and dipping his fingers into the puncture wounds on her neck. Hearing, Jag and Sky snapped into action, instructing the servants to clear the room whilst my family closed in, forming a protective circle around her.

'Fracture to her right wrist and considerable blood loss, presumably drained via the neck.'

'How much blood?'

'Too much. She is going into shock. If she doesn't receive a transfusion, her major organs will fail.'

He didn't need to continue. 'Get her a transfusion.'

'It's not that simple. The blood you have stored here is untested, whole blood, which is unsuitable for transfusion and it would take too long to acquire suitable blood from human blood banks.'

'Then turn her!'

Galen shook his head, laying her arm back down on the floor and rolling back until he sat upright on his knees. 'It's too late for that. Her body would not be able to cope with the change. I'm sorry.'

My mouth opened. I closed it again. Instead, I took her unbroken arm, stroking it, stunned at how she was colder than me. I heard somebody suggest going to the Sage, before another dismissed it.

'Couldn't we give her a small amount of our blood?' I

began, an idea forming in my head. 'Enough to keep her alive and let her body heal, but not enough to turn her.'

Galen looked at me sceptically. 'That would make her a dhampir.'

'So? It would save her life! Father?' I appealed, desperately, to my father's mercy. He did not say anything, but motioned for Galen and Eaglen to join him away from the circle. I caught snippets of their conversation I didn't want to hear, but was interrupted as Fabian appeared at the doors, joining me in a flash. He was still crying and when he glanced at me, his eyes told all.

'She's fading,' I murmured, and watched as my oldest and closest friend broke down, falling to the ground, sobbing. I looked on, unsure of what to do, unable to cry, as I told myself I would not, *could not,* cry for a human.

Her breathing was becoming more rapid, but her pulse was fading. Beads of cold sweat slid down her neck to the long slits he had given her across her collar and breasts; her skin was getting ever more icy.

'Come on,' I muttered, staring at the men huddled near the doors, catching my father's gaze as he glanced towards her.

You have nothing to say, Kaspar?

Her life is in your hands, father, so what would be the point?

I saw him sigh and turn to Eaglen, speaking aloud and raising his voice a little. 'This decision will gravely affect the fate of the Kingdom, will it not?'

'In more ways than you can imagine,' Eaglen revealed, smiling. *He knows things we can only dream of.*

'Arabella?' my father said, turning to her. She nodded, confirming what her blood father, Eaglen, had said, and strengthening her father-in-law's point.

If I let her die, we risk angering Lee and the human government and giving him his excuse to become aggressive. If I allow her to live, and become a dhampir, we risk the same. I must think of her too. Even if she were to consume a small amount of vampiric blood, there is no guarantee it will work. And of course, you must remember she despises us with a passion. Would she really want to be connected with the dark beings in even the slightest way?

His last words caught me and he knew it. She wouldn't. But neither would she want to give up so easily. She was a fighter.

Lee will never even know she's a dhampir. And this isn't her fault. She didn't choose this. She shouldn't even be a part of this world in the first place. I'll give my blood. I owe it to her.

I didn't know whether my words were working, but then his eyes did something unheard of: they turned blue.

'Do it.'

Galen snapped into action, hoisting her up into his arms and snapping for the servants to have a fire lit in her room. I froze in shock for a second, before grabbing Fabian and leading Galen up the stairs.

TWENTY-SEVEN

Violet

'Violet, it is time to wake up,' a musical voice sang from beside my knees. There was a gentle pressure on my leg from a tiny hand and I found myself wrenched back to consciousness. My eyes fluttered open to reveal a giggling little girl with wide emerald eyes, framed by tumbling blonde ringlets. Thyme. 'You have been human asleep-y for a very long time, Violet!'

My eyes continued to open, the haze disappearing. Dazed, I managed to discern that I was lying partially sitting up on my bed, soft pillows supporting my aching back. My wrist was wrapped in a support – but not a sling. Kaspar, Fabian and Lyla stood nearby, their backs to me.

'Violet's awake!' The girl dived at me, wrapping her match-stick arms around my neck, her knees digging into my stomach. I winced, groaning as my entire body erupted into joint-wrenching pain. She kissed my tender neck over and over, clutching me tighter. I felt her pass over fresh wounds on my body and I tried to cry out in pain, only to hear a screech. Immediately, the three vampires turned and Lyla rushed to pull Thyme off.

'Thyme! Can't you see you're hurting her?'

I breathed heavily as the pain dulled. Thyme's bottom lip quivered, and her lips swelled to a pout. She scuttled from the room, sobbing without tears. I watched her, before slowly beginning to prop myself up. I inched back, wincing as I put weight on my strapped-up arm. Kaspar stood a way back, seeming hesitant to move closer. His cold gaze lingered on me for a moment, before he averted his eyes and looked out the window. Fabian plumped the pillows behind my back, and remembering my last few moments at the ball, I scooted away an inch. He didn't seem to notice.

'Here, drink this,' he said, passing me a glassful of water. My throat was so dry I downed it in one and he poured me another from the jug on the bedside table. 'Violet, I am so sorry for what has happened to you.'

I made a small choking noise in the back of my throat, wanting to shake my head but finding my neck too stiff. There was an awkward pause.

'I'll go get Galen,' Lyla muttered, leaving the room. Nobody spoke for the next few minutes as I managed to sit fully upright with the help of Fabian: until the King entered the room, followed by a tall, imposing man, who I presumed was Galen. Behind him was Eaglen.

'I shouldn't be alive,' was all I could say. Fabian and Kaspar exchanged looks whilst Galan took my uninjured arm and pressed two fingers to my vein, taking my pulse. I tried to pull it away but he wouldn't let go, shooting me a subduing look. Fabian smiled in a reassuring way and I allowed the man to continue, as he had me clench and unclench the hand of my injured arm. I was amazed when it didn't hurt.

'How do you feel?' he asked.

Ashamed. Hopeless. Sick. 'Stiff,' I answered.

'You will be. You have been unconscious for the past three days.' I gawped. *Three days? That long?* 'She will be sore for a while,' he continued, turning to the King and Eaglen. 'And her wrist will need to remain in the support for two weeks. The wounds might take a little longer to heal, but other than that, she has made quite the recovery.' He left my bedside and muttered something to the King, in a volume he obviously thought I couldn't hear, but I could hear every word: 'The long-term mental impact is quite a different matter. And I would bear in mind, Your Majesty, that this may greatly influence her decision on turning.'

I cleared my throat. 'But how am I alive?' Again, looks were exchanged and everybody seemed reluctant to speak.

'You were drained of a third of your blood and went into hypovolemic shock,' Galen eventually said with a clinical detachedness that told me I wasn't about to hear good news. It was the same voice the doctors used when they told us Greg hadn't made it; that Lily had cancer. 'You required an immediate transfusion. Unfortunately, this meant there was not enough time to access human blood.'

My eyes bulged and the room went silent, waiting for my reaction. The only sound was the crackling of the fire in the hearth – lit for once – and the sound of my breathing, becoming faster and shallower.

'Turning a human requires just over half the blood to be replaced with a vampire's blood, which consumes the remaining human blood. A quarter of your blood was replaced with vampiric blood, meaning you are a half-blood, or what we call a dhampir.'

I didn't pay much attention. I frantically checked my palm, checking to see if it was any paler than I remembered it. It wasn't. In my chest, I could feel my heart beating.

'You're lying,' I growled.

'We're not lying, Miss Lee,' Galen countered.

'But my heart is beating! You must be lying!' I screamed at them all, refusing to believe it. Fabian stroked my arm but I wrenched it away so forcefully the joint clicked and I winced. 'I don't want to be anything like you. I'm human!' Anger, such extraordinary anger, built up inside me, to the point where I wanted to hurl.

Kaspar was suddenly inches from my face, grabbing my flailing shoulders and pinning them to the headboard. He knelt with one knee on the mattress and his face was unreadable. Angry, because his eyes were flashing between their emerald and black, but something else was there. *Pity?*

'Violet!'

I jerked away from him, thrashing about trying to release myself. 'Get off me!' I spat.

'Look at me, Violet!' I turned away, refusing to do what he said. 'I said, look at me!' he shouted. Still I refused. He grabbed my chin roughly and yanked my head around to face him; my neck stung where I knew there would be bite marks. I looked down at the sheets, not wanting to meet his eyes.

'For heaven's sake, just look! What's different?' Stunned, I conceded, raising my gaze to meet his. I reluctantly studied his face for a moment. Something *was* different. *The colours.* The green of his eyes was brighter, standing out more against the white.

'I—'

'Listen. Smell. Everything is better, isn't it?'

Yes. 'No,' I breathed. 'No!' I began thrashing around again, needing to get away. I screamed and screamed, without any rational thought.

Swiftly after my third 'no', however, a hand came into contact with my wet cheek and I squeaked, shutting up, stunned into total silence. My eyes widened and Kaspar breathed heavily on my face, looking shocked that he had actually hit me. He slowly released me, backing off to the corner of the room. I reached up with one of my now free hands to touch my stinging cheek. It hurt. But it worked.

'Fabian said vampires struggle to cry. I-is this the only time I can cry?'

'No,' Eaglen replied. 'If you would let us explain, it may not be as bad as you first thought.'

Galen stepped forward again from where he had stoked the fire. 'We had very little choice. The shock would have caused your major organs to cease functioning and your chance of survival without a transfusion was nil. None of the human blood supplies stored here are tested thoroughly enough for anything but consumption and, thus, vampire blood was our only option. And of course, vampiric blood has the added benefit of being able to heal wounds at an extraordinary rate. You are very fortunate that His Highness volunteered to donate some of his own blood to you.'

I looked at Kaspar, my eyes wide in surprise, but when I caught his eyes he turned away again, staring at something interesting on the window. *I owe him my life – again.*

'So, if I'm a dhampir, why is my heart still beating?'

'Because a dhampir is more human than vampire. You will function as before and you will not lust for blood in any way. Legally, you are still governed by humans and not the Kingdom. The only difference, as the Prince pointed out to you, is your slightly enhanced capabilities. Vision and stamina, for example. You will also live for longer than the average human.'

The King nodded. 'Thank you, Galen. You may leave us.'

'Should there be any problems, do not hesitate to send for me,' Galen muttered, and now I understood why I could hear them when they were stood on the opposite side of the room. With that he bowed and left with Eaglen.

'Fabian, Lyla, allow us a moment. Not you, Kaspar,' the King said as his son went to follow the other two. When the door had shut behind them, he continued. 'Miss Lee, you are under what we call the King and Crown's Protection, meaning that harming you in any way is a crime punishable by death. Ilta Crimson has fled, but we will endeavour to find him. When we do, he will stand trial. It was Kaspar here who found you and he has therefore been called as a witness. You have no objection to this?'

'No,' I replied, feeling my lips quiver. Below the sheets, I pressed my fingernails into my palm, finding it stopped the tears from welling.

'Then we will leave you. I suggest you rest. Someone will not be far at any time, if you are in need of anything.' They began to leave, Kaspar lingering for a second. The room fell silent, and swiftly, something clutched at my throat. *Fear.* I stared straight ahead, eyes bulging. I could not be alone. He would return to finish what he started.

'Kaspar,' I whispered. He turned. 'Please stay.'

'What?' he replied, going stiff.

'Please stay. I-I don't want to be alone.' I closed my eyes.

There was a pause where nothing penetrated the silence. But then the door clicked closed and I was sure he'd gone. The fear rose again, gripping me. I couldn't be alone. The floor creaked. My heart stopped. The sound of footsteps muffled by plush carpet, and then silence. Slowly, I cracked open an eye.

He stood there, leaned casually against the post of my bed. His dark, almost-black hair flopped lazily across his eyes – the sun-streaked tresses were fading now, as summer turned to autumn. The lack of light too had turned his skin more deathly, more haunting, although that may have been my eyes seeing more clearly.

'You stayed.' My eyes flitted up to his and he nodded slightly.

'I'm not as heartless as you think.'

There was silence.

'You saved my life.' I frowned. 'Twice.' He looked at the carpet. I looked to the sheets.

'Yes, I guess I did. But if you die . . . your father, so . . .'

I nodded hastily. Lips pursed shut, I averted my eyes out the window. I heard him shuffle slightly.

'Thanks, though. If you hadn't come, I don't know what he would have done.'

He waved his hand in the air, silencing me. 'You remember all of it?' He looked horrified.

I nodded sombrely. 'Everything, up until I passed out.' My vision glazed over and a shudder of disgust passed through me as I remembered Ilta's words to me.

When you are alive to feel the shame, Violet Lee, feel yourself violated, it makes it far more fun, you see . . .

But Kaspar had saved me from that fate – by the narrowest of margins. Kaspar had warned me away from him in the first place.

I was stupid, so stupid for trusting Ilta; for letting him close to me. Kaspar had been right. I should have stayed away. But I let him dance with me. I left the ball alone. This is my fault.

I buried my face in my hands, ashamed to let Kaspar see me breaking down like this. *I should be strong. I should just accept it.*

'Don't cry,' he said in a low voice. I looked up, surprised. His eyes were jet black and his fists were clenched. He had one arm wrapped around the post and was almost shaking. He might be staring at me, but he didn't see me.

'He will die for what he did to you. He'll be ripped and torn and burnt until he is begging for mercy, which he won't receive.'

'Please, don't say that,' I breathed, as horrific images rolled through my mind. Bile rose in my throat and I gagged. His eyes snapped back to emerald.

'Why? Don't you want revenge?'

I shrugged, his words bringing on a fresh wave of tears. To try to stop myself from descending into sobs, I focused on my clenched palms and shuffled under the sheets, noticing how hot the room was and how a layer of sweat and oil coated my skin. The mud and blood might have gone, but I felt unclean and not in a way I felt I could wash off, but I wanted to try anyway.

'Is there any chance I could have a shower?'

'Yes, of course. You can have a bath, if you'd prefer.' His eyes turned a faint pink colour. I nodded. 'I'll get one of the maids to run you one then.'

'Don't go!' I insisted.

He smiled lopsidedly. 'I won't.'

Closing his eyes for a moment, I was forced to look at closed eyelids. His lopsided smile, something I had rarely seen, remained on his lips. It was partway between a smile and a smirk.

'They're running one now, in the bathroom opposite.' He jerked his head towards the door.

'Thanks.' I twisted, throwing the sheets off and caught a glimpse of the clothes I was wearing: nothing but a long baggy T-shirt.

'I'll get you some clothes,' he said, disappearing into the wardrobe, appearing again a moment later, handing me a pair of leggings, a long, light wool jumper and fresh underwear.

'You need to keep warm,' he explained, facing away from me, looking out the French doors. I took the clothes, tucked them under my arm and inched off the bed, gripping the post for support. Feeling like a child trying to take her first steps, I got to the bathroom, blushing wildly at Kaspar's fussing.

'Will you be okay on your own? I will be in my room, if, well . . .'

I nodded. Scented steam hit me as soon as I stepped in, wafts of lavender escaping into the corridor. The mirror was coated in condensation and all the fittings were dripping with water – so was my skin as I hung my fresh clothes over the rail furthest from the bath. Reaching to shut the door, I noticed that the key for the lock had been removed.

I grabbed a towel from the rail and stripped down as quickly as I could, wrapping the towel around myself. I did not dare look at my body. I fiddled with the support on my wrist, struggling with the Velcro, which might as well have been glued shut.

When I managed to free my wrist, I wiped a patch on the mirror, holding my breath. I did not want to do this. But I had to.

I let the towel drop and gasped. Most of the smaller scratches and cuts had healed; so had the larger wounds on my right side, but on the left, five strips of shiny, mottled skin ran across my breasts and down my stomach. I touched the top of one of them, wincing as it stung, noticing that the scars on my neck that had been pinpricks were now each as big as my thumb. I sank onto the edge of the bath, covering myself back up again.

His face, his laugh, his slick, oily voice filled my head, and I could feel him touching me once more, hear his panting breaths, smell the reek of blood.

It is my duty to ensure you die before you ever fulfil your fate.

And he'll come back to finish me off. I know it. How can I carry on, knowing that? As I thought that, my eyes fell on something glinting on the side of the bath. A razor.

Think about it, Violet. What do you have to go back to? What is there left for you?

I had done it once. But I remembered the blood and how much there was of it; blood seemed too precious to go to waste now. Neither did I want to be sucked dry.

All of a sudden, the door burst open and Kaspar flitted in. He brushed past me and I sprang up as fast as the pain in my stomach and my stiff legs would allow, tightening the towel.

'Don't.' He snatched up the razor. 'Ever.' He turned and took another razor off a nearby shelf. 'Think.' He opened the bathroom cabinet and pulled out several sharp objects. 'About that.' He shut the cabinet. 'Again.' He wheeled around to face me, eyes ablaze with a thousand different emotions. We glared at each other.

'I wasn't actually going to,' I countered. I lowered myself back onto the edge of the bath, defensive and rechecking the mental barriers around my mind.

He raised an eyebrow. 'Just hurry up and get washed. I'm not taking my eyes off you any more.' He left, slamming the door.

'Fine!' I shouted after him. I dropped my towel with a humph and slipped into the water. It sent tingles dancing along my spine, and I involuntarily closed my eyes.

If he thought I was going to allow that stupid monster called Ilta Crimson get to me, then he better think again. At least, that's what I'm going to kid myself into thinking.

I flipped my wet hair back, having washed it twice and scrubbed my skin three times. My feet squeaked as I crossed the bathroom floor, but I didn't feel clean.

I opened the door to my room, to the sound of a tinkering guitar. He stopped as I walked in, his eyes following me as he sat on the edge of my bed. I walked towards the wardrobe, intending to find some warm socks.

'I meant what I said about not taking my eyes off you,' he called after me.

I flopped down on the bed, unravelling the socks as I did. 'You can sit down,' I answered, as he jumped up, backing away a little. 'I don't bite,' I continued. He chuckled and sat back down on the other side of the bed.

'No, but I do. Nice socks, by the way,' he said, raising an eyebrow at my fluffy bright yellow socks and continuing to mindlessly twiddle with the strings on his guitar. 'You seem perkier than earlier. Most people would have broken down if they were in your situation.'

'I'm not most people. Why should I let it bother me? It happened and there's nothing I can do about it . . .' I trailed off, wondering why I was even telling him this.

He continued to pluck the strings. 'Hiding it isn't always the best option.'

'I'm not hiding anything.' He just looked at me. 'What is there to hide? I should have listened to you and realized he was bad news, but I didn't. It's my fault.'

He set his guitar aside, meeting my eyes – it was a difficult gaze to break away from.

'Don't say that. It's not true and you know it.'

'It is. Anyway, why should you care?'

'So you don't want me to care? Well, in that case, I'll just go.' He slid off the bed and made for the door.

'That isn't what I meant. Please, don't go!'

He stopped, whirling back around. 'I won't go if you tell me why you're so afraid of being alone.'

I sighed, fiddling with the loose bits of fluff on my socks, wishing he would douse the fire because I was starting to sweat again.

'Well?'

'Because he's coming back,' I muttered, feeling my cheeks become warm and not because of the fire.

'He would be an idiot to do that.' He laughed. 'You don't need to worry about that. He would never get across the border. Honestly,' he added, seeing my face, which I knew was disbelieving. *You didn't hear what he said,* I thought. *You don't know how he said it. He meant it. He wants me dead.*

'Stop laughing.' I grabbed a pillow and chucked it at him. He, of course, caught it, and threw it back. It hit me square in the chest and I winced as it rubbed against the healing wounds. My eyes examined them, and so did Kaspar's.

'They'll heal.'

'I wish they would just go.'

He frowned, picking his guitar back up. 'They don't look that bad, you know.'

I raised an eyebrow. 'They do.'

'Don't.'

'Do!'

'Don't!'

'Get your shoes off my bed!'

And so it continued for hours, until the sun began to set. Relentless, pointless, witty banter exchanged back and forth until both of us had used up just about every comeback in the dictionary of sarcasm. It masked what was brewing beneath.

It was not until Kaspar reached across and switched my bedside lamp on that I realized how late it was.

'Do you think you'll be able to sleep?' Kaspar asked.

I yawned. 'There's your answer.'

He nodded slowly, but the silence was broken by a vibrating buzz. Kaspar darted up like he had been stung, pulling his phone from his jeans pocket. His eyes scanned the screen for a moment, before he cursed.

'What?'

'Look, I am going to have to go. There is something I have to deal with.' He got up off the bed, slipping his phone into his pocket again.

'Don't leave me! I don't think I can sleep if you go,' I pleaded, holding back the tears. The darkness was closing in, and every corner of the room seemed menacing. Outside, the sound of the wind roaring through the trees was chilling, because I knew what those trees could hide now.

His eyes widened. 'I have to sort this out. I'll be back as quickly as I can, okay?' He flitted out the room. Feeling very exposed, I rushed to the basin in the wardrobe, turned on the tap and began splashing my hands and face with freezing water.

TWENTY-EIGHT

Kaspar

'Kaspar!—'

'Charity,' I sighed, finding her standing against the frame of my door, looking completely overdressed in a short black cocktail dress.

'Where've you been, darling? Your mind is completely blocked off!' she whined, walking up to me and wrapping an arm around my waist. I felt my eyes go red, as lust pumped around my body. *Behave, Goddamn it.*

She placed her hands around my neck, and her lips brushed my ear. 'I have something special planned.' Her hands ran themselves down to my chest, pausing on my abs. 'Something *very* special . . .'

'What type of special?' I grunted, forcing my voice to stay steady. Her fingers were tracing the waistband of my jeans, teasing me as I became hard. *At least try to behave.* She linked a finger through a belt loop, pulling me into my room.

'I'll tell you when you tell me where you were,' she insisted and I grabbed her waist and pulled her closer. My eyes moved to her breasts, so ample they bulged out of the dress.

'How about you show me?' I chuckled.

What about Violet? my voice said, but I ignored it as I so often did.

I pushed her back towards the bed and, in an awkward manoeuvre, she managed to pull off my shirt. Her hands traced my six-pack. I grabbed the material of her dress and attempted to discard it too, but she backed away.

'Not until you tell me where you were.'

I covered the distance she had created, nibbling her ear and sighed in exasperated defeat. 'I was with Violet.' I moved down to her neck, ignoring the smell of her blood, acidic and foul – although that may have just been her attitude.

She backed off abruptly. 'What? You were with that human piece of trash?'

I shrugged. 'She isn't human, she's a dhampir.' I pulled her back into me, but she resisted again.

'Why the hell were you with her? How could you do that to me?' she screeched, backing away with a murderous glare that told me I was in deep trouble.

'She has just been attacked, Charity! What did you expect me to do? Tell her to sod off?' I replied, confused at her reaction.

'So you stayed with her, instead of being with me, your girlfriend?'

'Girlfriend?' I mouthed, taking a step back myself.

'That is normally what you call the girl you are in a relationship with!'

'Relationship?' I breathed, looking around dazed, like the walls could make more sense of this than I could. 'I don't recall us being in a relationship.'

She shrieked in frustration, tearing at her hair extensions.

'Kaspar, did you even bother to check Facebook? I applied to be in a relationship with you.'

'You have Facebook?'

Her eyes bulged and became black and she looked like she might launch herself at me. *Which would be amusing.*

'Yes, I'm one of your friends, which you would know if you ever bothered to check your profile! You're just trying to deny the fact that you cheated on me with that lying human slut who was apparently attacked. Well, if that's true, she deserved it. I hate you!'

I stood there for a full minute, feeling rather detached from my body. First, because we weren't supposed to use social networking – too personal – and second, because I couldn't take in what she had just said. But when I did, anger rose. 'Take that back,' I snarled, taking a step nearer to her.

'Which bit? The "slut deserved it" bit, or the "I hate you" bit?'

'The first bit. I couldn't give a damn whether you hate me or not!'

She flipped her hair. 'We are over, Kaspar. *So* over!' She straightened her dress and stormed from the room.

'We were never under!' I yelled after her. She didn't answer.

I couldn't move, reeling in disbelief. *I've just broken up with a girl who wasn't even my girlfriend. There has to be an award for that.*

I shook my head and grabbed my shirt off the floor. *How inconvenient. I'll have to find an alternative source of amusement.*

I went back to Violet's room, glad to see she had fallen asleep. I settled into the armchair beside her bed, frowning as I noticed the dampness of her clothes. I knew enough about humans from school to know she would get cold. I went to try to fold one of the sheets over her, but just then she winced in her sleep. I knew she was thinking of him.

Screw it: she can hate me for it later.

I crept into the bed with her, careful not to disturb her position. In an instant her face relaxed, and her feet entwined with me. Her breathing became more regular, and her expression more serene.

I reached over and kissed her on the back of her head. 'Sweet dreams, Violet.'

TWENTY-NINE

Violet

'You have three seconds to get your arm off me and move six feet away,' I groaned, as the sun glared through the rather pathetic voiles.

'Good morning to you, too,' Kaspar chuckled, taking his sweet time to extract himself.

My body was stiff and, as Galen had rightly predicted, sore. I groaned again, as he rolled me onto my back.

'Come on, you need to eat something. Doctor's orders.'

'I don't want to eat.' I rolled over, burying my face in the pillow. *I never want to move from here*, I thought.

'You can't not eat,' he retorted, prodding my pillow.

'Watch me. And since when did I let you sleep in my bed?'

This time he prodded me. 'Not a morning person, are you? Well, if you want to be alone, fine, I'm heading to the kitchen because I desperately need a drink.'

'I don't want to eat,' I repeated.

'You already said that,' I heard him call, before the door

slammed. I intended to stay where I was, but every sigh of the wind outside sounded like breath on the window, and the emptiness of the room began to bear down on me. So I jumped up, darting to the wardrobe and to the basin. I washed my face and brushed my teeth before grabbing the mouthwash. I was just pouring a mouthful into the cap when it slipped from my fingers, tumbling to the carpeted floor. Seeing it almost in slow motion, I stooped down and caught it – the right way up, not even a single drop spilled. I raised an eyebrow. *I certainly couldn't do that before.*

When I got downstairs, I found the entrance hall empty, both the doors thrown right back on their hinges. I paused, and then bolted across the marble expanse for the living room, like a child who runs up the stairs for fear of something running up behind them.

I found Kaspar had a drinking companion when I got to the kitchen: Fabian. They were in conversation when I entered, but stopped abruptly when they noticed me.

'Morning,' Fabian said. I didn't answer, hovering instead around the counter and avoiding eye contact. An apple rolled my way and Kaspar poured water from the kettle into a mug, a cup of tea following the fruit. I gingerly sipped at the hot drink, hit by a sense of déjà vu and a return to the day of my first sample of Varnley's fine breakfast cuisine. The uncomfortable thought was that now it was Kaspar who was looking after my human needs, whereas then I had desperately sought to avoid him. Now Fabian was the thorn in my side.

Fabian eyed me as I ate. I stared at the tiled floor. Kaspar raided the fridge, stuffing half a packet of ham into his mouth, washing it down with blood straight from the bottle.

'You all right?' Fabian asked. I nodded, lips tugged into a glum expression that said I wasn't. 'All right enough to talk?'

'About what? There are a lot of things we could talk about. Cheese. Chalk. Chocolate. The fact I was attacked. The fact I'm a hostage. The fact this whole situation is totally shit. Take your pick,' I replied, my voice surprisingly steely.

'About how *I* feel.'

'Well, how are you feeling today? Happy? Glum? Better than I am, guaranteed.'

'I'm being serious, Violet.'

From beside the fridge, Kaspar glanced our way; eyebrows raised, but said nothing.

I took a deep breath. 'Look, Fabian, I don't feel the same way about you, I can't, not when Lyla feels how she does, and I'm sorry about that, because you're a great guy, especially for a vampire. But you really shouldn't waste your time on me; go find some nice vampire chick that isn't totally different from you. Like Lyla. And this isn't my world. It wouldn't work.' I tried to be as diplomatic as possible, emphasising Lyla's feelings, but inside I was screaming, wondering why he had to bring this up now. *Couldn't it wait a few days?*

'But face it, Vi, you are not going to make it out of this human. Do you really think your father can get you out of this? Do you really think you can just leave? Do you even want to leave?' he finished, glaring at me as my mouth fell open.

'Maybe this isn't such a good time to talk about this,' Kaspar offered, leaning against the counter.

'Fuck off, Kaspar,' Fabian snapped.

The other man sprang up, hands in the air, whistling. 'Don't shoot the mediator.'

'You are going to be that nice vampire chick, Vi. Better than Lyla. Maybe not soon. But you will be, because I know you can't live like this for a lifetime. Don't you get it? This is all a waiting game. We are waiting for you to buckle. And I will wait until you buckle, whether you like it or not!'

I felt like I had been slapped. Kaspar gritted his teeth, running a hand down the side of his face as Fabian's chest heaved.

'It's Violet, not Vi.' Leaving my tea behind, I stormed from the room. *I don't need this. I don't have to put up with this.* However, Fabian darted after me and, just as I stepped onto the carpet of the living room, he grabbed my arm, swinging me back around.

'If you deny me your affections, then at least tell me one thing,' he demanded in a tone of voice I had never heard him use before. *Loathing.* 'You wouldn't deny Kaspar, would you?'

My face formed into a scowl. 'I would, and have!'

'I can't believe that,' Fabian muttered. 'I will wait for you. I will.'

I didn't hang around to listen to him. Darting back up the stairs, I hesitated before throwing myself through the door to my room, realizing I was being stupid. The windows to my room were locked; there was no way he could get in.

I found a fresh pair of socks and used them to replace the ones I was wearing, diving onto the bed and smothering my face in the freshly changed sheets. I enjoyed the complete darkness behind my eyelids, knowing it was only a matter of time before tears would start to fall.

He could have waited. He didn't have to bring it up now. Did he think I don't have enough to think about? Was Ilta not enough?

His name made me feel dirty; contaminated. It was as though he had singed the parts of my skin his hands and fangs had passed over, leaving me to burn and crumble.

You can't crumble, my voice said. *You're stronger than that.*

'Budge over, Girly; you're taking up the whole bed.'

I was prepared to spring up when I heard the voice, but relaxed back down into the mattress when I realized it was Kaspar. I didn't move. After a moment, I heard the bed springs at the end of the bed groan as he leaned against it.

'He's only being a bitch over this because he isn't used to being rejected by human girls, you know.'

'I'm a dhampir, remember?' I answered, voice muffled by the sheets.

'Tomahto, tomayto.'

I rolled over onto my back and dragged myself upright, propping myself against the pillows. *I won't buckle. They can wait all they like.* But I couldn't look at Kaspar whilst thinking that. Maybe I was afraid my face would betray my determination. Maybe I was afraid I would fall out of favour – and right now, I needed that favour.

I sighed. 'Are there many dhampirs?'

He nodded. 'About a thousand. A fraction of the total number of vampires. Most of them are hunters or slayers.'

'What's the difference?'

'Rank. Slayers are more skilled than hunters, but to be honest, they're all rotten bastards. I don't tend to discriminate.' Unsurprisingly, his eyes flashed black. I let my head fall against my knees, drawn into my own thoughts, trying to suppress the rising image of Trafalgar Square. *I know you don't discriminate.*

THIRTY

Violet

Kaspar didn't return for the rest of the day and, in the end, I figured he must have gone hunting. Fabian didn't come near me and everybody else left me alone. This was exactly what I didn't want. To lose the one vampire I was close to calling a friend.

With the daylight pouring in, the empty room didn't seem so menacing and maybe I even welcomed the time alone. But then, the next minute, I would perch on the windowsill, watching the edge of the forest and half-expecting a figure to appear from their cover.

Why had my *life turned upside down? I should be starting university, not stuck with creatures that shouldn't even exist.*

And Ilta. What had he said? *That I should die? That he was* saving *me?*

To top it all off, Fabian's words from earlier refused to leave my overcrowded, frantic mind.

'Do you really think you can just leave? Do you even want to leave?'

I should know the answer to that right away, but I didn't, and that was what bothered me. *I don't know,* I thought, as I forced my eyes closed, wanting to sleep. *I really don't know.*

I was still asleep, I knew that. And yet, I was aware of my surroundings, but not truly conscious.

I could feel the cold wind tickling my skin, hear it whistling against the glass, hear the floor depressing and creaking slightly. I could feel the sound of metal scraping against metal and even in my barely awake state, it made my teeth clench. The voiles rustled, as though blowing in a gentle wind – one that might blow through an open door. The clock ticked on and I could hear dust settling on the furniture. It seemed to become darker for a moment, like curtains had been drawn around my sleeping form.

I felt and heard the mattress depress, but still I did not open my eyes. I felt cold skin brushing my own, but I didn't move, or even think to scream.

I felt his weight held perfectly on top of me, heard his icy breath as I felt the burn of him gazing down at me. I felt every inch of carved flawlessness arch into my corpse, felt the lust and want, need, *no,* thirst, pumping through his veins.

When I did open my eyes, the first thing I saw was that the window furthest away, almost as tall as I was and normally securely locked, was now flung wide open, a chilly breeze passing through. Only then did it occur to me that something was not right. Then I opened my mouth to scream.

He snarled, hastily clamping a hand over my mouth. I attempted to bite at his fingers, but found myself quickly subdued.

'Play nicely now,' he mocked, pressing himself closer. I caught sight of the deranged, lustful glint in his blood-red eyes. My eyes widened and I was hushed to silence, terrified.

'Come on, Girly, just a little drop of blood. I'm so hungry. You'll enjoy it.'

I scowled, and thrashed about as he lay draped across me, pressing his crotch hard into my stomach.

'Kaspar, get off me!' I spat, as he removed his hand. He stared down at me, his eyes consumed by bloodlust and I could almost smell his throat as it singed, desperate to quench the thirst.

'If you scream, I swear I'll kill you, so I suggest you keep quiet,' he muttered, looking me in the eye, carefully pronouncing each word.

I scowled once more. 'But what about the Protection?' He faltered for a moment, eyes dulling a little.

'Give me your consent.'

I blinked. He said those words almost remorsefully.

'What's wrong with the donor stuff?'

It was his turn to blink. 'It doesn't taste as good as your blood,' he stated slowly, as though it were obvious. His eyes were rapidly fading, leaving crimson behind, emerald fast returning. But I could still smell the stench of burning flesh. He was still thirsty.

'Please,' he breathed.

His voice was so pleading, so desperate, like the piteous call of a starving child; and I whispered a word I should never even have thought of:

'Okay.'

Immediately, his eyes flared red again and I tensed beneath him. He chuckled, but it was not the cruel laugh I was used to; more one of quiet amusement. His eyes trailed over the tank top and shorts I had changed into earlier that night and he smiled slyly.

'Let me help you enjoy this.'

Slowly, very slowly, he allowed his full weight to rest on me and I groaned, feeling my chest compressing. He chuckled once more, but eased away an inch. His hand searched for mine, finding it pinned to my side. He stroked my fingers for a moment, before trailing a finger up the length of my arm. I shuddered at his touch, goose bumps forming.

I should not *be enjoying this. I was almost drained a few days ago. I should cower away from his touch, I should be scared.* But I didn't and I wasn't. *And he saved me.* Now, maybe, I could save him.

His hand trailed across my collar, brushing the tops of my scars. I squirmed away then, but he had worked a hand behind my back, pulling me into him. It dug into my spine and I winced, but he ignored me; he was occupied as his hand trailed the vein on my neck, his eyes intently watching its rhythm.

His head sunk lower and I stiffened, expecting pain to erupt. But it didn't. Instead, soft lips began kissing my neck.

'W-what are you doing?' I faltered.

'Just relax and enjoy,' he murmured into my neck. It sent tingles dancing along my skin and I suppressed an intake of breath.

You wouldn't deny Kaspar, would you?

Instead, I sighed, quietly, almost inwardly, and gradually relaxed. He leisurely trailed tender kisses down my throat, along my collarbone, until he reached my silvery scars, where he paused, breathing onto my skin before his tongue began to trace the indents. I jolted a little, as it tickled. He laughed and brought his lips back to my jaw line. His dark hair brushed my lips and I blew it gently away.

His head abruptly returned to my neck and I went rigid, sure he would bite this time. But again he began kissing my neck, his teeth grazing my flesh. But these kisses were deeper, more urgent and I shuddered under him.

'I know you want to moan, Girly,' he purred into my neck, and I could tell from his arrogant tone and full lips that he was smirking. 'Go on . . .'

I will get to you, Violet Lee . . .

His hands began rubbing my side. I pursed my lips, as his own delved frantically at my neck. I whimpered beneath him, fighting and flailing.

'Give in,' he whispered as his mouth brushed my ear. And I did. A small moan escaped my lips and I compulsively found myself arching into him, forcing every inch of flesh to meet his. He pressed me further into the bed and yet another moan slipped through my lips. He was smirking into my neck again as his hand slipped up my side.

Suddenly, he picked me up and pressed me hard against the wall; hard enough that the panelling dug into my spine, like it had done that first morning. 'You'll bleed less if you are standing,' he explained. 'Just relax,' he whispered, but I had gone rigid again, scared at just the sight of his fangs. He sighed, exasperatedly. 'It will hurt less if you relax.'

One hand wrapped itself around my waist, palm pressed firmly into the hollow of my back, pulling me to him. The other hand swept the hair from my shoulders, exposing my bare flesh.

He tilted my head out of the way, moving closer the whole time, head lowering towards the pulsating vein of my neck. I tried to pull away from him as his lips parted slightly, revealing his fangs.

His mouth met my neck and I heard him inhale my scent. His tongue darted out, licking the spot where he intended to bite, hovering over my vein. His lips parted a little more and he softly kissed my skin. A shudder of pleasure ignited me, sending my mind into spasm, my body falling into his waiting arms, as my resolve evaporated.

The instant he felt me wilt he sank his fangs deep into my flesh, blood surging from the wounds, trickling across and smearing my skin.

I opened my mouth to scream, but all that came out was a muffled cry. A hand was clamped over my mouth, forcing my jaws together, stifling the sound. I felt him drink, taking short shallow breaths, panting, eyes gleaming red, a trickle of blood running down his chin. I backed further into the wall, but he pulled me back quickly.

'Don't scream,' he ordered, lowering his head once more. I cowered away.

'It hurts,' I whimpered through his fingers, shaking. To my surprise his eyes softened, but he didn't ease up as his fangs sunk into my neck once more. As he continued to suck, my jaw tightened and tightened, attempting to ignore the horrifying drawing sensation. It was like a blood test gone very, very wrong.

The thought of what was actually happening made my vision waver, and, sure enough, seconds later I blacked out, falling forward onto his shoulder. He withdrew at once and my eyes flickered open as he caught me.

'Whoa there,' he breathed, steadying me. I felt myself straightening up, sandwiched between the wall and his cold body.

'You okay?' he asked, genuine concern in his voice. I nodded shakily in reply. 'I think I'm full.' He laughed, attempting to lighten the atmosphere. Again I nodded, taking a few raspy deep breaths. The tunnel vision was disappearing, the pounding in my head subsiding. There was a strange tingling on my neck, exactly where the wounds were and I reached up to touch them.

What should be two mangled puncture wounds were now small incisions, stitching themselves together.

'H-how is that p-possible?' I began, but he leaned forward to whisper in my ear.

'Vampires are fantasy, Girly. Anything is possible.'

'But—'

'It happens every time we take blood. Otherwise you would bleed to death. Haven't you noticed it before?'

I shook my head. 'But then when *he* bit me, how did I lose all that blood?'

'He drank it all,' Kaspar replied bluntly, averting his gaze. I lowered mine to the floor.

The blood was drying, caking itself to my skin and leaving bloody streaks all across my chest and neck. I went to wipe it away, but Kaspar caught my hand.

'Allow me.' His head lowered to the top of my breast and his tongue traced the line of my top. He gradually worked his way up towards my neck, lapping at the blood; and by the feel of his leisurely pace, he was savouring every last drop. His hand had begun to caress my side again.

'Damn, you're good,' I breathed, not intending for him to hear.

'I know.' He chuckled, his lips gradually moving further and further down, until he was pulling my top aside, revealing my bra. I froze.

'Kaspar.' He ignored me. 'Kaspar!' I pushed him away using the hand that wasn't strapped into a brace, all the while holding back tears. He looked up at me, frowning.

'What?'

'Just don't do that,' I stammered, still holding back the tears.

'Why?'

His ignorance triggered something and the tears began

flowing. I pointed at my scars, torn between anger and hurt, fear overshadowing everything. 'I was almost raped less than a week ago. Why do you think?' I screeched.

'You were all right before?' he said, frowning.

I shook my head, disbelievingly. 'I almost died! And I know it was all my stupid fault and I should have listened to you, and I was an idiot, but everything, it's just too much! And now Fabian's freaking out and I'm so bloody scared. I'm scared for me, for my family, for humanity, for you! Your family! I don't want my father to hurt anybody. I don't want a war!' I broke down in sobs, unable to continue. He just stood there, dumbfounded, staring at me as though I was a dangerous creature that should be treated with extreme caution.

'And you can't even say anything,' I continued between sobs. 'You stupid, arrogant, stuck-up, heartless vampire Prince!' I pummelled his chest, trying to hurt him but failing miserably. I tried to push him away, but he just pulled me nearer into a bone-crushing hug.

'I'm so sorry,' he murmured. 'So sorry.' He wrapped an arm firmly around my back, the other hand gently stroking my hair as I cried uncontrollably into his chest.

After what seemed like an age, I drew away; tears drying up, sobs receding.

'Sorry,' I mumbled to the floor, embarrassed. Breaking down in front of Kaspar was becoming a habit and it wasn't one I wanted to maintain. He shrugged his shoulders in reply, as though he had girls sobbing in his arms every night.

'Ashton will get Ilta, don't worry, and then you won't have to fear him ever again. The rest you'll have to figure out on your own.'

'Thanks for the help,' I mumbled, sarcastically.

He chuckled, shifting closer. 'But you have to admit, you were turned on back there.' He leaned his forehead against mine, characteristic smirk adorning that far too perfect face of his.

'No, I was not,' I replied defensively, punching him in the stomach. He didn't flinch.

Liar, my voice breathed and I detected an almost sinister tone, as though I *was* lying.

Kaspar suddenly drew back, his cool forehead leaving mine. His lips curled into their half-smirk, half-smile, revealing the tips of his glittering fangs. 'I'll seduce you one day yet, Violet Lee,' he breathed, letting out a faint sigh.

I closed my eyes, chuckling. 'In your dreams, Princey.'

'Fantasy *is* dreaming.'

I opened my eyes slowly to find him staring back, his lips just inches from mine. He was pressed into me, chests rising and falling in time, hands on the wall either side of my head.

Suddenly he snatched away from me, head jerking in the direction of the door. 'Someone's coming.'

He turned back to look at me, my heart palpitating. His face was a mixture of alarm and disappointment. It was a fleeting look – it couldn't have lasted more than a second, but it was there long enough for me to see it.

His hands wrapped themselves around my waist and flung me towards the bed; I landed surprisingly unsprawled on the soft sheets. He paused – his hands still wrapped around me – and shot me another look. I knew him well enough to know what such a look meant: never tell anyone.

I blinked and he was gone.

I heard footsteps approaching my door, creaking open, and panicked, I glanced at the open window, the voiles billowing in the wind. The door opened, revealing Fabian. I looked back to the window. It was closed.

I frowned, but quickly cleared my face as Fabian came in and sat on the end of my bed.

'Are you okay? I heard a noise.'

'I'm fine. Noise?'

'Yes, talking. Pleading, really. It's not those dreams again, is it? And why aren't you in bed?'

'Bed? Right, yeah. I guess I must have had a nightmare,' I said, rather lamely, hoping he would believe the hastily made-up excuse.

'Was it about that vampire again?' I shook my head. 'You're not all right, are you? Not at all. And you're all flushed.'

'I-I am?' I stuttered, reaching up to feel my face. My cheeks were warm, my palms a little sweaty.

'Do you want to talk?' he asked tenderly, and a wave of guilt for lying to him swept through me.

'I'm fine, really,' I replied, more defiantly than I intended. He narrowed his eyes slightly, but let it drop. There was silence for a while, the whole time of which I spent wishing him away, afraid he might realize who had been causing that 'pleading' earlier.

After a few minutes, he spoke: 'Look, Violet, I want to apologize for what I said earlier. It was cruel, I know you must be going through hell and I don't want to upset you any more. It was selfish of me.' He shook his head and my heart melted a little as I saw the genuine remorse in his eyes. 'And I know you would deny Kaspar if he ever tried anything with you; sex or blood. I know you're strong enough to not let him seduce you. So I'm sorry for that too.'

My lips parted and I drew back a tiny amount, my eyes darting to the window. They lingered there for a moment.

'Violet?'

I turned towards Fabian and realized he was staring at me. I looked to the sheets guiltily. *I can't let him apologize for something that isn't true. Something that had been proved wrong just moments before.*

What are you, a bloody martyr? my voice hissed. The sinister tone had not disappeared.

'Fabian, you don't have to say sorry. You were angry and we all say and do stupid things sometimes.'

I certainly had.

'That's exactly the point. I was angry at you because you don't have feelings for me. That's wrong. But please say we can stay friends?'

My mouth fell open a little, lost for what to say. I nodded, stammering over my words. 'Y-yes, of course.'

He dived towards me, wrapping his muscular arms around me, pulling me into a tight hug.

Why can't he just like Lyla? I thought desperately in my head. *Why did he let this happen?*

Because no man can control his passions, my voice replied bitterly.

Shut up, I thought. *In fact, get out of my head! Leave me alone!* I mentally screamed, and squeezed my eyes shut to stop myself from crying yet again.

I will never leave you, Violet; not for all eternity. I am a part of you.

Fabian drew back, his eyes searching my face, but I averted my eyes as my voice faded into nothingness.

'I'm sorry too, Fabian,' I breathed.

'What for?' he asked, surprised.

'You wouldn't know.' I shook my head and he reached a hand up to my face, cupping my cheek. His eyes watched me intently and self-consciously I swept a few strands of hair over my neck; over the still-healing wounds that Kaspar had given me.

'Violet . . .'

I caught my breath as I watched his eyes. They were dropping faster than a pin through the spectrum, every colour shining bright.

'Violet, I'm sorry, I can't suppress it any longer. It's killing me. One day you might understand, if you become one of us, but please forgive me.'

'Forgive you for what?'

He leaned in closer, hand still cradling my cheek.

'For this.'

His lips crushed into mine, and my heart stopped. Literally stopped. I totally froze for a moment, unsure of what to do. His lips tenderly pulled on mine, begging for some sort of response.

And respond I did, as perplexing, fantastical feelings erupted, seizing my heart and mind. The blood pumped through my veins, sending my body into a frenzy.

I had kissed lots of boys; men. But nothing even compared to *this*. Love . . . love didn't cover what I felt at that moment.

The Atlantic wasn't deep enough to contain the sinking feeling in my stomach. Happiness was far too colourful to even understand what I felt at that moment. Depression was overshadowed by the guilt surging through my chest.

And the most terrifying thing of all was the fact I wanted more.

His tongue traced my lips, seeking entry, which I gladly gave. His tongue swept into my mouth, over my teeth, withdrawing as I did the same, pleading entrance to his mouth, tongue running over his sharpened fangs as they scratched at my lips. He moved closer, pressing me into the headboard, legs straddling my outstretched ones, brushing the hair from my shoulders, hands twisting themselves into the tangled strands.

We broke apart minutes later, both gasping for breath. My chest rose and fell like I had just been subjected to school cross-country, as I waited for my mind to catch up with my heart; heart to catch up with my senses.

Only when they did, did it truly register what I had just done.

His hand slid from my cheek, reaching for my hand, which he took gingerly. I wrenched away, looking up to meet his gaze with wide eyes.

'Violet?'

'You should go now,' I replied coldly, ripping all emotion but hostility from my words. His face, full of hope, cruel hope, dropped, his eyes becoming a steely grey.

'Vi, I—'

'Go.'

He nodded, wordlessly disentangling himself from me. Before he left, he took one look back. One pitiful, despairing, wretched look back, before quietly closing the door. My chest tightened and my eyes stung with tears. My breathing was becoming shallower and anger was rising, along with shame and a mounting sense of hopelessness as the scale of what had just happened weighed down on my shoulders.

But not hopelessness. This is all my fault.

I wanted to scream at both Kaspar and Fabian for taking advantage of me; for using me – or better, wind it all back and stop myself. With that I threw myself towards the wash-basin in the wardrobe, using the water to cool off my burning palms.

Except they didn't use me. I was willing. I wanted it. I still do. I wanted it after everything that has happened to me.

But what – or who – did I want more?

THIRTY-ONE

Kaspar

The breeze ruffled my hair as I leaned against the stone railings of the balcony. *I shouldn't have done that. It was stupid . . . foolish . . . irrational.*

I almost smiled, as I realized I sounded just like my father. Perhaps the lectures had paid off. But the fact that I could admit I was a first-class idiot didn't mean I could take it back.

The upturned corners of my lips dropped and I sighed. Things would have been easier if I had killed her back in Trafalgar Square – a lot easier – but somehow I couldn't bring myself to regret the decision.

I still didn't know why I had acted that way that night. Protocol would be to kill her, suck her dry, and deposit the remains somewhere inconspicuous. It was the same for the hunters that night. We shouldn't have left a trace, but we did. *I* did.

I sighed, frustrated with myself. My father had been furious; more than furious when he had found out. So furious he had grounded all six of us to Varnley for two months. Of course, I had broken that rule a thousand times already, but he wasn't to know that.

Why did I let her live that day? Perhaps it had been her pale skin shining under the glow of the streetlights, much like ours did, as she sat there, stunned when I turned to her, catching her alluring scent as the wind changed direction. Or perhaps it was her violet eyes, such an unusual colour for a human; those eyes that widened when her gaze settled on the carnage we had created. Maybe it was her attitude. Even in the face of death, she had still managed to maintain the sarcasm. Or maybe it was just the idea of having a human around – a plaything and a constant source of food.

Even I could admire her strength. All through this she had kept it together; even after Ilta's crime she still had a sharp tongue on her; could still face Fabian; and could still hold her own. But what I had just experienced unnerved me. It had been a glimpse of something more: something not so strong.

I thumped my palm against the stone, groaning as the light from the moon was shrouded by dark clouds. Rain began to fall, slowly at first, but persistent, becoming heavier.

I sighed and turned back inside, but not before glancing at Violet's darkened windows. I knew Fabian was there.

Shutting the doors quietly behind me, I fastened the lock, and drew the curtains. Walking towards the bed I grabbed a slip of paper from the drawer in my bedside cabinet.

I didn't hold much sentimental value for things, but the piece of heavy, tear-stained parchment in my hands meant more to me than immortality ever would, or even could.

I sat down on the bed and under the watchful gaze of my mother's emerald eyes and my father's steely grey ones, silently read the first line. Their portrait loomed above me, dominating the mantelpiece, a constant reminder of happier times.

'My dear beloved son, Kaspar . . .'

I didn't turn the page. I couldn't turn the page.

THIRTY-TWO

Violet

Vampires are not gentle, loving creatures. It is not in their nature to change, or to adapt, to accept others. Their love is not what humans would call love, and lust consumes them on a level we will never understand. They do not grow old as we do, but age as stone does: they gradually weather, slowly perish, so slowly it is unnoticeable. But in the end, stone is a fixture forever, as are they.

I'd found that passage in a book in the library. It was a self-help guide for humans caught up in the vampire world – the existence of which had given me the first real reason to laugh since Ilta.

I couldn't become like that. I was a dhampir, a shadow of what they were capable of, and that's how I always hoped it to be.

What are you, a bloody poet today? my voice asked, filling my mind with a mocking snigger. I ignored it.

Fifty-four days, I had been at Varnley. Almost two months. I passed through the empty living room, heading for the kitchen. I shuddered, as the cold air rushed past. *It's getting wintry*, I thought.

I paused, as I heard a distant whisper of movement.

'You should really guard your mind better, Violet.'

It was soft and gentle, yet still menacing. *Female?*

I frantically looked around, searching for the source. I threw up huge barriers around my mind too, concentrating on the coldness of the passage and the coldness only.

'Behind you, Violet.'

I whipped around. Nothing. 'Who the fuck are you?' I screeched, my breathing becoming erratic and raspy.

'I know what happened with you and Fabian, you little human slut!'

My head was thrashed against the wall and I shrieked. My vision tunnelled, and I blinked, dazed. When my vision cleared, I managed to focus on the face in front of mine.

'What the hell?' I breathed. 'Lyla?'

She pinned me to the wall, her eyes a blazing jaded green, mixed with the awful crimson, pupils contracting as her eyes constricted to black and back.

'You kissed him, you fucking bitch! You know I like him and yet you still went ahead. What the fuck is wrong with you?'

I stood there dumbfounded for a moment, before anger rose. 'I'm not a bitch! And as to what the fuck is wrong with me, what about what's wrong with you?'

Her grip tightened around my arms, her nails digging in. 'You don't even deny it! Why the hell did you do it?' She scowled, wrinkling her nose. 'It's bullshit that a human can just walk right in here, cry a bit and get what the hell she wants!'

'That's what you think, is it? Well, let me tell you something.' I imitated her scowl. 'I would never touch any of

your kind. So maybe you should go and ask Fabian personally what happened, because I certainly didn't start it!' I shot
her a smile, making to break away. It didn't occur to me
that Lyla might be truly angry and that that anger could
drive her to bloodlust. I couldn't ever believe that Lyla would
hurt me.

'Liar! Your memories say everything. You enjoyed it,
didn't you? Probably the best kiss you've ever had, but
you're not getting any more of it. Stay away from Fabian,
or else . . .'

I raised an eyebrow. 'Or else what?'

She raised a finger to my cheek. Her deep purple nails
were sharpened and tough, able to lacerate flesh. So when
she slowly ran a single nail down my cheek, it gouged right
in, leaving a bleeding scratch behind. She took the finger to
her mouth, sucking on my blood.

'Sweet. And I don't know, maybe I will tell everyone that
a certain brother of mine spent some quality time with you
last night. I'm sure they would love to know that poor
attacked Violet is all better now.'

My mouth fell open. 'You wouldn't!'

She shrugged. 'I won't if you stay away from Fabian. Have
a nice day, Violet, you slut.' She smiled sweetly, turned on
her heel and disappeared, leaving me gobsmacked.

She's blackmailing me!

I had seen what jealousy can do to people. But never did
I imagine that Lyla was the type.

I don't have a choice.

I wiped the blood from my cheek and took several deep
breaths to calm myself. Composure was key. I slowly set
off in the direction I had thought I had come, still taking
deep breaths. I hoped and prayed that the scratch was not
that obvious and self-consciously fluffed my hair around

my face – nobody in the kitchen commented, but Kaspar's eyes never left my cheek the entire time I ate.

'Please play!' Thyme begged, grabbing hold of my knees. I shook her off, staring at the door. 'Violet,' she continued to whine. 'Pretty please play!'

'Thyme,' I replied, exasperated, and she tugged me by the hand as I sat on the bottom step of the staircase in the entrance hall, refusing to move. 'I keep telling you, I don't feel like it okay?' I wrenched my hand from her surprisingly strong grip and her lips trembled. But somehow, I just couldn't feel sorry for her as I usually did. Too much was running through my mind.

Thyme had recruited me to help her search for her absent nannies – neither of which we had found – and, resigned, I had agreed to look after her whilst the others attended a council meeting. The entrance hall was empty, devoid of the butler that usually guarded the doors. Most were attending the meeting. But that was the least of my worries.

I was more worried about what Lyla knew. If she knew about Fabian, what was there to say she didn't know about my father?

'I'll scream if you don't play, Violet.'

'Look, Thyme, if I give you a piggyback ride, will you stop asking?'

She nodded eagerly, and squealed in reply. Sighing, I picked her up and swung her onto my back. She shrieked excitedly as I spun around, her tiny arms choking me as she clung onto my neck. After a while I stopped, dizzy. The air had turned distinctly colder, and I wondered if they were finished with the council meeting.

The room levelled out and a quiet laughing seemed to

fill my ears. A laughing I recognized: a patronising, broken chuckle.

I turned slowly, letting Thyme slip from my hands to the ground. The double doors of the entrance were thrown open, three figures framed by the twilight. One held a bleeding body in their hands, the unfortunate victim limp, with arms twisted into positions that could only cause pain.

My eyes locked onto the man stood in the centre, his dark crimson cloak billowing in the wind. His manic laughing echoed around the room, as Thyme scuttled behind me.

'You just won't die, will you, Violet Lee?'

I opened my mouth and screamed.

THIRTY-THREE

Kaspar

'But Your Majesty, what do you intend to do with the rest of the Crimson family. Surely they cannot still attend court after their son disgraced them so?'

'Valerian Crimson has as good as disowned his son and will therefore be allowed to return to court in due time.'

I clenched my fist under the table. 'I don't think that's such a good idea. Violet keeps mentioning that Ilta Crimson will come back for her. She's terrified. She can hardly be left alone.'

Mutterings erupted around the room at that news and my other fist clenched as patronizing comments passed from person-to-person, most denying outwardly that Ilta would ever do such a thing. *But they haven't seen Girly. Whatever he said to her, he meant it.*

Ashton cleared his throat and stood to address the council, many of whom were missing as preparations for Ad Infinitum, the annual celebration for dark beings, began. Charity was one of them and I was thankful that was the case. 'The girl need not fear. I have personally searched the whole of Kent, far beyond the boundaries of Varnley. I am one of many doing so and we have contacts patrolling the borders of Transylvania, should he choose to return to Romania. Ilta Crimson has left the country, I am quite sure of that.' He bowed and sat down.

I spoke up. 'I don't disagree with you, Ashton, but think about the message we would send to Violet by allowing her violator's father into court. You say you want her to change of her own free will, but you're not exactly making it an easy task for any of us to convince her.'

Again, there were murmurs of agreement, mainly from the younger vampires who I knew would understand Girly's mindset better than the rest of the council.

Father shot me a scathing look I knew all too well. *It is better to keep our enemies close,* he said in my mind. *And I share Miss Lee's suspicions. I believe Ilta had a motive behind his actions.*

'The decision has already been made. The girl has no reason to come into contact with him, in any case,' he declared, aloud. His booming voice told all that no more was to be said on the matter. 'Furthermore, none of what occurred on the night of Autumnal Equinox can reach Michael Lee. I have no doubt that the Prime Minister would allow Lee to go ahead with his plans if they knew. News has already spread, so I can only urge you to guard your words, particularly around those with sympathies for the slayers.'

'What of Miss Lee, in any case? Does she show any signs of conceding?' Lamair demanded to know in his brusque manner. I sealed my lips, leaning back on my chair as far into the shadows as I could; glad I had chosen to sit in one of the corners. *She let me take blood from her last night. She's wavering. But was that her or what Ilta has done to her?*

'Kaspar, you are rather quiet. Do you not have any

thoughts on this?' Eaglen asked pointedly, turning his gaze to me. His unnaturally polite smile told me he was up to something again. *Heaven knows what. But why does he always have to involve me?*

'I have nothing to say.'

'Are you quite sure about that? You are far closer to Miss Lee than any of us here.' He gestured about the room and I followed his hand around. My eyes caught sight of Fabian, who sat on the opposite side of the room, fists clenched, clearly angry at Eaglen's false statement.

I sighed, knowing Eaglen would not give in until he had heard me out. 'No, I don't think she hates us. I believe she has a begrudging trust in us.' I crossed a leg over the other, resting my ankle on my knee, leaning back into the gloom once more.

'But do you think she would ever want to join us?'

I narrowed my eyes. 'I could not tell you that, Eaglen. I don't have the gift of seeing what is to be,' I snarled, letting my lips curl back; tensed until a spine-chilling scream cut through my anger. *Her scream.*

I remained still for an instant before leaping up and knocking the chair over, flying from the room, Fabian hot on my heels. Behind us, we left the shocked faces of the councillors.

Horrific thoughts sped through my mind. Violet was as good as alone. *Could it be possible?*

THIRTY-FOUR

Violet

My eyes locked with his for a moment, the scream ceasing to flow from my drying lips. They slid down to the dead woman lying in the arms of one his accomplices, who looked down at Thyme with a manic grin, revealing his reddened fangs. Her gaze was fixed on the woman and through the gore I could vaguely recognize a black-and-white uniform, complete with pinafore and laced cuffs.

'Nanny Eve!' Thyme wailed, her eyes emerald bulging, tears falling unchecked from them.

'Oh my god,' I breathed, seeing for the first time the woman's face. Her neck was pierced, blood staining her porcelain skin and white clothes, occasional drops sliding from her hand, which fell lifeless towards the floor. I felt bile rise in my throat and swallowed it back, gulping.

I pushed Thyme further behind me, hiding her from the atrocity before us, scurrying back.

'You cannibals,' I spat, at the figures framed by the setting sun.

He only laughed harder. 'Try telling that to your pretty little saviour back there.' He nodded behind me and I glanced over my shoulder, keeping as much of my gaze as I could on Ilta. There, in the corner stood Kaspar, the council members flooding into the room. He was visibly shaking, his fists turning purple as they clenched together, anger pulsating through his veins as his eyes faded to black. An arm was placed firmly on his shoulder and I saw Ashton physically restraining him. Another vampire I did not recognize stepped forward to help.

'Ilta Zech Valerian Crimson, second son of Lord Valerian Crimson, the Earl of Wallachia, you are hereby charged with the attack and attempted rape of a human under the King and Crown's Protection and shall await trial under the penalty of death. Henceforth, you forego any statuary rights held by a vampire, under the laws and treaties of the dark beings. Furthermore, I reserve the right to banish your family from the royal court,' the King declared in all his menacing glory, slowly moving towards me and Thyme. Six vampires stepped forward too, wary of the three stood before them.

Ilta too took a step forward. 'Vladimir. May I call you that now as I no longer have any rights? I see that as fair.' He smirked. 'And do you really expect me to remain silent? I would not stay silent if this were my last breath.' His eyes very purposefully slid down my body, lingering on the scars he had so delightfully given me. He sighed. 'It is a shame that such a pretty little thing – one day perhaps a beautiful thing – was ruined, don't you think?'

Ruined.

'You will die for what you have done to her,' Kaspar growled from behind me.

'I know I will, Kaspar. That is why I have come to the

conclusion that if I must die for such a pitiful creature, I might as well achieve what I aimed to do in the first place.'

I barely had time to scream before he was lunging towards me; his mouth spread wide, eyes intently focused on my neck. I felt Thyme being snatched from behind me.

Yet the pain never came.

On the dusty ground of the drive two blurs, rolled about – Ilta and Kaspar – each diving for the other's neck, frantically scrabbling for control as the two vampires who accompanied Ilta were thrown to the ground by Fabian and Cain, gasping for breath, their bulk nothing compared to the speed of the younger vampires. The corpse of the nanny was thrown aside, forgotten, still leaking blood.

I looked away as liquid spurted from the hearts of Ilta's accomplices, their faces forever etched with fear, and found myself looking at twenty or so bloodthirsty creatures, all eyes red, each slowly licking their lips; each intently focused on the bloodbath before us. A few inhaled the sickening scent hanging in the air, snarling and spitting as the stench burnt their throats. Yet they held back.

That is until Kaspar lowered his fangs to Ilta's throat and ripped his neck in half. I screamed as blood and sinew was ripped from Ilta's carcass, monster after monster now throwing themselves at the ravaged corpse. His stomach was sliced open by a single nail, vampires lowering their heads to drink the blood from the organs torn out and treated as offal. I clamped my mouth shut, gagging uncontrollably.

Thyme darted forward, but not before I grabbed her hand, shaking my head. Yet as she turned to me, her petite mouth opened to reveal her pinprick, thorn-like fangs. She sniffed at the air, tugging on my hand as she tried to edge towards the carnage before us. Suddenly, she whipped back around and plunged her fangs into my palm. I yelped and yanked my hand back, nursing the two tiny incisions. She flew outside, dress trailing behind, whipping at her ankles, coming to a halt beside the body of her nanny.

She stared at it for a moment before taking a hand in her own, raising it to her lips as though to give her one final kiss goodbye. Instead, she pierced the flesh, sucking her nanny of blood via the wrist, slurping it down like a baby would milk.

This time I was unable to control myself and I doubled over as bile poured from my mouth, causing my throat to burn and my eyes to sting as tears continued to fall.

I had wanted Ilta dead, but never like this.

My gut clenched one final time and I gingerly wiped my mouth, still gagging – but my stomach was empty.

My eyes rose to see Kaspar throwing what was Ilta, now just flesh clinging to bone, aside, unwanted organs littered about in a pool of darkening blood. The chests of his accomplices had been ripped open and the nanny's corpse was being raided for organs that might still contain the precious blood vampires worshipped.

'You never did deserve the name of vampire, Ilta Crimson.'

Ilta's bones clattered as they fell to the red-stained dust and gravel of the drive and I looked on through the double doors of the mansion called Varnley, paralyzed and horrified. Kaspar looked up, his shirt bloodstained and torn, tainted at the hands of the vampires he had just declared did not deserve the name.

My gaze locked with his, as he brushed blood-matted hair from his brow, his chest rising and falling rapidly, not even a drop of sweat falling. Thin black plumes of smoke drifted into the stinking air, as they burnt the remains of the four corpses.

A single drop of blood slivered from one of his fangs and

I wavered, unsteady. My eyes flickered and I just caught the concerned face of Kaspar before they closed. I was sent plummeting to the floor to land in a pool of my own vomit, my consciousness spiralling away from the scene, reminded of the true atrocity of the creature called vampire.

'Stop! Stop!'

'Vampires are not gentle, loving creatures. It is not in their nature to change, or to adapt, to accept others. Their love is not what humans would call love, and lust consumes them on a level we will never understand. They do not grow old as we do, but age as stone does: they gradually weather, slowly perish, so slowly it is unnoticeable. But in the end, stone is a fixture forever, as are they.'

'Don't come near me.'

My words pierced the silence as several pairs of eyes followed me as I folded myself into the ledge of the window. I felt as though I was under interrogation – incidentally it was not I who had committed the crime.

'Why are you acting like this?'

I exhaled loudly, caught between a laugh and a sigh. 'It was a shock, seeing that. Don't get me wrong, I remember Trafalgar Square . . . I just didn't expect you to be able to do that to your own kind. And now for you all to seem so unbothered by it . . . it's unnatural.'

'We drink the blood of our own kind. Violet, Ilta deserved everything he got. But I admit we lost it. I don't really know what happened.' Fabian glanced over his shoulder at the two Varn siblings behind him, both with their arms folded, perceiving me through sceptic eyes. He started to walk towards me, but my eyes met with Lyla's cold gaze and my breath caught.

But stood right next to Lyla was Kaspar, his eyes flickering between the three of us with blissful ignorance.

Fabian took yet another step towards me and I closed my eyes and turned my head away, holding back stinging tears. 'I said, don't come near me, Fabian.'

He must have paused, because the air around me remained warm. I took a deep breath. 'Stay away. Stay away from me.'

'What?

'Just do it.'

I buried my head in my arms, refusing to look. There was swift movement, and silence. I cautiously raised my head a little, peering through the curtain of hair. Lyla stood with a comforting arm on Fabian's shoulder murmuring something into his ear. Her face was masterfully plastered with fake concern, shaking her head disapprovingly in my direction as she steered him from the room. Yet as she passed my bed she glanced back, the tiniest hint of a smug, satisfied smile on her lips. I quickly lowered my head, not wanting her to see me looking. The door slammed shut and the forced indifference I had maintained since I had woken from unconsciousness not an hour ago loosened. I fell onto my knees, curling up on the cold sill.

'Why?' I whispered into the silence.

'Why? You tell me.'

I jumped, surprised. With his upper arm casually pressed to the wall stood Kaspar, his forearms folded across his chest, covering the unbuttoned part of his shirt. Anger that didn't reach his eyes was set upon his face.

'You weren't even in the slightest bit scared by what we did to Ilta, were you?'

I pulled my face into a grimace and shook my head. 'Just disgusted.' I nodded. 'Your disgust is only partly why you won't let Fabian near, isn't it?'

I froze, sensing dangerous territory. 'No.'

He sighed. 'Why do you delight in lying to me, Violet?' His arms remained folded and he jerked his head to the side, flicking his hair from his eyes.

It took a minute for me to grasp that I should reply and, not as defiantly as I would have liked, I retorted, 'I'm not lying.'

I blinked and he was stood in front of me, yanking my hair until my left cheek was exposed to his eyes. I tried to turn back, but he placed one hand behind my head. Slowly, he traced the scratch on my cheek, already weaving itself together.

'Then how do you explain that?'

'It's just a scratch. No big deal.'

His eyebrows lowered and wrinkles appeared along his brow, as he turned his head away slightly. He yanked my own head further over and I felt my neck strain until there was a click. 'Now are you going to tell me how you got that, or do I have to use other means to gain the information I want?'

I pursed my lips tightly and looked down at the floor, saying nothing. I didn't like the sound of 'other means', but neither was I going to tell him about Fabian's kiss or Lyla's threat.

He touched my lips gently with a single finger. I instantly recoiled from his cold and unusually soft touch.

'So it will be by other means then?'

'Why is it so important to you anyway?' I snapped, pressing myself against the damp window, away from him.

He raised his eyes to the ceiling. 'Let's see. Perhaps I was just wondering why my sister, my best friend since birth and my hostage are all acting extremely weird.'

He took a step closer and pressed two fingers to my temple,

tenderly at first and then more firmly. He closed his eyes.
Mine widened, as I realized what he intended to do.

I hastily threw up mammoth barriers around my mind,
hiding as much as I could from view, focusing on the coolness of the window and the condensation and the sound of
the wind buffeting against the panes of glass; on his steady
breathing, as he fought against my defences and his pained
expression, his forehead wrinkling from concentration; his
dark button-up shirt, only partly fastened, revealing smooth
chest underneath.

Rattle, rattle.

My thoughts were interrupted as a sharp stabbing pain
pulsated in my head, a thousand times worse than even
the most painful migraine. My legs weakened and I clutched
at my head desperately as it faded into nothing. Kaspar's
fingers left my temples and he looked down at me with
contempt.

'Privacy is a privilege I allow you, Girly, not something
you maintain on your own. And I know I'm hot – you don't
need to stare.'

I scowled up at him. 'But you can't get into my mind,
can you?'

He stooped down to my level. 'Oh, I can.' This time he
didn't bother to make any contact or even close his eyes.
Pain shot through my head again, quickly subsiding, and I
froze, unable to move as I concentrated on keeping what
I knew my father had done and the fact I had dreams buried
in their boxes.

The rest I sacrificed as images began to start flashing before
my eyes, mainly of the past few weeks: learning to dance,
the ball, Ilta, Kaspar taking my blood, Fabian . . .

'You kissed.'

I stared at the rug on the floor, refusing to meet his gaze.

A hand was placed under my chin and he tilted my head upwards until I could do nothing but meet his gaze.

'You kissed,' he repeated. Something about my expression must have been guilty, because he let go, his lips parting in disgust. 'You stupid girl.'

At that point I did not even have the dignity to try to defend myself, so I just sat there, unseeing.

'And Lyla is jealous and threatening to expose me?'

I tugged my lips into a grimace in reply. 'If Father were to know,' he muttered to himself, beginning to pace the room until he turned towards the door.

'Where are you going?'

He stopped and wheeled around, eyes wide and accusing. 'To sort this out! I'll talk to Lyla, but Fabian is down to you.' With that he left the room, leaving me sitting on the window-sill, unsure of what had just happened.

THIRTY-FIVE

Kaspar

The door slammed with a defiant boom behind me, separating me from the idiotic child sat on the windowsill. I leaned against the wall, taking several deep breaths.

She kissed Fabian.

I felt my eyes burn black and silently wondered why. Other than making things more complicated, what was so bad about it? *Why am I angry?*

I shook my head, pushing those thoughts to the back of my head. There were more important matters to deal with. Walking down the hallway, I could hear muffled voices coming from Lyla's bedroom and recognized the voice of one of my sister's friends. I was about to knock, when Lyla spoke. I paused, hand midair, intrigued.

'I just want to know what she has that I don't!' Lyla's raised voice drifted through the door, anger and frustration evident. 'I mean, I have the looks, the money and the status! And how can someone change their mind like that? He was all over me for what, twenty years? And then suddenly little Miss Living comes along, with her beating heart and seriously breakable *everything*, and suddenly it's all, "Oh, Violet, can I sleep with you? Let me shag you, kiss you, take you to the ball!"' she mocked, her voice peaking with resentment.

Her friend sighed. 'I'm sure if you weren't already committed to going to the ball with someone he would have asked you.'

'Oh, please, Cathy. He was always going to ask her. I even heard him talking about it with Declan.'

Silence. I could imagine the cogs turning in her friend's mind and I felt sorry for her. When Lyla decided something, changing her mind was impossible.

'You don't know that. I'm sure he likes you really. I mean she doesn't have anything you don't!'

'How about rosy cheeks? Irresistible blood? Vulnerability? Humanity?' Her voice rose in pitch and I heard exaggerated sighing, followed by what sounded like something being slammed onto a desk.

'Do you think I should have my nails done black or red for Ad Infinitum?' Cathy continued, oblivious to my sister's mounting despair.

'I mean, what the *hell* do they see in her? I am so much prettier and I know how to act in polite society!'

'Or maybe I should just go for a classic French manicure. What do you think?' There was a pause in the babble.

'Black nails. And Kaspar is such a dick of a brother. Why the hell he is heir, I don't know. I would do *such* a better job.'

I'd like to see you try, I thought.

'Because tradition says the fourth or seventh child is heir within the family,' Cathy explained. 'You're the third child. Even I know that and I flunked Vampires.'

Lyla sighed. 'I wasn't being serious, Cathy, of course I know why. And I thought you passed in the end?'

'Daddy bribed the headmaster. Like I was going to pass,' she scoffed, obviously finding her own stupidity hilarious.

'Suit yourself. But don't you think Kaspar is being a total manslut?'

Her friend paused. 'I think it's kind of hot.'

I raised an eyebrow and tried not to laugh as several disgusted noises floated down the corridor.

'Yuck! That is my little brother you're talking about!'

'Whatever. Anyway, I was thinking little black dress for the ball. What do you think?'

'Cathy! I keep telling you: steer clear of the short dresses! They don't do anything for your thighs. Go for an empire waist. Last time you wore a dress like that Felix totally went ditz!'

'Lyla, he went ditz because he was hammered. He was probably high as well.'

'I think he likes you.'

I think I need to talk to Felix. I couldn't take it any more. Not bothering to knock, I turned the handle and walked into the room. Both girls immediately spun around and Cathy curtseyed.

'Hey, Kaspar,' she said, with a roll of the tongue that I suspected I was meant to interpret as seductive.

I nodded in return. 'Catherine.'

'What happened to the knocking rule we established, Kaspar? How do you know I wasn't naked or something?' Lyla blurted out, hands on hips.

'Lyla, you're my sister. You were running around naked until you were two hundred years old,' I responded, amused at her pink eyes as she squirmed in embarrassment.

'No, I wasn't! Why the hell are you here anyway? I have things to do, unlike you!'

'What, other than bitch about everyone?' I retorted, raising an eyebrow.

'Perfectly amusing way to pass the time.'

I wasn't there to discuss her backstabbing character and so cut to the chase. 'Lyla, I want a word. In private.' I deliberately turned to Cathy, who flustered, gathered her things and left, but not before very deliberately brushing past me.

'Bye, Kaspar.'

I went rigid. 'Catherine.'

Slam went the door.

'Well, spit it out then! I don't have all day.'

'Stop being such a jealous over-possessive cow of a sister. Get over yourself and Fabian, stop putting me on the line and don't drag Violet into this.'

She spun around, eyes full of venom. 'What the hell did you just say?'

'Let me paraphrase it for you. Stop being such a bitch.'

'I know what you said, idiot. I just want to know why the hell you said it!' She practically shouted, seething. I raised an eyebrow. *So she is going to play innocent?*

'You threatened Violet. If she goes near Fabian, you will expose the fact I took her blood, humiliating both her and I—'

'Took her blood with her consent—'

'So you admit it then? Threatening us?'

'No.'

'But then how could you know I took her blood with consent? Nobody knew that but me and Violet. She wouldn't tell and neither would I. So, tell me, wise big sister, how could you know?'

She didn't answer, retreating into her wardrobe and

pulling more clothes down from the rack, which she held up to herself, silently pairing them together.

'You read her mind,' I said, cutting in on her browsing. 'Most likely when she was flustered and her barriers were weak; found out about the kiss, stumbled across what I had done and decided you were going to keep Fabian for yourself, despite him clearly not having the same feelings you have for him. Not to mention the fact you scratched Violet.'

Her mouth was hanging open, but as I paused for breath, she abruptly shut it again and began talking.

'Fine, I did. But so what? What can you do about it? Even you know it is for Fabian's own good. He can't get close to her, they are way too different. A vampire and a human don't go together.'

'They are different. But that isn't to say a relationship couldn't work between a vampire and a human. Look at Marie-Claire and John,' I retorted, leaning against the post of her bed, as she moved on to busying herself by clearing her desk, something she wouldn't normally do.

'John is turning in a few weeks anyway.' She turned to me and gave me one of her most contemptuous looks. I shrugged my shoulders.

'But he has been human for the entire, what, four years of their relationship? That has to say something.'

'Kaspar, shut up. It wouldn't work between Violet and Fabian and everyone knows it. And when he does wake up and realize what he has been wasting his time on—'

I cut in, interrupting her. 'You plan to be the one he goes running to.'

'Precisely. If Violet ignores him, he will just realize quicker. And then I get him quicker.'

To think I'm related to this.

'And you are going to do that at the cost of Violet's sanity?' I asked, scowling.

She snorted, lining her perfume bottles up in order of size. 'Stop being so melodramatic. She'll be fine.'

'Lyla, she needs Fabian like she needs air. He stops her going mad in this place. By all means, get Fabian. But if you snatch him away from her, who is going to win her around to turning? You are putting the whole Kingdom at risk. Remember that.'

She froze for a moment, before straightening up and turning to face me.

'You say that, Kaspar James Vladimir Eztli Varn.' I scowled at her use of my full name. 'But what about what you are doing? What about how you risk everything? You're heir, but you're the one who brought her here. You're the one who tries to force himself on her. And Fabian will kill her with his bloody kindness. If he'd never invited her to the ball, she never would have been attacked. You two are the ones putting her in danger and if anything happens to her, you know what Michael Lee will do.' She raised her hand to her neck and made a slicing motion.

I rolled my eyes at her melodrama. 'Come on, like he will have enough men to actually get to us.'

She had turned back to her desk, downing the rest of her customary vodka and blood. 'With slayers? Rogues?'

I shook it off. 'This isn't the point. The point is you're not going to humiliate me or Violet by telling anyone that I took her blood. Neither are you going to stop Fabian from going near her.'

'Aren't I?' she challenged.

I folded my arms carefully across my chest. 'You could if you wanted, but if you do, I will tell father that you lost your virginity to a rogue when you were fourteen. Seem fair?'

She gasped as her mouth fell open, her eyes tingeing pink 'How do you know that?'

'Met the guy. Now do we have a deal, darling big sister?' Grudgingly, she held out her hand and shook mine, the anger clear in her strong grip.

I left, feeling like a hypocrite the whole time. Because in truth, I was sure I was just as angry about the pair of them kissing as Lyla was. *At least my sister can put a finger on why.*

THIRTY-SIX

Violet

The temperature had noticeably dropped in the month after Ilta's death. In fact, as far as being kidnapped by vampires goes, things were pretty normal. Lyla apologized (I don't know what Kaspar had said, but it must have been good) and dropped her threat. Fabian cooled off and didn't try anything again, although it was still awkward to be around him as I tried to figure out what on Earth I had felt whilst kissing him. And Kaspar? Kaspar stayed away.

I changed into a pair of trousers and a jumper, knowing after the experience of the last few nights that sealing myself between the many layers of sheets on the bed didn't provide much warmth.

With a groan, I dragged the curtains across the windows, shutting out the worsening weather – the whole mansion smelt damp and I was sure it was going to rain. *Again. Never known a year like it,* I thought. *We haven't had a single hot spell, and now it's basically winter.*

I curled beneath the sheets, keeping as still as I could so

the air would form its own warm blanket around me. *Why can't they just light the fires? Or get bloody central heating?* But neither the warmth nor the cold could shelter me from the approaching dream.

The stench of death drifted through the air, not even disguised by the rotting damp in the valley that night. His feet sank into the ground with an unsatisfying squelch, soaking the hem of his cloak. Not that he cared. He had more pressing matters to attend to, such as how the damp masked every scent. *Why could the hunters not pick a dry night?*

Tonight, he was a true rogue. A feral smile appeared as he held onto that thread of thought. It was so liberating. Unrestrained by laws, morals and commitments, free to hunt when one liked, free to associate with whom one liked, free to enter Varnley and Romania; there were many, many benefits of relinquishing civility.

But something always held him back. To lose one's civility was to lose one's dignity. Many of the rogues still remaining in the country had taken to the forest of Varnley, seeking the seclusion and isolation it brought, as well as the obvious advantage of the bustling hunting ground of London being less than an hour's run away. But to live amongst the animals, as an animal was, well, *drastic*.

He paused as something caught his gaze, this evening as sharp as a knife from the fresh blood he had just allowed himself to indulge upon. Perhaps a few hundred yards in front of him was a dark shadow, three in fact, hovering about the border to the estate. Throwing the hood of his cloak about his dripping hair, he continued on with caution.

As he approached, he could hear hushed whispers, so softly spoken he could only make out every other sentence.

'Giles, remember we need the rogues . . . if you want

any chance of cocking a leg over this Lee bitch, then you'll shut up!'

His lips curled below his fangs in disgust at their crudeness, but he didn't lose focus, tugging his hood tighter, ensuring his face was cast into shadow and reached into an inner pocket, producing a letter sealed with the rogues' wax stamp.

'Good evening, my friends.' Startled, the three slayers reached into their own coats and he caught a glimpse of something silver and glinting. He rolled his eyes. 'Put your stakes away, I am no foe.'

'Then state your name and business, vampire,' the middle man demanded, stepping forward until he teetered on the border. He did not withdraw his hand from his coat.

'My name is of no consequence. My business is why you are standing here; I was sent in place of Finnian and Aleix, as they are indisposed.' *Yes, he indisposed of them yesterday, especially once he learned of this meeting they had planned.* He walked forward, careful to keep his gaze averted slightly downward so his hood would not slip and handed the slayer the seal. The slayer allowed his gaze to flick downwards, before it bounced back up and then down again. Seeming satisfied, he placed the letter into his pocket, his hand withdrawing from his long coat.

'Why has this meeting been requested, rogue? We have nothing of importance to share.'

He backed away a few spaces, allowing his elbow to rest on a nearby tree. He had little concern that they could overpower him, but he certainly didn't want a premature fight breaking out.

'Quite sure about that, slayer?'

'Of course we are sure!'

The second man stepped forward, his accent considerably

thicker than the accent of the first man. 'Romania is a long way from Varnley, no? And yet we have come all this way to hear you ask for information we do not have.'

He did not reply immediately, instead waiting and watching them squirm as he carefully chose his words.

'Not a wasted journey though, is it, my friends? I'm sure the English weather is quite enjoyable.' Careful to ensure his hood remained in place, he let his head roll skywards, where the stars were masked by swathes of clouds. He just needed to wait. Humans were so impatient – they let their secrets slip so easily.

'You know as well as I that Lee is waiting for the Varns to make a mistake. He needs an excuse to gain the support of the British government.'

The cloaked figure waved his hand dismissively. 'The Varns don't make mistakes.'

'Maybe they don't need to.'

His hand clenched. 'Must you speak in riddles, slayer? You just stated that Lee needs to wait for a mistake, and now you say the Varns don't need to make one? What do you mean by it?'

The slayers began to back away and the cloaked figure felt his eyes flash black. 'That is all you will learn tonight, rogue. We will send instructions when the time is nigh.'

'Of course,' he replied, fighting hard to keep his voice from wavering as he prepared to leap. With a bow of the head from the one man, all three turned and made an exit, retreating away from the border.

The cloaked figure forced air in and out of his lungs. *There are three of them,* he reminded himself. He couldn't afford to blunder. Stepping around the tree to conceal himself, he silently counted to thirty before beginning his pursuit.

Surprise was everything. He doubted the first slayer had

time to register what was happening as he appeared as a shadow behind the largest of the three, placing his hands as softly as a lover would on either side of the man's neck, fracturing it without so much as a moan from the man as he toppled face-first to the ground. His comrades took three or four steps before they even noticed what had occurred. When they did, a short, tapered stake materialized in the hand of the first man as he whipped around, thrusting the point in the direction of his assailant's chest. The cloaked figure was faster; he had already anticipated the man's move – *slayers were so predictable* – and stepped aside, leaving the weapon to strike thin air. The slayer stumbled and when the cloaked figure tore the stake from his hands, he toppled, landing at the feet of the dead slayer.

The third man was not so foolish. He backed away, holding his stake close to his chest and allowing his eyes to jerk between his two fallen comrades and the vampire in front of him. In their flecked hazel, he could see the reflection of the one slayer struggling to his feet, juxtaposed with the inner struggle of the third man as he battled between fight or flight.

The cloaked figure did not have the time or patience to wait for him to make a decision. With a languid effort, he pitched the stake in the direction of the man's chest, turning away to deal with the first slayer. He knew his aim was true when the scent of blood rose from the corpse, hanging like a heavy musk in the air between the trees.

He stopped just short of the slayer, watching as he hoisted himself up, his nose dribbling blood. It was a pitiful sight. But as soon as the man had straightened, he was thrust against the tree as the cloaked figure's hand clamped down on his throat.

'What do you mean, they don't need to make a mistake?'

he hissed in the trembling man's ear. The slayer didn't answer, instead throwing a ball of spit to the ground. The cloaked figure cringed. *Filthy habit.* He was disgusted, even, to bite such a filthy, grime-coated man and he toyed with the idea of using one of their stakes, but he dismissed it – he needed answers. So he sank his fangs into the neck, driving them in deep until his mouth was clamped around his throat. When he had quenched his mounting thirst, he withdrew, plugging each bite wound with a finger to prevent them from healing. Twisting them like a corkscrew, he worked his way through veins and sinew, earning cries of pain from the slayer.

'You're going to die, but there's still time to make you suffer,' the cloaked figure growled, plunging his fingers even deeper.

'Who are you? Who do you serve? You don't stink enough to be a rogue,' the man groaned with surprising defiance considering his legs were beginning to buckle from under him.

'I serve no one. Now why don't they need to make a mistake?' The cloaked figure raised his knee, pressing it into the other man's crotch, watching as his eyes bulged. When no answer came, he jerked his knee up. It had the desired effect.

'R-rumours,' the slayer choked, trying to press his hands to his crotch as tears rolled down his cheeks.

His heart leapt into his mouth. *Rumours about Violet Lee's attack? Could the slayers know?* 'Rumours about what?' The cloaked figure only gave him a second to answer, before kneeing him in the crotch again.

'The S-Sage.'

The cloaked figure could see he was losing consciousness and shook him roughly.

'What about the Sage?'

The man could barely speak and only managed to utter one word before he slumped onto the cloaked figure's shoulder, out cold.

'Prophecy.'

Frustrated, the cloaked figure reached down with one hand and plucked the stake from the other slayer's chest, pinning the unconscious man through the chest to the tree, like a flyer to a lamppost. There was no point attempting to wake him and he wanted to take no chances when it came to leaving witnesses.

Leaving the corpses behind – other rogues would enjoy the feast – he set off back west, feeling as though he had achieved little. *Prophecy? What did he mean by that?* Athenea had hundreds of prophecies, whole archives dedicated to them, and rumours circulated about them constantly. *And how is it a mistake? How can Michael Lee use it as an excuse?*

Either way, he knew he was not the person to make sense of it and took a running leap in the direction of Varnley.

My eyelids peeled themselves apart, and I blinked in the bright early morning light. My spine felt as though it had been wrenched apart with a hacksaw, and my neck had an unwelcome stiffness to the muscle. After blinking a few times I realized I was splayed across the floor, half-leaning against the bed, half-lying on the floor.

Groaning, I lifted myself up off the ground, using the bed as a support. Sinking onto the thick mattress I caught an unpleasant stink, like that of a sports kit gone unwashed for weeks.

Disgusted, I realized that I was the source of the stink – I was coated in sweat.

Then it hit me. *The dream.* In an instant, every memory

came flooding back, different parts vying for attention. Most prominent of all was the thought *he's coming*. Secondly, came the slayer's foul reference to what they wanted to do to me, and with a shudder, I resolved to step into the arms of none other than my father when I got out of here. Allies to the government they might be, but good they were not.

Scrabbling up, I darted for the wardrobe and hurried to get dressed.

Someone – the Sage, whoever that is – has made a mistake and a mistake is what my father needs.

I inhaled, paused, and stared at the wooden floor of the corridor for a moment, allowing the tiny bead of hope I had buried deep in my chest to grow bigger and bigger, bursting as I contemplated the idea that I could be getting out of here soon.

And he's coming here, to Varnley, to tell the King what I already know.

The house seemed hushed when I reached the stairs and I hovered on the top step, unnerved by the sound of the ticking clock – in fact it was the only sound, apart from my breathing which I noticed was speeding up.

The cloaked figure kills people, I reminded myself with a shiver. *He doesn't think twice about it either.* I'd lost count of the number of people he'd killed in my dreams.

I needed to find someone, but I wasn't sure what I was going to say. I couldn't tell them I had dreams – in a way, I wanted to guard them: despite the horrors they showed me, the dreams offered me information I wasn't getting from the Varns. Information like the fact that my father was still trying to find a way to get to me.

The click of a door closing snapped me from my thoughts. Kaspar had stepped from his father's study, breaking out into a smirk when he noticed me. In my chest, the bubble of hope shrank. He had passed me before he spoke, turning and pointing in my direction.

'Girly, almost forgot. Father wants to see you. He said wait in his study, he'll be there in a minute.'

My eyes bulged. 'See me? About what?'

He raised his arms at his side in an exaggerated shrug. 'You tell me.' With that he stuffed his hands into his pockets, carrying on towards the entrance hall.

I watched him go, feeling very sick all of a sudden. Behind me, the whitewashed, panelled doors to the King's study looked ominous. *See me?* The King never requested to talk to me – we more ran into each other, normally when I really didn't want to see him.

My stomach knotted. I couldn't help but feel this might have something to do with the cloaked figure and I was tempted to scuttle away and hide in the basement kitchens.

No. I wasn't a coward, and besides, I was intrigued to know what the King had to say. Taking a deep breath, I stepped through the door.

I was greeted by a manservant, who bowed. 'Please, Miss Lee, have a seat.' He gestured towards a high-backed wooden chair placed in front the King's generous-sized desk, today piled high with papers. I had heard the others mention he had a whole hoard of secretaries and assistants to help deal with the paperwork, but it still looked daunting.

'His Majesty is currently engaged with business, but I will inform him that you are waiting. Please, enjoy the refreshments.' He pointed towards a small side table, two separate jugs of water and blood placed beside several glasses and a plate of biscuits. He bowed again and disappeared through a door squeezed in-between two of the huge bookshelves that dominated the walls.

I gazed around, standing up to try one of the tempting

looking biscuits, which filled the room with the smell of baking. The room was actually rather pleasant, the curtains thrown open, bathing the room in daylight and the occasional ray of sun as it edged from around the clouds – though not enough to burn.

Business. With a strange thrill, I contemplated the possibility that right at that very moment, the cloaked figure could be talking with the King. But that would mean they would know that my father would come soon (I couldn't face using the word 'attack'). And if they were ready for him – it didn't even bear thinking about.

I took a bite of the biscuit and almost spat it back out, it was so bitter. It was like eating over-spiced gingerbread with grapefruit and lemon thrown in. Reluctantly, I chewed, searching around the desk for a bin to place the rest in.

Instead, my eyes landed on a partly folded letter on the desk, tucked below today's newspaper. But what really caught my attention was the signature at the bottom.

H.M. Queen Carmen.

My heart stopped. I placed the rest of my biscuit back on the plate, ignoring my voice who complained it was impolite to leave half-eaten food. Glancing back at the door, full of curiosity, I pinched a corner and slid it out, surprised at how thick and textured the paper was. I knew I should not read it and that the King could appear at any moment, yet I was unable to stop my eyes from moving from left to right.

Dear sweet Beryl,
First, I must ask how you and Joseph are? It truly has been far too long since we last met; I do believe I have not

enjoyed the pleasure of your company since the turn of the new year, and that was months ago now. Therefore, you simply must come over for dinner soon! I'm sure the children would like to see Marie-Claire and Rose again, and I know last time we met that Jag found John to be good company.

And you know, my dear friend that I am a prying creature, so I must ask how Marie and John are? From what Kaspar and Jag tell me, they have been courting for a year and a half now. I must congratulate them and you on such a union. It is not often that humans so seamlessly become integrated with the Kingdom.

Enough of me asking of you; perhaps you would be relieved if I babbled on about Varnley. Other than the usual happenings, I can't say I have much gossip to enrich your day with. Perhaps the only news worth reporting is the increasing appearance of Charity Faunder at the most unsociable hours. Whilst I am pleased Kaspar has come to his senses enough to move on from the vile von Hefner girls, I cannot help but feel that Charity is not suitable female company for him. I know I can't stop him, for he is not a child any more, but his superficial inclinations when it comes to the opposite sex do not exactly speak of the maturity I know he possesses. I know you had similar problems with Rose. Sometimes I think the way we were raised was far more appropriate. But then what can we do about this ever-changing world?

What else? I was thinking of perhaps going back to Spain soon, to show the children where I grew up. I am considering commissioning Flohr for another painting of the family too. We haven't had one done since Kaspar was young and I would really like one to include Cain and Thyme – now she is two years old I think we might be able to entice her to sit for long enough.

But that must wait until I return from Romania. It is just a

*day until I leave now, and the preparations do not seem to
even be near to a conclusion. Vladimir has also been suggesting
that I take Kaspar, but I refuse to entertain such an idea. The
entourage is quite big enough and Kaspar's quick temper is too
like his father's, which Pierre will not like. In truth, however, I
do not want my son and heir to be placed in the path of
danger, which there will doubtless be, although I have
neglected to mention this particular reason to my husband.*

*Do write back and I will reply in haste as soon as I return.
(Perhaps I shall take up Lyla's advice and start using email.)
I must go, for I still have strict instructions to leave Kaspar
whilst I am away (you can imagine, I'm sure). All my love
and greetings to your family.*

Your friend,

H.M. Queen Carmen.

My lips parted as I gaped at the letter in my hands, which
were trembling. I couldn't quite comprehend that I was
holding a letter – a letter never sent – written and held and
folded by the Queen who I had heard so much about; the
Queen whose death had torn the Varns apart.

Somewhere far away, the grandfather clock I always heard
but never found struck nine and I came back around, realizing that the King could return any minute. Folding the
letter back along the creases I slipped it under the newspaper,
hoping he wouldn't notice it had moved.

I lowered myself back into the chair, still feeling shaken
– I had to grip the hard arms of the chair to stop my hands
from trembling..

'Good morning to you, Miss Lee.'

Hearing the King's voice behind me, I sprang back up and
bobbed into a curtsey, feeling like my cheeks were on fire,
mainly from guilt after what I had just read.

'Your Majesty.'

He strode around his desk, settling into his own chair and indicating I should sit too. I did, looking at anything but the King.

'Miss Lee, in a few days time you will have been confined to Varnley for three months. In that time, you have been privy to many intimacies within my family and household, and, I hope, gained an insight into what life as a member of this Kingdom entails. Would you agree?'

I nodded. He shuffled his papers, shifting the newspaper and below it, the letter into a draw beside his chair.

'I appreciate that your time here has been difficult and at times very upsetting, and that the choice presented to you is not ideal, but I must urge you to make a decision.'

I tightened my grip around the arms of the chair, feeling my fingers meet beneath each length of wood. He paused in his arranging, eyeing my hands.

'Do not fret, Miss Lee, I do not mean now. But I feel it is my responsibility to inform you that you are at the centre of a growing political debate, both within the Kingdom, the United Kingdom and internationally, and that the only way to cool the situation is for you to willingly become one of us.' *No pressure.* 'I think it is also only fair to ensure that you are not entertaining any false ideas that your father or the British government will negotiate or fight for your freedom. In their eyes, your humanity is not a fair trade-off for the loss of life they would experience in return.'

I stood up so fast the blood drained from my head and stars appeared in front of my eyes. It took an enormous amount of willpower and a bitten tongue not to scream that he was lying. *My father is coming. He just needs an excuse. And by the sound of it, he's got one.*

'Miss Lee?'

'I thank you, Your Majesty, for your input. I'll consider what you have said,' I replied, speaking through gritted teeth before I curtsied and marched from the room. I went to slam the door behind me, but the manservant caught it with a grimace, softly closing it.

Outside, I slumped against the wall, breathing heavily. *What a liar! And if he thinks I'm going to turn because of politics, he can go and shove his choice up his—*

Language, my voice chided, interrupting before I could finish my line of thought.

I remained there until my breathing returned to normal and I was able to think more clearly, thankful that the dreams gave me an upper hand. It was just a waiting game now.

THIRTY-SEVEN

Violet

Grabbing the towel I rubbed it over my wet hair, shifting my weight from one foot to the other in a sort of dance whilst humming an Elvis tune. The King's talk of the day before was forgotten and I had woken up in an unusually good mood, partly from an uninterrupted, dreamless sleep and partly because the hope I had maintained in my first few weeks as a hostage had reignited.

'Girly, what the hell are you doing?'

Like a scared cat I sprang up and screeched, diving for the nearest something to cover myself up – I was only in my underwear.

Why didn't I get dressed? I mentally groaned. He chuckled, letting his eyes roam over my too-close-to-bare flesh.

'Girly, the voiles you are trying to cover yourself up with are translucent.'

I looked down, cringing. It was made even worse by the fact that my bra and knickers didn't match and that the knickers were more old-granny than sexy.

'You should prance about in your underwear more often.'
He turned and walked towards the door, calling back over
his shoulder. 'But if you are coming out with us, I suggest
you put some clothes on, it will be freezing for you outside.'

I let go of the voiles. 'Out?'

'Yes, out, Girly. Do I need to spell it out for you?'

'Out,' I mouthed. It seemed like an alien word, unspoken
for so long. 'Out, out, out,' I whispered, liking the way my
tongue flicked when I said it.

'Out. You know, outside?'

I nodded in a daze. 'Out where?'

'To London. Now, hurry up, I would actually like to leave
sometime today.' He turned and left, slamming the door
behind him.

I stood there in stunned silence for a full minute. *London?
Why the heck were they taking me to London? Wasn't that a bit
risky?*

Apparently not, my voice answered.

But I could just escape, I retorted. My voice mentally
chuckled in a mocking way that told me it would be eye
rolling if it could.

*Do you really think you can escape from several vampires? I
think not!*

'I could certainly try,' I mumbled back, aloud, getting
dressed and sorting my hair. 'But what if someone recognizes
me? I was on the BBC and everything!' I shuddered at the
thought of that cruel day when I had watched my family
suffer on the news.

*I doubt anyone will. It's London. Besides, no one will actually
think you are* the *Violet Lee. And you won't do anything.*

'What makes you think that?'

*It's too late for you to go back now, isn't it, Violet? You wouldn't
leave even if you could.*

It faded away, leaving me standing there, stunned and frightened at what it had just said. *Is it too late? Would I leave?*

Even as I thought those words my heart dropped. It was one thing having my father, well, *rescue* me, but it was another to actually make the decision to go.

Flicking the straighteners off, I ran my fingers through my hair, thinking it was sleeker than it had been in months. Coupled with the fact I had bothered with eyeliner and mascara, I actually looked presentable.

Descending the stairs I saw the same group that had been in London that first night, with the addition of Lyla and another girl, her mousy-brown hair tied up into a bun. Beside the tall, slender Lyla, she looked short and stocky, although I was pretty sure the Princess would be jealous of the killer cleavage the other girl had.

Fabian handed me a familiar black coat. I reached out, hand a little shaky as the rough velvet instantly brought back a thousand memories, the most recent being that of a certain night out in London.

I shrugged it around my shoulders, glad of the sudden warmth. My thin cardigan wouldn't have protected me much against the harsh breeze. There was a flurry of movement, as everyone unfroze and began grabbing various things from the living room, returning with car keys, purses and wallets, credit cards and handbags.

Kaspar walked right up to me, tucking a wallet into his back pocket. 'I'm warning you, Girly, I'm not leaving your side all day. So no funny business, okay?'

I nodded, rolling my eyes. *I've already had this discussion with my voice.* He flitted around me and poked me in the back, forcing me forwards but I froze. The blood drained from my face and I took a step back.

Walking out of the corridor was someone draped in a

black cloak, the hood thrown up, shielding the face from view.

Kaspar had frozen behind me too, finger pressed gently into my back. Every head in the room turned to him, and then me. At that very moment the King emerged from the depths of the corridor too, looking tense and uneasy.

Everything, including the cloaked man, seemed to become immobilized. He was tall, upright and with his appearance, the temperature in the room dropped. Kaspar grabbed me by the waist, pulling me into him and steering us towards the door, his face screwed up in concentration. I protested a little, but not much, torn between fear and wanting to know who this mysterious informant was.

His back was to us but at that moment his head tilted before he whipped around at a speed that should be impossible. His hood cast everything into shadow but his eyes, which were a dark indigo blue, fast becoming a flaming red.

'Get her out of here!' the King roared as the butlers stepped forward, placing themselves between us and the snarling figure in front. Kaspar didn't need telling twice. His arm clamped down tighter on my waist and his other hand grabbed my wrist, tugging me out of the doors. I caught a glimpse of Fabian dropping to a crouch behind us.

'Do not return before midnight, Kaspar,' the King shouted over the confusion, voices and the sound of crunching gravel beneath our feet filling my ears as my breath caught, focusing in on materialising figures at the far end of the grounds. They were too far away to make out and before they could near, Kaspar had yanked me around the side of the mansion to the tucked-away garages. His hand fastened to me, I could see it starting to redden under the sun.

I went to turn around but Kaspar tugged me back around.

'What's going on?' I asked, trying to glance over my shoulder as he let go of my wrist and placed a hand under my chin so I had no choice but to look at him. 'Kaspar, tell me!'

He grimaced. 'Girly, you've got to trust me, but whatever happens, don't look around, okay? Just keep on looking straight at the garages.'

'Why?'

'Don't argue, just do it. Promise. Please.'

There was such sudden desperation in his voice that I couldn't refuse this soft side of him that rarely appeared. I nodded. 'I promise.'

'Thank you,' he whispered. 'I'll explain what I can when we are out of here.' His eyes were darting behind me, watching something just to the right of us. 'C'mon.' He grabbed my hand and set off once more at a sprint. As we neared the garages, the doors opened, revealing hordes of expensive cars. We skidded to a halt, Kaspar pulling out a set of car keys from his pocket.

The others appeared behind and there was a frantic scramble as they decided who would go with who, and in which car.

'Who am I with?' I asked.

'You're with me of course. Aston. Now.' He was half-smirking and I felt my face drop a little.

Suddenly, all smugness disappeared from his face and the sound of footsteps reached my ears. 'Don't turn around,' he muttered, his eyes fixed on something behind me.

Fabian took a few cautious steps forward. 'What are you doing here, Fallon?'

'*Prince Fallon of Athenea* to you. And I'm curious.' I was surprised to hear an American – or maybe Canadian – accent; even more surprised to hear his title and fought hard with the urge to turn. 'So this is the young lady all the fuss is about?' I heard him taking a step forward and I mirrored his action.

'Young lady has a name.'

'I know you do, Miss Violet Lee.' The crunch of gravel told me he had taken another step forward and I saw Kaspar tense. The others were completely still, watching on with concern.

'Leave her alone, Fallon.'

He was so close I could feel his lukewarm breath on the back of my neck as he sighed. Yet, up and above that was an overwhelming sense of warmth that did not come from any breath. It was like the sun was beating down on my back, but that wasn't possible – it was October and freezing. Whoever this royal was, he wasn't a vampire.

Even I was surprised at how easily I could accept that. But then again, if vampires could exist, why couldn't other creatures?

'How long are you to protect her, Kaspar?'

'As long as the inter-dimensional council rules that we should. Which, I will remind you, your father heads.'

'I'm not my father. She will have to learn about our existence at some point if she turns, which is what so many people want.'

I sucked in a breath and gathered the courage to speak. 'I don't care if people want me to turn. It's my choice.'

I felt a pressure on my shoulder, a hand, although I did not look. I could not look.

'I wish I could say I agree with you.'

I felt the hand, surprisingly hot, brushing away the dark strands of hair from my neck. He pressed a finger into the tiny pinprick wounds that had never completely faded after I had consented to Kaspar taking my blood all those weeks ago. There was a quiet intake of ragged breath, so hushed only Kaspar and I would hear.

'Time is running out, Kaspar.' With that he withdrew his hand from my neck and I heard the crunching of gravel as he walked away. I loosened, but Kaspar remained rigid.

'Time is running out for what?' he yelled after the other man.

'Prophecy doesn't wait forever, you know.'

I gasped, whipping around. He had gone. I turned back around. Kaspar's face turned from a frown to a scowl and his eyes plunged to a glossy black. I noticed his hands clenching into fists, the veins on his arms protruding as he clenched tighter and tighter.

I didn't like that expression and walked away a little bit. *First Fabian, then the figure in my dreams mentioned Prophecy, now this.* I was no Sherlock Holmes but it didn't take a genius to work out that they were linked.

An arm snaked its way around my shoulders and spun me back around.

'Time to go,' Kaspar said.

I glared up at him, meeting his cold, uncaring black eyes. 'I want answers.'

He grabbed me by the elbow and started to pull me away. 'Want doesn't get, Girly.'

My mouth fell open. He pulled me towards his car, easily dragging me despite my resistance. 'I have a right to know! All this shit, it's about me, so don't keep me in the dark!' Kaspar pulled the door open for me and prodded my side until I clambered in. Slamming the door, he darted around to the other side and got in the driver's seat, wrenching the seatbelt around himself. The others were already pulling away and following them he accelerated down the driveway, speeding away from the place that had become my prison.

I refused to look at him. I could tell he was pissed. Very pissed. So was I.

As soon as Varnley was out of sight, Kaspar spoke. 'Fire away,' he said, exhaling.

'What's going on? You mentioned a council. It's going on right now, isn't it? What's it about?' I stopped myself, catching his expression. It was almost *mournful*.

He sighed, jaded. 'The meeting is about you.' I was taken aback by how weary he sounded – this wasn't the young, witty, arrogant teenager I knew.

'But why now?' I could take a guess at that answer, knowing it was something to do with the cloaked figure, but I couldn't tell him that and I wanted to know more.

Again he sighed. 'People are getting worried. They don't think your father will let this go on much longer. If he were to do something and we retaliated, we could have a war on our hands. And if we are involved in a war, so are the other dimensions.'

'Dimensions?'

'There is a reason I told you not to turn around.' he retorted, raising an eyebrow at me. I kept silent, finding the dashboard very interesting. He continued. 'We can't force you to turn into a vampire because you're a political prisoner. If we do, we breach treaties we have with both the humans and other dimensions. But we can't just continue waiting, because we have reason to think your father might make a move.'

'What's the reason?' I asked, unable to mask the urgency and intrigue from my voice. *Prophecy. What was meant by that?* But he didn't answer and I changed my tactic, knowing I had to take advantage of his sudden openness. 'What's there to stop me from just waiting until my father comes? Then I don't have to turn.'

He made a rumbling sound in his chest that sounded like the beginning of a half-hearted laugh. 'Don't bother even entertaining that idea, Girly. I highly doubt your father could raise a force large and dumb enough to face us and if, by some miracle, he did, we would just move to Athenea and you would be coming with us.'

He might as well have pricked me with a needle as my bubble of hope burst with a pop. I sighed and remained silent for a while, watching the trees rush by in a blur. They were thinning and the one-track road was widening out, a white line marking the divide between the two lanes.

'What's Athenea?' I asked after a while. He didn't answer. 'That Fallon guy was from there, wasn't he?' He nodded, mute. Realizing he was closing up again, I asked one more question. 'Who was that cloaked person?'

He pursed his lips. 'A very unpleasant man.' I edged away towards the window, alarmed at the force he used to jam the gear stick across. 'I'm not telling you his name, if that's what you want,' he added, glancing across at me.

I slumped back into the chair, disappointed and disheartened. It was a hopeless situation. Somewhere along the line there would be a war, and the worst thing was it would all be my fault. But even knowing that, I knew I couldn't face turning. *Not yet. I just need time*, I thought desperately. *Why is it the one thing I don't have?* I looked up at Kaspar, tears pricking my eyes. He seemed distracted, caught up in his own thoughts.

'There must be a way out. There has to be!'

I had to say it aloud just to believe it. I glimpsed Kaspar as he turned away from me slightly, as though he were guilty of something.

'Yeah, there is. If you turn and become a vampire willingly, your father would drop it. He couldn't do anything.

It would have been your choice. Problem solved.' He said it with a flickering of hope, although his tone told me he hardly dared to believe any such thing could ever happen.

I snorted. 'Then we're doomed. You don't know my father. He has the compassion of a walnut. He wouldn't care if it were my choice; he would still find some way to blame you.'

'Don't say that,' Kaspar muttered. 'Every father wants their child to be happy, and if vampire-kind was your happiness, then he would respect that.'

I shook my head. 'Even if that were so, how could I be happy as a vampire? There is no chance of me actually liking the idea of living forever. It's hopeless!'

Kaspar faced straight ahead, glancing in his side mirror. He spoke softly, something like caring in his voice. 'You don't know that, Girly. One day you might just find something worth living an eternity for.'

I sucked in a long, slow breath. 'You haven't. You're just as torn up as I am. Why endure the pain of forever?' I whispered.

The car slowed a little, as the tree line receded and we neared the coast. 'No. I haven't yet. But that doesn't mean I won't. Or that you won't. For all we know, we might just be staring at that something right now . . .'

I rested my head up against the cool window, watching as my warm breath coated the glass in a misty layer. 'You can't promise me everything will be okay, can you?'

'No,' he choked. 'No, I can't.'

It was some time before the conversation restarted, and he forced me into it.

'Did you just bloody go through red lights at ninety?!' I screeched, gawping at the speed dial.

'Yes,' he replied simply. I turned my open mouth to him,

tearing my gaze away from the speed dial, the needle fast approaching one hundred.

'You are so done in. There was a speed camera there,' I said as we passed a bright flash of luminous yellow – the dreaded speed cameras. 'Say goodbye to three points on your license.'

I thought I saw him roll his eyes. 'Will you relax, Girly, I am in perfect control. I have been driving since cars were invented. Besides, we have protected plates. So I'll just keep those three points.'

'What?'

'Don't you know anything? I can drive as fast as I like because the licence plate doesn't actually exist, so if the police catch it, their database will just tell them to fuck off. Little favour you get when you're royalty,' he smirked.

I shook my head slightly, looking out the window. 'Well, I'm sorry, we can't all be kaspary,' I said, settling back into my seat with folded arms.

'Pardon?' he snorted, half-laughing, half-grunting.

'I make up words. Don't you?'

He glanced at me sideways, taking his eyes off the road for a second to actually throw me a worried half-smile. 'And what does this particular word mean?'

'Kaspary: a level of awesomeness so high it kicks everyone's arse leaving them breathless and bewildered.'

He chuckled, a low pitched hum coming from deep within his chest. 'I leave you breathless and bewildered do I, Girly?'

'Don't flatter yourself.'

He hummed in disbelief, turning his full attention back to the road. I flicked my eyes towards him, trying to gage his reaction. He was smiling, but my stomach dropped as I saw the smile fall away from his face, meaning that the Kaspar that made me laugh, that teased me, that humoured my antics – and the Kaspar who had saved my life countless times and the Kaspar, who, occasionally, seemed to have a spark of caring in him – was fast disappearing.

I shook my head, ridding my head of the thought as a familiar frown encased his stunning features, unsure why a second bubble that had been swelling a few seconds before had popped even more painfully than the one before.

THIRTY-EIGHT

Kaspar

You told her too much, Kaspar, Fabian cautioned in my head, clearly displeased.

You sound like my father, I retorted.

More you tell her, more you hurt her. And I am pretty sure neither of us want that.

I don't know what I want, Fabian. But she asked a question, and I gave her the answer. It's not as though I told her about the Sage, is it? I just said Athenea.

Fabian sighed. *Just don't hurt her. She's fragile. And I don't just mean physically.*

Anger flared in my veins. *You think I don't know that? You think I would hurt her?*

Through our connection, I could feel him considering what to say next. When he did speak, it was with sorrow. *There was a time when I wouldn't even have considered it, but these past couple of years, I can't be so sure.*

Grief immediately washed through me. Thoughts of my

mother came to light and her joyous laughter echoed in
my head.

*Don't bring my mother's death into this. And besides, it's not as
though you can talk. You hurt Violet just by going after her!*

You say that as though not guilty yourself, he scoffed.

I'm not, I replied, puzzled.

Then perhaps you should examine your own feelings, Fabian
spat, abruptly. *Don't go thinking I haven't seen the way you are
with her. You flirt, you seduce and you spend more time with her
than any of us,* he fumed.

I don't! I protested. *I don't know what you are on about. So
get the hell out of my mind!*

Her tiny, frail body turned towards me, matching my
frown, looking down at my hands as they clenched tighter
and tighter around the wheel. I didn't know what he was
on about. I didn't feel the way Fabian did for her. But I
knew one thing for sure. I didn't see her the same way as
I had done three months ago.

You told her too much, Kaspar.

A familiar expression of subtle concern took over her
features as she noticed the scowl on my face that could only
mean I was otherwise occupied, as a fresh wave of self-doubt
washed over me; the self-doubt only my father's words could
bring.

I answered her questions, nothing more.

I sighed as I said it, not doubting that more than he could
hear my words.

You did more than answer her questions, young one, a third
voice said, which I recognized as belonging to none other
than Ll'iriad Alya Athenea, King of Athenea.

Great. Just great. My suspicion of my father allowing eaves-
droppers was confirmed and only out of begrudging respect
did I reply with a 'Your Majesty'.

Prince Kaspar, he replied with the same patronizing tone. *May I ask if you know the consequences of your actions?*

I sighed, exasperated, wondering how Fallon could hold such radically different views from his own father concerning keeping Violet in the dark. *Of course.*

Another unrecognizable voice interrupted and I was forced to believe every person at the meeting could hear me. Almost instinctively, my mind began shutting down, locking every secret deep within my subconscious.

Then, tell me, Your Highness, if you were aware of the consequences, why did you reveal what you did?

The anger flared within my veins. *I revealed nothing of the dimensions. But I'd tell her if I could. She deserves to know.*

A separate, powerful thread worked its way into my mind and I recognized my father's presence. *Kaspar,* he growled.

Smirking, I continued. I had no patience for them and their petty politics. *You can't hide everything from her forever. She is naturally curious and you can't change that either. If you deny her the truth, she will only learn to hate us and we need her on side, especially if the Prophecy does come true and Lee gets his excuse.*

I felt my father seething, beginning to boil. *Kaspar, how dare you? Apologize.*

No. I will not apologize for the truth. I would not apologize for simply going against the cosy status quo the inter-dimensional council had decided upon.

Take that back, or else, he hissed.

I knew I was tugging at an already taut string, but I didn't seem to be able to stop myself. *Or else what? You know I'm talking sense, you just can't accept it. Mother would be ashamed of you.*

My father growled, a growl that would not be confined to just our two minds, but a growl that would be heard in

every mind in Varnley and for miles around, until he closed
his mind off, speaking only to me.

From noon tomorrow, you won't touch that girl again, Kaspar.
Not a bite; not a finger; nothing.

I opened up my mind, ensuring everybody at the meeting
would hear. *Fuck off!*

I felt shock ripple through the meeting. Even Violet,
human and powerless, stood up straight, her eyes wide and
alert.

Pulling into the driveway of Charlie's townhouse we had
agreed to meet at, I cut the engine. I turned to her as she
glanced out the windows and reached out for her hand,
pulling her into an embrace.

'Welcome back to London, Violet.'

THIRTY-NINE

Violet

Cold arms closed themselves around my stomach and before I could protest, I was sitting in Kaspar's lap, side pressed to the steering wheel. He held me in an embrace for a second, forcing me against his chest. I could feel a vein throbbing in his neck, yet could not feel the beating heart that marked humanity; the heart in my chest that right now, was working overtime.

My words came out muffled as I cursed into his chest. 'What the hell are you doing?'

He pushed me away, pressing a single finger to my lips. 'For once, be quiet, Girly.'

I shook my head, meaning to say no, but failing. His enthralling eyes had caught mine and with a pained, creased brow, he took my hand in his and gently began rubbing his thumb across my skin, tracing the raised veins.

'I can't promise you everything will be okay, because I know it won't. I can't promise that you will make it out of this human, because chances are you won't. Time is running out and soon you'll have to make the decision. You have to choose.'

'Do I even get a choice?' I murmured, still lost within the piercing eyes. He shrugged his shoulders half-heartedly.

'Maybe.'

I closed my eyes, nodding solemnly. His cool breath tickled my ear, as his icy hands reached up and touched my burning, scarlet cheeks. He turned my head to face him, resting his forehead against mine. Outside the wind whistled and the permanently grey clouds of England rolled past. Inside there was deathly silence, shadows moving across us.

'Girly . . . Violet,' Kaspar whispered, choking on his own words. 'I should have killed you in Trafalgar Square. I didn't. And now you face the consequences and I-I'm sorry . . . so sorry,' he breathed, a single fang biting at his lower lip.

I sucked in a breath, instinctively leaning in to the hand cradling my cheek. 'You wish I was dead? Because I don't.'

'No.'

I exhaled sharply, pulling his hand away from my cheek, placing it again at his side. Fighting back tears I spoke. 'Why are you like this? Why do you hate me one second, and then the next it seems like you care? For God's sake, *why*?'

His fang broke through the skin of his lips and blood erupted from the wound, trickling across his lips. It coated his skin in a glossy layer, a salty stench making my nostrils flare, part in disgust, part in intrigue.

Leaning in, my hands worked their way towards his neck, tracing his collar, entwining themselves within his dark hair. I licked my lips in anticipation as forbidden emotions gushed within my system and my voice screamed.

Don't do it! You're not a bloody vampire yet!

But I didn't stop. All I had was the desire to be wanted;

to be cared about, and I had found that in Kaspar, just for a second.

We weren't even an inch apart when I paused, my heart racing and leaping as I looked up to meet his eyes, which I thought for a moment, a single, brief moment had flashed to red, yet they were their usual emerald as his hands reached for my waist.

Leaning in, he murmured as his lips met mine. 'I'm like this because I am just as torn up as you.'

With that he was gone, leaving me with his blood trickling from my lips.

I felt a cold breeze on my face and opening my eyes, I realized I was actually not in the car. A bitter wind whipped at my face, blowing my hair like it did the stormy clouds. I rested against the door, breathing deeply.

I slid my fingers across my chin, feeling the blood smear across my skin. Gagging, my legs lost their strength as horrific feelings filled my heart. *What on earth just happened?* I couldn't believe I had just tried to kiss him. *Kiss him!*

Moreover, I was alone, cast off in the middle of nowhere – the car was parked at the side of an immaculately maintained drive surrounded by a long, low box hedge.

I didn't have time to notice much more as several cars pulled up behind. I jerked my head towards the sound of dying engines and recognized the cars of the others, which Kaspar had overtaken on the motorway. Fabian jumped out of his Audi and darted towards me, pulling me into a tight hug. I collapsed into his arms, glad of the comfort they brought. He tugged me closer, until my face was buried in his jacket, muttering into my ear.

'It's okay. He shouldn't have left you . . .'

I nodded obediently, deciding it would be better to not mention that that was not the source of my distress.

'Where's he gone?' I murmured, looking up at him

His eyes flashed red. 'You're bleeding!' he exclaimed.

My eyes widened as I remembered the sticky red liquid coating my lips and quickly reached up to wipe it away. But before I could get to it, Fabian had caught my wrist, holding it in midair. My fingers brushed his lips involuntarily as he sniffed at the air.

'I-it's not your blood, is it?'

I looked guiltily at the floor, unable to hide the truth, let alone meet his eyes.

'Violet?'

I shook my head. 'I'm sorry.'

There was the shifting of feet, the whispers of the wind and two heart-rending words. 'Don't be.'

I wrenched my head up. His face had fallen and his eyes were grey. He nodded. He nodded because he knew even before I did, that I had made one of my many decisions.

I've chosen Kaspar. Not even Fabian's look of betrayal could change that. I didn't even know what choosing one or the other meant, but it had to be done.

As I thought that, he turned away, walking back over to Lyla.

FORTY

Violet

'Vampires take the tube? Seriously?'

'Keep your voice down,' Cain hissed, tugging me towards the ticket office. I tried to point out that we could use the machines, but he was having none of it. Reaching the glass of the office, we were faced with the accusing glare of a ticket woman, who I knew from experience was wondering why we hadn't just gone to a machine.

'Hi.' Cain turned around and silently began counting everyone, then puzzling over the ticket types. 'Could we have seven adult day anytime travelcards for Zone 1 and the same for a child, please.'

The woman peered cynically through the glass. 'Who's the child?'

Cain looked puzzled for a moment. 'I am.'

I peered sideways at Cain. He was sixteen and should be paying an adult fare. *He's a millionaire vampire Prince and he is seriously trying to save a couple of quid on the tube?*

'ID, please,' she droned. I frowned; I didn't know many

sixteen-year-olds that carried ID around. But sure enough, Cain pulled his wallet from his jeans pocket, flipped it open and revealed some sort of ID with a fake date of birth in the top corner. She didn't hang around: taking the note Cain was offering her and printing off the tickets.

'Sucker,' Cain chuckled, allowing the ticket barrier to swallow his ticket. Sidestepping a hurried business woman, I followed.

'You have fake ID that makes you younger?' I quizzed, slightly shocked as we descended the elevator, keeping to the right to allow rushed commuters to pass.

He smirked. 'Not only that makes me younger.' He flipped the card over and there, on the back, was another ID proclaiming that he was eighteen.

I shook my head in wonderment at what money could buy as I felt a familiar gust of cold air. Sure enough, a second later a tube emerged from the dark tunnel. Almost elbowing a man out of the way, I pulled Cain through the open doors, trusting the others to get on themselves.

As more and more people got on we were both thrust against a bin. In just seconds every inch of space was occupied and the sound of the racket of wheels in motion took over, save for the thumping bass of some inconsiderate soul who refused to turn their music down.

'Man, it's like being surrounded by a hundred-course dinner.' Cain's face was twisted slightly and he bit down hard on his lip, just like Kaspar did when he tried to resist temptation. I frowned and took a fairy step closer towards him. By this time we were accelerating, and out of practice using the tube I teetered off balance, almost crashing into Cathy, Lyla's friend.

'It's okay,' I murmured. 'Oxford Circus is only three stops along.'

'Suppose,' he replied, clearly trying to control himself. He didn't say another word for two stops, until we were just pulling away with a jolt from Warren Street.

A minute or two later we came to a halt and, grabbing Cain by the wrist, I pulled him out onto the platform of Oxford Circus. Buffeted by hundreds of rushing commuters and tourists we headed towards the escalator, slipping up the left side this time. I tugged him through the ticket barrier behind me before he even had a chance to get his own ticket from his pocket, earning myself a disapproving look from one of the men supervising. Spotting an alcove, I headed for it.

'You really need to hunt, don't you?' Spotting Fabian and the others dodging the crowd moving the other way, I suddenly had an idea.

He nodded weakly. 'I've never been in a crowd like that.'

When Fabian arrived, I grabbed him. 'Is there somewhere inconspicuous around here that you can go to, to you know?' I jerked my head towards Cain. 'Hunt,' I finished in an undertone. Fabian nodded, refusing to meet my eyes. My heart seemed to fall a thousand feet: he could not even look at me now.

'You boys go then and us girls will hit the shops.' I grimaced. *Talk about sacrifice.*

Fabian agreed and started to walk away, but Cain hung back, pulling something from his wallet.

'Here, you'll need this.'

I looked down at the little rectangle of plastic in his palm. I raised an eyebrow. 'Is that yours?'

He attempted a smile. 'No. I borrowed it off a certain someone a while ago.'

Comprehension dawned. 'Can I max that thing out?' I asked, an understanding smirk broadening on my face.

'You can try. But his account is pretty much bottomless,' Cain explained. Taking a step forward he whispered the pin number into my ear. 'Knock yourself out.' He winked and set off in pursuit of the others.

I followed Lyla and Cathy out of the station, facing the prospect of a Kaspar-free day: a day free of his mind tricks and unavoidable attraction. It was liberating as I realized that now he was gone, my spirits had lifted. Whatever he was doing to me, whatever he was making me feel . . . I didn't like it and it was frustratingly hard to resist.

Stepping out into the bustling streets of London, I inhaled the familiar stench of exhaust fumes and exotic food from every country imaginable. All around me people spoke in their own accents and native tongues and it was like music to my ears. I'd been surrounded by stiff-upper-lip posh accents for too long.

I beamed, feeling as though I was walking on air. *I'm home.*

Cain and Declan caught up with us outside Harrods, where Lyla and Cathy had spent endless hours. I had passed the time by donating to every single charity the department store supported, all using Kaspar's debit card. At first it filled me with glee, but the thrill of revenge quickly waned and I started to feel bad – even if he had kissed me.

My stomach saved the two boys from having to view every one of Lyla's purchases by growling loudly.

'What the heck was that?'

I blushed. 'That was my stomach. I'm hungry.'

Cain screwed up his face. 'Human stomachs growl when they are hungry? Wow! They never taught us that one at Vampirs. So what do you want to eat? 'Cause we're kind of full, if you catch my drift.' He winked cheekily at me, and I thought for a moment.

I grinned. 'I'd die for some chips.'

A few minutes later and I was opening up a greasy sheet of newspaper, the luscious smell of salt and vinegar filled my nostrils. Stepping out the takeaway I could still smell the stench of burning fat in the fryers and raw fish coated in batter. Waiting for the others, I took a single bite of one fat, crispy, piping-hot chip.

Now this was better than cheese sandwiches.

Trying not to burn my mouth I chewed the potato, swallowing and wincing as it burnt my throat instead. Cain stepped out into the fresh air closely followed by Fabian, both holding large portions.

'Full, eh?' I smiled, seeing the rest of the boys stepping out too with ridiculous amounts of food. It seemed as though Lyla and Cathy were boycotting the fat, each with a bottle of Diet Coke in hand and no food.

'So, where do you want to go? Because I can't eat standing up,' I prompted.

Cain shrugged his shoulders. 'Embankment?'

I nodded in agreement. Following Cain and not really focusing, I didn't notice when Fabian fell in step beside me.

'Can I talk to you? In private?' he added, watching as Cain turned and glanced from one of us to the other.

'Err, sure,' I replied hesitantly, silently begging Cain with my eyes to object. He gave me one last apologetic look before walking off, closely followed by the other five. As Lyla passed she glared at me, arms crossed defensively across her chest.

Suddenly finding the pavement extremely interesting, I hid behind my hair, praying he would not see the fiery blush tainting my cheeks. Brushing my toe across a crack in the stone he spoke.

'What happened earlier?' His voice was unnaturally calm

and controlled, as though he was barely containing his temper – something I suspected I had never truly seen.

'Earlier?'

'With Kaspar.'

I sighed. I should have known. Of course Fabian would want to know why I had his blood on my lips; why Kaspar had disappeared, which I did not even know the answer to myself. *Hates the tube, my arse.*

'Nothing,' I exhaled, knowing my ploy to lie would not last long.

He took a step closer, towering above me. And in the narrow side-street, surrounded by tall town buildings, the low hum of traffic just a few streets over, the grey, unexciting skies hovering above me, I felt extremely small. Extremely insignificant.

'Just tell me, Violet.'

'We stopped at that place and Kaspar, he seemed distracted, and suddenly he just pulled me towards him, a-and we talked, and then . . .' I trailed off.

'Go on.'

'He cut his lip, and I sort of, well, we-we kissed,' I said, surprised at how eager I was to tell someone; anyone. My head dropped to the floor because I knew I could not face seeing his expression at that moment. 'But only for a second and then he disappeared.'

A small, strained voice cut through the silence. 'Why?'

'I-I don't know . . . his blood just sort of . . . sent me crazy, and I couldn't stop it.' Taking a peep up towards him, I saw him too looking at the ground. 'What happened to me, Fabian? I-I didn't want that!'

Lies, my voice breathed.

'I don't know. But . . . tell me the truth. Do you feel anything when I do this?'

'Do what?'

He took a step towards me and tilted my chin to the side. 'This.'

Planting his lips on mine, everything forbidden, wrong and immoral came flooding back. And that was just me wishing it was not Fabian's lips on mine, but Kaspar's.

As my lips moved in time to his of their own accord I felt the wave of gushing love, longing, need and most of all happiness. Yet all the while . . . it just wasn't the same.

I knew that when we broke apart, that would be it and I would return to thinking of him as nothing more than a friend. And I knew that I was hurting him by allowing him to kiss me. Yet still my hands snaked around his neck, clutching the little bag of chips, pulling him down, closer. All of a sudden he broke away, holding me at arms length, hope gleaming in his eyes.

'Anything?'

'Yes. But . . .' I heard his breath quicken. 'I'm sorry, but it's only ever when I kiss you. I don't . . . it's not . . . I'm sorry, Fabian, but I never have and never will think of you as more than a friend, and I don't know why because you're so nice, and you treat me so well . . .'

And Kaspar doesn't, my voice offered.

'I just don't love you. I'm sorry . . . I don't know what happens when I kiss you.'

He closed his eyes. 'You experience what every other human would when they kiss a vampire. It's how we seduce our prey . . . sometimes. And no, it's not love,' he said. Impassively. Unemotionally. But underneath I could hear the strained tone in his voice, the true measure of how much he was hurting.

'And not what a relationship should be based on.'

Instantly, I regretted what I had said. Fabian's expression dropped from unreadable to rage in mere seconds.

'And what you and Kaspar have is? Should a relationship be based on lust, blood and desire? Is that what you want, Violet?!' he thundered, taking a step closer to me as I did the same.

'Who said anything about a relationship?'

'No one. Nothing. Nothing but the way you act!'

'I don't want a relationship. Not with a vampire, not with anyone! I had enough of men when my last boyfriend cheated on me, remember?' I screeched, breathing heavily, madly gesturing with my hands which were curled into fists, flinging the bag of chips around at precarious speed.

'Don't lie to me! You want him, and you know it.' His eyes narrowed. 'But hear me, Violet. When he breaks your heart, don't come running to me, because I won't have a heart to spare. Remember that.'

With that he turned and fled, leaving nothing behind but a whipped wind.

'I won't let my heart get broken, idiot,' I murmured after him. I leaned up against the railings of a nearby house, undoubtedly split up into flats and allowed myself to cool down. After a few deep breaths, panic set in.

Why the hell do I prefer Kaspar when he was such an arse, plainly put? Okay, an arse with his moments, but cruel all the same?

You prefer him, because like you said, it's not just because of the seduction that you kissed him, is it, Violet? my voice probed, in it's usual taunting manner. *Just follow your heart. What is the first name that comes into your head?*

I sighed. 'Kaspar.'

My voice chuckled. *Then you made the right decision.*

I closed my eyes, feeling stupid for seeking reassurance from a voice in my head. Yet I knew it was right. Because I knew I felt something for him, despite what he was, and despite the abuse I had put up with from all corners.

A shallow summary it was, but I wondered how I had rejected the good guy and found myself increasingly attracted to the jerk of a vampire prince. Who *kidnapped* me. *My life is one messed up cliché of a story.*

I sprung away from the railings and trailed in Fabian's wake.

Leaning back onto the bench I stuck my greasy hands deep into my pockets, having finished my chips and impatient for the others to finish. Cain, sat next to me, had long since fallen silent and so instead I watched the street performers dotted along the embankment.

Something further along caught my eye. Three guys, wearing zipped-up hoodies and baggy jeans held up by belts that clearly did not work, were leisurely walking along the pavement, swearing loudly and laughing raucously at the nearest mime artist. Beanie hats over jagged fringes, tight T-shirts, collars turned up, they swaggered closer. It was only when one of them looked up and glanced our (Lyla's) way that I recognized them.

Joel's friends.

'Shit!' I breathed, panicking. Cain turned to me questioningly, before following my gaze. His eyes landed on the three boys gradually getting closer. There were both staring at me, but stupid as they were, I did not think they had recognized me.

'What?' Cain flustered, yanking his head from me to them.

I raised my widened eyes to face him. 'I know them!'

Cain's eyes widened too, paling. 'Fuck.'

I nodded furiously. As they both passed behind a large group of tourists I leapt up, meaning to run for it. But before I could take a step forward I was pulled back down onto the cold wood.

'Where do you think you're going?' Cain hissed, sounding uncannily like his brother.

'I'm getting out of here! They'll recognize me!'

'You can't!'

'I can!'

'Then I'm coming with you,' he declared, jumping up too as I made to move. I pushed him back down onto the bench and replied rather too quickly.

'No! I mean, I'll be fine, I won't run off.' Hastily, I glanced up and saw the three guys, both glaring intently at me. They were gradually pushing their way through the crowds and I knew if they saw me properly they would instantly know who I was.

Cain's eyes followed the parting crowd like a hawk surveying prey, before he turned to me. 'Okay, okay, but please don't run off, Kaspar will kill me. We'll sort this out, just go!'

I did not need telling twice. I dove into a side-street and then through the crowds, feeling tears streak my cheeks. I didn't know where I was going, or even where I was; I just knew to keep running.

Elbowing someone out of the way I heard disgruntled grunts from behind me, followed by loud cursing. Glancing back I saw a man clad in an expensive suit shaking his fist at me, briefcase full of papers scattered across the pavement.

Fresh sobs caught in my throat and a new wave of tears poured down from my eyes. *Joel? Why now? I don't need this.*

Still pelting it down the pavement I ran to the one place I could seek comfort around here: Hamleys. A toy store. *Lame, but true.* The shelves and shelves of toys brought happy childhood memories flooding back – and happy memories were just what I needed.

Running up the escalators I passed screaming children,

all dragging peeved-looking parents towards expensive-looking toys. Tripping over at the top of what felt like the millionth escalator, I found myself staring at a room full of train sets.

I ducked behind a shelf and leaned up against a stable-looking pile of boxes containing model trucks. I took several deep breaths.

Joel's appearance had taken me off guard. That was for sure. And that had to be why my heart felt as though there was a vice clutching it, right? Because I was over him. *I'm over him.* That had to be the reason my heart felt as though with every faint pump the clamp around it was constricting, restricting the flow of essential liquid – blood.

Suddenly, something cold pressed against my back. 'I'm going to suck your blood,' a voice murmured against my neck, and I flinched.

'Don't do that!' I exclaimed as plastic fangs pressed themselves into my neck, arms clad in dark material wrapping themselves around my shoulders. 'Kaspar! Get off!'

'No,' he replied, pressing his chest into my back. 'I quite like it here.'

I struggled for a moment, trying to shrug his arms off. 'At least stop slobbering all over my neck and take those stupid fake things out, you have real fangs for Pete's sake!'

'Keep it down, people will hear,' he muttered, tone alarmed. But all the same he reached up and popped them out, placing them in his palm. He examined them, poking the rounded and exaggeratingly large incisors with the other hand – the one still wrapped around my chest. 'Stupid humans. We wouldn't be able to eat with fangs that size.'

'Just because you're jealous because you have puny little things.'

He pocketed the fake fangs and abruptly poked me in the

sides, causing me to jerk further into him. 'No need to get overenthusiastic, Girly,' he chuckled, pushing me away an inch or two. I flushed.

'But—'

'And we have tiny fangs so that no one sees them.'

His tone changed as he pulled me nearer. His head lowered and his hair tickled my cheeks, his lips brushing my ear. I shivered involuntarily, and thanked the heavens we were concealed by many shelves piled high with boxes – Kaspar would be considered X-rated in a toy store.

'Are you going to tell me what's wrong, Girly, or do I have to force it out of you, as usual?'

I sighed. 'Nothing's wrong.'

'Don't lie to me, Violet.'

'I'm not—'

He broke away, his cool arms leaving my chest. Snatching my hand in his, he tugged me deeper into the store. I blushed as tight-lipped mothers flashed us dirty looks, obviously thinking we were far too 'intimate' for their children.

You love it, my voice scoffed.

Totally, I muttered in my mind.

Bringing us to a halt in a shadowy corner sheltered beside rows of make-your-own jumbo jets, he whipped around, one hand on the wall beside my head, the other reaching up to stroke my cheek.

'You've been crying, Girly. Now tell. What's wrong?'

The vice tightened, but somehow my heart did not feel as though every ounce of life was being drained from it. Kaspar's touch was reassuring as he wiped a stray tear from my cheek. Yet I averted my gaze to the floor.

'I saw J-Joel,' I choked in little more than a whisper. I bit back tears, slowly raising my head, only to see his eyes falling through to black.

'Oh,' he mouthed. I nodded silently, biting down hard on my lip.

'He was at the embankment, and the others are there and I thought I was over him, Kaspar. I thought I had moved on, but I haven't, not even close.' I watched, eyes stinging, as his eyes regained their usual emerald green, if a little more luminous than usual; less rich.

Suddenly his hands clasped themselves around my arms. 'Did he see you? Violet, did he see you?' He demanded, gripping my shoulders, gaze darting from me to the escalator.

'I-I don't know.'

'What does he look like?'

I frowned, slightly disgusted. *Is that all he can think about?* But I was not used to the panicked tone in his voice, so answered. 'Dark blond hair, brown eyes, about six foot tall.'

'Then duck.'

Before I knew it, he had yanked both of us to the floor, leaving me to sprawl on the plush carpet.

'What the hell?' I screeched at him, but he dived towards me on his knees, clamping a firm hand down on my mouth. He raised the other to his mouth, pressing a single finger to his lips.

'He's here,' he mouthed. My eyes widened. I went to open my mouth, but he shook his head, pointing in the direction of the escalator, grabbing my hand and dragging me along behind him. Keeping low and darting between the shelves, he lugged us closer to the escalator, and ultimately, to our escape. But however much I despised Joel for what he had done, how he had hurt me, I could not help but crane my neck, trying desperately to catch just one glimpse of the boy I loved for two years, just to confirm he was real . . . that he was here.

And yet I knew deep down that if he saw me that would

be it: old life and new life would come crashing together, violently.

Kaspar stopped, listening intently. How he could hear anything through the cheesy jingles blaring through the speakers and the sound of squealing children, I didn't know. He pointed behind me, through the shelf, mumbling something.

'What?' I mouthed back.

'He's right there!' he muttered back a little louder.

'How right there?'

'Right, right there!'

'What are we going—'

Before I could finish he had lunged towards me, clamped a hand down on my mouth and sent me sprawling across the floor. He must have misjudged the distance though, because he landed right on top of me, earning him a loud groan as every bone in my body felt as though it were being squeezed into a pulp. He silently wrestled with me for a moment, as I tried to throw him off and he tried to shut me up.

'Sshh . . . sshh!'

Then he froze.

'Kaspar! What are you—'

'*Violet*?'

I froze as well. Peering over Kaspar's shoulder, I saw the one person I really did not want to see whilst a vampire was straddling me in the middle of a toy shop.

'Joel?'

Joel stood there, mouth wide, eyes transfixed on me – or rather, should I say, his eyes were fixed on Kaspar lying on top of me.

'I, err, it's not what it looks like!'

'That's them, right there! Those two! On the floor!'

'Well, what does it look like then, young lady?' a strange voice said.

Kaspar looked down at me expression that read 'we are in deep shit', an expression I was sure I shared. Peering timidly over his shoulder, I could see a uniformed man clad in a shirt emblazoned with HAMLEYS, a glinting badge pinned just above his breast pocket that read MANAGER. Beside him stood one of the tight-lipped parents, nose upturned.

'I can't believe this behaviour! In front of *children*! It's scandalous! They should be thrown out!'

I winced. Joel was here and now we were in trouble with the manager. *Wonderful, just wonderful.*

'Yes, yes, quite right, Mrs . . .?' the manager began.

'Charles-Pomphrey.'

'Yes. Out! Both of you! And don't come back! And you too, young man,' he said, turning to Joel. 'Young people these days, honestly, ma'am, I have never seen anything like it in all my days here.'

Kaspar's eyes closed and he relaxed into me slightly. He muttered something inaudible, before slowly, as though it took a lot of effort, clambering up and offering me a hand. I took it gratefully, gliding upright in his strong grip. I opened my mouth to protest to the manager, but Kaspar grabbed me by the elbow and marched us out, Joel hot on our heels, face still puzzled.

As we passed the manager, I thought I heard Kaspar mumbling an apology, passing him a slip of paper that looked suspiciously like a fifty-pound note.

We reached the entrance, the bitter air raising goose bumps on my arms. The clouds had finally cleared to reveal a glowing sun, low in the sky, even in the early afternoon. Dazzled by the light, I did not see as Joel stepped in front of us. But Kaspar did.

His arm snaked around my waist, pulling me close as he snarled faintly. 'What the fuck do you want?'

'And who are you? And what are you doing with my babe?'

I scowled. 'I'm not your babe!'

Joel's eyes flickered towards me before immediately returning to meet Kaspar's defensive pose, as he pushed me slightly behind him.

'C'mon, babe . . . you know I'm sorry. And I know that you weren't taken that night, Vi. I know you ran because I cheated. But that's over now.' He stretched out a hand for me to take, and sensing the risk, Kaspar snatched my upper arm, tightly grasping it to the point where my circulation was cut off.

He need not bother. *He thought I had run away because of the cheating?* That egotistical assumption caused anger to flare. Loathing, yet it was bittersweet: his eyes still made my heart to squeeze. It took a lot of self control to not correct him and just scream the truth about vampires.

'No! I'm not going anywhere with you! And for the last time, I'm not your babe!'

There was silence and even the street seemed to stand still, passers-by not bothering to hide their surprise at my outburst.

'You . . . what? What d'ya mean . . . not going anywhere? You mean you want to stay with him?' he jerked his thumb towards Kaspar and his eyes lowered to where Kaspar's arm was sneakily wrapping itself back around my waist, trying to steer me away. Comprehension dawned on his face. 'Are y-you two . . . together?'

My mouth fell open, appalled and I pulled myself abruptly out of Kaspar's grip.

'No! We're not anything. No, I mean, me and him? No.'

I giggled girlishly, blushing until I resembled a tomato. Kaspar draped his arm back around my shoulders, looking at me quizzically.

'Yes, we are!'

Again my mouth fell open, and I scoffed, half-laughing, half-making choking noises. 'No, we are most definitely not!' I stepped out of his hold, glaring at him.

He tugged me back. 'Yes! We are!'

I shrugged him off. 'No. We're not. And that's final.'

I thought I heard Kaspar distinctly breathe the word 'Idiot', under his breath as I turned back to Joel, whose eyes followed us like tennis, an eyebrow raised.

'Well if you're not with him, then come and be with me.'

He reached out and grabbed my arm, yanking me to his side. Not expecting it, I tripped over my own feet and stumbling, closed my eyes, expecting to have the pavement meet my nose at any moment. Yet the impact never came.

Instead, a wintry arm had locked itself around my stomach, leaving me teetering on my very tiptoes. Looking around, I realized Kaspar was my saviour. He set me right on my feet and then turned to Joel who was fast paling. Without even looking I knew Kaspar's eyes had darkened. He growled; a sound reserved only for times when he really was angry.

'You really should learn how to treat your "babes", Joel. Especially a girl as decent as Violet. Or better still, I'll teach you.'

Joel, obviously scared, tried to maintain some of his bravado. 'Oh, yeah? How about you teach me right now?' He raised his balled fist, preparing to punch. Kaspar stepped forward, meeting the challenge.

'Be my guest!'

I saw the crowds slowing as they stopped to watch the fight break out as Joel prepared to throw his punch.

Knowing he would not stand a chance against Kaspar, I intervened, stepping between them both. Instantly a fist flew towards my face, but reaching up I blocked it, pushing his arm aside. Snatching his wrist I twisted it, causing it to lock. He winced in pain, contorting to try to lessen the pain.

'That is for cheating on me the first time!'

I raised the other fist and punched him straight in the nose, not breaking it, but still drawing blood.

'That is for cheating on me the second time!'

He threw his head back and groaned, rather handily exposing a certain sensitive area.

'And that,' I said, raising my knee, 'is for starting on Kaspar!' Swiftly and without even the slightest ounce of remorse, I kneed him in the bollocks.

The effect was instant. Doubling over and grabbing his crotch he fell to his knees, crying in agony, blood trickling from his reddened nose. Passers-by looked on with varying degrees of disapproval and disgust, a few smirking – some even cheered.

Smirking to myself, I grabbed Kaspar's hand and flipping my hair dramatically, marched off, but not before I had one final say.

Looking down at the pitiful boy groaning at my feet, I was filled with an overwhelming sense of satisfaction. Bending down to his level, I smiled triumphantly.

'You know what, Joel? I am *so* over you.'

And with that we left.

I led Kaspar through a number of side-streets, eager to get away from the busy main thoroughfares in case Joel called the police – not that the police were likely to catch a bunch of vampires anyway, or even believe Joel's story.

'I can't believe we just did that!' I exclaimed when we were well away. He smiled the half-smile, half-smirk I so loved, allowing himself to be pulled along as giggled like a little girl.

'Remind me never to cross you. I want children.'

My laughs turned to a devilish smile. 'Better watch out then,' I warned, winking.

'Where did you learn all that anyway? You don't look like the type.' He looked me up and down and I blushed.

'My dad taught me a few moves . . . useless against vampires of course, but good enough for a human.'

His face fell a little at the mention of my father, his eyes dulling. 'Ah.'

We fell into silence for a second, and keen to avoid any awkward pauses, I carried on. 'That was so satisfying. I've never done anything like that before! And we got chucked out of Hamleys!'

He chuckled, mumbling something that sounded like 'Oh, you devil!'

'Hey!' I pinched him on the arm, but he just shrugged his shoulders. 'I've never got thrown out of anywhere before. Apart from some pizza place once for being too loud.' I smiled at the memory, when at the age of about thirteen I and a group of friends had devoured our way through four pizzas and the entire restaurant's supply of lemonade, causing us to become ridiculously hyper.

Kaspar tugged on my hand as I dragged him along, slowing me down a bit in my eagerness. 'Well, you better get used to it if you plan on sticking around. We don't have the best reputation for being good.'

I arched an eyebrow. 'Who said anything about me being good? And besides, I never said I was sticking around.'

I stole a glance upwards to see him slowly nodding, thoughtful. Guilty, I dropped his hand from mine, shuffling away a little.

'Kaspar, why did you say we were, you know, an "item"?'

He shrugged his shoulders. 'To unsettle him. It worked, didn't it?'

'I guess,' I mumbled. 'You don't think he'll tell the police I'm in London, do you?'

He narrowed his eyes. 'You almost sound concerned that he might. But if he does, they'll have a hard time catching us. I'm not worried.'

Now that is awkward. I'm not concerned . . . it just had to be asked.

'And why didn't you jump on Joel when he started bleeding like that?'

He snorted. 'I wouldn't drink that mongrel's blood if he were the last human on Earth. Foul stuff.'

I could not help but laugh, the mood instantly lightening. His half-smile, half-smirk returned, and he took a step closer.

I took his closeness as an opportunity to playfully slap him on the chest. 'You were prepared to beat up a guy for me. Some people would think that sweet. You said I was a decent girl too.'

'I did, didn't I?' he mused, raising his chin so he was able to frown at the space above my head. After a few moments, he chuckled, shook his head as though bemused and slung an arm around my shoulders. 'C'mon,' he said, slinging an arm around my shoulders. 'You were having a normal day, for once.' This time I did not protest as he dropped me off with Cain, Declan and the others again. 'I have to go do something.'

'Is he always like that?'

Cain shrugged. 'One thing you have to learn about Kaspar is that when you don't want him around, he will pester you until you give in to him; and when you do want him around, he will leave you. And you can't change it.'

*   *   *

'Change of plan,' Charlie said. 'The girls want to go to the fair.'

We were about to head into the underground back to Islington when we changed lines to head towards Hyde Park. There, a Halloween fair was in full swing, the sickly scent of candyfloss scenting the air.

Cain took my wrist and began tugging me along behind him, the excitement infectious. The neon lights swept around, the sirens wailing, men calling, 'Roll up! Roll up! Dodgems just a pound a go! C'mon ladies and gents!'

Guys no older than me were silently collecting the money, strapping the few visitors around into their seats, bored expressions permanent despite the pretty girls that occasionally emerged from the shadows in packs. The air was bitter and bit at my cheeks but the warmth of a thousand light bulbs stopped me from shivering.

'Oh my gosh, a funhouse! We have to go in, come on,' Lyla gushed, grabbing Cathy's hand, snatching Fabian's in the other (who did not shirk away), and dragging them both towards the booth. Cain rolled his eyes but followed, the other three boys not far behind.

We drew to a stop beside the counter where Lyla placed a handful of change.

They soon disappeared into the folds of the canvas entrance. Declan muttered something about not wanting to have to stick around to watch *that*, and Charlie was already hot in pursuit of Felix. I forced my face to remain expressionless and ducked in after him. I took a few steps in, cringing at the two-foot-high, six-foot-wide me staring back from a distorted mirror nearby. Cain didn't appear. Peeking back through the entrance, I found he was not there and figured he must have taken the same attitude as Declan.

I saw no reflection of any of the other four and had almost

reached a staircase, shunting up and down when I spotted Lyla. I froze when I realized her tongue was down Felix's throat; Fabian was on his knees, planting kisses and bites down her exposed stomach. Next to them was Charlie, fangs sunk deep into Cathy's neck, blood coating her hands as she ran her fingers through his hair. Soft moans escaped her mouth as a single trail of blood trickled down her shoulder, seeping into the material of her shirt where it feathered into veins and stained the pale fabric.

Disgusted and embarrassed I backed away, trying to get away without them noticing.

But Felix's head snapped around, his eyes deep red. A small smile spread across his lips, revealing pink fangs.

'Want to join in?'

I shook my head violently. 'No thanks.'

Back-pedalling, I hit something hard. Thinking it was one of the mirrors, I sprang forward again only to freeze and find a smirk caught on my lips as the familiar self-assured and arrogant voice of a certain vampire sounded behind me.

'Of course she doesn't want to join in your little orgy, idiot.'

'Chill out man, I was only asking,' Felix retorted, wrapping his arm back around Lyla's neck. I scowled as she giggled. Fabian never acknowledged my presence.

'And fuck it, learn to share,' Felix muttered, burying his mouth in Lyla's neck. With a disgusted groan Kaspar turned away, pulling me with him as Lyla whimpered beneath the two men.

Kaspar said nothing, despite my curious glances as we walked side-by-side towards the exit. He pushed the folds of the tent aside and stepped out into the cold without even a shudder, his dark shirt unbuttoned at the top and sleeves rolled up.

'I can tell you're dying to say something, so spit it out, Girly.'

I scowled. 'Where have you been?'

He looked sideways at me, lips parted and upturned, brow lowered; irritated. 'Somewhere, Girly, but I'm not going to tell you where because I have my own life and I don't have to answer the questions of some kid hostage.'

I stopped, affronted, staring at him. The lights glided over his alabaster skin, his eyes luminous in the neon air. I examined his hunched shoulders, watching as his hair flopped over one eye, his hands buried in deep in his pockets.

'What's wrong with you? You were actually verging on nice earlier.'

He shrugged his shoulders dismissively and I doubted he was even listening. Sighing with exasperation, I poked his arm and asked again.

He stopped and snagged my gaze. 'Quit asking questions or I'll get angry and bite you.' His mouth flat-lined, but I could not help but laugh.

'I'm scared: hollow threats are so intimidating!'

'I'm serious.'

'Sure you are, Kaspar.' I punched him on the arm and then sped off, glancing back and shouting, 'C'mon, I want to go on the waltzers!'

FORTY-ONE

Kaspar

She dived into the nearest waltzer, settling back into the fake leather. Reluctantly, I joined her, inching towards the warmth of her skin draped in her coat. The carriage spun as I stepped in, eyes stinging from the constant glare of the flashing lights humans seemed to love so much.

Yes, there was something wrong. Namely, the fact I knew I had just hours left of being able to touch her; to feel her glowing skin against mine, the feeling that I found myself craving with more intensity with every passing hour . . .

As I sat down beside her she began fumbling with the top button of her coat, a flush coming to her collar as a bead of sweat rolled down her neck. She was struggling, so turning away I reached over with one hand and unfastened the top two buttons, not exactly accidentally brushing against her now exposed chest. I felt her shiver below me, despite the fact that touching her skin was like pressing my hand to a hot stove. I sensed her face flaming, the blood rushing to her cheeks before she mumbled her thanks.

The sirens wailed and the floor rattled and began moving, our carriage beginning to spin. The bar that wrapped around the seats shook violently beneath my hand, and on impulse I wrapped an arm tightly around her slender shoulders. I half expected her to resist, but she didn't. Instead, she inched closer, allowing me to draw her into my chest, her hands leaving the bar without question.

With her body pressed to mine I could feel the heat of her skin on my bare arms – a heat that was becoming almost familiar to me now. It was a different warmth from that of the humans that became my victims: their heat would fade as I sucked them dry. But as I drew her closer her warmth would only increase; as I touched her she would not turn blue but red as blush coloured her cheeks.

I made my mind up months ago that I would have her, take her, please her and use her for my will. *I'm a man of my word. And her blood. Oh, her blood!* It was sweet – not as sweet as that served at the balls – but I didn't drink it for its taste. I drank from her because I craved her reaction. I wanted to hear her softly whimpering below me as I pierced her neck and veins; I wanted to see her blood trickling down her slight shoulders, seeping across her breasts, tinting the scars that Ilta had forced on her, still struggling to heal. I took her blood because unlike any other creature I had ever hurt she never cried out, never screamed, even when I set out to maliciously cause her pain.

It was that stubbornness that had always intrigued me, her steadfast and unwavering belief in what she thought was moral and righteous . . .

He won't physically stop me touching her. How could he stop us? Rip us apart?

A smile was spreading across her lips, which turned into a giggle as she wrapped her arms tightly around my middle, shrieking with laughter as the dizziness overtook her. It was infectious. I smiled too, despite my hate of the loud, beat-heavy music and flashing lights.

I couldn't have anticipated what happened next. In an attempt to pull her just a little closer, my hand must have brushed her side because she jerked away from my touch, the whirling motion of the ride causing her neck to wrench back onto my shoulder and exposing her fleshy throat and a single throbbing, purple vein.

My eyes changed to red and my mouth widened as I snarled softly, baring my sharp fangs. Her scent made my nostrils flare and my mind spun like the ride. *What I would give to just taste one innocent drop of her blood* . . .

My jaw lowered to her exposed neck, the thought of her blood cooling the burning in my throat. I was not an inch away from her throat when my voice, quiet for so many days, interrupted sharply.

Don't.

Her heart thumped, and I was gone.

FORTY-TWO

Violet

Gone. Again.

I straightened up from where I had collapsed onto the seat, drawing myself up on my elbows, waiting for the ride to slow down. My neck was stiff and ached and I most definitely felt very, very sick. I gagged a little, desperate for a drink. Closing my eyes and burying my head in my hands I waited for the ride to be over, regretting ever coming on.

Eventually the world slowed to a halt, and sucking in a deep breath I stood up, stepping out of the carriage as my head throbbed and my vision blurred for a split second. The low-cut collar of my T-shirt left me in full view, and I hastily buttoned it back up.

I scanned the darkness. The only people around were the ride attendants and the retreating backs of those that had just been on the waltzer. Convincing myself he couldn't have gone that far, I started searching behind the caravans.

Eventually I thought I heard muffled whining, and rounding a trailer, went to investigate. Fading moans floated through the air, and a low slurping sound reached my ears. Slowing down I eased forward, making out a shape in the corner formed by two caravans, sheltered by piles of empty boxes. My eyes adjusted to the gloom and pushing a box aside with a quaking hand I felt bile rise in my throat.

There, clutched in the arms of Kaspar was a girl, clothes torn and her skin lacerated. She was tanned, but becoming grey, eyes losing lustre. The only part of her that still contained any hue was her neck, which was flushed bright red and oozing blood.

Dead.

He stood up, allowing her limp body to tumble out of the cradle of his arms to the churned, muddy ground. He gradually turned to face me. Blood dribbled down his chin and his neck and cheeks were smeared with peach lipstick – a mark to prove how he had caught her.

I swallowed back the bile, forcing myself to breathe . . . *in and out, in and out . . .*

'W-why?' I managed to choke out, not wanting to back away but not wanting to go near him either. His eyes were crimson, becoming scarlet, then pink and eventually a murky, swirling grey to match her skin as a single fang bit at his blood-stained lips.

He looked down at her for a brief moment. 'She was called Joanne.'

'You knew her name?' I whispered, unable to tear my eyes away from the mangled body laying face down in the grass. He nodded, still biting at his lip with his fangs which were tinged pink, her blood crusting around the corners of his mouth. 'And that makes it better, how?'

'It just does.' He reached down and rolled her body over like she was a slab of meat, her arms twisted behind her back. He yanked her dress back down to cover her thighs and placed a finger on each of her eyelids, rolling them down to shut off her unseeing pupils, which stared up at him in permanent horror. 'Does that make it better?'

I cringed and looked away as the blood around his mouth continued to dry, turning an ugly brown colour against his ashen skin. 'You can't just go around killing people.'

I heard a growl from behind me. 'I'm a vampire, Girly, I have to kill to feed and I'd rather it wasn't you I was killing.'

I took a sharp breath and whipped back around. 'What?'

He didn't reply for a few seconds, his chest rising and falling. 'On the ride I nearly attacked you. And if I had you would certainly be dead. It was you or her.'

My mouth fell open. 'You should have just killed me!'

He took a step towards me and I took one back. My heart faltered as my senses shrieked that I should run. He snarled softly, his eyes pitch black. 'Wake up and smell the coffee, Girly! Your life is the only thing stopping us from descending into war! The first and last chance I had to kill you was in Trafalgar Square.'

He pushed passed me, knocking me back a step. But I whipped around and grabbed his arm, digging my nails in and using every ounce of strength I had to pull him back.

'Then why didn't you?'

He didn't meet my eyes, using the sleeve of his free arm to wipe his mouth. 'We have to go before someone realizes she's missing. C'mon.'

I tugged harder and repeated my question. 'Why didn't you?'

Instead of answering he prized my hand away and walked off, disappearing into the darkness. With one last glance back at the girl lying lifeless and blood-drained on the ground, I hurried after him, disgusted, but more sickened by the fact I couldn't bring myself to be truly horrified.

'I won't tell if you don't.'

'But you can't, that's seriously cruel!'

'Come on, it's not as though you two get on any more, why should you care?'

'But it won't damage his car, will it?'

'No,' Kaspar chuckled. 'Just delay him.'

He pulled the cables out and slammed the bonnet down. He moved around Fabian's R8 and I cringed, thinking it a crime as he moved on to Charlie's car.

'You're not going to do it to all of them, are you?'

He smirked wickedly, continuing to chuckle. 'Of course. I would actually like to have the run of Varnley for once. And with father away and this lot stranded it'll be peace and quiet at last. Besides, they'll just run back eventually . . . tomorrow morning, I should think.'

I scowled. 'Let me rephrase that. You mean *I'm* going to be stranded with *you*.'

'Yes.' He wrenched another set of cables out and slammed the bonnet down. 'Lucky you!'

'Lucky you,' I imitated under my breath. 'Won't they just be able to fix them?'

He slammed the bonnet of his sister's car down with so much force I thought the metal would buckle. Leaning across, his trademark half-smile, half-smirk appeared.

'Rich kids can't fix cars.'

I arched an eyebrow. 'Are you admitting you're a stuck-up arrogant jerk then?'

'I never denied it.'

I hummed sceptically, walking around the car and snatching the keys he had just pulled from his pocket.

'I'm driving.'

He made to lunge towards me, hand outstretched to grab the keys, but I jumped out of his reach. Wrapping my fingers tightly around the metal I hid them behind my back, side-stepping towards his car.

'Do you even have a license?' he grunted, darting around me.

'Yes.'

It was his turn to be sceptic as he continued to follow me around to the driver's side, playing along with my game – he could easily catch me if he wanted to. After protesting that I was perfectly capable of driving (he was worried I would hurt his 'baby'), he begrudgingly gave up and walked around to the passenger's side.

'I still don't forgive you,' I said.

He paused, his face faintly amused. 'I wouldn't expect you to, you're far too stubborn.' He opened the door and slid in. I wasn't far behind.

'And what's that supposed to mean?' I demanded.

'You really want to know?'

'Yes,' I replied, adamant.

'You don't give a damn that I killed that girl. You wouldn't give a damn if I killed a hundred girls. You only care because you just can't take the fact that it destroys your perfect little perception that we – I – am not a predator by nature.' He watched me, gauging my expression.

'I know you're a killer, I'm not stupid,' I sighed, jamming the keys into the ignition. 'You have fangs, for Pete's sake!'

I know he's a predator. I can never forget it, despite what he thinks. Scars and marks dotted my body; endless reminders of what he and others were capable of, and what a vampire would do to get his or her way. *But he's right about one thing. It doesn't really bother me that he killed that girl.* Of course I felt bad; she had died instead of me and I knew I would live with the guilt of knowing others were sacrificed on my part. But I had seen them slaughter and devour so many humans and vampires alike that I was almost numb to it.

'But do you?' he questioned, wincing as I thrust the car into gear.

'Yes! I have the bloody marks to prove it!' I pointed at my neck, pulling my collar aside.

Out of the corner of my eye, I saw him glance at my neck. 'I'm not convinced. You still think you can alter what we are and you can't. You just can't . . .' He trailed off, looking out of his window.

'I'm not trying to change you. I just don't agree with killing for food. I'm veggie, after all.'

'Whatever. Left here,' he mumbled as I turned out onto the main road. I sensed that the conversation was over and we fell into silence. Keeping my eyes on the road, I felt the quiet purr of the engine beneath my hands. It had been a while since I had driven; and then it was only my mother's car in the congested centre of Chelsea. I had never driven anything this powerful or expensive, and never on sweeping coast roads either. A jolt of anxiety shot like an electric bolt up my arm as I thought of what Kaspar would do if I got so much as a scratch on his precious 'baby'; of what he could do. I might have been bitten multiple times but it still terrified me and my breathing hitched as I remembered the pain and the drawing sensation.

I was transported back from my own thoughts as we entered a town, empty and still for the night. I followed the road around until we were trailing the sea again, passing a pier stretching out into the mud flat and eventually the murky waters of the Thames estuary.

'Where do I—'

'Head for the Isle of Grain but turn off at the sign for All Hallows. Then head for Low Marshes.'

'Right,' I muttered, surprised at his bluntness and sudden change of tone. I risked a glance his way to see that his eyes were fixed out of the window, his brow creased and his lips pursed into a thin line. I frowned.

His head snapped around. *'What?'*

I abruptly turned back to the road, blushing.

The night seemed to be getting darker, the sky losing the glowing halo of orange light the city adored so much. Here, it was clearer and the stars were dotted across the sky, like a child had sprinkled glitter across a dark sheet, only losing its sparkle when the occasional cloud wafted over. The roads were empty and we had already long left the main drag when the road started to narrow. I spotted the sign for Low Marshes and followed the arrow, gradually climbing away from the sea towards the rolling hills of Varnley.

It was strange to think it, but I yearned to be back within the thick walls of the mansion, tucked between cold sheets and inhaling stagnant air. It felt oddly safe – though it was far from – and I began to wonder if I was equating imprisonment with security. At Varnley, I made no decisions. At Varnley, I was just along for the ride.

But when I returned, much as I wanted the day to end, I knew there was a very real possibility that a decision on my humanity could have been made for me by this 'inter-dimensional council'. That was one choice that should be my own.

And then there was the thought that I had almost kissed Kaspar.

A glare in the mirrors caught my attention. Chasing our tail was a car, headlights on full beam. Unnerved by how close it was getting, I sped up.

The car behind us had dropped back, obviously taking the hint that I liked my space. Kaspar let his head fall against the window again, his fingers rubbing circles around his temples.

Suddenly he sat bolt upright. 'Slayers,' he hissed. Then he exploded. 'Pull over! Get out!' he roared, but it barely penetrated. 'Out! Violet, move!' I did as he ordered. *Slayers.* 'I'm driving, get in now!' *Slayers.* 'Violet!'

'Slayers,' I breathed. 'Here . . .' *The Slayers from my dream. It had to be.*

He threw his hands in the air from the opposite side of the car, thumping them down on the roof with a thud. 'Yes, slayers, here for you, now get around here!'

I thought I was looking at him but all I saw was the dark sky, grey, rolling and dangerous. I thought I was hearing him but all I heard was the howling of the wind as it picked up, rustling the leaves. I thought he was speaking but all I heard was my own voice, quiet and timid compared to the awe of the thunder that had just crashed.

'Here for me. I could go home . . .'

A quiet snarl escaped his lips. 'No.'

'I could go home and see my friends. I could go to university . . .'

'No.'

'See my family . . .'

'No . . .'

'See Lily . . .'

Cool breath tickled my cheeks and mist gathered in my hands as his forehead met mine. His fingers weaved their way between my own and I could feel the damp air swirling between them.

'I can't deny you that.' His eyes swept up to meet mine, grey, colourless, the dull shade of the sky an identical match.

He closed them slowly, taking a long, low, raspy breath as he did. 'I'll regret this. Violet; Girly. Go home.'

I wrenched away from him. 'W-what?'

'Go home. Escape this life that you don't want.' His words barely came out a whisper, strained and uncertain.

'But—'

'Be human.'

He clutched desperately at my hand as he shakily brought it to his lips, planting a soft kiss on my knuckles. Giving it one last squeeze he placed it back at my side and let go, backing away.

'Take good care of Lily. Look after her. Don't let her go.'

His eyes looked glazed, like light shining upon a pond, and for the smallest of moments I wondered if they could be tears – but this was Kaspar. Kaspar would not waste his tears.

'Just go before I change my mind! Go!' He yelled, his eyes burning, ash then fire. His taut, gaunt face lit up as the first flash of lightning cut through the mist hanging low above the sea, thunder rumbling not a second behind. Like carefully aimed bullets the second blade set a tree about a mile off ablaze, drums crashing and beating to the rhythm of the storm.

Back-pedalling and stumbling over my own feet, I retreated, not taking my eyes away from his as he scrambled for the handle of the car.

I knew that neither of us had long and fear clutched at my heart, terrified of what the slayers could do to him. But knowing they were after me I weighed up my options: I could go with the slayers or I could make my own way home from wherever we were.

The words of the slayer about cocking his leg over me filled my mind and I knew which I would prefer; I would take a forest full of vampires over them.

Frenetic, my voice was whispering in my mind, calling *hurry, hurry*, with an urgency I couldn't ignore. Staring at the trunks of the trees I prepared to delve between, I took one last glance back at Kaspar, frozen, watching me with an expression I had never seen him wear before.

As I met his gaze he turned away and began to slide into his car, the wind howling, whistling what I thought were the words, 'Goodbye, Violet.'

The thunder rumbled and tears streaked my cheeks, smudging my make-up yet again, eyes sore from where I was rubbing them to see. Tyres screeched as two sets of glaring headlights rounded the corner, ensnaring me like a startled deer. My heart leapt into my mouth as I watched the two cars close in.

This isn't the right time.

I whirled around and diving towards his car in a few short steps, I wrenched the passenger door open, just as he was firing the engine up. Falling into the seat I yanked the door closed behind me in time to hear Kaspar cursing loudly.

'What the fuck?'

'I can't leave, I just can't!' I gasped, spinning around to see the two cars not fifty metres behind us. 'Oh, my God, oh, my God, they're right behind us!'

'Okay, calm down, just put your seatbelt on,' he instructed, thrusting the car into gear. I didn't need telling twice and plugged the belt in as I was forced back into the seat, the car accelerating at a speed that had to be illegal. My neck hit the headrest with a sickly click and my hands gripped the edge of the seat like there was no tomorrow, which my mind was screaming at me there would not be if we ploughed into a tree at this speed.

Quit complaining! If you didn't want to die you would of gone back home to Daddy! my voice screeched in an oddly high-pitched tone, telling me it was as freaked out as I was.

Kaspar's eyes were constantly flicking between his mirrors, the road and me, alternating between anger, concentration and concern, and self-consciously I reached up to wipe my tears away, but decided I wouldn't bother as we rounded another corner and my hands flew back to grip the seat.

'We just need to get to the borders of Varnley. It's only a couple of miles,' he muttered, more to himself than me but I nodded anyway, unable to speak as we powered around a corner, tyres screaming and protesting as the dial inched towards a hundred – an impossible speed for a human to cope with on a normal, nice road, let alone a narrow, winding road with trees like concrete poles each side.

'What cars are they driving?' he demanded as we approached a horrific bend, twisted like a hairpin. Spinning the wheel to the right we drifted ungracefully around the corner, earning him a scream on my part as my door passed a tree with eighths of an inch to spare.

'What cars?' he repeated, straightening the wheel and causing me to slam into the door.

'I don't know, do I?' I shrieked, barely even glancing in my mirror. 'It's bloody dark! Why does it matter anyway? Shouldn't you be concentrating on the road?'

'I want to know if we can outrun them,' he explained, rather too calmly considering the situation. 'I don't want to ditch my baby unless I have to.'

'Right, well . . .' I spun in my seat, straining against belt. 'They're black?'

'Never mind,' he grunted. 'Just don't panic.'

I barely had time to process those word spun around in *his* seat and was gla window, in the *opposite* direction of what we were speeding towards, hands steering of their own accord.

'Oh, my fucking—'

The rest of my sentence was drowned out as the engine roared and the car spun out of control around the bend, straight towards the trunk of a gigantic tree.

I screeched as I hit the side of the door again as Kaspar straightened the wheel, thrusting the car up a gear, engine whining. My head throbbed from the impact but I did not dare take my hands off of the seat as I swallowed my guts back down.

'Alfa Romeo. Two of them,' Kaspar groaned, flicking his head so his fringe flew out of his eyes.

'That's bad?'

'That's bad.'

'How bad?'

'Very bad. We can't outrun them. I guess we could keep driving until they broke down though,' he joked dryly. Just as he spoke there was an almighty roar from right behind us and glancing in the mirror I realized one of the cars was gaining, fast. He pressed down on the throttle and we shot forwards but the car behind only did the same, continuing to close the gap.

'We've ⌐   ot to get to the border,' he repeated, slowing
                     we rounded a tight bend and continued
                     action was enough; the car behind us
                     e I could blink he had drawn level
                     in that direction; gut feeling told
                     iles would face me.
                     red as the slayer's car drifted
                     single scratch on my baby!'
                     st before, it was nothing
                     oing now as the roar of

engines filled my ears. Screwing my eyes tightly shut I began praying to every deity alive for my life, feeling the car break the peak of a hill and begin soaring downwards.

'Not much further now . . . not much further now . . .' Kaspar muttered with furious determination, braking hard and taking a sharp left.

'I'm gonna die, I'm gonna die,' I whimpered, eyes still shut tight.

'No, you are not!' Kaspar grunted and I heard the car change down a gear.

'I'm gonna die! I don't want to die!'

'There, we're—'

'I'm going to die, I'm too young to die, I can't die; I haven't been to Disneyland yet!' I cried hysterically, hardly registering the fact that the car had slowed considerably.

'Vi—'

'I'm gonna die!'

'Girly! For the last time, you're not going to die! We're back! They're gone! They can't get through the border!' he yelled above my sobs, cutting the engine and slamming his hands down on the steering wheel.

'Huh?' I opened my eyes tentatively, beginning to loosen my grip on the leather of the seats. We were indeed back: the floodlights of the garage gleamed off the paintwork of the cars, the comforting howl of the wind as it passed through the hills of Varnley echoing in the distance.

'They're gone. It's okay,' Kaspar cooed in what he must have thought was a comforting tone.

'Oh God,' I muttered, burying my head in my hands, taking deep breaths and attempting not to hyperventilate. 'Oh God, I think I need a cup of tea.'

FORTY-THREE

Violet

The kettle whistled as I settled gingerly onto a bar stool, letting my head fall into my hands. I was shattered, overwhelmed and the shrill whistling echoed painfully in my head, filling the room with the jingling of the pans hanging on the walls.

Shuddering, but not from the cold, I heard the sound of the gas being killed and felt the steam rising as the water stewed, the vapour tickling the tip of my nose.

Raising myself up onto my elbows I watched as Kaspar ducked down beneath the counter, rummaging in a cupboard for a second, cursing, and then mumbling that he would be back in a minute.

Resting my head back on my arms I listened to the gentle rise of my chest in the unnatural silence, the occasional wisp of smoke escaping from the kettle – the only other sound that my hearing didn't filter out.

The sound of another's breath joined mine and I peered through my curtain of hair in time to see Kaspar returning, a dusty bottle of liquor cradled in his arms.

'Finest Scotch whisky, 1993, and the last bottle in the cellar, so don't tell Father, he's rather fond of his spirits.'

And there was me thinking they keep coffins in the wine cellar.

In one fluid moment he unscrewed the cap and took a swig, gulping a ridiculous amount down that would have a human on the floor in seconds – to a vampire it was about as intoxicating as lemonade.

'I said tea! Not whisky,' I said, sounding weaker than I had hoped.

He set the bottle down with a clad, eyeing me the whole time. Not bothering to add milk or sugar he passed me the steaming mug, sliding it across the counter that separated us. In a blink he was by my side, bottle in hand and taking the mug straight back from me.

'Trust me, after the day you've had you need a shot of this,' he said, pouring a copious amount into my tea whilst I watched dubiously. 'You look like you've seen a ghost. And it tastes fine, stop looking so disgusted.'

I took it hesitantly. Taking a large mouthful I almost spat it back out it; it was smoky and combined with the herbal taste of the tea, just plain disgusting. It left my mouth dry as I forced myself to swallow and within seconds I felt burning down my throat, which I was sure had nothing to do with the heat of the tea. The room did a somersault and to stop myself from swaying I focused on Kaspar, who was knocking back the remainder of the bottle whilst settling onto a stool and watching me with vague concern.

I set the almost-full mug down, still feeling like I was spinning. 'I think I'm just going to leave the rest of that.' Sliding around to face him, our knees brushing, it didn't feel like the potent stuff had done Kaspar's intended job. I rested my chin on my hands, closing my eyes and willing tears not to fall as they stung and threatened to leak, almost beyond my control. 'God.'

I had made my decision and I felt terrible. I had just abandoned my sick and vulnerable little sister as well as my family and friends, not to mention my education and the promise of a normal, burden-free life.

And what had I chosen instead? A Kingdom full of sick, twisted, manipulative creatures that feasted upon humans, and the Varns' handsome, if egotistical, fourth son; the very pinnacle upon which this secret world would one day revolve. *I must be out of my mind.*

Yet the thought that I could have left it all behind still made my heart clench; whether in gladness that I had stayed or in protest that I hadn't gone was unclear.

I groaned inwardly, collapsing onto the counter, all too aware of the figure stifling a snigger beside me; all too aware of the gaze of his striking eyes and the shallow, almost unnecessary rise and fall of his chest that I could just glimpse through the gaps between my strands of hair.

What the hell is happening to me?

I do believe the term applicable here is Stockholm Syndrome, my voice offered, smug, like it knew best. *You've become indoctrinated. Congratulations.*

I'm not a mindless idiot yet, I snapped back and I sensed that if my voice possessed a pair of shoulders, it would be shrugging them.

Not yet.

'What have I done?' I asked, not really directing the question at Kaspar, but rather voicing my thoughts aloud. 'I've abandoned Lily. I abandoned her and all for—'

'For what?' he cut in sharply. I raised my head from my arms to see that his eyes were grey again. 'Why didn't you go? You had a chance to be free but you just came running back!' With his change of tone, all feelings of confusion fled as something far more sinister crept in, clawing and dragging at my chest.

'You're angry,' I murmured in a perfectly flat tone, sliding off the stool and drawing myself close to him. He got up and folded his arms across his chest, creating space between us as I closed the gap. 'Why are you angry, Kaspar? You got what you wanted, didn't you? A human pet for a bit longer. Someone to torment and play with, to muck up and break like you do with everyone else, because you just can't take the fact that you're hurting inside. Just like your father.'

Even as the words flowed from my lips I could not believe I was saying them, but I knew that I couldn't stop now. *How dare he be angry? What does he have to be angry about?*

Nothing betrayed his emotions but the cool emerald of his eyes, frustratingly unaffected. His gaze followed me as I stopped with my face level to his chest, looking down and perceiving me through a gaze that could be used to scold a naughty child. His voice was slow and measured, like I needed the concept of his anger explained to me as though I was that ill-behaved child.

'I'm angry because I gave you that chance, Violet. I gave you what you had longed for. But you didn't take it. Now you're stuck here and you'll come to regret it—'

'I won't—'

'You will. But you've blown it now; you know that, don't you? That was your purpose: to remain human. But you've lost that now, so it's when not if.' He shook his head. 'I just don't know what to think of you now.'

I stood on my tip toes, drawing myself up to my full height and refusing to be intimidated by the eyes that were now flashing red.

'That is not true! At least I'm not as cruel as you. I've

never known what to think of you. One minute you care and the next you hate me. Make your bloody mind up like I did!'

I turned away but he caught me, grabbing my shoulders and whipping me back around.

'At least I have good reason to be like I am. You don't. Why did you choose to stay?'

I narrowed my eyes. 'Why do you care?'

'Why shouldn't I care?'

'Fine, I don't know why I stayed. I had a moment to decide and I didn't trust those slayers,' I snapped with my eyes to the floor, still trying to ignore the burn that his gaze caused, cursing my heart for faltering when he implied that he had some sort of regard for my welfare.

'You're not telling me the whole truth, are you?' I closed my eyes, knowing I could not lie on that front. He sighed, pulling me closer into his waiting arms as I watched his eyes fade to emerald. 'What are you running from, Girly?'

'It's more what I'm running to,' I mumbled into his chest, his cold arms wrapped tightly around my back, the sleeves of his shirt rolled up.

I felt him freeze against me. 'What?'

'This place isn't so bad. I guess I'm kind of attached to it.'

Knowing he could read my mind and discover the truth, I fortified my conscious, hiding everything he should not and could not know. He laughed softly at my ruffled and slightly indignant tone and I silently breathed a sigh of relief.

'I'll tell you a truth.' He held me tightly to him and it seemed stupid that we had been arguing just seconds before – yet Kaspar was one big argument. 'I'm glad you stayed, Violet. I need someone to torment.'

'Thanks. Your sadism is appreciated.'

He chuckled quietly, leaning his head gently on mine so

I could feel his breath. His hand gently played with my hair and I lost count of the minutes as he held me there, both of us it seemed just glad that the nightmare of London was over.

After a while I could stand it no longer and pulled back, settling onto a stool. I felt my cheeks go warm. Intimate was not a term usually applied to Kaspar.

'Will the others be angry with you about the cars?'

'No, they'll find something to amuse themselves with.' I shuddered, feeling the hairs on my neck stand up. 'They'll be back tomorrow morning with sappy grins on their faces.' He chuckled wryly and I was taken aback by his change in emotion; but not surprised by it.

'And you're stuck with me.'

I expected him to respond, at least with some witty comeback or snide remark, but instead he just stared into space.

'Kaspar?' He didn't answer. Resigning myself to wait I simply sat as the minutes fell away, sipping on the lethal remainder of my tea.

'Violet, I have something to tell you.'

My heart stopped. I knew the tone he used; it was the tone the consultant used when she called Lily and my parents to her blank room, or the tone the policeman used when I answered the door to find him with his hat in hand, asking to speak to my parents about Greg.

'*I'm so very sorry,*' they said; as if sorry, lots of sorry, and sitting down and cups of tea would undo what was already done.

I raised my eyes to meet his, fear and dread clutching at my mind, heart and liver, tears welling in my eyes because I knew this was not going to be anything good.

His eyes fell through to grey. 'I did something really stupid.' He looked down at the floor, slowly, ever so slowly, backing away. 'The inter-dimensional council heard how much I told you of this world on the way to London. They said I told you too much and I got angry and told them to fuck off.' My eyes went wide and I did not bother hiding a gasp. He carried on, not able to look me in the eye as I slid off the stool and began inching towards him. 'I humiliated the Kingdom and now you pay the price for my actions.'

My breath caught and my chest felt like it was collapsing. 'What do you mean?'

He didn't meet my eyes. 'From noon tomorrow I can't touch you.'

A lead weight fell upon my shoulders and my heart gave up, exploding, bursting like a balloon; my vision shattered and I grabbed the steel counter, supporting myself as my knees gave way.

'My father knows how I lust for you. So as punishment he won't let me touch you in any physical way. We're the only sane people left here, and he just ensured we lost each other. I'm so sorry, Violet, I really am, because now he will make your life hell and it's not your fault. I'm so sorry . . .'

'N-noon tomorrow?' I managed to choke. Already images of what the King could do were rushing through my head, sending chills up my spine.

'I won't ever let him hurt you, don't ever think that,' Kaspar growled and I felt a rush of air behind me as my stomach dug into the edge of the steel, breathing deeply and trying to make sense of what he had just told me.

He was inside my head . . .

'Noon?' I glanced at the clock on the wall as it inched around, far later than I thought, the hands striving to *touch* one another at twelve. Arms ensnared my waist and the cool of his chest against my back sent chills of a very different kind racing along my spine and around my ribs.

'I will never let anyone hurt you.'

I drew a sharp breath, hardly daring to believe my own thoughts but knowing that what was sending silky tendrils dancing along my skin was right, and as I spoke I fought to keep my breathing from becoming ragged.

'But *you're* the one that hurts me.'

He withdrew a little, loosening his grip and I felt his pain. Seizing the opportunity I whipped around, knowing this was my last chance before everything changed.

Never thought I'd see this moment, my voice said, full of the same breathlessness I felt as I looked up at him.

Neither did I, I replied.

'Girly?'

'I give up.'

'What?'

I took a deep breath. 'I give in to you.'

FORTY-FOUR

Violet

He said nothing. For one agonizing minute we remained frozen, paralysed, the only movement the rising and falling of his chest. For one agonizing minute, I could only hear the ticking of the clock, nearing midnight. *Tick, tock.* For one agonizing minute, I thought he would say no. But I could see the restrained desire in the way he tried to control his breathing, and the way his eyes warred between emerald and red.

'Kaspar, I want you. Right here. Right now. And I won't ask nicely more than once.'

He didn't reply, but his lips crushed to mine, ferocious, anxious, with urgency incomparable. I was thrust back into the counter, the small of my back pressed painfully against the edge, hands instinctively breaking my stumble with an ominous click. He moved with unrelenting force, pushing me further into the marble; yet I returned every movement he made, drawing his lips to mine until I let out a soft hiss against his flesh.

'You're crushing me,' I winced, trying to free my arm as his body pressed to mine.

Breaking away he muttered an awkward apology, allowing me space to breathe as I slowly massaged my wrist. I let out a giggle, the pause allowing the desire to fade and uncertainty to creep in. But that quickly wilted as he reached up and brushed a single strand of hair from my eyes, tucking it behind my ear. His unusually feather-light touch sent tingles dancing to the very tips of my fingers, ridding any previous doubts.

This is what I want. And this is my last chance to get it. After noon . . . that's it.

'Sorry, I forgot you're not . . . built for . . . this . . .'

I chuckled nervously. 'No one is built to be smashed against a solid object.'

He cocked a half-smile. 'Then I'll make sure,' he rested his hands on my outer thighs, 'That you're out of the way of the solid object.' Lifting me up and gently placing me onto the countertop, his lips claimed mine once more. Somewhere in the back of my mind I registered that the metallic taste of blood still lingered on them.

His tongue traced my bottom lip, begging for entrance which I gave gladly. My tongue traced the tips of his fangs, sharp, pointed, slightly curved like the thorns of a rose and he growled longingly; his carnal desires barely restrained by the little control he could exercise. I felt the pressure as he began to bite down and yanked away. But he just smirked, following me back until I lay flat to the counter; he jumped onto the counter, straddling me. I could see the rippled strength of his muscles even through his shirt, and I fought hard not to lift the material and run my hands across his skin.

He seemed to pause halfway to my lips and my heart leapt.

The longing, the lust, the need had been suppressed for too long; but that was overshadowed by my heart, giddy and drunk, like a girl soaking up the eyes of her first crush. There was a huge satisfaction as well: I was kissing Kaspar, yet there was none of that fake floating; those soaring high feelings I experienced every time Fabian had kissed me . . . *no, this . . . this is more than that*. That feeling was designed to lure prey and to take control of rational thought. But this *was* rational. *I want this.*

I took in his eyes, emerald, flecked with red, fighting his desire on so many levels. He took in mine, violet; violet as always.

He leaned down and I thought he would kiss me once more, but instead his lips brushed my ear and he whispered: 'Do you trust me?'

I smirked. 'Not in the slightest.'

'Then that . . .' I felt his weight shift, and he pressed into me further. His full weight now rested on me, and though not small or brittle, it hurt. But I smirked nonetheless. I could detect a definite bulge in the crotch of his trousers, and his breathing was only becoming shallower. '. . . could be a problem,' he finished, purring, actually *purring*, like a cat indulged by a new owner.

So quickly that I could not see, only feel, my arms were pinned above my head, both wrists grasped in one of Kaspar's hands. He smirked like a child that had been given a new toy (in fact, I was rather worried that was exactly what he was thinking) and began to trail the other hand down my side, tracing the indent just below my rib cage. The corners of my mouth twitched and I squirmed away.

'You see, because you have so adamantly resisted me for so long, I would like to have my own way. And twelve hours is not a very long time to have my own way . . . certainly not long enough to show you what you have been missing out on.'

His fingers brushed my side and I bit on my lip. 'Cocky much?'

He arched an eyebrow. Gently pressing me further into the counter, the hem of my top slid up, the cool marble chilling my skin. His hands skimmed across the exposed skin, the smile fading from his mouth. He ran his hands in slow circles, higher, caressing my skin in taunting strokes. My breathing was becoming ragged. I was not even sure if I was breathing – he wasn't.

His cold hands urged the grey material higher, until they slipped under, so close to my bra now I felt my cheeks redden. Abruptly and without warning, he hooked a finger under the wire; my breathing hitched expectantly.

A devilish smile that I mistrusted far more than his fangs appeared and I immediately felt uneasy, temporarily forgetting all functions relating to my lungs. His hands creeped back down and suddenly, he was tickling me.

I shrieked with laughter, throwing myself around and gaining a few bruises, trying to avoid the onslaught of his hands as he tickled every inch of skin he could get to whilst wrestling me so I would hold still. I thrashed and writhed, squirming under his touch until with a bang I landed in a heap on the floor, gasping. I gulped great mouthfuls of air, and sprang up, tripping my way across the room with exaggerated awareness until I stopped at the doorway, turning back.

He was propped against the counter, casually surveying me as he had done the very first time we locked gazes in Trafalgar Square. I should have felt fear then, yet I felt lust. My heart had beat for two, just as it did now. I wanted to move, but my muscles refused, itching and stiff but frozen.

I was trapped under his spell, prey in his eyes, gripping the doorframe for dear life as my legs turned to jelly.

Nothing had changed. I might have thought I knew him better, known every etched scar below his left ear, known his every emotion just from the colour of his eyes, but I didn't. I knew no more than I had done that first night. I knew the truth now; I knew what he was, but I did not know him. Hundreds of stolen glances I didn't even realize I had taken had taught me about his species, not him. But now I longed to. I longed to know him . . . and that was why I stayed. This predator had caught me from the very beginning.

I'm his now. I'm giving myself to him.

A burst of laughter spilled from my lips as I registered what I was thinking. *What on Earth would my (feminist) citizenship teacher think about that?*

He shook his head, a bemused smile forming at my ill-timed outburst. 'What?'

'I just . . . when I said I give in to *you*, I meant I'm giving into my desires.'

He nodded, thoughtfully, as though picking that sentence to pieces.

Giving into your desires is a sin, you know. Still think you have made the right choice? my voice hissed in my mind, in the sinister tone it reserved for when it knew it could plant doubt in my mind.

Suddenly, the lights flickered and my treacherous voice was veiled in shadows. The break of eye contact with Kaspar and the realization that all I could see in the darkness were two bright, blazing red orbs, returned feeling to my legs and I turned and fled down the corridor, the torches that lit this part of the mansion snuffing out, dead, as I heard his frenzied pursuit of me. I burst into the living room, padding across the carpet and dodging the pearly white sofas. Slipping into the entrance hall I stumbled back, marvelling at how quiet the place was, even quieter than usual, and that was saying something considering clocks could be heard chiming from the other side of the mansion in the silence. There were no Varns and none of the servants seemed to be around. The single butler who had startled as I entered bowed low, before disappearing into a side passage.

They weren't ignorant to the goings on of the royal family.

I whirled around, still backing away, feet squeaking on the marble floor. Vases, expensive-looking and delicate, held glass flowers, folded from the torch light; a small porcelain cupid perched on one leg beside a snowy vase, a silver plate engraved in Latin beside that. All these objects were familiar to me, yet I was so much more aware of everything . . . everything new and afresh, sending a giddy excitement through my stomach. What settled that stomach, however, was what should not be there: a magazine was slung across one of the marble-topped tables, the pages open to reveal the glossy orange petals of a Georgia O'Keeffe painting. Carelessly misplaced, it would usually be whisked away by a passing maid. *Not tonight.*

I didn't allow my eyes to linger on the magazine and instead caught sight of my reflection in the silverware. My cheeks were flushed, rosy and pink, and I could see my chest rapidly rising and falling, matching my shallow breaths. My eyes were even brighter than usual, glittering and moist and alive, but the thick eyeliner that rimmed them was beginning to slip, sinking my sockets and giving me the dark circled look of . . . I quickly rubbed it away. The long, loose top I was wearing too had slipped off my shoulders, exposing the top of my flimsy bra. I raised my arm to cover it, but was cut short by his sharp voice: an order, brutal in tone,

but a voice I knew just well enough to discern that it was
not a command but an invitation; a rough wooing.

'No. Leave it.'

I jerked my head up to see him leaning against the closed
door (which I never heard close), silently surveying through
those same eyes that made me blush. His arms were crossed
against his chest, and even from here I could see his nostrils
flaring . . . as they always did when he was angry. Or aroused.

'How do you do it?' he asked bluntly.

I turned away, walking slowly past the staircase and
absent-mindedly admiring the marble of the walls. The click
of my ankle boots echoed in the silence, the only sound,
save for my breathing.

'Do what?'

He did not answer for a while, but I could feel his stare
on my back.

'Enchant us. Every male vampire . . . we all lust over
you. Me, Fabian—'

'Ilta,' I added quietly, looking over my shoulder to gage
his reaction. He nodded his head gravely.

'You're a human, a dhampir. This desire shouldn't be so
powerful. Fabian shouldn't have fallen for you and Ilta . . .'
He trailed off, not finishing his sentence for which I was
grateful. But then, quietly, so quietly I guessed I was not
supposed to hear, he added, 'It shouldn't drive me to this.'

My blush deepened. I carried on, pretending not to hear.
Trailing my fingertips across the table that held the vase, I
searched for the dust that was not there.

'P-perhaps it's because I'm not like any other vampire girl
you've met. Your wealth and status means nothing to me.'
My finger brushed the marble walls, veined in black. 'I don't
look on you and Fabian as a Prince and a Lord. I treat you
no differently and I don't try like those whores you have.'

Thoughts of Charity entered my mind, and obviously his as I snuck a look at him just to see him turn his head away.

'Unlike the girls of this Kingdom, I want nothing from you but respect.' I spun around to face him. 'And I know I'm not like any other human you've met. I don't fall for your seductions, at least not unless I choose to and I can, and have, said no to you.' I forced my gaze to remain steady in my bold lie. I hadn't resisted. Not when Ilta had charmed me, not when Fabian had kissed me, and not earlier in the car with Kaspar. 'And any man, human or vampire or otherwise, will always want what he can't get.'

In the blink of an eye, maybe quicker, he was there. His arms came to a rest either side of my head, palms flat to the wall, his hands large enough to wrap around my neck, strong enough to snap it in a heartbeat. My breathing hitched but I didn't even try to hide it. Just the thought of seeing such a creature . . . *knowing, such a creature . . . God, he's sexy. Dark, perverse . . .*

Somewhere deep within my mind I registered this wasn't right. This wasn't what I should think about him. Yet his eyes narrowed, like he knew my thoughts and was daring me to think otherwise; I sucked in another breath to remain upright and I would sigh from longing, if I had any breath left to. But no, he had stolen that too, along with my heart and resolve.

He leaned yet closer, arms taking his weight, muscles barely flexing under the strain. I reluctantly closed my eyes as his lips inched closer, the cool of his torso the opposite of my flushed, heated chest, rapidly rising and frustrated with the composure of his breaths, neither shallow nor ragged any more. Suddenly, in one swift motion he had grabbed both of my wrists in one of his hands and twisted them painfully above my head, pinned to the wall. I let out a faint whimper; but that was muffled as his lips, briefly, teasingly, brushed my own, and I felt sure he would be able to feel me melt and remould beneath him.

His kisses continued along my cheeks and my jaw until his fangs found my ear, nipping gently.

'But I already have you,' he murmured. I considered nodding, but that wasn't right either. He grabbed the belt of my jeans, roughly pulling me into him. I opened my eyes in surprise, but he just tugged me closer, his arm so close to my head I would curl into it if I had the nerve, but his eyes burnt 'move and this is over'. Without shifting his gaze he reached down for my top, seizing it and pulling.

I knew I would soon lose it, but there was no mercy in those eyes as he gathered the material high enough to reveal my bra, the long scars disappearing beneath the material. Not breaking his hold of me, he reached for my breasts, cupping and engulfing one in his hands.

A curse tripped to my lips and I remembered I should breathe, but it was futile, pointless, and I stopped bothering completely as I tried to tell him to be gentler, but it only came out as a pined moan, his forefinger beginning to drag my bra aside, grazing my nipple.

His eyes never left mine as I fought to keep them open, his sadistic smirk enjoying the sight of the inner conflict which I knew was painting itself on my face: doubt, mixed with want.

'Oh my, what – I – please forgive the intrusion, Your Highness!'

My eyes sprung open. There, open-mouthed at the tiny entrance to a servant corridor beneath the staircase was Annie, the maid. Her eyes were fixed on me, pinned to the wall by my wrists, his hand unmoved from my breast. I flushed deepest red, and went to pull his arm away but he held fast. Without turning to her he half-spat at her to leave, to which she quickly curtsied, never taking her eyes off us.

'Your Highness. Miss Lee.'

'For God's sake, just go!' he snapped, his teeth grinding together in a grimace of impatience as I watched her back away, trying to plead an apology to her with my eyes. Her expression of utter disgust did not change.

'It's ridiculous. Can't I get any privacy around here?' he growled, and with a flick of his wrist, my hand was in his and he was leading me towards the stairs.

It seemed an age since I had been in Kaspar's room. It still sent the same sensations creeping across my skin, not over-shadowed by my growing need or anxiety. But the eagerness and zeal I possessed earlier had gone, and gone far.

He let me wander into the room ahead of him, allowing me to take everything in. The bed, dark and imposing, loomed in the centre of the room and I had the sudden urge to avoid it – instead I skirted around, aware of the muffled silence of my footsteps on the once-plush, now faded, rug, and the contrast as I stepped onto the wooden floor. It was cold too, really cold, and the difference was extreme, like when you step from a hot bath onto a tiled floor. It hit me in one great wave, moving from my toes up, and I had the sudden chaotic thought that I might turn blue. I wanted to laugh at that crazed moment, but I still had not claimed my breath back from Kaspar. Instead, I shook it off and wrapped my arms around my middle, half from the chill, and half from the fear.

The little light that lit the room came from the moon, a day or two from full as it shone through the French doors, flung open to reveal the balcony. Like a moth to a lamp I was drawn to it, watching my shadow grow in the small rectangle of light. A gentle wind stirred the tethered drapes and I inhaled it gratefully – the room was bitter with the scent of heavy, rich colognes that burnt my throat and the musk of old, ageing wood.

I shivered. The view was magnificent over the gently sloping lawns and trees of the estate, but I had little reason to admire it, especially as I startled at the sound of a lock clicking. *Clicking shut.* I whirled away from the grounds.

He was resting against the door, one hand holding a small silver key. He raised it in his hand and it disappeared beneath his palm as he clenched his fingers. 'I'm not going to let you say no this time, Girly.' With that, he threw it straight outside.

It flew past, whizzing, sending a jab of exhilarated fear into my chest and as I heard it drop on the gravel beneath the balcony, I wondered just what monster I had unleashed, and what monster I was now locked in a room with. And what monster, frankly, I was about to shag.

I met his eyes; mine were wide from shock and a strange alien thrill. He chuckled, his eyes shining in the gloom, warring between emerald and red, beckoning me closer. I could not move. Instead he came to me, prising my arms apart as I tried to wet my lips. He didn't give me the chance. He reached for my T-shirt and tore it off, his lips crushing against mine in a deep, long, passionate kiss that left me greedy as he stepped back, his gaze sinking past my breasts, the flimsy bra and my now-bare stomach, to his next prize.

His hands went straight for my jeans – he growled something about the inconvenience of women's clothes – and I automatically kicked off my little ankle boots, knowing there was little else I could do, especially when he slapped my hands back as I tried to undo his shirt. All I could do was stand there, ragdoll, as he undressed me with unsuppressed desire and thirst, like a child ripping the packaging off a present at Christmas.

'Damn, you're beautiful, Girly.'

He stepped back and I flinched, surprised at such unwilling and impulsive praise. My eyes hit the floor, embarrassed at standing there in nothing more than my underwear – *God, why didn't I wear matching?* – whilst he remained fully clothed. I shivered, wrapping my hand around my neck and covered the hideous scars Ilta had given me not so long ago.

If the King hadn't forbidden you to touch, you wouldn't want this; you know that, don't you? my voice hissed, emerging from behind my previous thought. *But you're curious about his true touch, aren't you, Violet?*

I ignored it.

He stepped forward once more, brushing my arm aside and beginning to suck gently on my neck, never piercing the skin. I wrapped my arms around his neck, trying to pull him closer as I got greedier and greedier, needing his touch. He complied, one hand creeping under the wire of my bra, his fangs tugging on my skin. He clutched at my breast, his cold hands only heightening every sense as I pressed my chest into his waiting hand, arching my neck, exposing my vein . . .

He took the bait, his fangs piercing my skin so painfully I would have screamed if I had not been gasping as he tugged on my nipple. But he did not take any blood. Instead, he sunk his fangs in further up my neck, tugging on my nipple yet again . . . and again . . . and again, until I was a gasping, moaning mess in his arms. He lapped at the little blood that leaked from the already healing wounds, pulling me upright with a triumphant smirk.

'There's more where that came from, Girly,' he murmured, and I reached up, trying to undo his tie. But my hands were shaking too much from the cold and I couldn't do it. He didn't help. Instead, he picked me up, half-throwing me onto the bed, where I lay sprawled, scrabbling up, the ticking of the clock the only sound, save for my frantic breathing and his, rapidly speeding up.

He loosened his tie, tugging at it with one finger. It fell about his shoulders, resting across his shirt as button at a time he cast that off too, revealing his pale torso. Sitting on the bed beside me, his hands reached behind my back and expertly unhooked my bra. It fell away and he threw it aside, making me flush deep red – not that it seemed to matter as he smiled that half-smirk of his, one hand cupping my cheek, the other my breast. I reached up and kissed him as my hands trailed across his muscular arms, admiring their strength, knowing I shouldn't, knowing they caught prey; broke necks. His ego enjoyed my touch and he smirked into the kiss, placing his hand on my stomach, flatter than it had been a few months ago – too flat – and allowed it to slip down, pulling aside the elastic of my panties.

Suddenly, he sat up, straddling my legs, eyes examining every inch of my skin as though looking for faults. I flushed under the intensity of his stare – I could see the red lust overwhelming his eyes. I fidgeted, trying to cover the hideously silver scars, but quick as a flash my arms were pinned to the sheets above my head. Again.

'Don't.' His eyes scolded me, as though he was angry with me for being ashamed. Shame wasn't in his repertoire.

Yet it was prominent in mine. My body was rigid – legs tight together, breathing so shallow my chest did not rise and fall – as one of his hands started to flow over my stomach in a torturous circle, getting closer and closer to the burning sensation rippling up my thighs to my breasts and back down again.

'Relax,' he muttered, frustrated. His words were a command, not a request, and his tone almost made me push him away, stung by his insensitivity.

Relax? Does he not understand how difficult this is?

He kissed me again, his tongue seeking entrance, knowing that it would distract me, I suspected – *How could he do that?*

My arms slid over his back once more and curled around his neck, grabbing his tousled hair before changing my mind and letting my hands slide down his chest to the waistband of his jeans. I undid the buckle of his belt and he stilled, smacking my hand away and giving me the don't-move-or-else look for a second time. My eyes silently pleaded but he returned to kissing my collarbone and then the flat plane of my chest, before kissing and nipping his way to the mounds.

I gasped softly when his tongue passed over my nipple and even louder when he moved to the neglected one and continued his so-near painful onslaught there. He trailed his way down the valley of my breasts and kissed my scars – I wished he wouldn't – before moving on, not allowing me time to think or freeze. He trailed over my ribs and down my stomach, forcing me to suppress a giggle.

And then I felt him breathe softly over my thighs and I shivered violently, my nerves beyond alert. He kissed one thigh and I felt my muscles recoil under his lips, failing to escape. His hand then squeezed my other thigh, prising them apart. I wanted to moan so badly but refused to – couldn't – then as I screamed, a slash of pain ripping across my thigh – absurd pain: fangs tearing through sinew.

I groaned, tears pricking my eyes, gasping as I felt his tongue lapping at my blood, mixed with my own arousal. But then his grip on my thighs disappeared and he was above me, his red eyes gleaming in victory, his lips shining.

He bent down and kissed me and I licked his lips, feeling a chuckle rumble in his chest.

'You'd make a good vampire. You seem quite keen to taste all kinds of liquids.'

I smiled guiltily in reply. I could say nothing else. Words seemed to be losing their meaning. My hands made their way to his jeans again and I unzipped them, the belt already undone. He did nothing but press harder against my body.

It is my choice . . .

Abruptly, I felt his weight disappear and looked up and blushed deeply. Kaspar was even hotter naked – if that was even possible – and he was smirking at me, waving a condom box around, a little square of paper attached.

'Yours, I believe?' he growled, but there was humour in his voice. I reached up with my hand and took it from him, reading the note scrawled across the creased sheet.

'Always use protection, sucker!'

I laughed as I remembered how I had stolen all of his condoms and ruined them when I had first arrived here. Looking back, it was hard to believe I had the pluck to do such a thing so early on.

He raised his eyebrows, ripping a packet open. 'Surely you're the sucker in this relationship?'

I mocked an affronted scowl. 'Has anybody ever told you that your bedroom manner is atrocious?'

He chuckled, reaching down and pecking me on the lips. 'You can't blame a guy for asking.'

Shocked by the sudden, tender intimacy I stumbled over my words. 'I – fine . . . maybe later then.'

The red glint in his eyes that had begun to fade as he pulled the condom on gleamed bright again. 'I'll hold you to that.'

I felt his familiar weight on top of me, and he stared at

me a while, the tension in the air growing. I smirked but it was a façade: inside I was a nervous wreck.

He slammed his lips against mine and kissed me harshly as he slid in.

I felt the beads of sweat fanning out across the back of my neck, feeling the sheets dampen, hearing my occasional gasps and moans interweave with his grunts. It was a strange mix of pleasure and pain, and I wasn't sure which took precedent until a wince that became a cry escaped my lips and angst emerged from the desire in his eyes. Slipping a hand beneath my spine, he rolled over, pulling me on top, never breaking contact even for a moment.

He didn't move as I straddled him, regaining courage and knowing that he had finally relinquished the control he was so fond of. Briefly, very briefly, I wondered if he had ever allowed Charity the same, feeling my heart sink as I desperately hoped I was not what she had been to him: a whore; just another fling.

My thoughts did not remain there long as his hand slipped between my thighs, the other reaching for my breast, and the pleasure took over; I reached down, running my lips over his throat, tugging my teeth across his neck, knowing how different things would be if I could take blood. The gasps became moans as I sat back up, watching in satisfaction as his eyes fluttered shut and my own stomach fluttered in suspense of what I knew was coming as one hand joined the second between my thighs; hearing his groans my jaw locked as I gritted my teeth against a final moan, collapsing onto his chest as a searing pain shot along the lowest part of my throat, stars forming in front of my eyes. I felt myself slump against the hands engulfing my neck, before darkness intruded upon my thoughts.

*   *   *

It might have been minutes later, maybe hours when I came around. The room was a blur and I could feel the stiffness already forming in my limbs. I let out a shaky breath, hardly daring to smile as I rolled over to find him on his side, watching me and playing with a strand of my hair, twisting it in his fingers.

'I knew I was good, but no one's ever passed out on me before,' he said, smirking, his tongue running across one of his fangs.

'And in fairness, I don't think I've ever been bitten whilst climaxing before,' I retorted, rubbing my forehead, which was thudding as my eyes adjusted to the moonlight. I didn't have the energy to properly argue that it was more likely the bite which had caused me to black out.

He chuckled, his smirk growing triumphantly. 'I did tell you I would show you a good time.'

I smiled. Settling onto my back and staring up at the dark ceiling I sunk into the relaxed, almost numb state I had craved all those months back before the London Bloodbath, when the clubs had been my hunting ground.

But nothing . . . I mean nothing, could compare to Kaspar . . . and I would never feel it again, considering that in just a few hours the King would return and impose his new rule on touching. My heartstrings tugged, and I felt the tears well. I blinked them back, hoping he was not watching me.

'She would have liked you.'

I turned to him, confused. He was looking straight ahead, his eyes, a mix between emerald and misty grey, fixed on the painting above the fireplace.

'They're your parents, aren't they?'

He nodded. 'This was their room, right up until she died.' On the last word his voice broke and I instinctively took his hand, moulding myself to his chest and nestling up to him, trying to ignore the coolness of his skin. I was stunned though and trying to hide it. I had never heard him mention his mother in this way.

'She'd be proud of you.'

He turned to me, looking as though he wanted to laugh but his eyes betrayed him. They were grey. 'Proud of me for what? I'm heir to the throne but I don't want it, I hate responsibility and I fail miserably at everything a Prince should be, apart from being handsome. What the fuck is there to be proud of?' His nails dug into my skin, but I don't think he noticed. I winced quietly, hiding it.

'You're a good man. Look at how many times you've saved me – what's it, four times now? And you were prepared to suffer the wrath of the council and your father for letting me go home. It has to say something!'

'It doesn't. What's made you go all saintly forgiving anyway? I'm pretty sure you thought I was a sick, evil creature a while back.'

I averted my gaze away from the painting. 'Situations change,' I mumbled.

He glanced at me and I caught his puzzled expression. I thought he might press the matter, but he didn't to my relief and we lapsed back into silence. He began absent-mindedly fiddling with a strand of my hair again. Neither of us seemed to mind the quiet, both content to be in the other's arms.

Is that what he really hides behind the mask? A worry that he's not good enough?

'Why did your father move out of here? I mean, I know it would have been—'

He interrupted. 'He was driving himself mad in here. He couldn't take it. I know you think my father is cold-hearted and cruel, but it wasn't always so. She completed him. She made him good. That's possible, you know. You can make bad men good. When she . . . it ruined us . . . that night in Trafalgar Square . . . there was no need for us to even attack them, do you understand that, Girly? But it was his son – Pierre's son, Claude, that is – and I had to kill him. I had to take him away from his father like his father took my mother. The bastard!' I closed my eyes to banish the sting of tears, knowing I had more than overstepped the mark, hating myself for bringing it up and making him burst like this; hating him for reminding me of that night. I wrapped my arms right around his chest, hugging him close as he continued.

'My father as good as died with her that day. And John Pierre just sent us a message saying he was ordered to do it – paid to do it. And we'll never know who gave him that order. But I'll find out . . . I'll hunt him down, kill his love first, suck his children dry, rape his daughters, make the fucking heartless demon suffer. Because I more than hate him, Violet. He took my mother away.'

He fell into silence then, leaving me with dry lips and loosening arms. I was that daughter.

Rattle, rattle . . .

I threw up huge barriers around my mind, letting his horrific words sink in. I desperately wanted to tell him not to say such things – to take it all back, because he didn't mean it, he *couldn't* mean it – but I knew pushing the subject was far too risky.

'None of this matters. You'll be just as great as your father was before all this, despite what you say. I know you will,' I whispered into the dark. He did not answer, only pulling my hand up to rest on his chest where his heart should be and I soon slipped into sleep.

FORTY-FIVE

Tick, tock . . .

  'They know.'

  'What?'

  'They know we slept together. The servants told them.'

  'But—'

  'My father knows.'

  My breath caught, fear rising along with bile in my throat.
'She betrayed us. Annie betrayed us.'

  He nodded gravely, pulling me into his arms.

  'But what will he do?'

  'I don't know.'

  You don't want to know, my voice added. I silently agreed.
His wristwatch glinted in the light from the high windows
of the entrance hall where we waited.

  11:59 . . .

  The air was cold, the servants and members of the household assembling behind us in a long row, waiting to welcome
the Varns and the entire council; every member of which

knew. Fabian knew; Cain knew; the King knew. I felt the heated glares of the servants on my back, feeling their hate and disrespect, everything ounce of respect lost. I was one of *them* now in their eyes. *Whore.* I was his hostage. I was never meant to *know* the Prince. Especially not now.

Tick, tock . . .

'This Athenea is where they're coming back from right? S-shouldn't you let me go?'

He released me from his arms, but kept one hand in mine. 'Listen, Violet. Girly. I'm sorry about last night. I should never have—'

'Me too.' He seemed taken aback, but I nodded furiously, avoiding eye contact. I pulled my hand from his, feeling my heart squeeze painfully.

'I—' Suddenly his head shot up, his eyes blazing red, his nose flaring. 'They're here.'

He snatched my hand back and lifted my chin with the other, planting a soft kiss on my lips. He let me down and I felt my knees go weak I was so sore and stiff. And then I was stood on the other side of the room, breathless, wind knocked from my lungs, tossed away by Kaspar.

Tick, tock . . . Deep from within the mansion a great boom sounded; the first strike of a great clock and I counted each one, unable to block out the sound.

Twelve . . . I shuddered as the sound passed through me, my stomach churning with nerves. I wanted to cry but refused to in front of the servants.

Eleven . . .

The butlers stood beside the doors, immaculately clean gloves poised on the handles, ready to swing them open.

Ten . . . The dread and the horror was rising as my mind raced, reeling at what the King could possibly do to punish such disobedience; things never would have turned out well if we had slept together under different circumstances, but now on the eve of such anger, when Kaspar had already thrown so much shame upon his father, I didn't dismiss anything.

Nine . . .

What can he do to me that will be worse than not allowing the two of us to touch?

Eight . . .

He can't force me to become a vampire without giving my father an excuse to call upon the slayers and rogues. Turning doesn't seem so horrific now anyway.

Seven . . .

Why did I waste all that time hating him?

Six, five, four . . .

'Kaspar, what's Athenea?'

Three . . .

He didn't answer.

Two . . .

'Kaspar, what lives in Athenea?'

One.

The doors were flung wide open, the high noon sun masked by towering clouds. A group of thirty or so cloaked figures strode up the steps, flinging their hoods back and almost instantly becoming pink under the daylight, skin burning.

Furious at their head was the King, and I glanced at Kaspar, fear holding a vice-like grip on my heart. He stared straight ahead, passed the gathering crowd, all glaring at the both of us, his expression fixed and detached.

I felt a tear trickle down my cheek and turned back. The figures were gone. My eyes searched the room but I was cut off as the King came towards me, his eyes afire and raging. I let out a meek whimper as he came to a halt. I wanted to run. Instead, I curtsied.

His head turned towards Kaspar, eyes still fixed straight ahead but cringing now.

'Kaspar!' He did not speak the words. He hissed them. 'Go to Varns' Point. I will talk to you there.'

Then he turned to me.

'Do not touch my son again, Miss Lee, or I will ensure you never hear your heart beat again. Is that clear?'

When I did not respond he shouted, 'Answer me!'

I nodded, choking, holding back tears.

'You are not stupid. You realized that you were to never become involved with any of my children.' His mouth set in a firm line. 'This is the end of your freedom, Miss Lee. The end. And as a symbol of the end, I think we've found the perfect sacrifice at Ad Infinitum. Don't you think?'

Kaspar hissed and I raised my head. He immediately fell silent and steadily held my gaze with an intensity that took my breath away. And then he was gone. Yet again.

'Slut,' a voice hissed.

Lyla, hand in hand with Fabian stood in front of me, smug smile dirtying her face. She clung onto him – he refused to look at me but as she tugged him on I heard him mutter one word.

'Bitch.'

They all hated me now.

FORTY-SIX

Violet

I mentally kicked myself as I realized I was thinking about that day again, the events replaying themselves endlessly in my mind. I could still feel the bitter breeze around my ankles and the soreness around my legs, every word analysed; every thought churned over and every detail remembered.

It was almost two weeks ago, let it go, my voice advised and I was inclined to agree. Yet however much I wanted to, I couldn't.

Kaspar has been gone for two weeks. You try letting go.

My hands gripped the sheets of my bed again and I stared at the ceiling, reciting words that had become engraved on my mind.

'*Vampires were not gentle, loving creatures. It was not in their nature to change, or to adapt, to accept others. Their love is not what humans would call love, and lust consumes them on a level we will never understand. They do not grow old as we do, but age as stone does: they gradually weather, slowly perish, so slowly it is unnoticeable. But in the end, stone is a fixture forever, as are they.*'

Kaspar had become a fixture in my heart. I thought the King could not punish us any more than not allowing us to touch. But he had.

October had given way to November, the trees in the grounds bare now. But the forest was as dark as ever and tomorrow came the promise of yet more torture: tomorrow was the twelfth, and the twelfth meant it was Ad Infinitum.

I was the sacrifice. I had learned the steps and the dress had been measured and made. I had met John, the other sacrifice. He was a quiet guy, turning at Christmas to be with his love, Marie-Claire. That was the strange thing about sacrifice. It could be done for love – or for hate.

I played along at being the sacrifice, learning my part like a nice little human, but for one reason only: it was the only way I would be allowed to go to the ball, and Kaspar would have to return to attend. *Return from wherever he is.*

Wiping my dry eyes I swung my legs over the side of the bed, dragging the corner of the sheet with me. I grabbed a comb off the bedside table and ran it through my hair, ragged and knotted from almost endless days spent in this room, avoiding the rest of the house. That seemed to suit them just fine; nobody ever talked to me, save for Cain, who had lately picked up an annoying habit of asking about my family – particularly Lily. Always Lily. I couldn't take that.

So it was just me and my voice.

For a moment I wondered whether it was really worth going downstairs, but I was hungry and could hear loud talking. Pulling on a pair of socks from the wardrobe I quietly slipped out, creeping down the corridor. Just a few feet beyond my room I swallowed hard. *Kaspar's door.*

I had not gone near or in that room since that night. It was only two weeks, yet I was curious – I felt as though something must have changed inside, as though the room could not remain the same without its master.

A stupid thought, but I was having them with increasing vigour.

In contrast, at the forefront of my mind was a thought of a totally different nature. Try hard as I might, I could not stop thinking about Kaspar's naked body pressed to mine, or his firm grasp of me or his demanding, controlling nature that secretly, I sort of liked – although I would never admit it to his face. I could still reignite the perverted thrill that had shocked my system when he had thrown the key from the open doors, leaving me trapped.

My hand was already pushing the door to his room open when my mind caught up. Somehow I thought that not touching Kaspar included not going in his room. Which it probably did, but I *had* to look; I *had* to know.

The door shut quietly behind me and I took a deep breath before raising my eyes. The room was unusually light, winter sunlight flooding through the French doors. The dark drapes were thrown back and tethered, the sheets tucked beneath the mattress and the pillows straightened. Gone was the scent of cologne and the air was not tainted by the smell of blood either. Dustsheets covered most of the furniture, blanketing the room in white. The sheets were soft as my bare feet trod on them, cold too, like cotton snow.

Deep in the pit of my stomach, something ached.

I felt tears welling in my ears and back-pedalled, wanting the comfort and safety of my own room. But I stopped as something glistened in the corner of my eye. My steps slowed and I wiped my eyes. There on the mantelpiece, below the picture of Kaspar's parents, was a necklace.

I glanced towards the door, afraid someone might come bursting through. But all was silent and the shouting voices had faded. So cautiously I took a step forward, and then another, and another. I refused to look at the painting; the intensity of the eyes of the oiled figures was unnerving on a good day, and today was not good.

My feet ventured onto the cold flag of the foot of the fireplace and I stood on my tiptoes so I was level with the mantel. The necklace was coated in a fine layer of dust, tiny flakes clinging to the fine chain on which the pendant hung. It was placed on a piece of thick, heavy paper, which I ignored.

Gently lifting it, I stared in amazement as it caught the light – tiny, tiny lines of emerald engraved into the silver. It was a rose dripping with blood, a small V beneath: the royal coat of arms. In the centre was a minute emerald stone. I let it fall into the palm of my hand, gazing at its beauty. I was no expert, but something so extraordinary and delicate must be worth thousands.

Lifting it again, I gasped. It had fallen open and inside it there were eight miniatures, each enclosed by an equally small frame. *A locket.*

I instantly recognized the figures inside. It was the King and Queen and each of their children, eldest to youngest, sandwiched in-between. I flicked through the tiny frames, each suspended and strung together by hinges like spiderwebs.

I lifted it up to the light again, mesmerized as it spun on the chain. Behind it I could see the large painting that unnerved me so much, the scarily lifelike figures of Kaspar's mother and father, the King and Queen, staring down at me. But something caught my eye. Around the Queen's neck was an identical silver pendant, a jewel set in the centre.

I looked back at the locket in my hand, realizing that what I held belonged to the late Queen.

Lowering it I snatched the paper it had been placed upon, unfolding it and taking a moment to examine the broken royal seal. It was a letter, written in an elegant, curled hand. I quickly scanned the first few lines.

'Dear sweet Beryl,
*   First, I must ask how you and Joseph are? It truly has been far too long since we last met . . .'*

I did not need to read any more to know what the rest contained. It was the same letter from the King's study. Yet here it was, the Queen's final letter, weighed down by her locket in Kaspar's room. I admired it; still open, spinning and spinning . . .

The dream began differently that night. Usually it started almost peacefully, as though joining the mysterious cloaked man was an escape. It probably was – his thoughts seemed to revolve around liberty and being free of whatever restraints he hated so much.

Yet this night, I had to first endure tortured images. Kaspar and the locket I had left in his room swirled in my mind, more faces and voices and sound than actual images. Above it all, I could hear a clock striking twelve, and then nine, and then six, like it worked in reverse. But soon – not soon enough – the scene switched and was replaced with the thoughts of the King's rogue informant and the familiar forest.

Even thought was an effort and the cloaked figure yearned to enter the trance-like state that was as near to sleep as a vampire could get, but he would not allow himself. He *had* to return in time for the Ad Infinitum ball. He would not miss it.

His cloak billowed in his wake, the hem trailing in the moist ground. November and its damp air had descended quickly and he knew the humans felt the sudden drop in temperature. *Winter is approaching.*

Suddenly, he caught the unmistakable smell of a slayer through the dampness and in the blink of an eye they had taken to the trees. Creeping forward, he moved from branch to branch, inching towards the hideous smell, and as they got closer, voices.

'We want no more excuses, slayer. You can tell your precious Lee that unless he chooses to attack soon, we will have no more to do with him. We've waited long enough.'

Now this was an interesting meeting.

'Lee needs a reason to attack to ensure the Prime Minister's backing. So far he hasn't had one.'

'Perhaps you will change your mind when you have heard us out, slayer.'

The slayer, high-ranking judging by his dress and the array of weapons that hung from his belt, leaned forward into the light from the moon. 'I very much doubt that.'

The rogues, six of them in total shuffled. One sat further forward than the rest and seemed to be the spokesmen. He continued.

'Have you heard of the Prophecy of the Heroines?'

The slayer leaned back again. 'Of course.'

'And are you familiar with the first verse?'

The slayer simply nodded this time. The cloaked figure, high up in the canopy, sat rigid.

'And do you believe it?'

The slayer grunted, half-groaning his reply. 'It's a load of destiny crap made up by Athenea. Not worth your time or mine.'

The vampire smiled. 'Then perhaps you should reconsider that too.'

The slayer chuckled. 'Why should I? I do not buy into fate, and besides, what does this have to do with Lee?'

The rogue stood up. 'Everything, because the Varns don't know yet.' He turned away, scraping at the bark with a long, withered fingernail. The vampires around him shifted uncomfortably, rising too, almost as though ready to flee.

'Know what?'

'I thought it wasn't worth your time, slayer?'

The slayer's face was contorted with curiosity and he half-rose from his log. 'Spit it out, vampire, or I'll ensure my stake meets your chest!'

The rogue chuckled darkly, gouging out a large chunk of bark and tossing it to the floor.

'They've found the Sagean girl of the first verse. The Prophecy is true.'

The vampires began to move away, already swallowed by the darkness, save for their leader.

'*What*?'

The rogue stopped, turning slowly, his lifeless skin illuminated by the half-moon.

'They have found the first Dark Heroine. But after all, you don't believe it, so don't trouble yourself. We'll let Lee know before Ad Infinitum is over.' He smiled, like the thought amused him, and then turned and ran.

There was total silence in the trees for a full minute, as everything became frozen. Even the birds in their nests did not squawk at such a statement.

So it's true. Athenea had been right all along.

The cloaked figure leapt from the tree, dropping to the ground as a black blur. He had to get to Varnley. But first, he would feed.

The slayer did not have time to turn or draw his stake before the vampire dove on his back, pulling him to the ground. Fangs sank deep into the flesh of his neck and his expression twisted into one of agony, before it pacified.

Blood seeped from his lips and onto the ground as he tossed the body aside and ran.

The cloaked figure knew if he was swift he might reach the border before the sun rose, perhaps even a little before.

The King has to know. The Prophecy of the Heroines is true. The second verse rang in his mind, carved into every being save for the humans of this dimension. The first had been found. The vampires were next.

FORTY-SEVEN

Violet

Tonight was Ad Infinitum. Tonight, I was the sacrifice.

I wrapped my arms tight around myself. It would not be long now. John stood beside me, hands clasped behind his back as we both leaned against the wall, just waiting. The doors to the entrance hall were thrown wide open, the butlers stood silently beside several footmen dressed in their smartest black and silver uniforms, complete with powdered wigs.

My legs were bare, as were my arms and shoulders. The tattered, fraying white dress hardly provided warmth – it was made from layers of a scratchy, rough material and coarse lace, held up only by thin straps. It fell to just above my knees, with my feet encased in flimsy white ribbon and petite little ballet-like shoes, which made my enormous feet seem to shrink.

My hair fell about my shoulders, left to dry naturally, just as instructed on the card left in my room that morning. It fell in waves, frizzy and unkempt and beginning to form ringlets. I wore no jewellery, no perfume and no make-up.

'I hate waiting,' John said. It was a simple enough state-ment, but it cut through the air like a knife.

'I hate this.' I barely muttered the words, but he heard.

'So do I, and I don't get bitten like you.' This man, almost twenty years my senior, was clearly afraid of the family I would wager his love had taught him to fear. Already his loose linen shirt was sticky with sweat and his face was flushed. He wiped his brow, leaning against the marble wall. 'At least I have a reason for being here. You—'

'Are being punished? Yeah, I know.' Again I chuckled awkwardly. 'But it means I have a chance to see those who still don't think I'm scum.' I shrugged my shoulders, eyes focused on the door that would soon open.

'I'm sorry.'

That I did not expect. I stood up straighter. 'For what?'

He did not answer straight away as footsteps, echoing, were heard from the corridor that led deeper into the mansion. They faded again.

'For them treating you like this.'

My fists clenched. 'I'm used to it.'

'You shouldn't have to be.'

I had no answer to that, especially as the doors to the ballroom began to open, sending a surge of nerves through the pit of my stomach. I blinked a few times – the light of a thousand flickering candles lit the massive room – some burning blue, others orange. Black drapes framed the cathedral-like windows, the view through each pane of glass just as dark. The white marble of the walls, flecked with gold was cast in shadow, the tall pillars seeming to stretch into forever above the thousands of vampires – and it was thousands, all still. Perfectly, eerily still. Some were frozen in dance, some with drinks in hand, some poised to descend the stairs of the balcony that we would soon walk.

They all wore the colours and livery of their families, dark colours, mostly; immaculate make-up and smoked eyes, feathers, beads and withering lilies entwined in the hair of the women, swords hung at the hips of the men.

Waiters, frozen too, balanced trays carrying flutes of a red liquid that could only be blood, some tiny squares of raw, fleshy meat. Like the butlers, they also wore powdered wigs, stark against the gloom of the room.

But more stunning were the flowers tumbling in chains from the ceiling – roses, black roses with white leaves, strung together and hung from the beams far above the frozen spectacle below. They grew down the pillars and the far walls, some even wrapped around the King's black throne. Rows of them decorated the tables upon which punch bowls and wine bottles sat, petals strewn between the platters of food. Some were draped from the chandelier and a few had been tied to the stands of the orchestra, so large it occupied most of the far end of the room. They were the only occupants of the room not immobile, the music still flowing from their instruments. A woman clad in red, beautiful beyond comprehension stood at their head, also still.

'Violet,' John said, his eyes never leaving the scene in front of us. 'Only become a vampire for the right reasons. Don't be swayed.'

The music swelled and drowned whatever else he had to say out, and I refused to answer a statement that felt so oddly honest.

I walked forward, focusing on each and every step, trying not to shake, not wanting the fear and pressure to show. My hands felt the air in front of me, grabbing, clinging and clenching the banister of the small balcony that overlooked the ballroom, my eyes surveying the occupants with what should have been faked fear.

They were all as still as statues, immaculate and elegantly poised. But their torsos were tense, their arms stiff, like a hunter ready to pounce. My eyes darted about the room, looking for a characteristic pierce of emerald eye, or a smirk, my heart frozen as the couples were, but preparing itself to leap.

Not there. Something in my head told my heart to prepare itself for disappointment, and it sunk.

Suddenly, the couple below us began to move, whirling in an elegant waltz, never breaking hold. They circled the couple nearest them who in turn began to move, who circled the next, the hem of her dress brushing the foot of the staircase I would soon descend. Again and again the couples circled, around and around, more and more unfreezing. I watched, stunned, as the room awakened in a great wave, gathering momentum and moving away from us, continually whirling and spinning. It was like a machine coming alive, the cogs turning, faster and faster in time to the music. It did not stop, spreading further and further, sprawling outwards in all directions.

Distracted, I saw colour in the corner of my eye and turned towards the orchestra. The woman, tall, elegant, curvaceous – *perfect* – stepped forward, her red dress bright and vibrant compared to the rest of the room. As she moved, so did the rest of the room; those not dancing who had remained still shifted in one fluid movement, forming an oval, large; *inescapable.*

Only those at the very far end of the room near the throne remained in their places. But the wave was rushing closer, the dance gradually becoming more elegant, more complicated, more embellished.

I felt a single bead of sweat roll down my neck as I stared at the vampires there. They all wore black with emerald sashes. The Varns. My hand clutched tighter around the banister. There were fifty, maybe sixty of them, and that just a fraction of all the vampires in attendance. I spotted Lyla amongst the sea of black and emerald, lumbered with the same partner she had complained so bitterly about at the last ball.

A surge of sudden and irrational anger shot through me. If she had snared Fabian, then she should at least be dancing with him. I spotted him too, not far away, dressed in dark blue. I knew that wasn't how this worked, but it felt so wrong.

Deeper within the throng was the King with the same partner I had seen him with at the Autumnal Equinox. Her expression was as impassive as his. They were still. The rest of his family surrounded them and my eyes desperately searched, looking for him. The room continued to spin and I spotted a flash of yellow hair that looked like it belonged to Charity, and another figure that I could have sworn was Kaspar's ex, Charlotte. Jag was frozen, a girl that was not Mary in his arms, Sky with Arabella wrapped and held close beside him. Cain was there as well, his partner a girl I thought might be a cousin – he had joked that the ball was a keep-it-in-the-family affair. Even Thyme was in attendance – she was not dancing but waiting at the edge of the ring, her tiny fangs resting against her pink lips, curled into a small smile. But I could not see him.

The music quietened; the room hushed. Heads turned towards us, standing on the little balcony. The candles in the chandelier far above faltered as a breeze, icy and bitter, swept in through the open doors behind us, stirring my dress and tousling John's hair. I wanted to turn to see where it came from – I knew the main entrance was open but no draft was that cold. I never had the chance.

An arm had latched itself around my middle as the force
of a body slammed me into the banister, pinning me to the
marble. I felt the air leaving my lungs in a rush and I closed
my eyes, winded, taking involuntary gulps of air. The pain
clutched at my ribs but I had bigger trouble – a second arm
had grabbed my wrist and I felt my feet leaving the floor.
Instinctively my eyes burst open again and I lashed out,
kicking and clawing only to stop again.

The music was rising and as one, the Varns awoke. En
masse, the room glided as a sea of black and green, rising
and falling to the unnerving notes, drawn out and only
becoming more ferocious. My eyes never left the scene as I
was half-dragged, half-carried down the stairs, tripping and
falling, perhaps screaming; I would not know above the
music. We reached the bottom and as I fell forwards, unable
to stop, the same arm caught me. As it snatched me back I
caught sight of the sleeve; it was one of the butlers.

John appeared beside me, held by another one of the
butlers, struggling and fear, *real* fear in his eyes. Both of us
knew what was coming but nothing could prepare me for
the sickening jolt as the nearest couple broke apart, small
smiles on both their lips. The man, quite young by vampire
standards smiled, mouth widening to reveal two perfectly
chiselled incisors that marked him as the hunter; us as the
prey.

With his nod, we were thrown to the sea.

The room filled with sound, noise not music, a screeching,
blood-curdling shriek filling the room, coming from the
mouth of the woman I had thought beautiful. I flew through
the air, tossed towards the young vampire who caught me
in his arms. I smacked hard into his chest, hair over my eyes
and one of the ribbons of my shoes slipping down to my
ankles. But I barely had time to gasp before he had flung

me backwards over his arm, his open mouth lowering towards my neck. He swept the hair from my shoulders, his breath reeking of blood and wine. My eyelids quivered as I saw a flash of white, John, passing me, enclosed in the arms of the woman. I closed my eyes, feeling his hands roam towards the hem of my dress . . . The music peaked and I was back upright, the blood draining from my head in one dizzying moment. I felt myself being pushed away, into another's arms who threw me backwards, this new vampire's reddened eyes coming ever closer to my still exposed neck. I sucked in a breath, wanting to cover my ears, block out the shrieking but I couldn't; they were pinned to my side and the sick, dizzy feeling was getting ever stronger.

In a blink I was back on my feet and I felt the flush leaving my cheeks. A hand was placed on the small of my back and I was pushed to the next; John was sucked away in a mass of whirling silk and satin. I gulped down a breath of air as once again I was launched back to rest in the crux of yet another arm . . .

I squeezed my eyes shut, not wanting to look as I was passed from one vampire to another. I felt lace and muslin graze my exposed skin, tripping over my feet and falling, stumbling from one to another, new arms supporting me as fresh fangs lowered to my neck, throat, shoulders . . .

But they would not bite. I knew they would not bite. Yet it did not alleviate the feeling that I was bait amidst sharks, being torn apart, slowly and cruelly.

It stopped. The room froze once more and the music hushed. The couples around us – although it felt more like me, because only the freezing breath on my neck gave away the fact that I was not held by a statue – paused mid-step, becoming still again. My back was arched, the tip of my hair brushing the floor. I could feel my chest heaving and I screwed my eyes shut; I wanted to scream, it seemed so unfair.

A drum sounded and the music surged, the rhythm faster, the beat making my ribs pound as though a thousand stampeding horses were thrashing their way from one lung to another; with the drum I was upright again, swallowing back bile. The vampire who held me let out a heavy sigh and I started to turn towards him; in a flash he had placed both his hands on my shoulders and rammed me backwards. My mouth was wide open as I was flung away, watching as he was swallowed by the whirling figures.

As I was enclosed in waiting arms, I felt my temperature soar, my skin was flaming and flushing. Perhaps it was because I recognized the colour of the sleeve around my middle, crimson, and knew the emblem etched into the cuff links or perhaps it was because I could feel a tiny vial pressing into my back.

'We meet at last, Violet Lee.'

I swallowed hard, knowing exactly who this was. 'You're Ilta's father.'

'That's the Earl of Wallachia to you, human scum,' he hissed in my ear, throwing me back over his arm just as the others had done but with so much force I heard my joints click. My head dangled just inches from the floor – I could feel the cool marble as I stared into a pair of dark blue eyes. His lips pursed in disgust and I thought he might be considering dropping me onto the hard floor. I would not mind: his touch was sickening; unclean; it left scorch marks on my shoulders and in the palms of my hands.

'Your son was the scum, Crimson.'

He snarled at that, his mouth lowering to my ear. 'My son was doing this Kingdom a favour when he tried to rid it of you and your impurity. Your little Prince should have rewarded him that day, not killed him.' He opened his mouth a little wider and a single fang pressed to my neck.

I shuddered. His breath left a dirty trail behind, one that could not be washed away. 'What are you doing here? You were banished.'

He laughed: the laugh of someone who knew they stood on the higher ground. 'The King revoked his decision almost immediately. It seems I, like my son, know too much to be forgotten. I am of great use to them, you see.'

'How?'

'To put it plainly, little girl, I know too much about the Dark Heroines and I know too much about your future.'

Abruptly he pulled me upright, but before he could push me away I grabbed his arm. 'What do you know?'

He narrowed his eyes. 'That you don't deserve the path destiny has created for you.'

'Path? And what are the Dark—'

Before I could finish he had wrenched my arm from his and tossed me away, leaving me sickened and confused, but more than that, *intrigued*. That in itself was revolting. I should want to be far away from this man, but instead I wanted to return and get answers.

Vampire after vampire caught me and as I got closer to the throne I began to recognize more and more faces. Charlie, Declan and Felix had all had their turns mishandling me, Declan depressed, his eyes transfixed on a demure girl not too far away. Alex had winked with a friendly smile on his lips; his younger brother Lance was a little *too* friendly.

Fathers, sons and brothers of the vampires I had come to know all took their turn, mocking the bite coming ever closer. Izaak Logan had been by far the gentlest, whilst Fabian, his expression cold and distant, had averted his gaze and even dug his nails into my sides to the point where I thought they might draw blood.

It was your fault, Fabian, I thought. *You made it Kaspar or you. You pushed me away.*

I was incredibly near the Varns now and had figured that it worked in ascending rank; the only person standing between me and royalty was Eaglen, who snatched me with the strength of a much younger man.

Yet again, we paused mid-dance. My head was dangling precariously close to the floor and the couples that just a second ago had surrounded us seemed to disappear. Stars danced in front of my eyes but I kept them open, transfixed. A high window, cathedral-like in its construction was reflecting the eerie spectacle below of which I was the victim. According to the glass, the room was completely empty, save for two pasty, wide-eyed figures dressed in white. One had his arms pinned behind his back, totally rigid apart from his head which was lolling at an awkward, painful angle. The other was suspended mid-air, back arched, her feet just brushing the floor.

I closed my eyes for a second, stunned at what I was seeing. When I looked back at the glass, it reflected reality – a room packed with people.

I wouldn't fret, mortal child, because soon your decision will be made for you. My skin ran cold – colder than it already was. It was Eaglen's voice in my head; in my mind that I could supposedly guard and had done quite successfully against any other.

Get out . . . I started but was unable to finish as stars blinked behind my closed eyelids. I really needed to stand up or sit down; either would be better than being caught halfway between.

The music crashed. I screamed and had no choice as I

was yanked upright again; swaying, blood slipping down towards my feet and making them tingle. There were no other colours but emerald and black. I wanted to close my eyes, but I was afraid of what I could not see: sunken eyes and rough hands on my back, no compassion, no leniency, just hatred for a girl who had slept with their Prince and heir.

Faces, old and young, faster and faster, the music gaining momentum as the shrieks of the woman and the choir matched the pitch of my screams. My mind raced, almost keeping pace with my body, thrown from one to another. I longed for the bite, but only for it to be over.

Cain; a glimpse of Arabella seizing John who was taken away because he would not be bitten; Jag looked worried but his eyes were not focused in my direction; Sky fought to restrain me as I struggled, eyes to the floor, refusing to look. I knew it came ever closer, but at the same time I knew the hierarchy and who *should* be next.

I finally raised my eyes. A circle was forming, a circle of swirling, whirling couples. In its centre was the King, his partner abandoned in favour of me. She was standing close by, her usually serene expression twisted with bloodlust as her eyes bore into me.

Two people broke from the circle, their backs to me. Both were dressed in black, emerald sashes around their shoulders. One wore a long sweeping dress, backless, lace floating about her ankles. Her hair was twisted into a knot; a flower, just like those dangling from the pillars, was tucked in-between the loose strands. The other was a man wearing court dress, sword hanging at his hip, his dark hair dishevelled.

I already knew who they were as I found myself staring at two pairs of green eyes.

One pair stared back.

A small smile upturned the corners of my lips and my limbs unconsciously became still. My heart jumped, warming and growing. But my mind was ahead of my heart. He was next yet I knew I could not touch him, and I tore my eyes away from him to the figure standing just behind, whose grey eyes were darting between his son and me. Kaspar met my gaze, caught my expression and whipped around to face his father.

The King's gaze was fixed on me and as I watched, his eyes fell through to black, tinged with red – deep, lustful, lecherous red. The palms of my hands burnt.

Kaspar hissed and his stance dropped. Nobody but us would hear it over the music, but it grew as he backed towards me, on my tiptoes, about to be thrown to the centre of the ring.

Abruptly, Sky let go and I fell, lurching towards Kaspar, who whipped around, lunging towards me as his father did the same, hissing and snarling. I opened my mouth to scream, fighting to try and regain balance, scrambling away, half on my knees in a futile escape from two predators who possessed a hundred times my strength and speed. Tears soaked the front of my dress as I tried not to watch, still scrabbling backwards. They came ever closer, both blurs, just a foot away when the King reached out and grabbed the lapels of his son's jacket, tossing him away with a single hand.

The King spoke whilst he reached down with the other hand, grabbing my arm and yanking me upright. His voice cut through the confusion, a low hiss at his other son, Sky. 'He does not touch her, not even for this!'

All eyes were on us and I stopped struggling, feeling the blood colour my cheeks, which I cursed, knowing it just added to the allure. Standing behind me, the King took the opportunity to grab both my wrists in just one of his hands, yanking them above my head. With the other he swept the hair from my right shoulder, a quiet snarl coming from between his lips.

I could feel his breath, so cold it seemed to burn my skin as he moved closer, like the way my palms burnt. The vein in my neck throbbed uncontrollably, pounding against my skin as though it was desperate to escape, but I knew it was because my heart beat for two as it sped wildly out of control. A few tears leaked from the corners of my eyes and I scrunched them shut, not wanting them to see me cry.

'Open your eyes,' he hissed in my ear, and reluctantly I prised them open. I felt like demanding to know why I had to watch them watch me suffer, but did not have to as the crowd to one side of us jostled and swayed, parting a little. Sky darted to the commotion where Cain had appeared, wrestling with Kaspar, whose expression was one of a man knowing he was fighting in vain: lips parted, fists clenched, brow lowered; hopeless. Without a word, Sky grabbed his brother's arm as Cain did the same, both clearly worried that he might dive forward.

I knew he wouldn't. It was too late. His eyes met mine and I managed the briefest of smiles as the King tightened his grip around my waist, preparing to throw me back and bite. My eyes fluttered closed. I plunged towards the floor, his fangs sinking into my neck as the room, as wide, tall and high as a cathedral was filled with the echo of a scream, not faked, not acted, like they had instructed, but real. *Very real.*

FORTY-EIGHT

Violet

'You okay?' Cain asked, pulling a handkerchief from his breast pocket, dabbing at the wound that I could feel stitching itself together already. We were outside, the gentle breeze cooling the sweat that covered my body.

'I think so.'

It was a breathless reply and didn't sound okay but it was all I could muster. The previous few minutes (although, according to the clock set high in the wall, it had been half an hour) had shaken me more than I expected and restored the fear of these creatures – although restored didn't seem to be the right word, because it was a fear that had never truly existed.

'Good,' he said, stuffing the handkerchief into his trouser pocket. He looked like he had more to say, but I interrupted him.

'Where's Kaspar?'

Cain shot me a weary glance. 'Talking with the King. You would think two weeks in Romania would have taught him a lesson.'

My ears pricked up. *Romania?*

'Don't feel too sorry for him,' Cain replied. 'He spent it boozing it up at Sky's summer castle with his old mates from Vampires.'

Romania? So that is where Kaspar had been banished to over the previous two weeks; and there was something about 'mates' that made me uneasy – something told me they were mates of both genders. My heart sunk. He had wasted no time. *Yet here I am, moping about, waiting for my Prince to return.* It was pathetic. *What did I expect? I'm just another notch on the post. After all, I'm human scum with a future I apparently don't deserve.*

Yet I couldn't help but remember the way he promised to not let anyone hurt me – the way he had pulled me across into his lap on the way to London. He seemed like he cared in those moments, but then he would flip and the jerk would reappear. *Talk about Jekyll and Hyde.*

'Do you want to go back in?'

'No, you go ahead. I just want to be outside for a bit.'

'Suit yourself. Shout if anything happens.'

Walking around the pillar I slipped into the small alcove beside the doors, a smaller replica of the balcony above, tonight lit up with lanterns rather than torches.

I knew being alone should unsettle me more than it did, but I needed time to think without being bombarded with more information.

I had barely spared two thoughts about my dream the previous night. I knew I should have because whatever this Prophecy was, it was providing an excuse for my father to put his plan to get me out of here into action. And Valerian Crimson had said the same thing. Dark Heroine.

I also knew how I should feel about that. *Relieved. Hopeful. Exuberant.* But I couldn't reconcile those feelings – which I did feel, in moderation – with the growing attachment I had to Varnley which I had openly acknowledged to Kaspar by refusing the chance to leave.

Yet what is there to justify me staying here? Most people despised me for sleeping with Kaspar – who I couldn't touch in any case, which, according to Cain and Jag, hadn't seemed to bother him that much in Romania. To top that off, I had a voice and nightmares about very real events. *This place is sending me mad.*

I wiped my mind clean, focusing on the water trickling in the fountain as something pushed against my barriers and attempted to pry. It persisted for a minute, and then its touch fell away.

'A penny for your thoughts, Girly.'

I let out a deep breath and with the air went my worries. 'My thoughts are mine, Your Highness, and are worth far more than a penny.'

He chuckled. 'There you go again, denying the Prince of the Realm. You really should learn not to do that.'

'I did.' I turned, coming face-to-face with Kaspar, *finally,* after fourteen long, arduous days. 'But it landed the Prince of the Realm in Romania for two weeks, which I heard he was not too pleased about.'

'No.' He walked around me, leaning on the stone banister. 'He was not too pleased. He finds Romania quite beautiful, but there happens to be something far more beautiful here, if a little annoying and very outspoken.'

I flushed deep red and my stomach fluttered at the compliment. 'Nice to see you too, Kaspar.' I leaned against the banister beside him, careful to keep far enough away to not run the risk of accidentally touching him.

'Did I ever say it was nice to see you, even as stunning as you look in white?' He asked, quite sincerely, but his eyes twinkled mischievously and I mocked insult.

'So rude! And white washes me out, it's hardly stunning.'

'Precisely. It makes you look like a vampire.' He turned away as he spoke, but not before I caught the pink tinge in his eyes. Again, I knew the correct emotion to feel would be upset, but I couldn't help but feel flattered. 'But seriously, it is nice to see you. Turns out you're what makes life fun,' he said, chuckling quietly.

'Thanks. I guess I missed you too,' I mumbled, hoping that the lanterns were dim enough for him not to see my blush, becoming permanent.

'What?'

My heart dropped. 'I missed you,' I repeated.

He laughed. 'I heard you, Girly, I just wondered if I could have that in writing?'

I frowned. 'What do you mean?'

'I mean that I never thought I would live to see the day when you would say that.' He twisted so that he fully faced me and I smiled half-heartedly at his comment as I felt my eyes wander without permission down his torso to linger below the tails of his waistcoat.

God, I've seen you naked.

'Violet?'

I shook my head and felt an embarrassed smile spread across my face. I shifted my gaze to the grounds. 'How was Romania?'

Out of the corner of my eye, I could see his smirk fading away as his face became serious again. 'Beautiful, as I said. I wish I could take you there; show you home. It would have been nice to have someone there who shares my passion for alcohol too.'

I raised an eyebrow. 'You drank a lot?'

He sighed and his eyes dulled to a mint green. 'It's hard to know how much you've had when you're drinking alone.'

My heart and hopes lifted a little. *So he didn't go off with other girls?*

'Alone?'

He returned to watching the grounds, glancing at me every few seconds, as though torn between what he should be looking at. 'You seem surprised.'

'I just thought . . .'

He did not pressure me to finish my sentence and we lapsed into silence, yet the absence of talk was not an awkward barrier between us. Instead, it seemed comforting, knowing that we were at ease with the quiet. I closed my eyes for a while, listening to the odd chirp of a bird and the continuous pattering of water on water in the fountain. Even behind closed eyelids I could see a suspension of red and gold – the tiny flies floating above the pond and the tongues of flames in the lantern.

'You're cold,' he whispered.

I opened my eyes, brushing a stray strand of hair from my eyes. 'Only a little.'

He raised an eyebrow, brushing his own hair from his brow. 'I can see the goose bumps on your arms.' He removed his sash and unbuttoned his jacket, which he handed to me. I took it gratefully, careful not to touch his hand. Slipping it on I felt the immediate warmth around my shoulders, which had been frozen for most of the evening.

I stretched my arms out. 'It's a little big.' The sleeves were inches past my fingertips and the hem fell almost to my knees. 'Thanks.'

He nodded. 'Walk with me?'

He stepped around me and led the way down the steps, the few passers-by gawping. I could read the same thought in every face; wearing his jacket didn't help to ease their shock either.

'Damn, I have a stone in my shoe,' I said as we stepped from the gravel onto the grass. Stopping, I reached down and pulled on the ribbons wrapped around my calf, undoing them. Slipping the shoe off, I hopped on one foot, emptying the flimsy thing of a pebble. Kaspar cocked his head, watching me with amused bewilderment.

'Girly, you really are the very definition of elegance.'

I faked a laugh before almost falling flat on my back whilst attempting to tie the ribbons back around my leg.

'I would help you,' he continued. 'But I can't touch you and besides, I'm rather enjoying the spectacle.'

I had the feeling he was not looking at my foot, but rather my cleavage, exposed and not exactly supported by the thin material of the dress as I bent forward. Eventually I managed to slip the shoe back on, giving up on making the ribbons look tidy. Standing back up I marched off in front of him, heading towards the pond at the bottom of the grounds.

In fairness, you were staring at his crotch a minute ago, my voice reminded me.

Yeah, well noticed, voice.

He quickly caught up, matching my pace but letting me silently brood, the half-smirk, half-smile on his lips. I reached the pond, entranced by the flies flitting about, coating the surface of the pond in a glittering cloud of dust that hummed softly.

'Beautiful, aren't they?' Kaspar said, nodding towards the flies. 'They only come once a year, for Ad Infinitum. It's silly, but people say they feed on the joy.'

'Wow,' I murmured, not truly watching the flies.

'Mother loved them.'

The silence fell again and after a few moments I followed the edge of the pond to where yet more chains of roses fell from the trees, linked like paper-chains. They were identical to those inside, the petals darkest black, the leaves utterly white. I stretched out a hand, wanting to touch the petals – they looked to be made from velvet.

'I wouldn't do that if I were you.'

I snatched my hand back as Kaspar appeared right in front of me.

'Why?'

His face became incredibly sincere. 'These roses are called Death's Touch; they're lethal to any human or dhampir who touches the petals.'

I scrabbled back. 'You're kidding me?!'

He shook his head. 'Deadly serious. If you had touched one just now, you would be on the floor, snuffed by now.'

My eyes widened and I took a few cautionary steps back. He chuckled, turning around and plucking one from the stem, admiring it in his hand, straitening the outer petals so they conformed to the perfect circle the rest of the flower created. 'Here, smell one.'

He offered it in the palm of his hand and I shook my head. 'No way!'

'Trust me, Violet,' he sighed.

I frowned but leaned down. I did not even have to be close to catch the scent.

'What does that smell like to you?' he asked.

I scrunched up my nose. 'Like rotting vegetables.'

He nodded. 'But to me,' he lifted the flower to his nose. 'They smell almost as sweet as you.'

I snorted. 'Is that some cheesy vampire pick-up line?'

He feigned surprise. 'Damn! Is it that obvious?' He tossed the flower into the pond, where it floated like it was sat atop a lily pad and wiped his hand on his white shirt below the waistcoat, leaving a black smear.

We started walking. 'So if they are so deadly to humans

and dhampirs, why is the whole place decorated with them?'

He slowly exhaled as though it were obvious. 'There are only two humans at Ad Infinitum and they are being constantly watched, so why not? Besides, they are the flower of the Kingdom. It's what you see on that.' He pointed towards the rose part of the coat of arms on his jacket that I was wearing. 'They represent everything we are about. They're lethal to humans, yet to us they are a thing of beauty and value. They even make perfumes that contain the scent, which can't be much fun for any humans who catch a whiff.'

I nodded. 'So they are symbolic to vampires?'

'No. They're symbolic to the dark beings.'

I shut my eyes, reminding myself not to be exasperated at his answer. Considering I knew nothing about the dark beings, that hardly meant anything.

We had reached the fountain and Kaspar sat down on the edge, patting the stone rim beside him. I sat down, convincing myself to have the guts to get answers.

'What are the Dark Heroines?'

He turned to me, back straight, eyes wide and mouth agape. His eyes burnt black for a split-second. 'Who told you about that?' he demanded.

My mind raced, trying to find a plausible excuse. I couldn't tell him about the dreams; not if his father might find out. 'No one. I heard some people talking inside about how the Athenea had found the first Sag-e-an girl or something.' I sounded the word 'Sagean' out, barely remembering how the rogue had pronounced it in my dream.

He relaxed a little, but alertness and curiosity continued to burn in his eyes. 'Sagean. Spelt with an A, pronounced with an E. Sage-en,' he repeated, breaking it down into sounds.

'Sage . . . en.' I attempted to imitated him, but found it difficult to make the same sound he did when he pronounced the last two letters.

The corners of his lips upturned slightly. 'Do you know who you overheard? Because no one but the council is supposed to know, let alone talk about it.'

I shook my head, lying through my teeth. 'I don't know. I didn't recognize them.'

'Ah.'

I sighed, letting my exasperation show this time. 'You're not going to tell me what the Dark Heroines are, are you? Or what the Prophecy of the Heroines is. Or why the vampires are so surprised. Or why the vampires are next.'

He cringed. 'You heard all of that?'

'Please tell me. What harm can it do? It's not as though I'll tell anyone I know what it is.'

He shook his head. 'You do know that it's been agreed by both the Vamperic council and an inter-dimensional council that you should have no knowledge of any other dimension but this one until you turn, right?'

'That's what that meeting was about when we went to London, wasn't it? And that Fallon guy. Was he Sagean? He knew about this prophecy, didn't he? How long ago did you find out that the girl had been found? Was it recently? I've not heard anybody mention this all before.' I threw in the last couple of questions to test him; I knew the answer from my dream the night before, but I wanted to see how truthful he would be.

'Slow down! I'll tell you, okay?' His eyes darted up and back down again, his hand running through his hair. My heart stopped, finally anticipating answers.

'Right, where to begin?' He took a deep breath, lowering his hand, and then launched into speech. 'There are nine dimensions, parallel in almost every way; each is populated by humans as well as a much smaller number of dark beings, which I am not going to explain about.' I was about to protest, but he cut in. 'It's worth more than my life, so no.'

He carried on. 'The humans of each dimension have never really got on with the dark beings, other than in this dimension, where, with the exception of government officials, you are all pretty much oblivious to our existence. But about five thousand years ago, a Sagean scholar and prophet, yes, Sage-en,' he said as I sounded it out once more. 'A Sagean scholar claimed to know of a future age. Sure of his own abilities, he wrote what he had foreseen down in his scrolls.' He raised his gaze to meet my own, his eyes flecked with grey at the edge. 'He knew about the world wars and climate change and even about the invention of the atomic bomb. He knew that the treaties struck between the dark beings and the humans would fail and that war would be an ever-looming prospect. He knew of our world, Violet. He knew where we would go wrong.'

Enraptured, I remained silent and he took that as a sign to pause.

'Sure you want me to carry on?' I nodded and he let out a dry chuckle. 'But he didn't entirely leave us without hope. At the same time, he came up with the Prophecy of the Heroines, and in that he predicted that during this dark age, nine women would ascend to become kinds of . . . deities, I suppose. Above all Kings, they are meant to restore the balance with humanity we lost.'

I could imagine it. It was a fairytale, a hero's tale, but this was real. *This is real.* My voice was quiet as I spoke; wrapped up in a story I was so intrigued by. *The story of my world.*

'But you don't believe it. At least, you didn't.'

He shook his head. 'Not many did, other than the Athenea – which is both the Sagean royal family and an actual place – and the Sagean people. It was disregarded as rubbish at the time anyway, because it placed women in power.'

I shifted closer, eyes wide with intrigue and slight disbelief, my voice no more than a whisper.

'But now it's coming true?'

'Yes. I don't want to believe it, but how can I not?' His question was more directed at himself than at me, so I did not reply, memories of my dream last night still fresh. *It's true. It's real.*

'The Sage of Athenea found their girl,' I breathed and broke off in wonderment. My father had brought me up to be rational, but my experience here had changed that. I was ready to believe this, crazy and way-out as it seemed.

'Do you know who she is?'

He shook his head. 'The first Heroine? No idea. Nobody knows. The Sage have shut their borders so there is no way into the dimension and no way out. We can't send messages and they certainly aren't telling us anything. We have to wait on them to tell us. As usual.'

I frowned. 'But how long could that take?'

'Who knows?' he answered. 'Days, weeks, months maybe. They'll bide their time and when they are ready, she will come. She will have to at some point, because she was born to awaken the other Heroines.'

I gripped the edge of the fountain, the cool spray chilling me again and spotting Kaspar's jacket with water. 'What do you mean?'

He shut his eyes, sighing. 'The verses are in order. The first is about the Sage, the second about here, the third about the Damned, and so on. The first explains how the first Heroine must search out each Heroine. As the second is supposedly a vampire, she will come here first, find the second girl and then . . . well . . .'

He trailed off, shaking his head.

'What is the first verse? Do you know it?' I asked, doubting he would actually tell me.

'Of course. Everybody knows it, apart from you puny little humans in this dimension.' I scowled at his reference. 'It's far more beautiful in its native tongue, Sagean, because in English it's been altered to make sense and to rhyme, but you can get the gist of it.' He leaned back on his elbows, staring up at the starry sky, the words flowing from his tongue as though they had been spoken a thousand times.

> 'Her fate is set in stone,
> Bound to sit upon the first throne.
> The last of her line and a symbol of the fine,
> She is the last of the fall; a deity among all.
> Her teacher, her love, her lie,
> Alone, the first innocent must die,
> For the girl, born to awaken the nine.'

He finished and his lips came together, his eyes down-turned from the stars now.

'Alone, the first innocent must die?' I quoted, feeling the hairs on the back of my neck stand on end.

'Haunting, isn't it?' he murmured. 'Forty-five people will die if the entire Prophecy is true.'

I shivered, the intrigue for the subject fast become an unnerved chill. 'I wouldn't want to be that Heroine girl right now.'

He shook his head. 'Neither would I. It's not something I would wish upon anyone,'

'What if it was someone you knew?'

He stood up abruptly, turning back to me, his form blocking the light from the house and moon, casting a long shadow across the grounds. 'Then may fate have mercy upon her heart.'

When he looked back at me, a second shiver passed down my spine; gone was the amusement and the smirk. Instead, it looked as though just laying eyes on me seemed to hurt him.

'Maybe we should go back in,' I murmured, getting up too. *I've got enough answers for tonight.*

'You're right. C'mon.' Together, we headed back in, ignoring the many stares of the onlookers. We were just passing the alcove beneath the balcony when he stopped. 'Violet, wait.'

I froze in front of him and turned back to find him ducking into the alcove. I was taken aback, but quickly remembered I was still wearing his jacket.

'Jacket. Here,' I said, quickly slipping it off and handing it back to him.

'No, it wasn't that, but I do need it back,' he chuckled. He pulled it on and reached into the breast pocket. 'I have something for you.'

I knew my cheeks were moving from washed out to purple. 'What? You shouldn't have!'

He smirked. 'Yes, I should. Think of it as a sorry I screwed up your life gift.'

'I didn't think you showed remorse?'

'No, I don't. If I regretted what happened in Trafalgar Square, there's no way I would give you this,' he clarified, and from his pocket he pulled a long chain, a pendant – *no, a locket* – hanging from it.

'My God,' I breathed, not believing what I was seeing. My eyes became glued to the tiny, sealed album, watching the emerald stone disappear and reappear again as it spun on the chain.

'It was my mother's locket. And inside it contains miniatures of my family. She gave it to me the week before she died and told me to give it to the woman that I felt would keep this family together. And . . . and I figured that was you.'

My voice caught in my throat. 'I-I . . . you can't!'

'I can,' he replied, already moving behind me to fix the clasp.

'But—'

'No buts.'

He lowered it over my head, bringing the chain behind my neck. I froze, afraid he might accidentally touch me. He fiddled for a moment and I could feel the locket against my skin, the metal unnaturally cold and not warming as I pulled my hair from underneath the chain.

'There,' he breathed, sidestepping around me. 'Look after it.'

Slowly, ever so slowly, he brushed his fingertips across the emerald, gradually tightening his grip around the pendant. I stopped breathing as he brought the locket away from my skin to his lips. He kissed it.

'Look after it,' he repeated and then replaced it, just as I took a single, slow breath. His fingers, as cold as the locket, just for a moment, *a second*, traced across my skin. But it was long enough. Kaspar met my gaze, the sudden fear I felt bubbling in my chest reflected in his eyes as he turned away and looked past me, beyond the alcove to the doors. I followed his gaze. I knew what I would see.

Standing beside the doors, his eyes darker than the night beyond the lantern-light, was the King.

FORTY-NINE

I took a step away from Kaspar, clutching protectively at the locket; more afraid he might take that from me than of his actual anger.

'You just don't understand, do you, son of mine?' His words were calm. Controlled. *A threat.*

'Understand what, Father?' Kaspar replied in the same tone.

The King took a few steps forward, bringing himself into the shadow of the alcove. Folding his arms across his chest, he observed his son through black eyes – the only thing that betrayed his anger.

'The philosophy of look but do not touch.'

A gentle breeze blew across the veranda and through the alcove, stirring my hair. The lanterns swayed, chasing the shadows away and spilling light across both the King and Kaspar. For a moment, I was struck by how much they were alike – from the way they stood to the arrogant smirk they shared; even the determined line of their brows was identical.

Kaspar chuckled hollowly. 'I understand that perfectly. You gave me that lecture earlier. But this is about more than that, isn't it?'

'Far more,' the King answered. 'I have many reasons, one of them being that you need to take responsibility and learn that your actions have consequences.'

'I know that,' Kaspar snapped. 'I know it far too well.'

A small crowd was beginning to gather on the steps, watching the scene with interest.

'No, you do not. If you did, you would acknowledge that you must stay away from her.'

The words were out of my mouth before I could stop them. 'Her has a name.'

His eyes snapped to me, as though he was noticing I was there for the first time. His eyes settled on the locket and I snatched the pendant back in my hand, unsure of his reaction. The chain tugged against my neck, so taut it threatened to snap. The locket itself was still cold in my hand, despite having rested against my warm skin for quite a few minutes. His eyes widened in recognition and I tensed, ready to move, but instead of hissing or snarling as I expected, he spoke with a calm tenderness I didn't know he was capable of.

'Miss Lee, may I have the pleasure of the next dance?'

'No,' said Kaspar.

I glared at him, knowing he was creating even more of a scene in front of the growing number of onlookers.

'I don't have any choice,' I mouthed back, dipping into a curtsey for the King. With a grimace, he stepped aside. The King was already halfway up the steps and I trailed behind, trying to ignore the stares of the crowd.

The King swept straight into the centre of the room as I passed through the shadow of the double doors. Immediately, the music ceased to play and those who were dancing came to a halt. The crowd sprawled out to form a ring.

So just us dancing then. Great.

The orchestra looked towards the King, who called out a simple dance that I knew from Sky's dance lessons; even better, it was one that did not involve being in hold. My tense shoulders lowered, only to tighten again when my eyes flickered towards Kaspar, who had worked his way towards the front. He looked concerned.

The ring closed around us, sealing me into its centre. The violins struck up; the babble died, and I curtsied, long and low, whilst opposite, the King remained upright.

The music began; I took a few steps forward, as did the King until we met in the middle, coming within inches of each other.

'Miss Lee.'

'Your Majesty.'

We backed away and circled one another, returning to our original positions before coming together again.

'Do you intend to dance in silence, Miss Lee?' He took my left hand in his right and again we circled, the distance between us quite apparent.

'Forgive me, Your Majesty, but I don't make a habit of making conversation with someone who abhors me.'

He took up my other hand, taking a step back as I also took one back until he brought us together again.

'But, Miss Lee, what makes you so adamant in your belief that I abhor you?' We broke, circling once more, weaving between one another and the imaginary couples surrounding us.

I almost laughed at his question, but thought better of it. I swept around, waiting until we were close to speak again. 'Because you won't let me near your son.'

Again he took both my hands in his, let go, and then circled me. 'I have my reasons for that. It is by no means because I loathe you. You simply assume that to be fact, when in truth, it is not.'

I frowned, becoming lost. 'But I slept with the heir to the throne. Your heir.'

We both took a step towards the other and a step away whilst he chuckled. 'Do not flatter yourself, Miss Lee. My son has slept with many girls – many human girls. Your scenario is no different. But by ignoring my explicit order that neither of you should touch, you worsened your situation. As you have done yet again this night. It's a basic instruction, Miss Lee; follow it and I will cause you no harm.'

He brushed past, sweeping in a long circle around me, his eyes constantly burning into my back. 'It is for your own good.'

He returned to his original position and I skimmed past him, taking my turn to circle around.

'Care to explain that?'

His grey eyes, duller than a London morning followed me around, burning holes in my skin despite the fact they lacked lustre. *They lacked life.*

'That is quite a gift my son bestowed upon you.'

My hand followed his eyes and found the locket, realizing he was not going to offer an explanation, but change the subject instead.

'Yes, it is.' I let it rest back on my skin, cool as ever as we continued to dance.

'It belonged to my late wife.'

'I know.'

Repetitive as ever, he grasped my hands, rather too tightly as we turned on the spot.

'You do, do you? So you are familiar with how Kaspar acquired it?'

She gave it to him the week before he died.

'Because she knew she was going to her—'

He broke off. His firm grip on my hands was tightening even more, like someone who was fighting the urge to break down.

'I'm sorry,' I whispered, giving his hand a light squeeze back, unsure of what else to do.

'You wouldn't understand,' he snapped, his face recovering; he almost threw my hands from his grip and broke away, circling me like I was prey. I didn't take my eyes off him, feeling a moist trail run down my cheek as a few tears escaped.

When he returned to my side and took my hands I answered. 'My brother died. I understand.'

His head snapped up to look at me and his eyes fell through to black again. 'No, you don't. You cannot even grasp understanding. You have no idea what it is like to have to hold back tears so as not to waste them as you do!'

We both froze and I yanked my hand from his grasp – a struggle, because his grip was unbelievably tight. His hand left white marks behind, each gloved finger leaving an imprint on my skin.

'What?' I whispered, hastily wiping the tears away and increasing the distance between us.

'You take those tears for granted child. So liberally you let them fall, but look around. Look at my Kingdom. Here there are men and women who can shed so few tears. You should treasure your own, Miss Lee, before it is too late.'

I narrowed my eyes, ignoring Kaspar whose mouth was slightly agape, watching as both of us abandoned the dance.

'It will *never* be too late. I will never join your sick Kingdom!' I spat, the words out before I had time to think about what I was saying. The crowd shifted uncomfortably and I could see Kaspar cringing at its forefront.

The King took several measured steps closer, closing the distance, dwarfing me. 'Do not insult me, Miss Lee, or you will come to regret it.'

I took a final step to close the gap between us. Just inches apart, I stood on my tiptoes to meet his glare. 'I'm not afraid of you.' An audible gasp swept through the watching room. Shocked, the crowd erupted, the room coming alive at once.

Yet he chuckled darkly. Bending down, he murmured into my ear. 'No. But you are afraid of your feelings for my son.'

My heels lowered to the floor, everything else motionless. *He knows.* He knew and he was going to cross hell to ensure those feelings were not returned by his son, heir and Prince. *He knows.*

'Everything has a consequence, Miss Lee.'

I took a few shaky steps back, staring at the floor as the music drew to a close, the violins striking one last note. *I have to get out of here.*

And so I curtsied and fled. Away from the room. Away from the ball. Away from the King. Away from Kaspar.

FIFTY

Kaspar

She walked away, not even lifting her eyes as she hurried right past me, so close I could reach out and touch her. I didn't. She strode from the room, head held high but avoiding the gaze of anyone she passed. Disappearing amongst the milling and shocked network of hushed tones, I only just caught a glimpse of her sprinting up the stairs, hands over her face, crying.

'You may think that I am heartless, my son.' I jumped at the sound of his voice beside me, muttering in my ear as the crowd gradually dispersed back into a waltz. 'But truthfully, I am just trying to protect you, and more importantly, her.'

I nodded, wordlessly, recognizing in his gaze a look he saved only for moments when he wished to make an impression. 'Her feelings for you will only cause her pain.'

With that, he walked away.

Bollocks. That's what it is. Bollocks. All of this. Duty, and responsibility and consequences. What happened to free will?

'Feelings'. I knew what that suggested. And what one heck of an emotion that was.

It wasn't a total surprise: I had long suspected she was attracted to me; it would be hard for her not to be. I knew she had sacrificed her friendship with Fabian for me too. Putting two-and-two together didn't require a huge amount of effort.

But *that*. 'Feelings'. *For her to return the sentiment when I have been a jerk all along . . .*

Not that secretly I wasn't pleased. Just not shocked. *No . . . flattered . . . and pleased. Beyond pleased. Ecstatic even . . .*

'I've got to tell her,' I said aloud, as though that confirmed the matter. It didn't. It wasn't that easy.

You don't want to break her heart, do you? Because you've been denying it for months, haven't you, Kaspar? You like her. Always have. Always will. Prophecy or no Prophecy, you want her.

My voice was right. *Of course it is right.* But my duty was not to her. It had never been to her. It was to another. And it had always been to another. I just never knew.

Feeling my grip clench too tightly around the china wash-basin, I pushed away. 'But I'll be damned if I don't get her,' I told my voice and the empty bathroom. I just had to hope that the first Heroine didn't show herself too soon.

I pushed the door open silently, shutting it behind me as quietly as possible to not wake her. She lay on top of the dishevelled covers, still wearing the white dress from the night before. It had ridden up, exposing her thighs. But unusually, that was not what my eyes were drawn to. Instead, I looked to the locket resting on her chest, rising and falling in time with her slow breathing.

FIFTY-ONE

Violet

I heard the clattering of curtains being thrown open, as loud as the wheels of a train on a crossing. The pale yellow light of dawn poured in, the darkness behind my closed eyelids becoming bright, blotchy orange. My instant reaction was to fling my arm over my eyes, the crook of my elbow sheltering me from the piercing light. I groaned, not attempting coherent speech. I had been woken up far too abruptly for that.

'Morning to you too, Girly.'

I moaned in reply. This was not a pleasant wake-up call, however much my stomach was twisting itself into knots. 'What are you doing here? It's barely even light.'

He grinned, walking towards the wardrobe as I grabbed a pillow and jammed it firmly over my ears. I would much prefer it if he just treated that as a rhetorical question and left me to sleep.

'Waking you up. And correct. It's barely light. Which is why you need to get your arse out of bed.'

I lifted the pillow a little, feeling the bed depress as a pile of clothes landed beside my feet. I turned my head, glancing at the tiny clock that occupied the bedside table. I hadn't even managed to catch six hours of sleep.

'Nuh-uh. Not happening.' I rolled over and buried my head in the mattress.

'C'mon, Girly!' The duvet was whipped from beneath me, almost pulling my dress with it. I spun around, sitting up.

'*What?*'

He threw the clothes towards me. 'Moody in the morning, aren't you? But I'm asking nicely. Please, get up and get ready. We've only got fifteen minutes.'

I narrowed my eyes, instantly suspicious. 'Get ready for what?' He took a couple of calculated, cautious steps back. I crossed my arms and legs, not caring if he caught a flash of my knickers.

'You might not like this,' he began, to which I laughed.

'Cut to the chase, Kaspar.'

His mouth settled on a grim expression. 'Suit yourself. We're hunting. You're coming.'

I chuckled into the silence. 'And what makes you think, Kaspar, that a vegetarian will come on a hunting trip?'

I only just had time to throw myself back onto the bed as I saw him move. In a second, he was poised above me, his legs either side of mine, not touching, hands just an inch from a few stray strands of my hair splayed on the pillow. He was close, so close that I could feel the ice cold air searing into my quickly warming skin and his eyes bore down into mine in a gaze I couldn't break. My heart involuntarily sped up and I prayed that at that moment Kaspar couldn't hear it.

'Wake up, Violet Lee! Before this year is out your heart won't beat and your blood will turn cold. You're going to become a vampire. You're going to have to hunt humans and animals. You'll have to feed off them. You have no choice. You never did! Nobody chooses their fate when they get involved with dark beings. Nobody!' He paused, gulping for breath, his eyes closing briefly before that smouldering look returned. 'Wake up, or die dreaming, Girly! I just hope to God you wake up, because I can't lose—'

He stopped.

His mouth was left slightly agape and I was sure mine matched his. He didn't move. Neither did I. We were totally frozen for a full minute, the clock counting down the seconds. Sixty-three had passed before he finally moved, springing away as I scampered up to see him standing beside the window, his hands resting against the ledge, his eyes fixed on the glass. He didn't look at me as he spoke.

'Go get a shower. I'll tell the others to wait.'

This time I didn't argue. I scrambled up, grabbed the clothes and dashed from the room. I didn't turn back. In seconds I was in the shower, thousands of cold water droplets cascading around me, not knowing whether I should let my heart leap because he had started that sentence, or fall, because he never finished it.

Barely ten minutes later, I stepped out of the bathroom to find clothes laid out for me: a thick black T-shirt, polo neck jumper and tight-fitting dark jeans for me to wear, as well as a pair of woolly socks and old battered converse. Next to them was a scarf and long, black coat – the latter mine from the night of the London Bloodbath.

When I was dressed, I met Kaspar at the bottom of the stairs.

'How am I going to keep up with you? I'm nowhere near as fast.'

'We're walking. It's a chance for us to show you what we really are.'

I scoffed. 'Maybe I don't want to see that.'

'And,' he continued. 'It's a chance for me to show that you don't have to kill every time you feed.'

I stopped for a fleeting moment. 'That's possible?' I breathed, more to myself than him.

He slowed so I could catch him, glancing down at me, his expression scolding, but his eyes twinkled and I felt my tense shoulders lower, realizing he wasn't *that* angry with me. 'Of course it is. Do you die every time I've taken blood from you?'

'Well, no—'

'Do you feel excruciating, crippling, heart-stopping pain when I bite you?'

'Well, it's a little painful—'

'Do you walk away with only a tiny scar and an aching neck?'

'Well, yes—'

'Precisely,' he finished. 'Perfectly possible.'

I stuffed my hands into my pockets and pouted, eyes downturned but a small bubble of hope forming somewhere around my breastbone. 'Why didn't you tell me this before?'

Out of the corner of my eye, I could see him watching me, gauging my reaction. 'Because I didn't want you thinking that you'll never have to kill an animal, or never have to hunt humans. You will have to, at some point.'

Watch me, I thought, but didn't press the matter, knowing he would only insist the opposite.

Kaspar had been right about how cold it was: even sprinting flat out I could feel the chill of the early morning air battering my cheeks in waves, and hear the sound of frost crunching underfoot. I heard the sound of quickening footsteps behind me and stole a glance. The others were gaining on us as we raced on towards the forest, but they kept their word. They weren't running any faster than a fit human would.

It took no time to reach the forest and a few metres in, after leaping over several logs and leaving brambles to whip back in my face, Kaspar came to an abrupt halt. I wasn't expecting it – I grabbed a nearby tree to stop myself tumbling into him and inevitably touching, shrieking as I seized a handful of moss, bark, and thankfully, trunk.

'So graceful,' he said with mock wistfulness, turning towards me. I was about to reply when the others stopped just as abruptly behind me.

'So where shall we camp tonight?' Cain asked, gesturing vaguely about at the trees. 'The clearing near the catacombs?'

Kaspar inhaled steadily. 'I don't think the catacombs are such a good idea.'

The circle that had formed went silent as Kaspar jerked his head towards me. I looked away, pretending I hadn't seen.

Again there was more murmuring, more jerking of heads and a final nod of agreement, at which point they turned, the chinking of bottles heard from the bags they carried around their shoulders. I trailed behind a little, following the winding path as it weaved its way deeper into the trees. The ground underfoot was damp and littered with leaves, as the natural debris of autumn was churned to a faintly red mud – I had to watch where I put my feet, nearly slipping several times where others had already trodden. Behind, the pale walls of the mansion became less and less visible as trunks encroached and as we gradually descended – the ground sloped slightly – it became difficult to even spot the uppermost spires through the pine trees, which had replaced the fiery foliage. With the pines came a more unkempt landscape, beyond the care of the gardeners, where brambles teased my skin and the juice of rotting blackberries smeared across my hands as I pushed the chains aside, snagged and strung between the lowest hanging branches.

Kaspar dropped back, waiting for me on the path. He fell in step with me; Alex was not far ahead, a guitar case strapped to his back.

We moved further and further into the forest. I had no idea how large the estate or forest actually was, but I wouldn't be surprised if it went on for miles. Yet the trees around us weren't that thick, the trunks stripped of all needles until about halfway up, two or three times my height above our heads. The spindly poles and sparse canopy meant plenty of light was still able to filter through – this didn't seem like the forest I had first encountered when I tried to escape, or the forest of my dreams.

Suddenly, we broke into a clearing, the winter sun glaring down on a glassy surface and I immediately retracted my previous thought.

'Recognize it?' Kaspar asked with a smirk.

Oh, I recognize it all right. I had seen the glossy, oiled surface of the lake before, seen the rainbow palate along the banks and felt the mist rising between my fingers. Moreover, I recognized the slimy, slippery tentacle draped over the banks of the lake.

I paled, but laughed. 'You know, you never did tell me why you have a giant squid in your lake.'

Alex turned to me, puzzled. 'You've met Inky before?'

'It has a name?'

He nodded his head, quite serious. Kaspar grinned. 'Violet decided it would be a good idea to run away and fall in on her first morning here. I had to ruin a pair of trousers to save her.' He clicked his tongue disapprovingly, rolling his eyes at me.

'You didn't have to,' I grumbled.

'Save you? Yes, I did. You can't swim, can you?'

I inhaled a sharp breath and glared at him, mouth agape, blushing profusely as Alex sniggered. 'How do you know that?'

'Educated guess. And Inky was a gift, as you ask.'

'From?'

Out of the blue, his eyes locked onto something over my shoulder, and distractedly, he muttered, 'From a particularly idiotic leader of a dimension I can't tell you about.'

Just as he said that, Alex cleared his throat with a meaningful look at Kaspar. 'I'll go round the others up. We should probably get going soon.' They both froze: Kaspar's brow lowering as Alex presumably said something to him in his mind. The former stuffed his hands inside the pockets of his dark jacket, slowly beginning to follow the other man who was striding back around the lake.

I fell in step beside him. 'Are you going to explain that?'

He did not answer. I sensed he was gathering his thoughts, so didn't pester. Across the clearing the others had come together as a group once more and were filing back into the forest. I noticed Lyla's hand was firmly clasped in Fabian's.

Out of the blue, he sighed; a long, low sigh. 'Fate's a cruel thing, Girly. It tears people apart and breaks hearts; it hurts the innocent. Time does the same: it rips people up, limb from limb, until they are too weak to remain upright; to stand and to live. You'll appreciate that better than I do.'

I glanced at him. 'I will?'

He chuckled, but his laugh was lifeless; flat. Inside my pockets, my fingers clutched at the lining of the coat. The serious tone he used was more than unnerving – it filled me with dread.

'Before you had to have the blood transfusion, you were entirely mortal. If you were lucky, you would have made it to ninety. Now you are a dhampir, you will live longer than your human counterparts. Before all this, death was still very real to you. But now you know you have to become a vampire and millennia stretch out in front of you.'

I shrugged my shoulders, unsure of where he was going. 'To be honest, I never thought about death. Even when Greg died and Lily got ill, I still thought I would live forever. It's a teenage thing, I guess.' I paused, thinking. 'The first time I really thought about death was when I got here, when I had to make the choice between a lifetime as a prisoner and becoming a vampire. It spelt death either way.'

He stopped abruptly. 'You think becoming a vampire might as well be death?'

I spun around, walking backwards so I could face him. I could see the hurt in his eyes, clear as day – an overcast one, for they were a smoky grey.

'I did. Not any more.'

His eyes didn't fade but he managed a feeble smile in return. 'That's a sudden change of mind. Not something to do with my outburst earlier, is it?'

I shrugged. 'You were right. I've got to accept the inevitable. I never had any choice, because remaining a part of humanity is what will kill me, not stopping my heart to become a vampire.' Behind him, I could see a tentacle slip back into the water noiselessly, dragging a chunk of muddy grass verge with it. Above us in the trees I could see a squirrel cautiously approaching the end of a branch, about to leap to the next. 'And you cleared something up for me earlier.'

'Which was?'

I took a deep breath, knowing that in years to come I would look back on my next words with either bitter regret or a warm, contented smile. Yet all the hype and the inner debate that had been present in me since the first day of August didn't seem to have any effect on that which was around me. The birds still twittered their early morning song, the trees still swayed and the squirrel still did not leap. The ticking of Kaspar's watch went on, uninterrupted.

'I know now that I don't have to kill to feed, which was my major objection to turning.'

It took a few seconds for my words to sink in. When it did, the expression on his face – a mixture between surprise, confusion and disbelief – was one I burnt as a brand to my memory, determined to remember it, whether I was going to be bitter or glad in the future.

'Wait . . . are you saying . . . you *want* to become a vampire?' He collapsed up against a nearby tree, looking like he might pass out from shock if he could.

'Yes.'

'Shit,' he breathed.

I nodded. *I might never have had a real choice, but the truth is I'm doing it for him.* I couldn't help but hold out a glimmer of hope that if I turned, the King might just allow us to touch. I didn't know if we'd ever make it in a relationship; I didn't know if it was even allowed, but I had to believe that everything would work out fairytale style if – *when* – I turned. I had to. It made it feel as though I was in control of my humanity.

'Shit,' he repeated, pushing his hair back from his forehead. 'I-I never thought I would hear you say that. Violet Lee, *a vampire*. You really are sure? You made your mind up so quickly.'

Adamant, I began walking once more. 'Yes. I've been

thinking about it a lot the last few days,' I lied. I hadn't really considered it until a few minutes ago when Kaspar had desperately, just inches from me on my bed, uttered that unfinished sentence. It really was a decision based on the hope that he was going to finish it with '*you*'. The ability to feed without killing was a massively welcomed bonus.

I continued. 'But I was wondering, are there rules? About turning someone?' Side-by-side, we entered the forest, a fair way behind the others now. I could see their darkly-clothed figures, draped in coats, weaving between the trees, far out of earshot.

'Not strictly, no. Not for vampires, anyway. But a vampire who turns a human is expected to give their charge – the turned vampire,' he explained, seeing my expression, 'a rite of passage and teach them the laws of the Kingdom, that sort of thing.'

I felt like I had swallowed a cherry stone whole. His tone was so distant; there was no joking or pleasure, or even surprise in it, like I had expected, and I already felt that bitter regret creeping up on me.

'A rite of passage?' I managed.

'God, you have so much to learn,' he groaned. 'There is no such thing as a poor vampire, Girly. The Kingdom is made up of wealthy families and their charges. A respectable family will treat their charge well, allow them wealth and introduce them into society. Some charges aren't as lucky and end up as rogues or servants. You see? But I still don't think you're sure about this. And why are you blushing?'

His question was blunt and the rich colour of my cheeks only deepened. I took a deep breath. 'Will you turn me? I don't fancy anyone else taking a chunk out of me and you've bitten me before and well, it's just – well – I don't know,' I gushed. I waited a couple of seconds before I looked his way.

At first he looked surprised, but then his eyes betrayed him and his expression became darker.

'You don't have to,' I faltered. *Oh God, but please say you will. Say you will and you'll pluck this lump beneath my ribs right out.*

'I'll have to talk to Father about it, considering his touching rule and he'll take it to the council, who will decide if it's . . . *appropriate* for you to be my charge or not. It's not up to me, sorry.' He briefly glanced at me and I knew I must look crushed. 'Like I said, there's no room for free will here.'

That lump seemed to lodge itself somewhere in the vicinity of my heart, but I accepted it solemnly, knowing he spoke the truth about decision-making.

'Kaspar, are you all right? You don't seem too pleased about all this?'

His step faltered. 'Not pleased? Of course I'm pleased. You really are funny sometimes, Girly.'

He glanced behind us uneasily before pulling his collar up around his neck. I followed his gaze, staring back at the clearing, just visible between the dark pillars. The trees that just moments ago had thrashed about like they were caught in a livid storm were now perfectly still, but the sun – the welcomed winter sun – had disappeared, shielded behind a mass of grey clouds. They rolled in, snatching at the blue skies, blown along by the absent wind. Stealing glimpses between the canopy, I could see each bank rising higher and higher as ascending steps to some hellish place, white tufts caught up in their extending claws, churning them until they too were part of the monotone mix. It was not normal, and neither was the decision I had made in the clearing. Something strange was happening, and I did not like it.

FIFTY-TWO

Kaspar

You needed to tell—
  You didn't tell her?
Two voices unanimously rung in my head: one my voice,
the other belonging to Alex.
  You heard?
Alex knew. It was Alex who I had confided in the moment
I had returned from Romania. It was Alex who had coun-
selled me through it – he beat discussing it with father,
Eaglen and Arabella, the only others who knew.
A guilty image flashed through my head of him dropping
back, allowing my sister and Fabian to get ahead until he
was close enough to hear us.
  Sorry.
  *I couldn't do it, Alex. I can't hurt her. She wants to become a
vampire and I know it's because of me. She wants me to turn her,
for Christ's sake!* My fists clenched and I stuffed them into the
pockets of my jacket so she wouldn't see.

The longer you leave it, Kaspar, the more you will hurt her; the more you'll hurt yourself.

I know, I groaned in my mind, frustrated and feeling more helpless than I had in a lifetime. *How have things changed so quickly?* A few weeks ago she had been a game. Now, without me even noticing, she was closer to my heart than it seemed anyone had ever been.

Think of it this way: if you don't tell her soon, she will become a vampire and she will have nowhere else to go but Varnley. I'm no emotional expert, but do you really think Violet could live under your roof after you betray her like that? She would never forgive you. She would want to know why you let her fall for you, why you slept with her, why you saved her and why you're showing so much affection for her when you knew damned well you couldn't be together. Do you have the answers to those questions?

My silence answered his reasoning. Ignorance was my only plea, and that only applied to before I had been sent to Romania. It didn't apply now.

If I had known it was possible to become so infatuated, so quickly – for a plucky little human teenager, of all things – I would have guarded myself better. But I didn't, and now we both had to pay the price.

She deserves better than to be betrayed, Kaspar. Alex said.

I know, I moaned again, hopelessness becoming over-whelming. Whether I told her or not, she would end up hurt, but I knew what the right thing to do was. She shouldn't have to endure prolonged suffering. Yet my own selfishness told me that I could wait a little longer, just until the end of the hunting trip. I only wanted to get close to her once more, like I had done in her room, so nearly revealing that I couldn't face losing her, to death or to her father.

Tonight . . . when we set up camp. I won't touch her. I just need to get close. Just once more.

Once more won't hurt, my voice added, laced with encouragement.

Just until tomorrow, I reaffirmed.

Alex sighed heavily in defeat. *I've known you since we were at school, Kaspar, and I have known all that time that you are a great man. But unless you sort this, you are never going to be a good one.*

With that he severed our mental connection, disappearing into the midst of the consciences surrounding us. He left a sizzling trail of anger and disappointment behind which I did my best to ignore. I had enough on my mind without his disapproval troubling me. I closed my eyes briefly, letting my senses guide me as we descended further towards the estuary.

Fate is our enemy, but time is the danger.

FIFTY-THREE

Violet

If I had thought vampires were predators before, then my experience joining them on the hunt only convinced me that they were perfectly adapted killing machines.

'See, look here, tracks,' Kaspar whispered, pointing to the ground where there were several hoof marks. 'What do you reckon made them?'

I scrunched up my face for a minute, pretending to think. 'Feet?'

He groaned dejectedly, exasperated of my antics. For the last hour they had been slowly tracking their prey. Kaspar had attempted to teach me a few things, but I wasn't interested after learning that once he had showed me it was possible not to kill when feeding, he was going to go ahead and kill anyway.

'What animal, Girly, what animal?'

I rolled my eyes and took a guess. 'Deer?'

'Finally,' he muttered. 'And how old do you think the deer that made this print is?'

'Just turned twenty-one. Celebrated with champagne.'

He buried his face in his hands, groaning even louder. 'Lords of Earth, give me strength!'

I cocked my head. 'Sorry, but I'm vegetarian and the thought of seeing dead deer just isn't filling me with excitement. Can't you *just* show me how you *don't* kill the deer?'

He removed his hands from his face slowly, dragging them across his hollow cheeks rather dramatically. 'Okay, but if I do, will you pretend to look interested?'

I put on my best interested face, at which he chuckled dryly. 'Stick with the bored expression. Okay, it's an adult doe – that's female by the way,' he added.

'I know that. How do you know it's an adult?'

He pointed to the track again, imprinted into the soft soil and pine needles. 'The size of the track. It's too large to be a yearling and it's definitely a female because of the tracks here.'

I took a step forward, peering at the tiny impression of a hoof through the gloom that was fast descending as dusk approached. 'Baby deer?'

He nodded. 'They're quite fresh too. I can smell the herd. Not far now.' His voice descended to barely more than a whisper. 'Girly, I'm not going to kill because you asked me too, but the others will, okay? So don't freak.' His voice became even lower. 'And if you're really considering turning, you will have to accept that at some point, you will have to kill your prey. It's more merciful in some cases, okay?' he justified before I could open my mouth to protest that that would not happen.

Without waiting for a reply, he edged forward; I stumbled. Every time I stepped on a twig he would cringe, waving his hand for me to be quiet.

'Shut up!' he hissed as I froze behind him.

'I didn't say anything!' I protested, the force of the state-ment losing its power due to the fact I only mouthed it.

'You were thinking, it's distracting!'

I double-checked my mental barriers and made an outraged face, which he dismissed, pointing towards a small patch of grass about five metres away. A herd of maybe nine or ten deer were feeding, totally oblivious to our presence. Opposite, Cain, Alex, Declan, Lyla and Fabian were closing in, and, to my amusement, Felix and Charlie had taken to the trees.

I started as a voice sounded beside my ear. 'We're going to spring on them. I'll catch the doe and show you how we feed. Come forward when you're ready.'

With that he was gone. In an instant, eight figures had sprung from the shadows, sending panic rippling among the deer; they turned to flee, only to be blocked by one of the vampires. In perhaps a second or two half of them were lying on the floor, necks broken and blood pouring from the freshly punctured wounds.

It was worse than I had imagined. I had seen the cloaked figure feed in my dreams, but there was no way a dream could prepare me for the smell: metallic, like copper; like the butcher's shop I was taken to as a girl of five. It was that butcher's shop, and a school trip to a sheep farm, which had turned me vegetarian. *And I'm choosing this life?*

Slumping against a tree I took a few deep breaths, knowing that the quicker I got this over with, the less the doe would have to suffer. Hesitantly, I began to edge forward to where she lay struggling, legs flailing, making a sort of shrieking sound in sheer terror. Its fawn bleated back from the edge of the clearing, where it had been left alone by the vampires. Kaspar held her with one hand on her flank, his other stroking her neck in slow circles until gradually, she calmed.

ABIGAIL GIBBS 401

'They're quite tame,' he murmured without looking up. 'When you treat them kindly.'

He removed his hand from her back to pat the ground and I dropped to my knees beside him, not looking up for fear of seeing the others feeding. He asked me to carry on stroking her and I mimicked his tender touch, feeling the slow rise and fall of her ribs below me, though I could feel a very prominent, strong, rapid heartbeat.

'Watch her legs, she might kick,' he warned, beginning to lower his mouth. With one swift bite he had created two puncture wounds. Unable to tear my gaze away I watched, wide-eyed, as he drank from a live deer who lay content beneath him. After a minute or so he drew away.

'That's enough; I don't want to weaken her.' Even as his mouth left her neck the skin stitched itself together at an incredible rate. He stepped away, not a drop spilled.

'How come you're not that neat when you bite me?' I asked with a small, awed smile. The doe scrambled to her feet, shaken but alive, and scampered off in search of her fawn.

'I enjoy making a mess with you. And I told you it was possible to feed—'

'Kaspar!' His eyes snapped up immediately. The night had descended quickly: whereas moments before I could see the others, now they were just outlines and tracings between the trees.

Alex appeared beside Kaspar, his eyes as white and pale as a ghost. His stuttered on his words, and for the first time since I had entered Varnley, I heard fear in a vampire's voice.

'Sage.'

Cain grabbed me, blood still on his hands and guided me behind him and Kaspar, who took two cautious steps forward. Alex stumbled to the right and the other five gathered around, forming a loose but clearly defensive circle, Kaspar at its head.

The trees above us creaked and swayed, groaning and filling the silent forest with the sound of protesting giants, basking beneath the moonlight. The wind, missing for the entire day whipped up, swirling into a gale that started to rage through the tiny clearing. The air was freezing, yet warmth began to creep up from my toes as a spark travelled up my leg and through my veins; it gushed in my blood and paused at my heart, beating at twice the normal rate, stopping then starting as the ember disappeared, only to be replaced with another, and another, and another . . .

'H-how can they be here?' Kaspar stammered, the confusion and *terror* in his voice far from hidden. 'Their borders are closed!'

I tensed my muscles. The sensation was becoming unpleasant, painful even, as it worked its way between the layers of my skin, like some sort of fictional scarab beetle designed to disgust and my mind, usually so closely guarded, felt as though every wall had come crashing down; every lock was being turned by key after key . . .

'What actually are the Sage?' I cried, tripping over my own feet to try and get away. 'What can they do?'

The very roots of the trees sounded as though they were being torn from the ground when the noise and the warmth and the wind abruptly ceased.

'Rather a lot, Miss Violet Lee,' a voice said.

FIFTY-FOUR

Violet

A Canadian voice. A voice I knew.

'Fallon?' Kaspar choked, utter disbelief in his voice, tinged with relief. 'And Lady Sage,' he added quickly, as though it was an afterthought.

Two figures stepped forward from the night. One a man; the other a young girl of perhaps sixteen.

There was silence. Kaspar was the first to break it. 'Violet, this is His Royal Athenean Highness, Prince Fallon,' he introduced shakily. 'And forgive me, Lady Sage, for I do not know your name.'

The girl stepped forward to curtsey and for the first time I caught site of her face.

'Autumn Rose, of the House of Al-Summers, Your Highness.'

Stillness fell upon the clearing. The girl, if she was a girl, stood bathed in the light from the moon, a cloak around her shoulders, the hood thrown back to reveal long, golden blonde tresses, tightly curled and streaked with warm honey and auburns. Her skin was ashen and pale, although a few fading freckles adorned her left cheek only, because her right cheek . . . *no*, her entire right side was coated in an intricate, waving, swirling pattern of scars. Strokes of colour, raised like ribbons of twine spun a web across her skin, twisting and spiralling as raised veins of yellow, orange, ochre and red, darker across her neck, lighter as they encircled her face, gold as they reached her forehead until they faded into nothingness on her left.

Her companion, Fallon, stepped forward and her eyes, liquid amber in colour flickered towards him for the briefest of moments, as though seeking reassurance. They quickly returned, where they surveyed the clearing with marked caution.

'Autumn?' Kaspar choked. 'Wow, I didn't recognize you. You've grown. And you're Du—'

'Forgive me, Your Highness,' she cut in, near singing, her voice sweet and pleasing to the ear like music; entrancing. But even through that I could hear that she spoke with a very pronounced British accent; a posh one. 'I have not had the pleasure of your company for nigh on three years. I have grown much in that time. And I would be obliged to you if you did not use that title.'

I sensed the tiniest hint of sarcasm, so subtle I might have imagined it. Her hand clenched and unclenched as she said it, and her lips, full and pink, twitched like she was irritated but trying to hide it. She was not entirely comfortable speaking of her body either – a light blush tinged her cheeks and she pulled her dark cloak a little tighter around her middle where it had fallen open. Beneath its folds I could see that her hips were rounded, her waist tiny and her chest . . . full, to say the least. Her legs were clad in a pair of dark tights, ripped and laddered, worn underneath a pair of loose shorts and a dark tank top. Her boots, lace-up and calf-high were coated in mud.

I stared openly at the curious marks upon her skin, feeling a tiny pang of jealousy as Kaspar gawped at her. Suddenly, her gaze met mine for a moment, questioning, before she averted her prominent almond eyes, slightly pinched so they slanted up at the outer corner, and looked timidly towards the ground. But I felt that in those seconds she had looked on me with as much curiosity as I did her.

'Well, you never were much good at introductions, Kaspar,' Fallon, said, stepping forward and grasping his hand in a hearty handshake. Kaspar returned it, meekly, still dazed and shocked by their appearance if my own emotions were anything to go by. For the first time I turned my eye towards him. Kaspar had introduced him as 'His Highness' and he was clearly on an equal footing with Kaspar – he had not bowed.

He was certainly handsome, despite the strange markings that he also bore. His skin was tanned; a total contrast with every other occupant of the clearing. His scars were a deep blood red, burgundy and russet, and creeped as much as they swirled, whilst his eyes . . . his eyes were the most electric shade of cobalt blue I had ever seen; brighter than Fabian's even. His hair, flaxen and dark blond in colour flopped messily over his forehead, unkempt and untidy. Around his throat there hung a shark tooth on a leather thong, framed by the open collar of a dark grey shirt; and over that he wore a black V-necked jumper. He also had a cloak.

Neither was like anything I had ever seen. They were ethereal. And from both of them radiated tingling warmth: a dancing, shimmering heat encasing their figures in intense energy, so compelling I could see why the vampires feared these strange creatures.

The Sage.

His gaze glided towards me, where it settled as he slowly approached. Cain edged aside to let him through, eyeing him warily. The tight circle that had surrounded me broke and Fallon came to a halt in front of me.

'We've met before I believe, Miss Lee.' He stooped down to take my hand but I snatched it away, not wanting to touch his, particularly where it was marked. I remembered well when I had heard his voice before, just two weeks ago. It seemed far longer. It had been before we had left for London, just as the council had been gathering for a meeting about my fate – amongst other things.

He seemed taken aback by my reaction and turned towards Kaspar, something like surprise written in his strong features. 'You followed through the council's instructions then?'

Kaspar nodded sternly. 'We told her nothing.' His eyes searched for mine, and all the doubt and jealousy ebbed away. His eyes, white from fear just a minute ago were now their natural vivid emerald, and I took courage from their colour.

Slowly, I offered my hand to Fallon and curtsied. To my surprise, instead of shaking my hand, he took it and lightly kissed my knuckles. Immediately, a spark ignited where his lips touched my skin, throbbing before it hurtled through my veins, sending a chill up my spine; distracted, every wall, every barrier around my mind seemed to fall away and a foreign conscience invaded mine. I hastily tried to throw barricades back up in defence but it was useless and instead threw my efforts into the lock around my father's box. The musical mind of this creature was in mine, and carelessly sifting through images of my life like an album, pausing at those concerned with the vampires.

Then as quickly as he had come, he was gone. I returned

to the present in time to meet Fallon's eyes, twinkling with intrigue.

'Yet you told her about the Prophecy of the Heroines,' he said, turning to look over his shoulder at Kaspar, my hand still in his.

It was a statement, not a question and Kaspar, floundering, looked from my wide-eyed expression to Fallon's small smile.

'You were in her mind?!' Kaspar spluttered, a look of outrage crossing his face.

Fallon chuckled. 'Curious, Kaspar, just curious.'

Kaspar, appalled, took a step towards Fallon and the girl, Autumn Rose. Even in the gloom I could see his eyes flashing dangerously black.

'You cannot just arrive here and enter our minds at liberty, Fallon. At a time like this I should have you locked up and brought before our council for invading Violet's mind; if it were not for your title I would ensure you were dragged there.'

Fallon shook his head. 'Being a Prince allows one such a liberty, Kaspar, you know that. And, as you say, at a time like this we should be united, don't you think?'

'And how,' Kaspar scoffed, 'Are we supposed to be united when your Kingdom won't tell us who this Heroine girl is or how you plan to find the second? Besides, closing Athenea's borders more promotes division, don't you think, Fallon?'

Fallon chuckled dryly for a few seconds, before his mouth became a set line. 'Ask and you will be answered, my friend.'

Autumn's eyes flicked between the two of them, grimacing slightly. Suddenly, her eyes moved to me and her face became unreadable again.

'So who is the Heroine? Is she of noble blood or not?'

'I don't know.'

Kaspar swore fiercely under his breath, turning and punching a nearby innocent tree. The bark splintered, falling as shards to the mossy ground.

'You don't know? Not even a name?' Cain interjected, glancing at his brother.

'No. My father has not told me. All I know is she is far from under the control of the court. She's beyond our influence. The court closed the borders in an attempt to keep her from leaving the dimension; force her to pay them a little visit.'

'But you opened them again?' I asked.

Fallon drew a long breath, glancing at Autumn as he did. 'No.'

Comprehension, swiftly followed by shock, seemed to spread around the clearing. Autumn's eyes had become averted again, her gaze firmly locked on the ground. But every few seconds, perhaps when she thought no one was looking, her eyes would sweep around, still cautious until they came to a rest on me. I frowned, hoping to catch her eye but she didn't look up again, as though she knew I was watching.

'You mean?' Cain began.

Fallon nodded, his face solemn.

Lyla laughed nervously, stepping forward into the moonlight. 'But . . . that's not possible. It's just not possible.'

I glanced from one to the other, not following the broken conversation. 'What's not possible?'

Kaspar, leaned against the tree he had taken his anger out on, opened his eyes for the first time in a full minute, stirring once more.

Fallon sighed, turning his attention to me again. 'The girl – the Heroine, opened the borders. By herself.'

I shook my head. 'So?'

He continued. 'The borders are what divide the dimensions. Dark beings are able to move freely through them, provided they are open. But they are not physical divides. They are made from energy, so opening and closing them takes immense power: hundreds of dark beings, at least. An entire court.' He paused for a moment. 'Yet this girl, even if she had help, must be powerful; so powerful that she could wield enough energy to be able to open the borders.'

I frowned. 'But what do you mean wield? Wield what?'

Autumn raised her eyes.

'Oh,' Fallon cooed. 'You really do know nothing.'

I folded my arms across my chest. 'Then tell me.'

He held out the hand that was scarred. 'I'd do better to show you.' Kaspar hissed all of a sudden but Fallon cut him off with a wave of his hand. 'You already know what it is, Miss Lee. It's what keeps the blood gushing through a vampire's veins, despite a deadened heart. It's what allows every dark being to use their minds to communicate. It's what caused the Death's Touch to flower. It's all around us; you feel it now.'

The burning, tingling sensation returned, skipping from fingertip to fingertip. The trees swayed once more and the beams of moonlight streaming between the canopy disappeared, like the light of a candle blown out by the rising breeze.

Fallon smiled. 'All dark beings are born with it,' he said, gesturing around the group, to which a few nodded. Kaspar stared at the ground, arms crossed, defeated. 'And the Sage have the power to manipulate it.'

He paused, then held his hand out and smiled.

'*Incendia*,' he breathed. His lips barely moved but from the very air he had just exhaled sprung minute, dancing sparks, champagne coloured and effervescent, cascading with so little effort that they looked to be lighter than air. They spun and spun in his hand, a tiny whirlwind until suddenly they disappeared; in their place was a flickering ball of fire, perfectly shaped into a flame and floating a few inches above his skin.

'Energy in its very rawest form; or what you, Miss Lee, may know as magic.'

My eyes widened. He waved his hand and it followed, becoming a flaming tongue, interweaving between his fingers as they clenched and his fist became a ball. When his fingertips met his palm, it was gone.

Magic. I believed it all, utterly and entirely, my reasoning simple: if vampires could exist, then what he had just produced from thin air could too.

Fallon stared at his hand for a moment, his eyes glazed and unfocused before he seemed to remember himself. His eyes drifted upwards and he continued.

'The borders are comprised of complex, dangerous magic. It is not something a normal young Sage could master. Yet she has. We're dealing with something new. Something powerful and perilous contained within one girl. She opened the borders and only heaven knows where she is or what she plans to do.'

Kaspar stirred. The brooding expression on his face, the downturned eyes, the folded arms – they were parts of his character that I recognized and was so familiar with now that I knew something was bothering him.

'Find the second Heroine, perhaps?'

Fallon shrugged his shoulders. 'Maybe. But that doesn't narrow it down. The second girl could be any woman, anywhere. She could be in any part of your dimension. Besides, what is there to say this girl accepts her fate? She is young, after all. She may ignore her duty.'

Alex dropped his guitar case to the ground, unzipping the top part. His fingers twiddled with the strings and I shifted, wishing he would stop.

'No. I can't believe that. Wherever the second Heroine goes, so does the first. No sane person would want to be stuck alone with a fate like that for long.'

Kaspar glanced at him, obviously thinking the same thing that I was. Alex picked up the hint, mumbling an apology. I glanced at Fallon's hand. A few sparks were still clinging to his fingertips, red this time.

'Then why are you here? An odd time to visit, surely?' Kaspar asked. The distrust and curiosity were evident in his voice.

'We wish to visit Eaglen and with your permission, would travel and camp with you tonight,' Fallon began, with a little more tact than before.

Kaspar narrowed his eyes. 'Eaglen? At a time like this?'

'Is Ad Infinitum not the time for visiting family and friends?'

Kaspar's eyes flashed black and I inwardly groaned at the insensitivity of his next statement. 'Eaglen is no relation or friend of yours.'

Quiet rained down on the clearing and for the first time, Autumn Rose stepped into the circle. Her eyes never left the ground and she spoke timidly and quietly, yet her voice rang clear through the air, musical in sound, so varied in pitch it was almost a song.

'I can explain that, Your Highness.' She paused, seeming to gather courage. 'Eaglen was a close friend of my grand-mother many years ago; I wished to spend such a time with someone who knew her well. I have no one else.'

Her eyes flickered upwards, coyly gauging his reaction. Kaspar seemed taken aback and his expression softened.

'Forgive me, Lady Sage. I did not know.'

He bowed stiffly and she nodded her head in return, seeming to gain a little confidence.

'And might I offer my apologies for not attending your late grandmother's funeral. The timing was unfortunate.'

She curtsied. 'A funeral is bitter to the grieving heart. It is no matter, Your Highness.'

I watched the exchange with interest. I felt a pang of sympathy for her. By the sound of it she had no family left. Yet the courtesy and respect Kaspar allowed her sent another type of pang stabbing through my heart.

Green doesn't look good on you, Girly, my voice snickered.

'No objections then, Kaspar?' Fallon continued.

Kaspar shook his head. 'None.'

'Then might I suggest we get moving? As I'm sure Violet will testify it's a little chilly just standing here.'

I nodded vigorously, hands already buried deep in my pockets. Alex swung his guitar back over his shoulders and with that, Fallon led the way into the trees, leaving the corpses of the unfortunate deer behind.

As early evening moved to night the clouds dispersed, blown away by the cold wind that had gradually intensified as we moved deeper into the heart of Varnley forest. The stars twinkled high above and occasionally, when we climbed to higher ground, I could make out the orange glow of London.

Crickets chirped in the undergrowth as I weaved my way through the treacherous maze of roots, tired and ashamed of my stumbling antics. Ahead, the two Sage leapt elegantly from root to root, hardly touching the ground and never so much as brushing a single thorn nor leaf. It was almost as though the forest moved with them, fluid and lithe to their swift pace.

The vampires were grouped in-between, stamina and strength pushing them on and guiding their feet. Kaspar had dropped back, staying behind with me, but he barely talked and when he did it was to warn me not to trip or to stay close.

'Where did you say we were going?' I asked for the umpteenth time, hoping he might elaborate on his reply compared to the last time.

'The brook,' he replied in a monotone. I sighed, resigning myself to the fact he did not want to awaken from his deep-thinking stupor.

Although his answer did not help, I got the feeling this was not an area that was ventured into much. Thick curtains of ivy were suspended like cobwebs between the mighty oaks that dominated this part of the forest. The ground was earthy and the grass sparse – only the odd bush sheltered life. Creepers snaked across the loose path, perfectly positioned as trip hazards for my ungainly feet.

As we walked on, I watched Autumn Rose. She was truly unlike anything I had ever seen. Her pale skin, intricate tawny scars and fine, straw-coloured hair were so exotic; so strange and alien, her amber eyes so wide, innocent and unknowing . . . and then there was the power she possessed within. The magic she could wield, shape and conjure at will. The possibilities seemed endless, even frightening.

'Is she an orphan?' I asked tentatively, wondering if I was pushing the boundaries too far.

Kaspar sighed. 'As good as.' Again he sighed, almost remorsefully. 'Her grandmother died about eighteen months ago, some months after my mother. Her parents are not Sage and she has no close relations that are either. Since then she has kept far from Athenea – away from the Sagean social circle.'

'How did she die? Her grandmother I mean. Old age?' I probed.

Kaspar stopped, turning to me with reproachful eyes. 'Violet, it was murder.'

Immediately, I felt terrible for asking. I glanced after her and then bowed my head.

'And you'd do better not to mention it to anyone,' he added before starting off again. 'Some things are better left buried.'

I closed my eyes, slowing breathing out. Dark beings buried everything, just never deep enough. Swallowing back my wounded pride, I carried on after him, hopping over another particularly large root in the dark forest.

We must have walked on another hour before the scenery began to change again. The trees narrowed and the oaks were replaced with great swathes of orange and red. Patches of autumn-flowering snowdrops broke through the hard earth, scattered between plots of grass. I could faintly hear the sound of trickling, gurgling water.

Suddenly, Felix clapped his hands together. 'Right, fire-wood. Any volunteers?'

We had come to a halt at a tiny clearing, ringed tightly by trunks. In the centre was a little circle of stones, enclosing a heap of wet ash. The group was gathered around, dumping their bags and settling down. There was a general disgruntled murmur and no one raised their hand.

I looked at the fire circle sceptically. 'Surely it would just be easier to use that magic of yours?'

I looked at Fallon, who smiled amusedly. Cain chuckled, muttering, 'City girl,' under his breath.

'It won't burn as bright or as warm.'

'Which is why we need wood,' Felix put in. 'I'll go if anybody nice wants to help?' Autumn sort of half-smiled and raised her hand. 'Anyone else?' he continued.

'I'll go,' I said, taking a step forward. Autumn seemed taken aback and Kaspar looked as though he was about to protest. But Felix was already striding away, heading in the opposite direction to which we had come. She recovered her unreadable expression and turned after him. I hurried behind.

I didn't know quite why I had volunteered, but something about this Autumn girl fascinated me. The Sage fascinated me. Magic fascinated me.

We approached the brook, a tiny, babbling stream flowing over mossy rocks and perfectly smooth, glinting pebbles. The banks were lined with snowdrops and luscious grass as it flowed down towards the Thames estuary.

Felix jumped the stream and disappeared into the trees, shouting for us to hurry up. Autumn followed, crossing in one graceful step. I edged downstream a little, strategically picking a spot with stepping-stones. There was certainly no firewood here. The branches were high up and what little wood did litter the ground was covered in moss or rotting leaves. However, it wasn't long before we were back within the confines of the great oaks. The night darkened and here there was plenty of dry, dead wood. I began picking up handfuls.

'Cold night,' I began, directing it at Autumn, hoping to strike a conversation. I received no answer, but persevered. 'So, how old are you?'

I bent down and picked up a few twigs. Her back was to me when she answered.

'Sixteen.'

'You look older,' I lied.

She turned, examined me for a moment and then curtly nodded, in gratitude I assumed. She continued on in silence, her arms already bundled high with sticks.

'So where do you come from? All the places are the same in the dimensions, right?'

She nodded. 'I grew up in London, but I come from Devon.'

Encouraged by her longer reply, I carried on. 'I grew up in London too.'

This time she took longer to reply and she averted her gaze again, eventually turning away and heading deeper into the forest.

'I know. You were born in Chelsea.'

I stopped, slightly dumbstruck. 'How do you know that?'

She paused, turning back to me. 'Everybody knows.'

She shifted her pile of wood into one arm, reaching into her cloak and pulling out a glossy magazine. She handed it to me.

I looked down at the cover. It was titled *Quaintrelle* and dated for the first week of November. Subheadings were splashed across the page: HOW WILL YOU SPEND YOUR AD INFINITUM?, OCTOBER'S TOP SOCIALITES and WHAT'S HOT, WHAT'S NEW AND ON THE RISE all featured around the edge of the page. Beneath that was a picture montage – the smiling faces of young Sage, vampires and other, unrecognizable creatures stared up at me, all dressed in suits and dresses.

But what really caught my attention was the heading at the bottom, written in red:

THE LATEST ON VIOLET LEE – TURN TO PAGE 5.

I yanked the magazine open, almost tearing the pages as I searched for the right page. I found it and began reading.

'Violet Lee – kidnapped and held hostage for months: her story has reached millions of dark beings and humans alike and touched many hearts. We discuss what it means for the second dimension and whether this tale will have a happily ever after – namely in the form of HRH Kaspar Varn.'

I could hardly bring myself to read on, feeling my cheeks glow red. Below the text was a picture of me at the Autumnal Equinox ball, surrounded by vampires. Inwardly, I cringed, closing the magazine and handing it back.

'No, keep it. It might be interesting for you,' she said, expression still perfectly unreadable. With that she carried on, occasionally stooping to pick up a handful of twigs. I followed, unsure of how I should feel.

A small part of me was flattered. A magazine – and one that was circulated around all the dimensions – was following me, along with a lot of the population by the look of it. But another, much larger part was humiliated. I didn't have to keep reading to know what it would go on to talk about.

That was private. It was between Kaspar and me. It was bad enough that the entire court knew.

I sighed. A different, more rational part was telling me I should have expected it. It was not as though vampires kidnapped humans every day.

We carried on in silence and I began to wonder when we were going to return. My arms felt like lead and my feet were beginning to ache. The path was leading us into a thorny thicket and the ground underfoot was mossy and damp. I gazed around and shivered, but not from the cold. A sudden sense of déjà vu had passed through me and with a sickening thump I realized where we were. Where we were heading.

We broke from the thorns and sure enough, ahead there was a stone building, ivy creeping up the walls and invading the huge cracks. Steps, broken in the centre, led up to a plinth, two stone pillars guarding the entrance to a huge, open door. From inside came the stomach-churning smell of decomposing flesh and the dust hung in great clouds, coating my arms in seconds.

I stopped. That was where the cloaked figure had feasted upon a young girl. Killed her. *Sarah. She was called Sarah.* It was here I was sure the Queen was buried, deep beneath my feet. *Carmen.* It was not far from here that he had attacked me. *Ilta.*

I swayed a little on the spot, feeling sick and quite light-headed.

'Can we go b-back?' I stuttered, eyes struggling to focus. 'I'm kind of cold,' I lied.

Felix, oblivious to my plight carried on. 'But it's only a little further and there's a whole load of dead trees.'

I swayed, dropping a few sticks. As they fell, Autumn abruptly whirled around, her eyes following them until they hit the ground before her gaze bounced back up to mine. Something warm and alien brushed against my mind, before I vaguely heard another voice.

'I'm cold too.'

I heard Felix sigh exasperatedly. 'Okay, okay . . . I get it . . . we'll go back . . .'

I closed my eyes for a few moments, taking a few deep breaths. When I opened them, the other two were already heading back up the path, the sticks that I had dropped at my feet gone.

The moment I stepped back into the clearing, Kaspar's eyes shot up from where he was silently whittling a piece of wood with a penknife. Questioning, they swept across me before they returned to his carving.

I dumped the wood beside the fire and dropped beside him, leaning against the trunk of a great tree.

'What's the time?'

'Mr Wolf.' He smiled at his lame joke, but his flat tone told me his heart wasn't in it. This Dark Heroine business had wiped the smile clean off his face. 'Almost midnight,' he added, not glancing up from his work. He stared at it, intent, tiny curls of wood floating to the ground at our feet until eventually all that was left was a shard of useless bark. He dropped it to the ground and folded the knife back up, watching as Felix and Cain arranged the sticks into a rough pyramid in the stone circle. Fallon knelt beside them, whispering words into the cradle of tinder.

Autumn gravitated around her companion, seeming reluctant to get too close to anyone else. Eventually she settled against a nearby tree, a little way out of the circle. Her eyes feasted on the smouldering beginnings of the fire, never leaving it, even as Fallon's face shone with a child's glee as flames sprung from the damp wood, or when the boys let out a satisfied shriek of surprise.

Yet again I found my gaze could not be torn away from her and I watched, even more fascinated now after her sudden act of insight and kindness towards me, a virtual stranger. The flames were reflected in her amber eyes and they were taking on an even greater depth – too deep for a shy girl of sixteen. They were the flickering eyes of an adult who had endured pain and torment; who understood the world and what she had to do.

I had seen those eyes before. They were the eyes of the King, of my father, of Eaglen, yet here they were, encapsulated in a young Sagean girl.

The clearing settled as the fire grew higher and higher; warmth spread outwards, creeping slowly across the ground until it reached my toes, then my legs and as I leaned forwards towards it, my face, which glowed and began to burn.

Fallon, content with his handiwork, held his hands out to the fire, warming them. Autumn shifted closer and joined him. Immediately, the fire quite literally bent towards them both, becoming brilliantly orange and distorted. She pursed her lips as though about to whistle and blew gently, forcing the reluctant fire back like a chastized child. Fallon just chuckled as the fire sprung back, trying its luck again. His serious companion did nothing this time, but continued to stare into the depths of the fire, even as the falling leaves landed in a little ring around them.

The vampires, on the other hand, scuttled away from the flames. Kaspar hesitated for a few minutes, staying close by my side but it wasn't long before he too succumbed to the burning heat and withdrew into the shadows.

It was mostly quiet for a long while, other than the occasional giggle from Lyla from the shadows – it did not take much imagination to know what her and Fabian were up to. Felix and Charlie occasionally whispered a few words to each other but their conversations were short. Alex eventually took out his guitar and retreated even further away from the fire and began strumming half-heartedly, competing with the crackling of the fire, Cain interjecting every now and then.

I sensed that everyone was lost in their own thoughts, just like I was: it was odd to think that the people sat around me were at the centre of everything that was happening to the dimensions, as things started to breakdown.

As are you, my voice said.

I scoffed in my head. *Hardly. I don't even understand the Prophecy.*

Then maybe you should ask.

I contemplated its suggestion for a moment but decided

I didn't have the courage to ask – I felt such a fool with the Sage around. I turned around, wondering if I could quietly question Kaspar but as soon as I met his eyes he stood up.

He walked around the fire, grabbed one of the bags and reached into it, pulling out a handful of chocolate bars. He chucked a couple of them my way and gave the rest to the two Sage. Autumn ripped hers open and devoured it hungrily, making her seem more human than her vampire counterparts; seeing that, Fallon handed her the rest and with a wave of his hand, conjured an apple from midair.

Kaspar handed the beers around which Autumn politely refused and settled back down behind me. I moved back a bit and joined him, tired of the burning heat, taking a few sips of the beer.

'How do you do that?'

'Do what?' Fallon asked, taking a second bite out of his apple.

'Produce food from thin air.'

He took a third bite. 'Magic.'

'But how is that possible?'

'Just is,' he said, shrugging his shoulders.

There was a pause. 'Then nobody starves.'

Fallon frowned ruefully. 'We feed our own.'

'What do you mean?' I asked, knowing full well what he was implying.

'We can only conjure what nature provides, and nature cannot provide enough to feed the expanding population of the world; of each dimension.'

My face cleared with comprehension but my mouth fell slightly open, aghast. 'So millions of humans – innocent children – die whilst the dark beings wallow in wealth?'

'I wouldn't say wealth,' Fallon argued, but I turned to Kaspar for back-up.

'You said yourself that there's no such thing as poverty for dark beings.'

He nodded solemnly. 'But it's more than that. There's too much politics involved between dark beings and humans.'

I straightened up. 'Clearly,' I retorted, knowing that my situation reflected that perfectly.

'Kaspar's right,' Cain said. 'Co-operating is basically impossible. Mother's proof of that. There's no trust.'

My eyes guiltily slid to the ground and the box rattled. 'Well maybe that is what needs to change,' I ended, defeated.

'I agree with Violet,' a quiet voice suddenly said.

All eyes turned to Autumn as her gaze briefly met mine. Quickly, she hastened to explain herself. 'The wealth could be more evenly distributed.'

'But Miss Lee,' Fallon begun. 'Who do you suggest could implement such a change?'

I flushed. 'The Dark Heroines? Isn't that what the Prophecy said they would do?'

The clearing went silent and Fallon cleared his throat, glancing sideways at Autumn.

'We'll tell you the first and second verse of the Prophecy, but no more. You don't know enough about the other dimensions to understand it.'

That stung but Fallon's mouth was set in a line and I knew not to argue.

'I've heard the first verse before,' I said, still hearing the hallowing penultimate line in my head.

'From Kaspar, I presume?'

Kaspar nodded and rested his head back against the trunk of the tree, looking resigned. His hands rested on the ground beside him and his nails dug into the earth, his arms tensed. My heart dropped, longing to know why he had become so withdrawn all of a sudden and almost instinctively I moved my hand as close as I dared to his, our little fingers almost touching. Perhaps he felt my warmth because his arm relaxed.

'Just the second verse then.' Fallon shrugged his shoulders and took a long swig from his can of beer. Finishing it, he crushed it in his palm, the metal disappearing beneath the crevices of his fingers. When he opened them again, all that was left was dust, which he scattered onto the fire.

Autumn glanced his way and then began to speak in her native tongue, Fallon weaving a translation in-between.

'Her fate is set in stone,
Bound to sit upon the second throne.
Destined to betray her kin; she lives in his past sin,
Bathed in the blood of the black rose above.
No birth, no time, no choice,
So as martyrs, two innocents must die,
For the girl, born to impassion the nine.'

Her last words were spoken with a severity and urgency there hadn't been before and she gave a small gasp, as though surprised at herself. Fallon didn't question her behaviour, but lay there patiently, his eyes roaming across the dark sky, as though counting the stars. With her gasp came silence, the fire the only one to speak as the wind raced through its mouth, sighing through pursed lips as the air escaped and hurried on, zipping between the trees and leaving only a whistle behind.

I nestled further into the tree and stared up too, wondering whether, perhaps, with its strange, airy, even earthy language that the stars were more familiar than the first dimension and its even stranger inhabitants, the Sage.

Fallon sighed and propped himself up on his elbows. 'That verse is a true declaration of war.'

'But this is peacetime?' I questioned, confused.

'No, Miss Lee,' Fallon cooed again. 'If this were peacetime, you would not be sitting here, a prisoner of politics, faced with a decision you hardly dared to consider until recently.'

My eyes lowered to the ground.

'If this were peacetime, no child, whether a descendent of magic or not, would starve.'

My hands clenched together.

'We have not been at peace for millennia. I highly doubt we ever have and things are now coming to a head. You just can't see it yet, Miss Lee.'

Autumn's eyes lowered to the ground.

'And you're hoping that the Heroines will sort it all out?' I snorted. 'Good luck with *that*!' Chuckling, I leaned back against the trunk of the tree. A quickly stifled laugh came from Kaspar beside me, who sobered as soon as Fallon disapprovingly looked his way.

'Was that some sort of backhanded insult, Miss Lee?'

I shook my head innocently but rather exaggeratingly winked at Kaspar who resorted to biting his bottom lip with his fangs to mute his laughter.

'I don't see this as a laughing matter.'

'I-it's not,' I choked, trying to subdue my giggling. And it wasn't funny, I was just glad to see Kaspar smiling and laughing again. 'But seriously, if I know anything about people with power, they'd rather die than accept change.'

Suddenly, Autumn stood up and muttered something that sounded like 'tired' to Fallon who replied in their native language. She shook her head and began to walk away but in one fluid movement he had stood up and grabbed her hand, stopping her mid-step.

Immediately, I stopped laughing.

Fallon called after her and she stopped, her back to us.

'You forget yourself, Autumn. You are in the presence of royalty, remember.'

Her shoulders rose gradually and fell as though she was sighing, before she slowly turned and in a show of manners or mockery, I wasn't sure which, bowed to the ground in a full curtsy.

'Your Highnesses. Lords. Sirs.' Her eyes glided across each person until they came to me. 'Madam.'

Her gaze turned to Fallon, reproachful, and lingered there for a moment like she was searching for his approval. But she didn't wait for it because she sprang back up, her hair flung from about her neck to her back and in one leap; she had disappeared into the thick canopy of leaves.

There was stunned silence at her departure. An acid-y, sickly feeling settled in the back of my throat. I had only met this girl a few hours before, but I felt as though I had insulted a close friend; the jealousy I had felt when Kaspar had shown her kindness earlier seemed trivial; my thoughtlessness childish.

Fallon stared into the forest and slowly turned back to Kaspar, a rueful look on his face. Niceties were exchanged as he apologized profusely for her behaviour – '*So inappropriate*' – before he turned into the darkness after her with the assurance the vampires would keep watch for the night.

The last thing I saw before sleep enveloped me sometime later was Fallon's swirling scars through the many lashing, lusty tongues of the fire as he returned and a hand – Kaspar's hand – creeping closer to mine, palm facing the stars.

FIFTY-FIVE

Kaspar

The hands of my watch moved achingly slowly as the night wore on, tiresome and troubled. Below me, Violet's soft breathing was the complete opposite: calm and even but still agitating.

I had kept my hand near hers for the first half an hour or so, but was forced to move it as she rolled over in her sleep and moved dangerously close. We were many miles from my father but he would know. And even if he didn't, I couldn't touch her. The King was right.

My responsibility was not to Violet. It was to another. It had always been to another. I may not have known about it, but it was my duty. It was Prophecy.

Here Violet was, prepared to sacrifice her humanity for me and what did I have to give her in return?

I was a fool for letting her get this close. A fool for not stopping and realizing what was happening. A fool for not realizing what I felt for her until we were apart for two weeks. *It's crazy, it's wrong and it's going to hurt her.*

*Yet she brought you back, Kaspar. She brought back the 'you'
your mother knew,* my voice reasoned.

And what me was that?

It did not answer.

I looked down at Violet's frail frame and felt a pang of guilt.
I had wronged her and worst of all I couldn't bring myself to
tell her why. I knew I would never work up the courage either
and that she would find out the hard way: as fate played out.

It was so close now. *So real.* Athenea had their Heroine,
whoever she was, wherever she was, and the second would
follow.

Sighing, I pulled a crumpled, roughly folded piece of paper
from my pocket and opened it, thumbing the darker parts of
the page where tears had fallen. *Mother's letter. One of a pair.*

Dear sweet Beryl,

I didn't have to read on to know what it said. I had studied
it so many times now that tiny tears had appeared along the
folds where I had repeatedly folded and unfolded it. It was
the other letter I was interested in, which I extracted from
the crumpled mass and flattened out on my bended knee.

'My dear beloved son, Kaspar,

*A warning, sweet child: I leave for Romania in a week and
I will not leave without entrusting what I know to you. But I
would advise that you don't read on until you must – if you
are at peace, my son, do not turn the page. I know you are
wise and true enough to heed my words.'*

I had been in possession of that letter since the day she
died; the first time I ever turned that page was when father
had given me her letter to Beryl – one we all treasured.

'That letter is one of a pair,' he had said, resting against the stone atop Varns' Point, the morning after I slept with Violet. 'It is time for you to read the other.' And then he told me. *Everything.* Why we couldn't touch. Why he was sending me to Romania.

I ran the whole way back, taking the stairs two at a time, bursting into my room, maids bowing and making hurried excuses as they dropped the dust sheets from their hands, fleeing from my snarls as I flung the white coverings away, pulling drawers from their runners until I found the second letter. *Flinging my mother's letter to me onto the unmade bed, untouched since she had slept in it. Reading it. Hearing Violet's heartbeat as she slept next door, collapsed and stunned, not peacefully as she does now.*

That letter changed everything. Even as I realized that Violet was no longer just a prize won and thrown away, but one to be treasured and revered – she wasn't just another notch on the bedpost. That letter changed everything.

I took the second, hidden part of the letter with me to Romania, along with her last letter to Beryl. *Drinking myself delirious. Drowning my sorrows.* Selfishly hoping she would return my feelings but knowing it would be so much better for her if she didn't.

Returning, desperate to see her before the ball but distracted and swept up by the politics as the news that sealed so many fates fell upon our ill-prepared ears.

They found her. The first girl. The Sagean Heroine.

Athenea closed their borders and refused to give news. But the ball went on. *I'll never forget her face, as my father sunk his fangs into her neck. Never.*

The locket should have been farewell. I should have let her go, but I couldn't. Not when Father announced her feelings for me.

I can't let her go and I can't break her heart.

After a while I realized I couldn't sit there and listen to her sleeping. So I got up, crushed both letters into a ball in my pocket and walked away, leaving the questions of the others unanswered as they called after me.

FIFTY-SIX

Violet

The forest brims with life this night, he thought. *Not that life is quite the right word.*

Gone were the rogues and the slayers, driven away by Varnley's guards in anticipation of Ad Infinitum. Forgotten by the council too, for a few days at least, was Michael Lee's plan to rescue his daughter. To replace it had arrived lore and legend: the Prophecy.

He sighed. Leading a double life had left him weary. It was a relief simply to walk in the forest as his true self, and not the cloaked figure the forest had learned to fear.

The persona he had taken on in his younger years was gone. He'd taken to this life to become as much of a rogue as he could – a rebellion, perhaps, against authority – but it had backfired and the ultimate irony was he had become exactly what he had been trying to escape: a man, not a boy, ready to shoulder that authority.

A rabbit scampered by his feet, but he ignored it, not thirsty after drinking from the doe earlier.

He vowed, silently to himself, that the days where he would prowl the catacombs and the marshes would be only memories now. He had exacted enough revenge on the slayers and hunters of the forest.

His mind reeled. He was sure it wouldn't be long now before Michael Lee came for his daughter. It had been months and he was a man of strategy – this was the perfect opportunity to attack, whilst the Kingdom's back was turned to face the Heroines. Violet Lee would not be forgotten, as she had forgotten them.

Home was the best place for her.

But she would never move on; never let go. How could she? A whole world-within-a-world, so near to her grasp: one she almost joined.

But Varnley will be a worse place for her.

The old part of the forest gradually became new as the cloaked figure – no longer cloaked – began to slow as he approached the clearing. And knowing she would hear him, he spoke in his mind, his voice more than familiar to her.

Forgive me, Girly, please.

Forgive me, Girly, please.

I sat bolt upright. The air left my lungs in one breath, suddenly leaving my chest painfully empty. My eyes flew open and reluctantly the light flooded in, revealing the scene before me.

Kaspar. It's Kaspar.

Ten pairs of concerned eyes drank me in and I immediately became aware of one set: emerald and belonging to a figure strolling back into the circle.

He can't be. How can he be?

Kaspar, uncloaked, his hands buried deep in the pockets of his black jacket, the collar still upturned, slipped past the fire, almost unnoticed by everyone but me. Their attention had returned to their work as they doused the fire and gathered empty beer cans . . . everyone's attention but one: Autumn's gaze still burnt into my back.

Kaspar cannot be the cloaked figure. It just isn't possible.

My mind reeled. But my heart tugged. I knew the voice that had rung in my head just seconds before. It had called me 'Girly'.

Nobody else calls me that.

But the rational side of me spoke the loudest. I believed in my eyes and my eyes had seen Kaspar and a cloaked rogue in the very same room just before we set off for London, a couple of weeks before. It didn't make sense.

My eyes bore into him as he rounded the remains of the fire. I scrabbled up.

'Don't stare, Girly, it's not very polite.'

I knew my gaze was one of an accuser, but I hoped I would see confusion in his face, or at least some sort of recognition at my anger; even the pleading eyes of a man who had just begged for my forgiveness. But there was nothing. His smirk faded and he shrugged his shoulders, setting off after Alex and Charlie who were already carving a path away from the brook.

I watched him go, the outline of a figure swathed in a black cloak pursuing him towards the hill. In the figure's arms was the limp form of a half-naked girl, neck pierced and dripping blood.

Faintly, I saw a golden blur pass and I shook the image away, my eyes focusing to see Autumn Rose, flinging a cloak about her shoulders and hurrying to catch the others. Taking a deep breath I pushed the dead girl's name from my mind and followed.

Please God, don't let it be Kaspar.

*   *   *

With one last painful step I broke from the trees into the clearing that was Varns' Point, which continued to grow to a shallow mound of earth topped with an enormous boulder. The ground was covered in heath and was damp with an early morning frost. It crunched beneath my feet, gradually retreating from the light as the sun rose. That light slid along the boulder, twice as high as it was wide, casting a long shadow. Grooves were chiselled along its side – just large enough to be hand or footholds.

Kaspar took a few steps back and surged forward, completely unfazed. With one leap, he stood at the top of the boulder, staring smugly down, his eyes almost daring the others to try and do the same.

With a chuckle Alex followed, jumping four times his height and joining Kaspar at the top. Before long, the others were doing the same. Looking doubtful, however, Cain opted to climb and gestured for me to join him.

Dubious, I approached. I wasn't usually afraid of heights or falling; I was afraid of making a fool of myself. Unbuttoning my coat, I let it fall to the ground beside the bags. It would only get in the way. I knew I must look a state and that I would probably freeze in just a T-shirt and jeans, but the coat was too bulky to climb in.

I slotted my foot into a crevice. Cain smiled encouragingly and began to hoist himself up, pointing out the best hand-holds as he did. When he reached the crest, he offered his hand, which I took gratefully. With one easy tug, he pulled me over the edge and onto my feet.

The view was incredible. The sun rose in the distance to the east, a ball of fire floating just above the beginnings of the North Sea and the end of the Thames estuary. The water was not blue but black; the sky was completely cloudless, hovering over a strip of orange thrown out as far as the eye could see by the sun. A little closer, the Thames River snaked inland, marshes at its fringes which eventually gave way to pines which sloped uphill until they suddenly broke into bare and baron oaks, which in turn gave way to a blur of lighter green and white – the main grounds of the Varns' mansion, far below us. Over the tops of the trees I could just make out a few of the pale towers.

'Beautiful isn't it?' A voice said behind me.

I didn't need to turn to know it was Kaspar, stood unnaturally close . . . so close I dared not move for fear of touching him. 'Something is wrong, isn't it, Kaspar?' I muttered, not taking my eyes off the glow the sun cast over the water.

I felt his coldness withdraw a little. 'No.'

'Don't lie,' I chuckled flatly. 'You're crap at it.'

There was a pause. Then I felt an icy chill on my back once more as he bent down to my ear. 'You've heard my father talk of responsibility.' It wasn't a question – we both knew I had. 'And you know that my responsibility lies with the Kingdom.' I swallowed. 'I don't want to rule that Kingdom alone, Violet.'

My heart skipped a beat and I cursed it, afraid he would hear the effect he had on that particular organ.

'I want someone alongside me who knows when I'm lying, who will stand up to me and who knows me at my very worst. But what I want and my duty do not always coincide and—'

I turned me head sharply to the right. 'What is your very worst?'

'You know what my worst is, Girly. You've seen it.'

'No,' I breathed.

He couldn't be. He just couldn't.

'I had known someone was tapping into my mind for a while and when Fabian told me about your dreams, it all slotted into place,' he continued. His voice was a drone. It did not sound as though he were reasoning with something extraordinary. 'It can't be a coincidence considering you contain my blood; it's unusual but not unheard of for dhampirs to be able to enter another's mind.'

His explanation fell on death ears. I couldn't even bring myself to correct him on when the dreams started – before I became a dhampir.

This man . . . this man I have learned to trust and have feelings for; the one I am prepared to give up humanity for is not the same brute that prowls the forest as a rogue. That monster was not the Prince of the Kingdom; the heir to the throne. But even as those thoughts crossed my mind, I could see the greying body of the girl he had killed at the fair, not so different from the girl in the catacombs.

'No,' I repeated.

'You don't want to believe me, do you, Girly?'

I shook my head and took a step back.

His eyes fluttered down. 'I wish you would accept me as a vampire and let go of this illusion that I'm something I'm not.'

I took another step back. 'Don't play mind games with me, Kaspar.' *Don't play games with my heart.*

'I'm not.'

That was all I heard as the ground fell from beneath my feet and I screamed; screamed as a hand caught mine, mottled and scarred, a pair of amber eyes briefly fixing on mine before I was tumbling through the air, pulling Autumn Rose with me.

But the ground did not hurtle towards us; neither did I land awkwardly. Instead, I came to a gentle rest on my back amongst the damp heath, not even winded. Autumn was already on her feet, completely unharmed. Gingerly, I propped myself up on my elbows and felt a pain shoot down my wrist, as though somebody had run a knife down my inner wrist. Supporting myself with the other arm, I forced myself to look.

A jagged gash running from my hand to my elbow had opened up, coated in grit, stinging as though someone had poured vinegar over the length of my arm.

I scrabbled to my feet just as Autumn grabbed my unharmed elbow and steered me away at such a pace my feet caught on the uneven tufts of grass, and I would have toppled if she had not been supporting me, seemingly unaware that I was almost dragging her to the ground. She shouted something over her shoulder to Fallon in her language and rounding the rock, I stole a glance back.

The vampires seemed unaffected. They were grouped beside the edge of the forest, not even looking our way. *So what's the urgency?* Tugging me along, she didn't say a word until we came to a halt near the pile of coats.

'Put pressure on your inner elbow,' she said, indicating to my arm. I did so and she began running a finger down the length of the cut, making it sting even more.

Muttering something under her breath, a pool of water appeared in her cupped hand, which she poured over my arm. I winced as the cold water trickled through the wound and looked away, clenching and unclenching my hand in an attempt to combat the stinging.

'Was that you, back there? That stopped us from falling?' I asked, trying to ignore the pins and needles sensation passing through my fingers.

'Yes,' she said, as a particularly painful stab shot through my arm.

I mumbled a thank you through clenched teeth, silently wondering how she could have acted so quickly – she must have been standing nearby. *Did she hear what Kaspar said?*

It bothered me, somehow, that she might know me and Kaspar were – well, I wasn't even sure what we were – and I definitely wasn't sure what we were if he *was* the cloaked figure. *But how could he be?* He was standing in the same room as a cloaked figure before we left for London. But doubt was entering my mind. *Why would he claim to be the figure if he wasn't? After all, the figure in the entrance hall could have been anyone.*

A minute passed and the tingling sensation increased. Needle after needle felt as though they were being thrust into my arm – but I didn't mind, because as the sensation increased, the bleeding receded.

More importantly, can I forgive him? He had killed so many during his night-time prowls: the rogues and hunters in the name of the Kingdom, but the image of the girl in the catacombs, Sarah, refused to leave my head. Yet I knew the answer to my question. It was no less sickening for it, but my heart had already forgiven him without ever consulting my rationality.

What does that make me? What he did to her was worse than what Ilta did to me. He killed her.

'You have dreams about a cloaked man, don't you, Violet Lee? And a voice too.' The sound of her voice so surprised me that I yanked my arm from her grasp. When it registered what she had said, I took two steps back until I hit the rock.

'How do you know that?'

She smiled. It wasn't a reassuring smile, but something more sinister; a knowing smile, except her eyes betrayed her: they were as wide as mine and full of the same fear.

Suddenly, she lurched forward and grabbed the hand of my injured arm, clutching it in two of hers. I looked down, astonished at the contact. As I did, I caught sight of my arm. Not a trace of the wound remained. My skin was completely unblemished, as though I had never fallen. Reluctantly, I looked back at her.

'Oh, tell me you have a vague idea?' Gone was her composed, unreadable face. Replacing it was a barrage of emotions – fear, desperation and urgency, formed in the shape of her wide eyes and parted lips.

'Of what?' I asked slowly.

Her grip on my hand loosened and she took a step back. 'Eighteen years ago, a second child was born to a rising MP and his wife, in Chelsea, London. That same night, a group of young vampires were out hunting in Westminster. Amongst them was Kaspar Varn, who that night, first heard a voice in his mind that would plague him for the next eighteen years.' She paused and took another step back. I didn't say anything. I couldn't say anything. 'Almost from the moment you arrived at Varnley you started hearing a voice in your mind. You started having vivid nightmares too.'

'Stop it,' I breathed, pushing my back into the rock as though hoping it would swallow me.

'You were that child, Violet Lee, and Kaspar is both the figure of your dreams as well as your voice, as you are his voice.'

Through lowered eyes she gauged my reaction as she had done with Kaspar the day before. Behind her, I could see the light advancing towards us as the sun rose higher in the sky and emerged from behind the rock.

'You're lying.'

'I'm not lying, Violet Lee.'

I gripped the handholds in the rock. The cloaked figure I could believe. *But to be a voice in his mind without knowing? For* eighteen *years? My* whole *life?*

'You're lying because I would know if I were his voice.'

She sighed. 'Your voice is subconscious. You are not aware that your mind is tied to his, as he is not aware he is tied to yours. But I wish it were a lie, Violet.'

Her voice trailed off into silence, pitying at the end. But the pity only doused my emotions, already tattered and on tenterhooks. My head fell into my hands, defeated.

'Why are you telling me this?'

'Because there's no time left.'

'No time left for what?' I raised my head out of my hands, slowly raising it up to meet her eyes, golden and full of sympathy.

'To choose.'

'What do you mean?' I breathed. *That word again. Choose.*

Her eyes lowered to the ground, not raising her gaze once as she spoke, almost guiltily. 'The first Heroine is indeed of noble blood, Violet. Neither is she is far from the control of the Athenean court; although as Heroine she takes precedence over even the greatest of Kings.'

Last night she had no reason to curtsy . . . You forget yourself, Autumn. You are in the presence of royalty, remember.

'Her grandmother died alone so she could awaken the nine, leaving her the last Sage of her family.'

An innocent must die . . .

'In short, Violet, she is the last of the fall.'

In front of me stood not a girl bathed in sunlight, but a girl I had only just met, covered in a cloak and curtseying with the smallest of smiles in the gloom of the night.

Autumn Rose, House of Al-Summers, Your Highness.

'You,' I whispered. 'You're the first Dark Heroine.'

She nodded to the ground. For a minute I could only stare at her, before I closed my eyes, reeling in stupidity. It was *so* obvious. It had been staring us in the face the entire time.

'I . . . why didn't you say anything earlier? Why did you lie?'

'Because . . . because . . .' She wrung her hands together. 'Because I have to doom another to the same path as mine. Now. Here.'

'It is my duty to ensure you die before you ever fulfil your fate . . . You will have no choice, Violet Lee. So do not weep, child, for I am saving you this night.'

As Ilta's words echoed and then died, a sort of quiet acceptance came over me. I let my head slowly fall back against the rock, running my fingers through my hair.

'You know why I am here,' she said softly.

'Wherever the second Heroine goes, so does the first. No sane person would want to be stuck alone with a fate like that for long.'

'But the only person I know who has died is Greg, that's not two innocents,' I reasoned quietly, clawing around for flaws in what I knew she was about to tell me.

'Your brother was the first. Queen Carmen was the second.'

'But I'm not a vampire,' I muttered to the darkness behind my closed eyelids.

'No birth, no time, no choice, Violet. The second Heroine was never meant to be born a vampire. But you must become one to fulfil the Prophecy and become the second Heroine. And soon.'

The early morning dew was fast melting, as was the sun. Already it was becoming a feeble blotch behind dark, menacing clouds that almost certainly constrained the rain. I stared up at them, willing myself to remain calm.

'I don't want this. I can't be a part of this. I don't know a thing about the dark beings, Autumn.' My voice sounded oddly serene compared to my inner turmoil. 'Four months ago I didn't even know this whole world existed. I won't be dragged into this.'

'You have no choice.'

'You have no choice. You never did! Nobody chooses their fate when they get involved with dark beings. Nobody! Wake up, or die dreaming, Girly!'

She pushed a few stray curls from her forehead, turning so that her back was to me. 'If you choose to ignore the Prophecy, Violet, your two worlds will destroy each other, taking most of this dimension with them.' She shook her head, as though clearing her mind. 'Your father's sin is surfacing and if you do not betray him as the prophecy states and pledge your allegiance to the vampires, then your family will die at the hands of the man you care for.'

'I'll hunt him down, kill his love first . . . suck his children dry . . . rape his daughters, make the fucking heartless bastard suffer.'

The black box rattled, its seal tearing at the edges.

'I have no choice,' I whispered, feeling my legs begin to buckle beneath me.

'I-if I could give you time, Violet, I would. But I can't and I'm so sorry . . .'

As she spoke she looked past me, beyond the rock and the trees of Varnley. She looked into the distance, her eyes focused on a flickering orange dot on a far away hillside. Another appeared to the left, larger, closer.

'They're lighting the beacons,' she murmured, hesitantly taking a few steps around the rock. Her eyes were fixed on the dots, as though she were completely mesmerized. 'I have to go. They know I'm here.'

She backed away a few paces, before her expression softened and she hurried forward again and grabbed my hand, clutching it with an unnaturally tight grasp.

'Do not tell them what you are until I send word. But I can only buy you a few hours of normality, no more than that.'

'A few hours of normality to do what?'

She glanced over her shoulder frantically before turning back to me and grasping both my hands.

'To follow your heart.'

'What if it was *someone you knew?'*

'Then may fate have mercy upon her heart.'

With that she swung around and marched towards the trees, her eyes fixed on Fallon. Kaspar followed close behind, his gaze sliding from the one Sage to the other before he swung around, staring across the treetops to where a third beacon had sprung into flames.

Is that all she was going to leave me with?

As she grew nearer the group she threw her cloak about her shoulders and I backpedalled, grabbing my coat. Something fell from the inner pocket and looking down, I realized it was the magazine she had given me the night before. Staring at it for a moment, I snatched it from the ground and stuffed it back into the pocket.

Meeting in the middle, Autumn and Fallon exchanged a few words before the Sagean Prince turned to Kaspar, waving off his wide-eyed protest. Before anyone could say another thing, Autumn curtsied – her final curtsy – and throwing up their hoods, they disappeared in a whirling mass of black cloth.

Nobody spoke. An identical picture was painted on every face as eyes slid from one to the other. It was one of complete disbelief – a feeling I shared, but for different reasons.

Dark Heroine? But I didn't have time to wallow in doubt. Already, the adrenaline was kicking in and I felt a strange sort of determination. *I am not going to let fate destroy anyone I care for.*

Kaspar's eyes moved quickly between the beacon and the spot where the Sage had just stood. Behind his eyes, fast falling through to white, I could see his mind turning things over. His lips mouthed the word 'beacon' over and over; his eyes searched the sparse heath for answers. After a minute, his expression became perfectly placid. Realization was dawning and it almost hurt to watch his hand running through his hair, clutching at strands as he spun around and mouthed the word 'beacons' one final time.

'She was right here,' Kaspar choked, utter disbelief in his voice. 'They duped us.

And the council will know by now. But why would she come now?'

'Second Heroine,' Alex answered, his words clipped and impatient. He glared at the other man, his brow creasing when, to my surprise, his gaze moved to me. 'She has a duty, just like you do, Kaspar.'

Kaspar didn't seem to be listening because he motioned for Alex to follow him and instructed the others to return to the mansion. He glanced at me.

'Cain, with Violet. You won't be slowed down as much. And *look after her*.'

I was about to protest that I didn't need 'looking after' but Cain beat me to it. 'We're going back? But the sun's barely risen. What's the rush? It's not as though we can do anything. Father will deal with it.'

Kaspar sighed, his irises a cloudy white – a shade worse than red, or black. It was a shade that robbed his eyes of humanity. 'You're not old enough to remember the last time the beacons were lit, Cain. That's because they're only ever lit when things get bad. They're a call to court. In just hours, the entire Kingdom will be flocking to Varnley and expecting answers about the Prophecy. Answers we don't have.'

Cain's eyes flickered to the orange flames on the horizon and he shut his mouth, subdued into nodding.

Kaspar, on the other hand, opened his mouth as though to say something and my heart seemed to constrict in the middle, partly in dread, partly in anticipation. But he closed it again and turned his attention away from me to Cain.

'Look after her,' he repeated. With that he and Alex shot off into the forest.

My heart deflated. I could have stood there, staring after them for hours, trying desperately to piece together everything that had happened in the past fifteen minutes, but that wasn't an option. The others were dissipating and Cain glanced at me, adjusting the strap of the guitar case on his shoulder.

'Do you mind if we run? It's only a mile downhill and I've got a feeling we don't want to be missing this.'

I shrugged my shoulders, buttoning up my coat, feeling the magazine press against my side in the inner pocket. Taking a few steps, Cain broke out into a jog, gradually speeding up as we slipped in-between the trees. It occurred to me suddenly that I would probably regret this half way down, but I did not have the capacity or the time to care.

My brain was working overtime. I was a Dark Heroine and however much I wanted to not believe it, I knew that there was too much at risk to just ignore it.

Hours. I had *hours*. I didn't even know what I had to do in those hours. I was completely at the mercy of the Sage and Autumn Rose. I knew nothing of this world; of the dimensions; of Vamperic politics. *All I know is that I can't let my worlds destroy each other.*

Moreover, in mere hours the Vamperic Kingdom would descend upon Varnley as the beacons flamed, news of the first Heroine spread and thoughts turned to the second Heroine.

Me.

*   *   *

Sweat dripped down my face as we emerged from the trees, bare of the vibrant covering they had possessed in earlier months. Those leaves that had once been plush and alive were now as devoid of life as the inhabitants they surrounded; they were swept into rough piles at the very extremities of the grounds, out of site and view of the entrance as though they had never provided colour and pleasure.

But beyond that was a more curious sight. Lined up on the drive were dozens of the servants, their trim uniforms looking out of place against the disarray of the grounds. Even the disciplined butlers were amongst them, their crisp white gloves a complete contrast to their skin, burnt a deep red by the morning sun.

Cain meandered through them, attempting to chivvy them back inside, but at most he earned himself a few desultory bows. Instead, they all stared across the treetops, a few talking animatedly in little enclosed groups of two or three. As I moved closer, I caught a few words of the nearest group.

'Found the first Heroine . . . Varnley . . . back to Athenea . . .'

Suddenly, one of them caught me looking and nudged her two friends who immediately hushed. I recognized one as Annie. She straightened up, squaring her shoulders and glaring defiantly at me. Unable to hold her gaze I shifted and moved to join Cain.

'They're watching the beacons,' he explained. 'They won't hear sense, c'mon.' He left the servants behind and progressed through the open double doors. Leaving Kaspar's guitar beside the staircase, he turned to me.

'I'm going to try and find someone who knows what the hell is going on. You better stay in your room.'

I nodded, not intending to follow his advice: as soon as he had disappeared into the corridor I bolted for the stairs and took them two at a time, dashing into Kaspar's room. It was empty. My heart sank.

I took a few hesitant steps in. The door slammed behind me and I jumped, always on edge in this room below the gaze of the realistic, piercing eyes of the King and Queen, immortalized in oil and canvas above the mantle. I shivered. This was not a welcoming room: if wood could be cursed then the panels lining the walls were damned.

Most of the furniture, bar the bed, was still covered in dust sheets, adding to the eerie, unlived-in feel of the room. There was another draft, too: the French doors to the balcony were wide open, the dark voiles fluttering in the breeze and filtering the mid-morning sun. The few untampered rays fell across the floor as slits of light that I moved into as I reached out and grasped the material. Drawing them across I balanced on the lip of the doorframe, where my heart sank for the second time in a minute. He wasn't there either.

I retreated back inside, question after question tumbling from my mind into my chest, where the dread mounted. *I'm only human, what on Earth can I do?* From that dread spilled resentment. *Why did Autumn leave me? Doesn't she get it? I have no one. No one but Kaspar, and where the hell is he when I need him?*

Right here, a voice said.

I spun around so quickly that I stumbled and had to grab the voiles to keep myself from falling. *That sounds exactly like—*

So poised, Girly, the same voice said . . . wait, *my* voice said.

'Oh God,' I muttered.

You did ask where I was, it or *he* responded.

So you're referring to yourself as Kaspar now? I asked cautiously in my mind.

It chuckled. *Girly, I am Kaspar. Always have been, always will.* It stopped and corrected itself. *Actually, I'm a diluted version of his personality embodied in your sub-conscious since birth, but let's keep it simple.*

'You've known all along?' I spat as it occurred to me that I was having a conversation with my own mind – a mind that contained all the sass of Kaspar. *Great.*

Not really, it replied. *I'm still your mind and I can only learn things as you do.*

'Well, diluted Kaspar, would you mind shutting up?' I asked the empty room as I flopped onto the bed and fell back onto the sheets. My feet dangled off the edge and I swung them, my heels hitting the mattress over and over, remembering the last time I had lain here, stark naked, in the arms of Kaspar. A small smile crossed my lips.

I sobered quickly. I couldn't forget what had been revealed to me that easily, and I was fully expecting to start panicking if I didn't tell someone soon.

But what use is there in panicking?

I kicked my shoes and socks off, glad of the cool breeze steadily blowing through the open doors to the balcony. I let my head fall to the side and I was just contemplating going to look for him when a triangle of white tucked beneath the pillow, stark against the black covers, caught my eye.

Rolling over, I pinched it between forefinger and thumb and pulled, moving the pillow aside.

A ball of heavy, almost-yellow paper rolled into my hand. It was so creased that tears had begun to appear at the folds and where the paper had worn thin I could read inked words in reverse, written in an elegant, sprawling hand. Astonished, I folded it out flat on the bed.

As I did, it became apparent that it was in fact two sheets of paper and that they were both written in an identical hand, with an identical signature and coat of arms at the bottom. I picked up the nearest; the writing was difficult to discern because the paper was so battered, but as I made out the first few words I almost dropped it in surprise.

Dear sweet Beryl,

Sure enough, besides the royal coat of arms it was signed 'Queen Carmen' and swallowing an uncomfortable lump in my throat, I lowered the Queen's last letter to the bed. Here it was, for a *third* time.

I took up the other sheet of paper in my hands. It too had been folded and refolded, but had not worn as much: the paper was thicker and had a faint musky smell, like it had been stowed away for a long time. The torn edge of a wax seal clung to one end of the paper and the sheet showed two defined creases where it had been folded, quite precisely, into three.

I turned it over and saw that there was writing on both sides of the sheet, although far more on the inner side. The handwriting was undeniably the same as that of the other letter. Beginning on the side with less writing, I noted the date: it had been written on exactly the same day as the other letter.

A shiver ran through my spine as I realized who it was addressed to: Kaspar. Sitting up straight, I fingered the paper in my hands.

My dear beloved son, Kaspar,
  A warning, sweet child: I leave for Romania in a week and I will not leave without entrusting what I know to you. But I would advise that you don't read on until you must – if you

are at peace, my son, do not turn the page. I know you are
wise and true enough to heed my words.

A second chill ran down my spine and again I wondered
whether I should turn the page. But Kaspar had turned the
page – the letter had been opened – and I couldn't let go of
the desire to know what had compelled him to disregard his
mother's wish.

Just do it, my voice snapped impatiently and spurred on,
I turned the page and began to read once more.

I will assume, Kaspar, that if you are in possession of this
letter that I have passed from this world and am no longer
able to convey my knowledge to you with a mother's embrace
– an event for which I am deeply sorry. It is my own mistake
that has led me to writing this letter, for I should have been
sincere and honest with you from the onset. But I could not
ruin your happiness, my son, and I ask firstly for your
forgiveness for my weakness.

Secondly, I ask that you do not be angry with your father,
as you undoubtedly will be. I know that what he will say to
you will make no sense and may seem to be another
superficial whim of his, but you must understand that what
he does is for your own well-being. Understand that I
instructed him to act in such a way, as well as to prompt you
to read this letter when it becomes apparent you must. How he
does that is of his choosing, but do not be angry. He is your
father and he does it out of love.

Before I explain to you what could warrant such words, I
will tell you that you may trust Eaglen and Arabella as
confidants about what I will shortly tell you. Of course, your
father also knows. On my request they keep a silent vigil but
all three will gladly hear your questions.

To truly appreciate what I have to tell you, I must take you back to many millennia before you or any of your siblings were born. During a particularly warm Romanian summer, your father and I paid a state visit to Athenea, where we were received by the then young King Ll'iriad Alya Athenea and his wife, pregnant with their first child.

The court at Athenea was a vibrant place, full of the most praised philosophers, academics and astrologers; it was the centre for all deemed revolutionary within the nine dimensions. One of these famed thinkers was a certain Nab'ial Contanal, rising in standing after receiving a royal patron for the Prophecy of the Heroines that you are quite familiar with. Upon our introduction, I was immediately struck by his devotion to the belief that man and woman should be bestowed with equal status – something very few of us had entertained at the time – and found myself listening intently to his talks during the many dinners and dances that occurred.

As previously mentioned, the season was unnaturally hot and one afternoon, when walking alone, I profess that I found myself overcome from the humidity. Contanal, passing, saw my plight and offered to let me rest in his nearby quarters, which were shaded and faced away from the noon sun. Although inappropriate, I accepted his offer – to this day I do not know why.

It was here, half in a daze, that I was witness to a most extraordinary speech. Contanal, pacing between his cluttered shelves, began telling me in a most agitated way that his visions about the Heroines had not ended with his twelve previous verses. A new work he had begun, starting with the second Heroine, the heart of which he was the most fascinated by.

For the first time since Autumn and I had talked at Varns' Point, a truly uneasy feeling passed through me. This was real. I was one of the Heroines this prophet, Contanal, had written about, thousands of years before.

He then began to detail, with what I would discover years later, uncanny accuracy, events which I could not have foreseen or dreamt of at the time. He told me that I would have six children – four sons, two daughters – before proceeding to tell me the names your grandfather would give to you and your exact birth dates. But it became apparent quickly that it was only the fourth child, a son – you – he was concerned with.

I am not naïve to the power of fate, but what he told me next was near unimaginable. Neither do I pretend to understand the ways of the Sage, nor how they wield the magic in their veins, but his perception was unnatural. In truth, I thought his ideas to be warped, but in my heart I knew them to be true.

He described that during the lifetime of my fourth child, a girl would enter his life – a girl bestowed or perhaps cursed with the title of second Heroine. This girl's life would become irreversibly tied to the Kingdom and to the fourth child, heir to the throne. To you, Kaspar. He explained that resistance would have no worth, for the girl's status would bring the two of you into constant contact. In short, you and the second Heroine are tied together by fate.

The paper fluttered to the ground. My hands dropped to the sheets and gripped them, tightly. *That's why.* It explained everything: why the King would not let me and Kaspar touch; why he talked of responsibility – Kaspar was duty bound to his Kingdom's Heroine; why Kaspar had become so withdrawn since he returned from Romania: the King must have told him to read this letter. My voice and the dreams too – Kaspar, again.

He is tied by fate to me. He just didn't know it was me yet.

A strange mixture of emotion rose in me and I didn't know whether to be elated or sickened. I had no choice, *yet again*, and the idea of being tied to someone I barely knew and had hated until a few weeks ago was unnerving.

Yet . . .

Compulsively, I reached and snatched the paper from the floor.

> *This will not seem fair to you. It will seem a great injustice. You may not love this girl or even be acquaintances, but you must accept your fate, for the good of the Kingdom and her heart, whether she loves you or not. She will need you. To become a Heroine will be a lonely plight and she will need someone to trust. It is your duty; your responsibility.*

I'd need him. I already needed him.

> *But not all is entirely lost, sweet child. Two people who are thrown together often learn to love, over time, and she will possess many of the qualities you admire – if she did not, she would not be a Heroine. In some ways, it may be a blessing to you: if you choose to marry her and make her your Queen, you will be in an extraordinarily strong position politically. Whatever you choose, this girl will remain in your life. But you must make what you can of this. Remember your duty to her and all will be well.*
>
> *Contanal died before he ever published his second prophecy on the Heroines and his papers were burnt or else hidden deep within Athenea. Many say that he was murdered by the Extermino to ensure the Prophecy never became truly complete – a rumour I am inclined to believe: Contanal was not an old man and the Sage rarely ail. Therefore, what he did discern*

*about the Heroines (other than the main Prophecy) was long
forgotten, save for what was passed down by word of mouth.
For that reason, I do not know whether you are alone in your
plight of being tied; not even the wisest of prophets know
anything near to what could be called the whole truth about
Contanal's Prophecy. So we will never know, until the time of
the Heroines is here.*

*I have come to the conclusion that I will not live to see such
a time. If I were to live longer, then logic would state that I
would have been blessed with a seventh child, and as danger
approaches in the form of visiting the Pierre Clan, I have
taken the decision to write this letter. But you will see such a
time, Kaspar. So do not grieve for me or for the past; for
acquaintances lost and times changed, because these must be
sacrificed in order to create a better future.*

*Fate moves in strange ways, but know that the end is only
truly the end when all is well. You are a good son, Kaspar; a
great man and you will be the greatest of Kings. Do not fear
the future.*

I love you, sweet child. In life and death,

> *Your mother,*
> *H.M. Queen Carmen*

I let the letter fall into my lap. She had known she was
going to her death. The whole time, she knew. When she
wrote that letter to Beryl, she knew she would never read
her friend's reply. She knew she would never find out how
John was, and that she would never commission a painting
of her whole family. *How could she possibly have sat down and
wrote that letter to Kaspar? How could she have said goodbye?* It
was unthinkable.

A fresh wave of respect for her courage washed over me and I studied the painting above the fireplace where the Queen sat, poised, her husband behind her. A small, dignified smile upturned the corners of her lips as she stared with an unsettling gaze towards what must have been the artist, now the bed. Her hands were clasped in her lap amongst the folds of her deep jade dress and around her neck was the locket I now possessed.

I pinched at the skin around my collar until my fingers found the chain. Gently, I pulled it from beneath my T-shirt and let it rest in the palm of my hand.

'You knew you were going to die in Romania, didn't you?' I whispered into the stillness, letting my eyes slip from the real locket in my hands to the one immortalized in the painting. 'That's why you gave Kaspar the locket the week before you left for Romania. You knew he would give it to me; to the second Heroine.'

I picked up the other letter, addressed to Beryl, searching the paper for a particular line. I found it, near the bottom.

I do not want my son and heir to be placed in the path of danger . . .

'And that's why you wouldn't let Kaspar go. You never intended for this letter to be sent. You wrote it so nobody would ever suspect that anything was wrong, didn't you? So nobody would think that you knew you wouldn't come back from Romania.'

My mind reeled at my epiphany and I turned my gaze back to the motionless figure of the Queen, as though expecting her to tell me I was right. But of course, she didn't. She was just oil and canvas.

Another thought struck me as I clutched the locket to my

breast: the letter had been opened and read, but how long ago? It looked well-read. *How long has he known he was tied, and when was he planning to tell me?* My feelings had not exactly been hidden from him these past few days. *Was he just going to let me wait and find out, and suffer that way?* A surge of anger shot through me. *How long would he have let it go on?*

Why are you complaining? You care for him and you're tied. Isn't that a good thing? my voice questioned.

You wouldn't understand.

Being tied will just take some getting used to, that's all, my voice reassured, as though it was that simple.

Suddenly, there was a noise from the balcony and startled, I jumped up. Seeing a shadow move behind the voiles I hastily stuffed both letters back beneath the pillow and glanced at the painting again.

'One day you might just find something worth living an eternity for.'

I glanced down at the locket resting on the collar of my T-shirt. Whether I liked it or not, Kaspar was going to have to be worth it. I bounded forward, brushing the voiles aside, balancing on the lip of the doors, hands grasping the frame either side.

'Who was the cloaked figure in the entrance hall before we left for London?'

There, leaned against the stone railings of the balcony was Kaspar; below him, yet more figures were strolling across the grounds, heads bowed away from the sunlight.

He sighed. 'Valerian Crimson.'

I leaned against the edge of the wall, hands clasped behind my back. It made sense that it was Valerian Crimson who we had crossed paths with that day. I don't think any other family of vampires could possess such demonic eyes when they lusted for blood. I had been stupid for assuming that the figure in the entrance hall had been the same figure of my dreams.

I let my head fall against the stone and soaked in the warmth of the sun which would be burning Kaspar's exposed hands and face.

There is so much to say, but no way to say it.

'The dreams will go once you become a vampire,' Kaspar said quietly, not turning his attention away from the grounds. 'You'll never be in a deep enough sleep to have them.'

I couldn't confess to being disappointed. I didn't want to see any more of the darker side of Kaspar which the dreams brought to the forefront of my mind.

I joined him on the railings. Below us, figures, mainly men, ascended the steps to the great marble double doors I knew were below. They came in pairs and small groups, dressed in the colours and livery of their families. Occasionally, an expensive-looking car with tinted windows would wind up the driveway and butlers and valets would rush out to open the doors.

From here too I could see where Kaspar's gaze was directed. To the west it was possible to see two of the beacons, flickering on the horizon like stars in a night sky. But these were far more sinister. *A call to court.* It wouldn't take more than a few days for the entire council and court to be here, at Varnley.

I didn't have *days*. I had *hours*.

Tell him you're a Heroine, my voice urged. *Tell him now.*

'You forgive me then?' Kaspar asked with a small smile.

I shook my head slightly and came back to my senses. Propping my chin on my hands, I rested my elbows on the stone railing. 'Not really.'

He hummed a note deep in his chest, sounding unsurprised.

For the first time, I noticed he had changed into a formal shirt and trousers – the court was descending, after all.

Tell him, Girly!

No. I have to set everything else straight first.

Then on your own head be it.

'That girl in the catacombs: Sarah. You didn't kill her for food, you killed her for fun. That's wrong, Kaspar.'

He looked down at me, eyes as emerald and piercing as the first time I had met him. 'I know,' he said.

'Then why do it?'

'I don't know . . . I was pissed off.' His fingers tightened around the stone before he raised it to his hair, combing it with his fingers, neglecting to offer a fuller explanation.

'You can't kill people because you're pissed off.'

He slumped, slapping his palm against the stone, looking as though he was about to shout, but noticing another figure passing below he lowered his voice. 'I get it! Okay, Girly? There's no need to preach,' he added.

I stood upright and folded my arms. 'I don't think you do, Kaspar.'

He studied me through his lowered lashes, his mouth parted just enough so I could see the two pointed teeth that were his fangs. He sighed and turned back to the railings, his head dropping down into his hands.

'What do you want me to do, Girly? I can't turn human for you. I can't stop lusting for blood. I can't stop killing. So what do you want me to do? Tell me!'

His eyes darted around my face, searching for answers, a mixture of desperation and exasperation on his face. I averted my gaze, unable to meet his eyes.

'You could start by being honest.'

You're not being honest, either. So what if he wasn't going to tell you about being tied? Tell him. Tell him now, Girly.

'You know what, Kaspar? You're just selfish and self-absorbed and you don't think that anyone can suffer like you do. And seriously, look around at what you have! It's incredible!'

I gestured around the grounds but he didn't look.

Instead, he looked at me with a peculiar expression almost identical to the one he had worn when I was clutched in the arms of the King during the Ad Infinitum ball: the face of a man fighting and losing. He stared at me for a moment and I shut my mouth, forgetting my next train of insightful insults. I whipped my head back to stare out at the grounds, wide-eyed, finding myself falling back on the taunts that had regularly spilled from my mouth in my first weeks.

'You're an arrogant, stupid, stuck-up jerk of a Prince with a serious ego problem who should really go and shove—'

My sentence ended in a high-pitched squeak as I was tugged around, an icy hand on my shoulder.

'Fuck fate,' he growled. Then his lips were on mine.

I was so shocked by his touch that I froze for a moment as he sucked gently on my lower lip, before I found my arms wrapping themselves around his neck, kissing him fervently back. I felt him smirk into the kiss before he drew back. I rolled onto my tiptoes, trying to reach his lips but he held me back.

'Missed my touch then, Girly?' He ran his thumb along my jaw and down my neck, pausing at my throbbing vein, pulsating far faster than it had been the minute before.

'Ego problems,' I murmured.

I heard him chuckle before he drew me closer again, lifting my chin and softly pecking me on the corner of my mouth. I followed him and he yielded, letting me suck hungrily and greedily at his lips as his tongue begged for entry, which I gave without hesitation. I let my tongue slip into his mouth too, gliding it across the points of his fangs.

I could taste blood and my heart picked up – he must have noticed because he chuckled, his fangs just clipping my lip as his hands worked their way slowly down my spine. Effortlessly, he picked me up and placed me on the railings as though I were a china doll – a doll he admired as he stepped back, his eyes raking across my body. His gaze was so intense I could almost feel my skin tearing away as it burnt hot; vaguely, I was aware that there was a fifteen-foot drop behind me.

He drew close again and clasped my hands behind his back before joining his own hands behind mine. I let my head rest on his shoulder, my mouth just brushing his neck, the Queen's locket – my locket – trapped between his collar and mine.

'Your father is going to kill us,' I chuckled, but he shrugged.

'He'll have to deal with it.' He sighed, his hands tangling themselves in my already-knotted hair. 'Violet, don't ever leave me. Whatever happens; however bad things get, just don't go. Please.'

I pulled away, studying his face. I knew what he was referring to. 'Kaspar, I have to tell you something.'

He frowned for a moment but then shook his head. 'No, it can wait. Just enjoy now.' I opened my mouth to protest but he pressed a finger to my lips. 'Wrap your legs around my waist,' he murmured in my ear.

I did so and with a muffled shriek on my part, he lifted me up in his arms. Stepping into the shadow of his room, he pecked me on the cheek, before kissing me again with an urgency that wasn't there before.

It was an urgency I felt too and as his tongue delved between my lips I wriggled free of his grasp, though he quickly grabbed my hand and tried to tug me towards the bed. Yet I remained still, eyes transfixed on the open door.

In it stood the King, the irises and even the whites of his eyes entirely consumed with anger. He stared with an unwavering gaze at me, a soft growl escaping his mouth. Beside him stood a vampire I recognized as Ashton and another, unfamiliar to me. Both of their eyes were warring between black and red.

Kaspar yanked me to his side, hugging me close but I hardly noticed. I couldn't tear my gaze away from the King's eyes as tears began running down my cheeks.

'Not this again,' Kaspar growled. 'Forget my duty! It's my choice whether to touch her or not!'

But the King didn't hear, or maybe he didn't care because he gave no reply. Instead, he motioned to the vampire I didn't know, who moved forward.

'Take her outside.' His voice was flat.

Kaspar immediately moved in front of me and I began backing away.

'What the fuck?' he cursed, but quick as a flash Ashton had grabbed him and twisted his arms behind his back at a painful-looking angle; Kaspar was stronger and quickly broke free, elbowing him in the chest.

I back-pedalled, arms grasping at the air behind me until they hit something solid, my back following. The other vampire smirked, beginning to close the distance between us. But there was a sudden groan and the vampire glanced at Ashton, pinned against the wall, his neck encircled by Kaspar's hand.

Seeing an opportunity I began sliding along the wall to reach the open French doors. The ridges of the wood panelling snatched like clawed hands at my shirt and though I knew I was running my feet didn't seem to be moving; even

as the vampire lunged towards me, I still had time to let my eyes wander to the painting of the Queen and her husband, her eyes as dead and lifeless as the living King that stood before us. My eyes found the locket around her neck as my hand found it resting against my collar and closing my eyes, I braced myself.

Hours.

The vampire's weight thrust into me and I shrieked, yet heard no sound. I struggled, but I couldn't move as his entire body pushed me into the wall, rapid breaths tracing a pattern along my throat. When I opened my eyes, I could see nothing but blotches until they gradually refocused and I could make out the King's lips soundlessly moving as he stared in the direction of his son, who backed away from Ashton and spun to face me, a look of utter defeat on his face.

The King motioned and I was dragged out as Kaspar silently watched; something cold like a knife was pressed to the skin just below my jaw. I let the feel of that touch wash through me, cherishing the rush; the heavy scented air, rich with cologne; the light, the dark.

As I passed the King I stared at his unfeeling face, unmoved and indifferent as tears trickled down my cheeks and doors flew open, pleading and shouting filling the hallway as I watched his empty eyes follow me.

'But, Miss Lee, what makes you so adamant in your belief that I abhor you?'

I tried to free my wrists from the vampire's grasp as he lugged me down the stairs, but other hands tightened around my waist and the knife pressed harder into my neck. Amongst the confusion I made out faces – Cain, Fabian, Alex, Kaspar, Jag, even Lyla – but the only sound louder than my own heartbeat was the ticking of a clock and the giggling of a small child . . . the only face I could pick out amongst the sea of cloaks and black eyes gathering in the entrance hall: Thyme.

She wound between the legs of the onlookers, her black dress frilled with white and trailing silver ribbons. She came to a stop at the base of the stairs, clinging to the bottom banister as she stared up at me. Her eyes were wide with wonderment and her mouth ajar, but her lips quickly widened into a toothy smile.

'Don't look the Princess in the eye, scum!' a cold voice said at my ear, and the knife – which, as I glanced downwards looked more like a dagger – was pressed further into my neck.

I looked away hastily as noise flooded my ears once more. I could hear the frantic protests of Cain and Kaspar, pleading and desperate, amongst the reasoning of Jag and Sky as whoever held me tossed me down the steps outside and caught me once more by grabbing my hair. I screeched, only for the dagger to silence me as it rested against my windpipe.

As they spun me around to face the steps I watched as Lyla tugged at her father's sleeve and Fabian halted on the steps, frozen in horror as the household poured out around him, engulfing his form. Mary turned away into the arms of Jag, whose mouth was moving wordlessly as Thyme broke through the throng of onlookers: the family and their friends; the servants; the council . . .

Outside, it was hardly brighter. The sun no longer showed, instead colouring the clouds orange as hot, licentious chants filled the autumn air, curses for my name rising with the smoke from the beacons.

Two hands rested on my shoulder, another two on my arms and pressed down, forcing me onto my knees. I dropped down but they did not ease the pressure, instead taking a wrist each and twisting them behind my back until I screeched and begged for them to stop. They didn't.

Gritting my teeth I lifted my eyes and found Kaspar, who slowed and stared at me, a thousand unreadable emotions written in his face – but horror was uppermost, evident and distinguishable.

'I said don't look!' the same cold voice said as a hand met my cheek. I winced, but kept quiet, as blood, alongside tears, trickled down my cheeks. I tasted it on my lips and grimaced.

As the hand lifted once again, Kaspar broke free from the crowd and surged forward, only to be grabbed by his older brothers and Ashton, who lugged him back, their voices vying to be the loudest as each shouted, grunting as they fought one another.

'It's a wondrous thing knowing you will die at the hands of a man so adamant to fight for you now, is it not, Lady Heroine?' a voice hissed beside my ear. I shuddered. Twisting my neck I came face to face with Valerian Crimson, kneeling, one hand clawing my wrist, the other holding the knife to my neck. Restraining my right arm was the other vampire.

'You knew,' I spat, droplets of blood pooling between the gravel.

He chuckled. 'Oh, I have known you were a Heroine all along. You see, my dear son Ilta was gifted with foresight, much like Eaglen. But instead of being a bumbling fool, he took action.' He tightened his grip around my wrist as Kaspar continued to struggle. 'You see, a human should not be bestowed with such a title as Heroine. You have no right to it. Unfortunately though, his plan was fooled by his own desire for you, and your pretty Prince saving you over there. But I think it's rather apt that he will finish what Ilta started, don't you?'

I scowled. 'You're sick,' I muttered.

'Now, now,' he chided, with false politeness. 'I was just about to compliment you on how well-guarded your mind is: for us not to find out about your father's little secret all this time is a clever trick.' His voice lowered and out of the corner of my eye I could see him smiling. 'But you were betrayed. Somebody sent a note.'

He pointed to the King as he raised his hand, silence gradually falling. Clutched in-between his fingers I could see a tiny slip of paper.

Valerian laughed.

'Open your mouth about being a Heroine and I'll slit your throat. Do you understand, My Lady?' As if to prove he would do it, he pressed the blade right up against my flesh and I flinched away, believing him.

Silence fell and I let my gaze rest on the gravel, not daring to meet Kaspar's eyes because I knew what the King would say next.

He opened his mouth, his voice a harsh whisper. 'She deceived us. It was her. Her father ordered my wife's death. And she knew. *She knew all along.*'

FIFTY-SEVEN

Violet

Spots of blood were still appearing on the gravel.

I closed my eyes and let my head droop forwards. The pain was easing in my arms, forced behind my back, but only because they were going dead. The knife pressed under my chin seemed warmer and I could see a lonely droplet of sweat – my sweat – trailing down its length and pausing momentarily at its tip as a perfect teardrop, like rain on a leaf waiting to fall. But it could not hang so precariously off such an edge for long and after a second it fell, mixing into the tarn of blood.

I was too scared to look up. I didn't want to see Kaspar's face.

'Do you deny it?' the King barked against a refrain of murderous words whispered by the council and the servants; but not the family. They remained deadly silent.

The blade of the knife pressed against my neck and so with the sort of guilt impossible to hide on my face I raised my gaze, then my eyes, and shook my head.

'No?' the King croaked. 'No? You lie to me and my Kingdom for so long and yet you do not deny it?'

I paid little attention to him. Instead, my gaze had become transfixed on one person: Kaspar. On his eyes. Black. But not just black. Glistening. The tears that were trickling down my cheeks were matched on his.

He's crying.

My lips parted and closed again as I gulped. 'I'm sorry,' I mouthed. 'I'm sorry.'

The wind nestled in his hair as pride raised his chin slightly and exposed his neck, pulling taught the skin across his throat. His eyes stared into the sky and I followed his gaze to where two crows were circling, dipping and diving amongst one another, opening their beaks and shrieking.

I brought my eyes back down to him and in one blink, he had averted his gaze. He made no effort to wipe the tears away and I saw them plummet, falling and fracturing into tiny droplets on the stone steps. Slowly, they dried on his pale cheeks until they became nothing.

He did not turn back and with that, my tears fell uncontrolled; not withheld, not restrained but free to fall: not for my father's sin, not for myself, but for him.

'Do not look at my son,' the King murmured, even the quietest of whispers audible in the still air – the chants had eased to a murmur at the King's words. 'Do not look at him.'

I spat blood onto the ground as Valerian pushed on the back of my neck and I was made to stare at the gravel at my knees. Fear, real fear, was beginning to rise again as the murmur of chants became a babble and the babble a chorus. But that was nothing compared to the sound my shattering heart made.

With the little lustre I could manage, I spoke. 'Then who would you have me look at?'

There was no reply and Crimson grabbed a large chunk of my hair and wrenched my head back, straining my skin against my exposed throat not with pride, but with humility. I thrashed in his strong grip, fighting as he reached around and pulled the Queen's locket from my breast, holding me still long enough to undo the clasp. He reached down and pulled the pendant from beneath my shirt. The locket fell away. The skin it had rested upon seared, naked without the cold metal resting upon it. I struggled, but the grip around me tightened and slowly I stilled, recognizing the hopelessness of fighting. Valerian was a thousand times stronger than I was and half the bloodthirsty court stood in front of me; if I tried to speak up the knife would be driven through my neck.

How can you prepare to die on a perfect Autumnal morning?

Yet surviving did not seem so appealing either. I was tied to a man who could not even watch me die. *A man who will let me die.*

I let my eyes fall on Kaspar's back before raising them to the sky. Just before I closed them I saw the blurs of the two crows, continuously circling, around and around.

'We won't hurt you, you know.'

The bloodbath would not end here. They would kill my father; his junior ministers; anyone that was associated with him and I didn't want to think about what they would do to my mother and Lily.

I couldn't help them. I couldn't warn them. In my mind I began praying to anyone or anything that would listen.

'You do not need to do this, Vladimir. The girl has done nothing wrong.'

My eyes flung open and rested upon Eaglen. The crowd recoiled and I did the same, staring at his wizened hair and wrinkled hands, hardly daring to believe that I had heard correctly.

The King hissed.

It must have been coherent to Eaglen's ears, because he chuckled with mild amusement. 'No, you do not. You are blinded by anger and it is preventing you from understanding the irrationality of your actions.'

The King pushed through the crowd. His face was twisted with menace and he bared his fangs, sneering. 'Stand aside, Eaglen.'

I stared, frightened for the old man, wise but frail. I didn't need anyone else to die for my father's actions, least of all somebody who – although I did not know why – was defending me.

'No.'

The King seemed taken aback, as did the crowd – a steady stream of whispers flowed from the steps.

'You do not need to die for a scum of a human,' he spat.

Eaglen chuckled again and adjusted the cloak around his shoulders, impervious to the King's foreboding glare. 'I am an old man, Vladimir. Death does not scare me; I will die a martyr if you insist upon it.'

The taunting wit in his voice was clear and it only served to anger the King even further. He gestured behind him and hesitantly, Ashton and another vampire came forward. They lingered behind the King, seeming reluctant to get too close to Eaglen.

'I command you as your King, and beg you as your friend, to stand aside.'

The King's expression softened but hardened again as Eaglen closed his eyes, sighed softly and bowed his head.

'I like to think I have been a loyal and faithful subject and mentor for each and every one of your many, many years walking this earth, but alas, this day, I cannot be.'

The King raised his hand and with two fingers, gestured

first towards Eaglen and then to me, as he nodded curtly to Valerian. My eyes widened and realizing this was it, began to fight, managing to struggle to my feet within Valerian's grip. He cursed, releasing my arms but wrapping one of his own around my middle. His other reached up, clasping the knife in his hand as he fought to reach my neck, my fingers scrabbling at his wrist and the knife, whatever I could get a hold of, leaving searing slashes across my skin. But the other vampire surged forward and together with Ashton, pinned my arms to my side. Valerian pulled me back to his chest and pressed the knife into the skin below my jaw. In desperation, I reached down and bit down, hard, on his fingers.

'You little whore!' he cried, dropping the knife. But instead of going to pick it up, he wrapped his free hand around my waist as Ashton brushed the hair from my neck. Blood, sweat and tears trailed down, following the curve of my skin; with complete disgust I tried to recoil from Valerian as his tongue darted out, lapping up each drop, hungry for the river he would find below my skin.

Vaguely, I heard the sound of Eaglen's voice, calm demeanour gone and replaced with an urgent plea. 'Carmen died *for her*, Vladimir! Your wife died so that one day, your son would meet Violet Lee. If you kill the girl, your wife will have died in vain. Hear sense!'

But the King did not even acknowledge Eaglen's begging as he was pulled aside, others moving forward to help restrain him. The King nodded in approval, and then turned back to me.

'Any last words, Violet Lee?'

I could barely see through my tears and I was too frightened to even swallow, let alone speak under Valerian's eager fangs. But I stared at Kaspar until he turned my way and I could lock eyes with him.

'Fuck the day I first met you. Fuck you and everything you have done to me. I hate—'

I couldn't finish as my voice broke and I was reduced to sobbing, fighting and muttering prayers for mercy. I had expected my terror to abate at my words, or my heart to stop shattering over and over, but it didn't. It just made it worse. Guilt washed through me and all I could think about was dying with Kaspar thinking I regretted the past four months. *Because I don't. God, I don't.*

Neither do I, my voice murmured.

I raised my eyes and tried to scream the truth through my sobs but all I saw was Kaspar weaving through the crowds towards the doors, his head turned firmly away. I shut my mouth and stilled as Eaglen began a fresh wave of protests.

'For the sake of your Kingdom, Vladimir, *listen*! She's the Dark—'

He stopped and stared behind me. I was able to focus long enough on his face to register a brief look of relief before suddenly, my feet had left the ground and I was wrenched from the grip of Valerian, Ashton and the other vampire into another's arms. I screamed as I was pulled backwards, half on my feet and half-dragged away from the King.

Just as abruptly I was dropped as we reached the grass. Whoever held me pulled me fully to my feet and I flung around, ready to struggle or run if I needed to. But to my astonishment, it was Arabella who clung onto me. Her eyes were as wide and astonished as mine as her gaze flitted from Sky to her father to the King and she turned back to me, looking shocked. I felt her gaze linger on the cuts littered over my neck and hands.

'Are you seriously hurt?' were the first words from her mouth as her eyes scanned my body. I shook my head but even if I had been hurt, I wouldn't have acknowledged it because I was staring in the direction of the King: pointing directly at his throat was a sword.

'King Vladimir Varn, I am required to inform you that under the Terra Treaties Act of 1812, the harming of Miss Violet Lee, henceforth known as the Lady Heroine, is an offence punishable by immediate execution, without trial.'

A gasp as loud as a howling wind spread through the crowd and many dropped to their knees as Sage appeared from nowhere, right sides encased in vibrant scars, swords in some of their hands, magic in others. They grabbed the guards and freed Eaglen, who dashed to Arabella's side. Daggers appeared at the throats of the Varns and Kaspar was marshalled towards his family.

Valerian was dragged back and pushed to the gravel, magic circling around his wrists as restraints and a sword pointing at his chest, held by a girl. She looked a few years older than I was; her scars a deep burgundy red and startlingly similar to Fallon's. She glanced up as I stared and nodded in my direction.

The speaker – Canadian, judging by his accent – held the sword to the King's neck, waiting silently for a response. The King, however, didn't seem capable of speaking as he looked wordlessly from the man in front of him, to me, just as shocked as everybody else.

'Her?' was all he managed.

The man nodded. He waved his hand and a large rolled up sheet of parchment appeared in his hand, sealed with wax and a deep red ribbon. 'Confirmation of the removal of the Lady Heroine from the protection of King and Crown in the second dimension, to be replaced with the protection of King Ll'iriad Alya Athenea.' He handed it to the King who snatched it from his hands and ripped the seal open.

His eyes scanned the paper. 'Does your father no longer have any respect for the power I wield within my own Kingdom, Henry?'

The man took the roll back into his hands and lowered his sword. 'I believe I speak on behalf of the Sagean people when I say we have no respect for a man who would murder an innocent girl for the crimes of her father.'

The King said nothing and the man – Henry – sheathed his sword. 'Do you accept the terms?'

The King raised his head with an air of pride, but it seemed hollow at his next words. 'I have no choice.'

Henry nodded and with a wave of his hand, the Sagean girl lowered her sword from Valerian's chest and the gleaming restraints around his hands disappeared. He shot her a filthy look, but said nothing as he darted back to the crowd.

'I suggest you wait for the remainder of your court to arrive and hold a council meeting this evening. There is much to discuss,' Henry said and with that, turned and walked towards us. The girl joined him and slowly, the other Sage backed away from the vampires, but not by very far. None of the vampires moved.

I stood, rooted to the spot and not really sure of what had just happened. As they neared, they both dropped into full court bows.

'My Lady,' they said and I stared, flushing as they both rose and took a further few steps forward. From here I could see that the man had scars of a similar colour to the girl's – deep red and brown – and that both their eyes were the same brilliant blue.

'I-it's just Violet,' I choked, unsure of how to react, stealing glances at where the Varns stood. The man nodded.

'Henry,' he said. 'I'm Fallon's older brother. And my sister, Joanna.'

He gestured to the girl and I realized that they must be a Prince and Princess of Athenea. I didn't pay them any more attention as I locked eyes with Kaspar. I stared at him. He stared back, until he turned on his heel and disappeared inside.

As my vision began to blur I could just see Henry whipping about to follow my gaze before he darted forward to catch me as my knees buckled. I felt myself sink and I could sense the cool dampness of the grass soaking into my shirt.

I knew I was becoming unconscious and the last thing I registered before I retreated into my mind was a voice.

'No, Henry, leave her. Too much has happened for her mind to cope with. Leave her . . .'

Wherever I was felt oddly familiar. I knew the feel of the rug beneath my feet, plush but worn beside the door and beneath the bedposts. I knew the wood of the walls. The smell. The way the light loitered around the French doors.

I dropped down onto Kaspar's bed and threw myself back, utterly convinced I was dreaming – I was too calm to be awake.

Everything was so clear now – the course of my life, before a puzzle, had slotted together to make a straight line; one that led to here; now; the beginning of my life as a Heroine.

Greg, an innocent, had died and I had turned to Joel. Joel had cheated and I had turned to clubbing every weekend, and that had pulled my line right across Kaspar's. The Queen had died so he would kill Claude Pierre and create the Bloodbath. And at that moment, the two lengths of string we both trod knotted and we became tied.

'But now he hates me,' I whispered to the stillness.

'My son does not hate you. I highly doubt he is capable

of it,' said a voice, eloquent and undoubtedly belonging to
a woman.

I sat bolt upright and stumbled up from my bed – which
wasn't even my bed anymore – and back-pedalled into the
wall. I hit the wood panelling and stared dead ahead, a
breeze stirring the black voiles around the French doors,
open to reveal the balcony outside.

Stood in front of the mantle was a woman, dressed in a
long emerald dress which clung to her waist, cinched by the
bones of the bodice. Her wavy brown hair clung to the curvatures of her neck and breast, long enough to reach her hips.
She was smiling in my direction, revealing the tips of two
small fangs. Although a woman past the years of youth, she
was beautiful – most stunning of all were her eyes, which
were a bright, vivid shade of emerald.

'Your Majesty,' I spluttered, bobbing into a curtsy.

Her lips came together and the corners of her mouth
upturned, her eyes seeming to sparkle with the same amused
half-smirk, half-smile I had seen Kaspar use on so many
occasions. Her head bowed and she gathered the sides of
her skirt, dropping into a low curtsy. 'You have no need to
bow to me, Lady Heroine.'

I could only stutter as she straightened, still smiling – a
smile none of the portraits I had seen of her, including the
one behind her, had ever done justice.

This was one hell of a dream.

'I . . . How . . . What do you mean Kaspar doesn't hate
me? My father ordered your death.' The words seemed
surreal and stupid even as I was saying them. She bowed
her head again and gracefully sat on the edge of Kaspar's
bed – her bed – and stretched out her hand, inviting me to
do the same.

'Kaspar, although often callous and devoid of civility, is a good man. His heart is true and I am in no doubt that it belongs to you. He is angry, I do not deny that, but his hurt will abate, in time.'

I clasped my hands together, uneasy. 'You mean he will forgive me?'

She shook her head. 'He has nothing to forgive you for.'

'But—'

'Hush,' she breathed, taking my hands in hers. Her skin was warm too, as though she had bathed her hands in hot water. 'Here,' she added, pressing something cold into my palm. I looked down. Resting on my hand was the Queen's locket – her locket – the chain dangling between my fingers. 'My son chose correctly when he bestowed this upon you. Valerian Crimson had no right to take it.'

I closed my fingers around it, feeling the ever-cool metal burning my skin. 'Is this really just a dream?' I asked, believing that nothing was impossible anymore. *Even the dead walking and talking.*

The Queen did not answer immediately, but seemed to think for a while. 'You must decide that for yourself. But we do not have long.'

'I don't want to wake up,' I breathed.

The Queen shook her head. 'You must, Violet, if you wish to keep your family from harm.'

I squeezed the locket in my hand and stared at the floor I was so familiar with now. 'And how on Earth do I do that? I have to betray them to fulfil the Prophecy and I will turn if that is what I have to do, but I don't think that is going to be enough.'

The Queen didn't answer, standing up and rounding the bedpost, hurrying towards the French doors. I sprang up and followed her. The sun had appeared once more from behind the cloak of grey clouds and the morning was fast reaching its height. She stepped out, devoid of the elegance now and rushed to lean over the banisters of the balcony. I did the same, just in time to see my limp body being carried inside by one of the Sage.

That clears up whether this is a dream or not.

I recoiled, whilst the Queen leaned even further down, her hair dangling in mid-air. Slowly, I placed my weight back on the stone and listened as below the balcony, Eaglen and the Sagean prince, Henry, talked in undertones.

'I understand, Henry, but the girl's father will come tomorrow along with the Pierre clan and maybe even the Extermino too. We *need* you and your men, to keep the Varns from harm as much as anything else,' Eaglen pleaded, pausing as two of the Sagean men he talked of walked past – the crowd of vampires that had gathered earlier had gone. 'To keep the girl from harm.'

The Prince shook his head. 'Can the vampires not fight their own battles? I have orders, Eaglen, and those orders are to remove the Lady Heroine from the second dimension to our own. The human family will be forsaken and the Prophecy fulfilled.'

Eaglen smacked the stone pillar he stood beside. 'And you think that is the way to introduce the mortal child to her new life? Death and her removal from the man she is tied to?'

The argument continued but the Queen sprang back up, staring at me wide-eyed before dashing back inside. I followed her as far as the doors to see her scribbling something on a slip of paper that looked a lot like one of her own letters. She dropped the paper on the bed and hurriedly placed the pen back on the bedside cabinet before flitting back to me. She grabbed me and wrenched me away from the doors, out of view of the room. Her hand clamped down on my mouth just as I heard the door of the room opening and the sound of footsteps and Kaspar cursing loudly. Then the footsteps retreated and the door slammed, rattling the glass of the French doors we stood beside.

The Queen breathed a sigh of relief. 'I cannot be seen, but you can,' she whispered in my ear, pushing me down behind the railings as she leaned back over. I nodded, not quite understanding what had just happened.

'Eaglen, the Lady Heroine will go to Athenea and that is not negotiable—'

Abruptly, the Sagean prince stopped talking and a third voice joined the conversation.

'Violet is not going anywhere that I do not go, and as the heir to the throne, my place is here.'

My lips parted into a smile as I recognized Kaspar's voice. Shifting a little closer to peer through the gaps in the stone railings, I could just see him beside Eaglen, who chuckled.

'Well, that settles it then. Henry?'

I watched as the Sagean prince appeared and descended the steps, heading towards a young Sagean boy who had been standing aside from the conversation. 'You are a messenger boy?' The boy, who couldn't have been any older than twelve almost squealed in fright as the Prince first addressed him and then gruffly relayed a message.

'You are to go straight to King Ll'iriad and inform him that we intend to remain at Varnley until further notice.' Henry turned back to look at Eaglen and Kaspar. 'And that the Lady Violet Lee will remain here too. Do you understand what I want you to do? Hasten and do not relay the message to anyone but the King or the Lady Autumn Rose.'

The boy scampered away and Henry retreated back under the balcony. Kaspar and Eaglen followed; as the latter climbed back up the steps, he looked up towards where the Queen was standing. The most fleeting of smiles crossed his face before he disappeared too.

The Queen turned back to me, seemingly unaffected. 'There are ways, young Heroine, of fulfilling the prophecy and ensuring those you love are safe.' She reached out and pulled me to my feet, leading me back inside. 'This is what you must do . . .'

Consciousness came quickly as I became aware that something cold was being pressed to my brow and that my cheeks were tingling. A pillow had been placed beneath my head and I lay on something soft. All around there were voices. Trying not to move, I listened, keeping my eyes closed.

'Are you that foolish, Vladimir? Are you so naïve to think that this girl's coming to us was a mere coincidence?'

A voice, undoubtedly the King's, responded in an undertone. 'I do not question fate, Eaglen, but fate's choice. A girl – a *human* girl – who has not been brought up at court, nor even in our Kingdom must act on behalf of a people she despised until a few weeks ago. And that is not to mention her treacherous father. How can she possibly live up to what is expected of her?'

Someone, who I presumed to be Eaglen, replied. 'She is young and she will be of new blood when she turns, for she must turn, but in her I see the youthful spirit of your late wife, and with it will come the faith of the Kingdom. She can learn our ways and as to her father; when he comes, she will betray him, as the Prophecy tells.'

There was a long pause. The tingling ceased and I felt warm breath across my face, before a few words were whispered in what must be Sagean.

'I cannot let that man into my Kingdom. I cannot.'

'You must.'

'Then I do so unwillingly and without courtesy.'

Eaglen chuckled. 'Do it however you like, Vladimir. I doubt the man will give a damn.'

There was a sigh. 'And Kaspar?'

'He will come around. But he needs time.'

'He does not *have* time. No one does.'

My heart skipped a beat and I decided I wanted to hear no more. Beginning to fidget, I heard whoever bent over me hiss for the others to hush. I slowly opened my eyes, blinking furiously at the sudden light and looking around, trying to look dazed.

I was lying on a divan sofa, propped up by cushions. The person leaning over me was the Sagean Princess, Joanna, who smiled at me as my eyelids fluttered open. Looking around, I vaguely recognized where I was: the King's study. Bookcases lined the walls and a huge mahogany desk was framed by a window on the back wall, the curtains partly drawn across to block the light. Behind that desk stood the King, his hand resting on the high back of the desk chair and with him, Eaglen. Henry stood a little way away, examining a book he had pulled from the shelves.

Locking eyes with the King, I tried to feign surprise at his presence – although it was not entirely faked: as he turned towards me, a jolt of adrenalin shot through my chest and I scrabbled to sit up, but Joanna pushed me down.

'Calm, Heroine. He will not harm you.'

I shot her a disbelieving look and the King stepped around the desk. Wary, I sat up again, tightening my grip around the edge of the sofa. As I did, I felt something press into my palm, cool and round. I glanced at my hand and through the gap between my finger and thumb I could see the Queen's locket. My eyes widened.

So the dream was real.

Panicking, I tightened my hand even further, hiding it from view. The King slowly came forward. With each step my heart seemed to jump into my mouth. But I held still. Henry closed his book and watched, tense. Joanna stood as the King bowed his head and closed his eyes.

'I cannot forgive your father,' he began, his voice strained. 'Because the pain he caused in this Kingdom and in others is far too great. But I will tolerate him, because I must and I will ensure your family comes to no harm, for your sake. But I cannot forgive.' He shook his head and Eaglen came forward, resting a hand on the younger man's shoulder. I just stared, trying to absorb the enormity of his words. The locket seared even colder in my hands – so cold I struggled to keep hold of it.

I just bowed my own head, finding myself unable to find the right words, or to settle on the correct emotion. Part of me wanted to hate this man, so ready to murder me, but the other half of me sought to pity a man driven to such grief.

'We have an understanding then, young Heroine,' Eaglen said, smiling. 'There is much to be discussed at the council meeting this evening.' Henry murmured his agreement. 'But for now, you—'

He was interrupted as the door opened. One of the King's manservants entered and bowed. 'Prince Kaspar, Your Majesty.'

The King briskly rose at the servants words and my heart fluttered furiously. I pleaded with it to calm, for I had no doubt the vampires would hear its beat. Eaglen glanced at me.

'We will take leave of you, My Lady.'

He bowed and the two Sage followed suit. The King hung back for a moment and then bowed too, sweeping from the room. I heard the door shut and took a deep breath. Gradually, I turned towards where Kaspar stood in the centre of the room, the back of the divan separating us. As my eyes settled on him his arm swept behind his back.

'Don't,' I began, but he dropped into a low bow.

'My Lady.'

I turned away, embarrassed and hurt by the formal address. Twiddling the chain of the locket between my fingers, I waited for him to say something. But he kept quiet and glancing towards him I saw that he had not moved.

'Say something,' I snapped, in a tone more harsh than I intended.

He lowered his head. 'What would you like me to say, My Lady?'

'Anything but "My Lady",' I murmured and I could see from the slight twitch in his lower lip that he heard.

'Then what would you have me address you as, Lady Heroine?'

I scowled at his use of 'Lady Heroine' (which was even worse) and continued playing with the locket, letting the chain run like it was fluid across my fingertips.

'The same as you usually do: Violet or Girly.'

A low groan escaped his lips and his weight shifted slightly. 'Then what would you have me say, Girly?'

I sighed and rested my head against the back of the divan. 'That you don't hate me.'

'I don't hate you.' I sat up and frowned. He continued, clasping both his hands behind his back. 'I doubt I could hate you, even if I tried. I cannot face you as I did before, but I do not hate you, and never will.'

I slid one leg, then two, off the divan, steadying myself on the arm of the chair as a few stars danced in front of my eyes.

'But in time?' I began.

'Sit down. You should rest,' he said, taking a step forward as I swayed a little.

'But in time you could face me as you did before?' I repeated. 'I know we're tied, so please say you can, for both our sakes.'

He nodded. 'If there was ever a time for the truth, then now is it. We are bound by fate, but that does not matter because as far as I'm concerned, I chose you.' His eyes closed and then flew open again. 'Violet, I cannot suppress what I feel for you, but at the same time I can't deny that I feel deceived.'

Beneath my feet, the wooden floor felt cold as I stepped off the rug and cautiously rounded the sofa.

'I'm sorry,' I mouthed, hating his formal tone and choice of words; wishing he would just tease me and make light of what had happened, like he had done with so many other things.

'How long?' he murmured. I knew what he meant.

'Since you and your family went hunting and I was left with Fabian. He told me about how your mother died and the dates fitted. I didn't know for sure and I was scared, Kaspar. After what everyone said . . . you said . . . I thought . . .' I trailed off, not really wanting to voice what I had thought, particularly as what I had thought had so nearly happened.

I slumped against the back of the sofa for support, not daring to move any closer as the remnants of unconsciousness refused to leave. Kaspar walked forward, as slowly and deliberately as his father a few moments before.

'Just give me time to work all this out in my mind,' he murmured.

I shook my head, a few tears escaping from the corners of my eyes 'I don't think we have time.'

'Hey, don't cry,' he cooed, brushing his thumb across my cheek and wiping the tears away.

I half-heartedly smiled. 'Hey, you cried, so I'm allowed to as well.'

He mouth tugged into the half-smirk, half-smile I had seen reflected in his mother's face and his eyes, emerald, sparkled with dry tears that could no longer fall.

'Fuck fate, remember? Well, fuck time too.'

I chuckled and his hand enclosed my fingers, turning my palm over to reveal the locket. He didn't question how I had acquired it back from Valerian, but took it in his own fingers and allowed it to dangle between us, the locket swaying in midair. Gently, he rested the other hand on my shoulder and twirled me around. He reached over my head, bringing the chain around my neck. I felt the coolness of the pendant, even through the material of my T-shirt. He fiddled for a moment, and then rested his hands on the back of my neck. I shuddered beneath his touch as he ran his hands across my shoulders and down my arms, tugging me until my back rested against his chest.

This isn't fate. I chose you. I've made my choice.

Slowly, I turned in his arms and rested my head against his chest. He remained rigid, but gradually, his body loosened and I felt his cold breath on my hair as his head came to rest on mine. Between us, the locket lay, cold.

After a minute, I broke from our embrace and took both his hands in mine, letting his fingers slip between my own. In that moment, nothing else really seemed to matter. My heart was swelling and I was exerting huge amounts of self-control to stop myself from jumping up and down and squealing – or kissing him – but I knew he wasn't ready for that yet. Nevertheless, I couldn't prevent a grin from spreading onto my face as I soaked up his emerald eyes and stupid good looks.

Screw the Heroine part because damn, I am tied to this guy! Tied *to him.*

'Stop looking so smug,' he muttered, a small smirk creeping onto his lips. His words only caused my grin to widen and I bounced on my heels. 'No, really,' he continued, tightening his grip around my hands. 'this is just the beginning.'

I nodded, sobering. *I know that.* But I also knew what I had to do, and more importantly, how to do it.

Yet there was something I did need to know. 'Can I ask you something?'

'You just did,' he replied dryly.

I shot him a disapproving look. 'I'm being serious.' I paused, thinking of the best way to phrase my next sentence. 'Back there, outside. You were – I mean, you just stood there. Were you going to just watch as they . . . killed me?'

He groaned softly. 'I don't—'

'You were, weren't you?'

He averted his eyes and stared at one of the bookshelves. His silence revealed more than a thousand words.

I wrenched my hands from his grasp. 'How could you?' I questioned, recoiling away in disgust.

'I said I need time,' he breathed, still not facing me.

I scoffed, trying to suppress the sudden wave of anger I felt surging through my veins. 'Time? I didn't *have* time back there.' I gestured out of the partially screened window. 'If the Sage hadn't come at that moment I would have been your dinner, for Christ's sake!' My voice rose at the end and took on a screeching pitch. 'Do you even understand what was going through my mind when I thought I was going to die?'

He took a step back. 'And can you understand what it's like to have a member of your family torn from you?'

I cocked my head, stunned by his insensitivity and the emotionless tone he used. 'Yes, I do actually. Greg, remember?'

'Well, what was I meant to do? They wouldn't let me near you and nothing I could have said would have changed anybody's mind.'

'Eaglen did something!' I hissed back.

'Eaglen knew what you are,' he grunted.

I felt my heart tug. 'It shouldn't matter who or what I am.'

With that he took off, and I followed him to his room and out onto the balcony, mutterings of his title and then mine an echo of our footsteps.

'You might be a Heroine, but you still don't have much choice in things. They'll eat you alive,' he said when I settled against the banister beside him. I shook my head, not sure of what he meant or who 'they' were. He took a long, slow breath and gazed out across the grounds to where the sun was beginning to lower. 'The Sage's orders were to take you back to Athenea for your own protection.'

Of course, I already knew that – I had eavesdropped in on Eaglen and Henry's conversation whilst I was out cold. But I did my best to feign surprise. 'When?'

'Immediately. Athenea would be the best place for you right now.'

I laughed nervously. *Athenea is really not the best place for me right now,* I thought.

'Then why am I still here?' Again, I knew the answer to that but I was interested to see what he would answer.

'Because it would be impractical. You're not a vampire and crossing the borders is difficult for humans. And you need the support of the council. And . . .'

'And?'

I glimpsed a pale pink tinge appearing around the rims of his irises as he stole a look at me. 'Whilst you were unconscious I went and told Henry that I wouldn't let you go.' The corners of his lips upturned a little.

'I thought you were angry?' I asked.

He nodded. 'I was. Still am.'

'Then why tell—'

He cut me off, walking to his bed and snatching a piece of paper from under his pillow. I knew it must be one of the Queen's letters but he turned it over, pointing to what should be the near-blank side. Instead, interweaving between the wax seal and several blotches of ink was a scrawling message, written in an identical hand to the letter.

Don't give up on her.

My eyes widened. *That's what the Queen had written.*

Kaspar pointed to it, his mouth forming the words but no sound coming out. He turned the paper over, revealing the main part of the letter. 'It's a letter my mother left me about being tied to the Heroine.' He turned it back over. 'But that part wasn't there before.' His voice was soft and cracked a little on the word 'mother'. I reached out and placed a hand over his, folding the paper into two.

'I know,' I murmured.

He raised his head, surprised. 'How?'

'When we came back from Varns' Point, I came looking for you and found it. Autumn had just told me about the Heroine thing and I couldn't help but read it. How else do you think I found out about being tied?'

He shook his head. 'I thought Eaglen had told you. But why didn't you tell me? None of this would have happened.'

'I tried, but you wouldn't listen.'

His brow creased as he thought back. Then he cringed. 'Well, why didn't you scream it down there?' He gestured down to the gravel of the driveway. 'You didn't have to wait for Eaglen.'

I closed my eyes. 'Valerian Crimson knew I was a Heroine all along. He would have driven a knife through my neck if I so much as squeaked.' I rubbed my throat as I said that, able to feel the cool metal still pressing against my skin. I stepped out onto the balcony and Kaspar followed, grabbing my wrist and yanking me into his chest. I felt a little weak at the knees as he raised my chin and scrutinized my face, his eyes back to their usual shade of emerald now.

'Why aren't you angrier with me? I'm angry at you and it's your father who is to blame, not you.'

'I am trying,' I replied dryly. 'Why, do you want me to be angry?'

A perfected pout appeared on his lips and his eyes twinkled with mischief. 'Well, you are kind of hot when you're angry.' I glared at him and wriggled in his grip until he let me go. 'Inappropriate?' he questioned, breaking out into a sheepish grin.

'Just slightly,' I laughed, running a hand through my hair to brush my fringe from my eyes. 'God, we have issues,' I added.

'Major issues,' he echoed and at that moment, there was the sound of crackling, followed by a roar. We both rushed forward; I leaned over the railings and whipped around to face the mansion again. High on the hill behind the building, a plume of smoke was rising and below it, I could just see a few tongues of fire lapping at the air above the treetops, near Varns' Point.

'The beacon,' Kaspar breathed, a look of realization dawning on his face.

A sense of foreboding rose in my stomach. There was a reason the Kingdom was being called to court: the full council was going to assemble, and I would be there. I knew what I had to do at this meeting – the Queen had told me what to do – but actually seeing it through might not be so easy.

'I'm sorry,' Kaspar said. 'For everything.' He was leaning against the railing, his hands resting either side on the stone, his eyes watching the fire grow steadily higher and the smoke thicker and blacker – I could taste soot and the smell of burning filled the air, settling on my clothes.

'Me too,' I murmured, watching the fire as well. I placed my right hand on his left and he turned it over, letting his fingers slip between mine. Neither of us said anything and at that moment, the door to his room opened and a maid – Annie – slipped in, dressed in her dark dress. But today, she wore a black not a white apron, lined with emerald and emblazoned with the Varns' crest. She stepped out onto the balcony, dropping into a full curtsy.

'Lady Heroine; Your Highness. Your presence is required immediately at the council meeting.'

My heart leapt and Kaspar's grip tightened around my hand.

FIFTY-EIGHT

Kaspar

I entered the council meeting alone. Eaglen had taken Violet aside to talk to her – hopefully to discuss some sort of plan, because this lot would eat her alive. *Literally.* I gazed around at the thirty or so men and women sitting around the table, careful to meet the eyes of the more prominent members of the council. But there were two notable absences: Ashton and Valerian Crimson. Their chairs were instead occupied by Henry and Joanna, and the chair Ilta had once sat in opposite me was empty, ready for Violet. Either side of that were two empty chairs for Eaglen and Arabella.

Whatever Eaglen has planned better be good, I thought. I had a feeling of what he might propose, but whether it would be accepted or not was a completely different deal.

'We have enough men combined with the Sage to secure the border. No rogue or slayer will cross it,' Lamair declared in his usual aggressive manner. 'We can concern ourselves with the human government later. This is a time for defence, not diplomacy!'

There were several calls of 'hear, hear' and it wasn't hard to see that my father half agreed with them.

'Lamair, the defence of Varnley is my main priority, but I beg you to remember that the father of the girl is one of those in the human government. Not only is he a rash man, but we cannot run the risk of upsetting her. She is the Heroine, after all.'

Lamair was taken aback. 'Forgive me, Your Majesty, but are you implying that we should let the man who ordered your late wife's murder escape without punishment?'

The room held its breath. *Nobody* mentioned mother. *Nobody*. My father ran a hand down the back of his head and studied the ceiling, his face pained. 'No,' he eventually sighed.

'Violet won't want to hear that,' I muttered, leaning back in my chair.

Faunder, Charity's father, scoffed whilst his daughter scowled. It was no secret now that his master plan was to marry his daughters off to as many royals as he could. *If only I'd seen that at the time.* 'Forgive me also, Prince, but I think you are unfit to give impartial judgement on such matters. It is common knowledge that you are, how do I say it?' He paused, turning to smile at Lamair as they formed a cosy little faction. 'Emotionally compromised by the girl.'

I sat back up and rested my arms on the table, grasping my glass of blood to prevent them from seeing my clenched fists. 'Do your research, Faunder. I'm *tied* to the girl.'

'Yes, Eaglen did mention it to us. Is that why you slept with her? In that case, I commend you on your foresight, Your Highness, because you knew she was a Heroine long before any of us.'

I went to stand up but my father grabbed my sleeve and yanked me back down. *Don't rise to it,* he growled in my mind. I pulled my sleeve out of his grasp and sank back down into my chair, watching with disgust the satisfied grins of the Faunder family.

Sitting to my left, Henry, up until now just an observer, spoke. 'You have the promise of our best guards, who will be more than able to deal with the hunters and rogues. As to Michael Lee, I believe the best course of action would be to interrogate him by bringing him here—'

'Bring him here?' Lamair near screeched. 'To the very heart of the Kingdom? How foolish!'

My father smacked the bare wood of the table and Lamair looked like he might topple off his chair as my father turned to him, eyes ablaze. 'You *will* remember your betters, Lamair.'

So much for not rising to the bait, I thought. At that moment, the door opened and Eaglen appeared, followed by Arabella and, lastly, Violet. Chairs scraped against the wooden floor as they were pushed back in a hurry, everybody rushing to get to their feet. The women sank into curtseys and the men bowed, holding their positions as the trio rounded the table. Once they neared, I raised my head a fraction to watch her. Her face was beetroot red as her eyes darted from one person to another, taking it in. She was under-dressed in the same T-shirt and jeans that she had been wearing earlier, but then again, so was I. Nobody would question it. Nobody dared question it.

Girly, a Heroine. It still hadn't sunken in. The feisty human girl who I had stolen from London; the woman I had learned to care for; the dhampir who had faced so much, now a Heroine, about to face even more. The odds seemed ridiculous. But there were no chances with fate.

Her eyes found mine and I cracked a small smile. Her lips upturned at the corners but she looked too terrified to smile: her eyes were wide and her pupils were dilated, so large that hardly any of her peculiar violet irises showed. When she sat down, the rest of the room followed. Every face turned towards her, whilst she stared into her lap.

Eaglen nodded and my father continued. 'Henry, do carry on.'

The Sagean prince nodded and began to suck the tip of a pen. 'As I was saying –' he looked pointedly at Lamair – 'it would be easy enough for us to restrain the hunters and rogues, without too much force even, if they don't make this difficult. The rogues can await trial in either your courts or ours; the hunters, of course, we can do little about. Lee, as a human civilian, is different.' Violet's head, full of hope and fear, popped up. 'Unless he directly uses force or infringes upon your boundaries, we can't touch him because it would breach the Terra Treaties and that is something we cannot allow.'

Girly's face lit up as the room erupted into speech. Of course she wouldn't want him to be hurt. But she still had to betray him and he still deserved punishment.

'You might not be able to touch him, but the Terra allows us to,' Eaglen began, taking a long drag from the glass set in front of him. He motioned for one of the manservants to come forward, who filled it back up: one part whiskey, two parts blood. 'I have a proposition.' Father motioned for him to carry on. 'Provided the Sage keep any of Lee's accomplices away, it would not be hard to bring him here. My suggestion is that once he is here, we place the King and Crown's Protection over him and the Lee family.'

There was a great roar of objection and I frowned, unsure of where he was going. Violet's face fell and she went back to staring at her lap, fiddling with a loose thread on her shirt. I edged forward on my chair as near to the table as I could and reached across with my foot – the table was long, not wide – until I found her leg. I nudged it slightly. Her gaze shot up.

'Are you all right?' I mouthed. She nodded and smiled, but not very convincingly. 'Really?' She pulled a face and grimaced. *No*. I hooked my foot behind her leg and pulled it towards me. Not exactly gently, she kicked me as she started to slide off her seat. 'Sorry,' I added, hoping she would know I was apologising for a whole lot more.

How did I nearly let her go? What would I have done if they had . . .

'Let me explain,' Eaglen called over the noise. He took another mouthful from his glass, seeming unfazed. 'The Lee family need protection. Once news of Lee's deed reaches the wider dimension, their lives will be in danger. If we place the King and Crown's Protection over them, it will act as a deterrent to anyone planning revenge, shall we call it.'

Faunder's son, Adam, spoke up. 'So what if they die? They are traitors and it fulfils the Prophecy, doesn't it?'

Violet's hands balled into fists and her eyes burnt with rage. She leaned forward and glared down the table at him. 'That's my family you're talking about,' she snarled in such a menacing voice she could pass for a vampire, any day. A few eyebrows were raised, but Adam said nothing.

'Nobody beyond the innocents needs to die. Violet will fulfil that part of the Prophecy by becoming a vampire and thus denouncing her family blood,' Eaglen continued.

'That's all very well,' Henry said. 'But I still don't like the idea of having Lee in government. He's dangerous to us all.'

'Let me get to the good bit, young one,' Eaglen chuckled. 'We will instruct Lee to resign from his post as Secretary of Defence. If he doesn't, we remove the King and Crown's Protection and the Lee family . . . how shall I say it? Become dinner.'

I laughed, shocked rather than amused. 'But that's black-mail. Did you agree to this?' I asked, turning to Violet.

Before she could say anything, Eaglen cut in. 'It was Violet's idea.'

My mouth fell open, as did everyone else's. 'Is that true?'

There was something unreadable in her eyes and expression as she nodded. 'He'll agree to it,' she said, defiantly. I ran a hand down the back of my head. I had to hand it to her. She had guts. 'He might be family, but it's a risk that has to be taken. He can't stay in government, I know that.' Her words were not directed at everyone, but at me, and me alone.

Father leaned back in his chair, sighing in one of those rare moments he was stunned. 'It's flawed, but we don't have much choice.'

The talk descended into logistics – the general consensus was that Lee had arranged for the rogues to be at the borders at one o'clock the next afternoon. Nobody knew if he was aware of who his daughter was.

It was another hour before anything definite was agreed. Violet would stay within the walls of the mansion, despite her protests. Most of my family would too, save for Arabella, who would join the Sagean Princess, Joanna, and Eaglen, alongside some of the more trustworthy members of the council who had been charged with bringing Lee back. In theory, it would work. In reality, a lot could go wrong. We didn't know what Lee's plans were. We didn't know how he would react. We didn't know how *Violet* would react: she couldn't go soft on her father. There was a mounting sense of unease in the pit of my stomach. This had been too easy and I didn't like it.

'There is one more thing,' Joanna said, standing up as the meeting headed towards a natural close. 'As the Lady

Heroine has declined My Majesty's protection, the Lady Autumn Rose has requested the presence of Lady Violet and the council at court, in Athenea, as soon as possible. I understand that it is inconvenient, but we have the capacity to welcome as many as—'

Father cut her off with a wave of his hand, standing up. 'The court will spend the winter season in Athenea.' A wave of shock passed around the room. I stared, aghast, at my father. The court had not moved from Varnley since the Forties and even then, that had only been for a few weeks. 'I suggest you communicate with your families to inform them to ready themselves. We leave in two weeks. You are dismissed.'

Most seemed too stunned to speak and silently filed out. I remained rooted to my seat until one of the attendants appeared by my father's side, as he instructed him to inform the sizeable court of the move. Distracted by that and Henry, beginning to formulate more detailed plans for the next day, I didn't notice as Violet slipped towards the door. But my father did.

'Violet,' he called, not bothering to look up from the notes he was writing. She froze, hand on the door. 'You cannot leave this dimension and enter Athenea as a human.'

Her eyes widened. The meaning was implicit. She had to turn, and she had to turn soon.

FIFTY-NINE

Violet

I think Kaspar saw the fear in my eyes when he told me he was going to hunt. I think he knew I would sit on my bed with my arms wrapped around my knees, curled into the most uncomfortable position so I wouldn't fall asleep. I didn't want to follow him in my dreams, which was irrational. I knew that soon, I would have to hunt too. I had to turn. I had no choice now. Whether I wanted it or not – which God, *I did* – was irrelevant. But it was more than that. I didn't want to know his thoughts. I didn't want to know what he wanted to do to my father and I certainly didn't want to know what he had been thinking when he left me to die.

Maybe that was why as he swung his cloak around his shoulders, he caught my hand and said sorry.

There was so much to think about and yet he was thinking about *her.* Not that he minded hugely. It was better than lingering on the thought that in twelve hours, Lee would be within a hairsbreadth of Varnley's borders. It was not an event that he would ever have foreseen before the previous July and he felt a familiar anger rise towards the surface, which he didn't try to quench. There was no point trying to hide it from her. Lee was the man who had consigned his mother to death; he had a right to be angry. It was bad enough staying restrained in public. He couldn't do it in private as well.

He was thirsty but most of the deer had fled to where the Sage camped, drawn to their high-pitched laughs, which settled amongst the canopy. It sent a shiver down the figure's spine. The Sage might move in harmony with nature, but they were not of this Earth – no creature that could kill a man with one word was of this earth. The cloaked figure sighed. It wasn't hard to see why Athenea was the most powerful Kingdom. Nobody dared question their authority. Either way, he was glad he was not a slayer having to face them later that day.

But what he really needed was human blood. In fact, he needed the city.

A small smile broke on his lips. That's where he would take her, when all of this had died down. To Victoria, on the south coast of Vancouver Island, or the bigger Vancouver. It wasn't so far from Athenea. In fact, any city in the first dimension would do, because the humans knew about vampires. Some were willing to be bitten; most would panic when they knew vampires were about. There was nothing like hysteria on a hunt.

He stopped, realizing his thoughts were straying to where they shouldn't. She would be following him, if she was asleep. But he couldn't stop his tongue from gliding over his lips in expectation, especially as he glimpsed the white flash of a tail amongst the trees to his right. Only a rabbit, but it would do. Without making a sound, he etched nearer to the creature, which was completely oblivious to the predator until the light from the moon, creeping between the pines, was blocked by a large shadow. Startled, it kicked at the earth with its hind legs, making to run. But the cloaked figure stooped down and grabbed it by the scruff of its neck before it could get far.

There was a snap. *Might as well be merciful.*

I woke up in a cold sweat, half-naked on top of the sheets, patting the bedside table with my hand until I found the lamp.

Will I ever get used to the killing? I thought, struggling to shrug the dream off. I doubted it. I knew it was possible to not kill to drink, but it still felt like I was betraying my vegetarianism. As to drinking from a human . . . well, that was plain cannibalism. He could take me to every city in the world and I would not kill a human.

Yet you are worried about controlling yourself, my voice added. *And you have no qualms about drinking donor blood. What is so different about drinking from a human?*

I didn't answer the voice. What was I meant to say? It had a point and it knew it. They were all questions that would be answered when I turned anyway.

I threw myself out the bed and scampered across the room to grab a pair of socks. The floors were always so cold here. Icy, icy cold. *They will feel warm to me when I turn. So will Kaspar. Will I miss that?*

Knowing there was no way I would sleep now, I turned and started to make my way through the darkness – the lamp only lit the one side of the room. But as I neared the opposite wall, my feet tangled in something and I stumbled, hopping along like my laces were tied together.

It was my coat, dumped on the floor the previous morning when I had rushed back in. I shook my head, pulling the sweaty T-shirt I had changed out of away from it and dumping both on the bed. As I did, the magazine that Autumn had given me fell out. I scowled at the faces beaming up at me, all dressed in black tie. *It's all right for some.* But my curiosity burnt and I picked it up, examining the photos. I could pick out the vampires, gaunt and drawn; and the Sage, their scars bright and obvious across their right sides. But then there were others. They could all pass for humans at a glance, but there was something different about them. Their eyes were too colourful, or too large; their cheekbones too pronounced or their hair too fair; their was something ominous about the black ribbon tied around the arm of one girl and something wild about the eyes of another; and tucked in the hair of almost every girl was a black rose with white leaves – Death's Touch.

I shuddered and rolled it up, deciding I would read it downstairs. Flicking the lamp off and feeling my way towards the door, I managed to get out without hitting anything else. In the entrance hall, I settled myself a few steps from the bottom of the staircase, leaning against the banister and working my way through the magazine, page by page.

Sage, vampires, the Damned, wolves, shifters, . . . other creatures with names in Latin that I couldn't pronounce; all with grand titles like Lady or Duchess, Earl or Elder; all clothed in dresses with trains and ladies in tow, or suits with cumber bands and ties, inscriptions below each of the photos stating who it was, what event, when . . . all there, laid out like a fairytale concealed in gossip columns, agony aunts and articles featuring the latest trends in formal wear. I would have laughed if I hadn't been so worked up about what was to come.

My thoughts wandered to the humans of the other dimensions. From what I could discern from my dream, they knew about all of this. *What do they think of vampires? Are they accepting? What would happen if the humans of this dimension found out?* But at the end of the day, vampires were predators and the humans of this dimension could never know about their existence – they caused enough panic in other dimensions and they didn't even live there.

The weight on my shoulders grew heavier. I was a Heroine, but I barely even knew what that entailed and to top that off, I barely knew anything about the dimensions, and this was a world I was about to become part of.

On the bright side, my voice chirped in a tone so cheery I would slap it if I could; *you get to see your father soon.* That didn't seem like such a bright side. It just filled me with dread and mounting anxiety. I hadn't seen him in – I paused, counting the weeks back – three and a half months. I had changed. *Will he approve of what I am?* I mentally slapped myself. *Of course* he wouldn't approve.

I was yanked from my thoughts by the sound of the doors being pulled open by one of the butlers. Kaspar entered, his cloak wrapped in his arms, nodding his thanks to the butler who glanced in my direction and promptly disappeared down a servant's corridor.

Kaspar's gaze followed the butler's and he frowned. 'What are you doing up so late?'

'Sleeping wasn't really working out for me,' I admitted.

He bit his lower lip. 'I tried not to think of your father and all of that, but I can't help it.'

I shook my head and half raised and then lowered my shoulders. 'Don't worry about it.' I patted the step beside me and he came and sat down, slinging the cloak over the banister. 'Is this what it's like, being a vampire? In each other's heads all the time?'

He smiled. 'Not really. We keep ourselves to ourselves.' He picked the open magazine up off my lap and flicked through it. 'You shouldn't read this stuff. It's just a load of gossip and crap.'

I took it back, a little annoyed. 'I was just curious about the dimensions. Autumn gave it to me.'

He sighed, resting his forearms on his knees. 'You can see what the other dimensions are like for yourself when we get to Athenea.'

'I'd like to have some idea what the world I'm joining is like, you know,' I muttered and he chuckled as I pouted.

He picked the magazine up again and flicked to the back page, holding it up and arching an eyebrow. 'And Aunt Agatha is going to do that, is she?'

I shrugged, as if to say 'why not?' 'Besides, I've been thinking,' I murmured.

He wrapped his arm around my waist and pulled me closer, until my side completely rested up against his. 'Thinking about what?' he asked, the corners of his mouth upturned into a smirk as though the idea of me thinking was amusing.

I took a deep breath. 'About what your father said earlier. About turning.'

He froze. 'Oh,' he breathed.

'You'll turn me, won't you? I don't think I can face it if it's not you.' I entwined my fingers with his and looked up at him, my eyes wide and pleading as I felt a few tears prick their corners. When he didn't answer I lowered them back to the marble of the staircase. 'It's crazy, this. I feel like I'm betraying everything. My vegetarianism, my humanity, my family . . .'

That's because you are, my voice sneered, so callous, and I felt a tear slide down my face.

Kaspar reached up and brushed his thumb across my cheek, catching my tears. 'Name your night, Girly,' he whispered.

I pulled my hand out of his grasp, tugging the Queen's locket out from beneath my shirt and letting it rest on my palm. I could feel the weight of her legacy just by holding it. She had died so I would sit here, in her son's arms. So had Greg. My whole life had just been leading to this moment. I closed my eyes, letting the pendant fall back against my breasts.

I had promised my father I would not turn. But I had no choice. I never had any choice.

'Two nights from now,' I muttered, shivering. Deciding on a date cemented it. It was happening.

'It doesn't have to be so soon,' he murmured back, rubbing his thumb in circles across my hand, which he had taken in his again. 'You have two weeks before we go to Athenea, remember?'

I pressed the back of my fingers to my lips to hide the fact they were quivering as I fought back a flood of tears. 'I know. But I'll lose my nerve if I don't do it soon and I want to be in control of the thirst in Athenea.'

'You will be,' he reassured, wrapping his arm around my waist. 'It's not so hard, I promise. But do you think it's a good idea to turn so soon after your father is captur—' He stopped mid-sentence. 'I mean, so soon after he arrives?'

I let my head fall against his shoulder, appreciative of the fact he had corrected himself. 'I don't know. He can't do anything, can he? He'll just have to deal with it, I guess.' I sighed and asked a question that had been bugging me all evening. 'Is it wrong than I'm nervous about seeing my own father?'

'You are?' Out of the corner of my eye I could see him cocking his head, looking puzzled.

'You seem surprised.'

'I just thought you would be happy. Isn't this what you have wanted all along?'

I frowned. 'It was at first. I was scared and homesick and I hated you all. No offence,' I added, catching sight of his affronted expression. 'I had just seen you murder thirty men, after all. But at some point that changed. I don't know when. I just stopped missing my family and I stopped thinking of Trafalgar Square as murder and I stopped . . .' I trailed off as he leaned in, tilting his head to the side and pausing just short of my lips.

'Stopped what?' he asked, his voice so low I only just heard him.

My breath caught. 'Stopped hating you,' I replied and without hesitating, he pressed his lips to mine. It was only brief, but it was like kissing cool metal – I could taste the blood of the rabbit on his lips and I pulled away, shocked at the fact I *liked* it. He lowered his eyes but I raised his chin with a single finger, meeting his eyes, so bright and vivid, worthy of the most precious stones.

'On August 28th, eighteen years ago, you first heard your voice, didn't you?'

He inhaled sharply, his eyes wide. 'How the hell do you know that?' ·

I tried to smile, but I only managed to grimace. 'Autumn told me because I have a voice too. And I first heard it in Trafalgar Square.'

'My God,' he mouthed, running a hand down the back of his head, ruffling his already messy hair.

I nodded. 'The night I was born, you hear your voice. The night I meet you, I hear my voice. When I get here, I start following you in my dreams. If your mother had never died, you never would have killed the hunters in Trafalgar Square and I never would have ended up here. You should have killed me that night. But you didn't. You've saved me god knows how many times after that. Is that why we're tied? What does it even mean to be tied? I just don't get it. I don't get any of it.' I slumped against him, frustrated that voicing what I did know and did understand wasn't solving anything. *Why me? What do I have to do?*

He sat listening with a polite but detached expression, staring past me to the closed doors to the ballroom. I followed his gaze until my eyes rested on the black veins that ran through the white marble, thicker there than anywhere else.

'We're in a chess game,' he muttered. 'But we're not in control. We are just the pieces.' His voice trembled and a chill ran up my spine, like a ghost had passed through me.

'Then who is in control?'

'Fate. Time. Things we don't know about,' he whispered. 'We're not meant to understand any of it. So don't try and make sense of it. Just play along.'

'You make it sound like they are actual people or something.'

He shrugged, pulling me towards him as he stretched out his legs on the stairs, tugging my leg until I straddled his thighs, facing him, knees resting on the cool marble of the step below the one he was sitting on. He wrapped his arms around my lower back, his hands slipping just below the waistband of my jeans and tracing patterns along the elastic of my knickers. I felt a blush rush to my cheeks and my heart pick up.

'I've been thinking too,' he said and I could see his tongue running itself across the tip of his fangs as his lips parted. 'The Athenean court is a lot stricter than here. Morally stricter.'

I shook my head, not following his meaning. 'So? I can be good.'

It was his turn to shake his head. 'They have a different definition of good. Lots of things are considered scandalous that we consider normal.'

'Like?'

'Like . . . like how two people can't be publicly affectionate or sleep together unless they are officially courting. So, considering that, I thought that maybe, after things have settled down obviously, because there will be a lot of attention from the press if we're together, well, maybe . . . only if you want, obviously—'

I cut him off with a wave of my hand as the irises of his eyes were tinged with a pale pink. I half-laughed, half-smirked, and he pouted.

'Don't smirk, you'll turn into me.'

'This is too good not to smirk,' I breathed, breaking into an even wider grin. 'Kaspar Varn, are you asking me out?'

He grimaced and his eyes became an even darker shade of pink. 'I think we have skipped the dating stage, so I was more thinking girlfriend. But we don't have to publicly announce it right away, maybe around Christmas time—'

I cut him off again by placing my hand over his mouth and shifting forward in his lap, using my other hand to push him onto his back. I followed him, hovering just above.

'In a relationship with the daughter of the man who ordered your mother's death. How controversial.'

'In a relationship with a girl I'm tied to. How sensible. In fact, how *responsible*,' he replied, chuckling. I joined in. But my laughter turned to a muffled squeak as he pressed his hand to my mouth and started to roll over, the hand behind my back cushioning me as I rolled onto the steps. He appeared above me and brushed a few strands of my fringe out of my eyes. 'In a relationship with a girl I would have been an idiot to let go yesterday. A girl who breathed life into this place. A girl who made me feel again. How *natural*.'

My heart clenched and my eyes stung as a thousand different emotions hit me in one wave, overpowering the fear, the uncertainty and the anger at him for the previous morning. It was a mixture of emotion I recognized, but hadn't felt in a long time. And this was stronger. It was real. It was palatable: it tasted metallic as he pressed his lips to mine a second time. It was cold too as I wrapped my arms around his neck and he tried to press his entire body to mine; and as his hand slipped under my T-shirt, it was a jolt of desire.

He pulled away, his smile fading as he cupped my cheek. 'Girly, I—'

'Sorry, was I interrupting something?'

I sat upright as quickly as Kaspar rolled off me, flushing beetroot red as the doors closed behind Henry, who stood frozen and watching us, blushing too.

'No, not at all,' Kaspar said in his usual smooth tone, trying to discretely pull my T-shirt back down over my exposed hip.

Henry nodded, but looked sceptical. 'You should probably get some rest,' he said, looking at me. 'Tomorrow will not be easy.'

I nodded and began to clamber to my feet, reality feeling as though it was tumbling down to crush my shoulders once more. Kaspar stood up too, taking my hand and pulling me close enough to peck me on the cheek.

'Try not to worry,' he murmured, before giving me a little push up the stairs. As I neared the top he joined Henry at the bottom and both started talking in undertones, heading towards the main downstairs corridor.

Rest? How the hell am I going to rest? I thought. But to my surprise, as soon as my head hit the pillow my eyes became heavy and I fell asleep within minutes, head full of images of Kaspar and twisted dreams of everything that could go wrong the next day.

SIXTY

Violet

The following morning was grey but dry. A strong breeze had whipped up and as I perched on the bottom of the staircase, jumping at the smallest of noises, the cold wind kept rushing through the open doors, stirring my hair and making the hairs on my arms stand up.

My hair was washed and I had attempted to put make-up on, but my hands had been shaking so much that applying eyeliner was just too much of a chore, so I had given up. I wore a fresh buttoned black shirt and a pair of boot-cut jeans, both laid out for me first thing. *I haven't worn boot-cut for years,* I thought. *If ever.* I had been wearing shoes too, but Eaglen had told me to take them off because he didn't want anyone getting the idea I was going anywhere. *Anyone.* We all knew who that referred to. But all in all, I looked more presentable that I had done in weeks. I was pretty sure that was due to the fact they didn't want 'anyone' getting the idea I had been mistreated.

But I could look like the best turned-out princess – *the*

irony – and it wouldn't improve how I felt. Sick. Waiting, just waiting, was more nerve-racking than Ad Infinitum had ever been. In fact, it was worse than getting my exam results and I had thrown up that day.

I glanced at the face of Kaspar's watch: 12.40 p.m. The Sage, just thirty in total, would have taken out the rogues and slayers on the south side by now. I had heard Henry, heading out that morning, murmuring to Eaglen who was going towards the north side that he didn't hold out much hope of 'just immobilizing' them. *Blood will be shed.*

'Are you all right?' Kaspar asked, sitting beside me on the same step as the night before. He wore a black shirt as always, but today it was tucked in and buttoned up. He had even combed his hair. Mute for several hours now, I just nodded. 'Not long now,' he said, stretching his legs out. I was stiff too, but I couldn't bring myself to move.

The rest of the Varns had retreated into the King's study to wait, leaving Kaspar, the two butlers, ten or so of the guards of Varnley and I in the entrance hall. Every so often, they would stiffen and mutter urgently in Romanian to one another, before relaxing again. Once or twice, they directly addressed Kaspar, who would tense, a flash of red crossing his eyes. After a while, I figured that it must be when a slayer managed to evade the Sage and slip across the border. But they obviously were not getting far. In the back of my mind, I knew the death toll was rising.

12.50 p.m. The Sage would be working around towards the north side now, to meet Eaglen near the village of Low Marshes, which was where my father was waiting. *What if he isn't where he is meant to be? Could he have got wind of what we were planning?* That was unlikely because the plan had only been finalized the day before, yet it still worried me. But there were worse eventualities: the vampires involved might not respect the King and Crown's Protection; they could kill him. That was far more likely. I would just have to trust Eaglen. He wouldn't kill him. He wasn't that type.

Who will he have with him? Bodyguards? Advisors? Ministers? Endless questions bounced around my mind.

12.55 p.m. A particularly strong wind swept through the doors, sending the black cloaks of the guards billowing across the entrance. The green-and-grey landscape outside was draped in black cloth until the gust passed. The cloaks sank back around the forms of those who wore them, encasing their pale, translucent skin once more. I bit my bottom lip. *How much will he know about the Heroines?* I assumed he would know quite a lot, because that must be why he had chosen now; now, when the dark beings were preoccupied. *Or so he must think.*

12.58 p.m. The second hand of Kaspar's watch inched around, seeming to be slow enough for my heart to thump twice every time it moved. 12.59 p.m. All of a sudden, the guards straightened and their forever-red eyes turned not to Kaspar, but to me. My breath caught and I scrambled up, feeling my stomach knot.

'They have got him,' a voice called and I turned to see the King entering, along with his entire family as well as Fabian, Declan and the others; several members of the council accompanied them, including, I realized, with another sick twist of my stomach, Valerian Crimson. *I will never be rid of him.*

I felt a hand enclose my own. 'Just focus on what you have to do,' Kaspar murmured, untucking a chunk of hair from behind my ear and letting it fall around my face. It curled itself into a coil – the reason I had pushed it out of my face in the first place. I nodded and said nothing. *I should have straightened it,* I thought. *I always wore it straight at home.*

I forced deep breaths into my lungs. The clock struck once; the minutes continued to pass like hours. Nobody made a sound. The air could be cut with a blunt knife, tenser than the guards who lined the outside steps or the fingers of the butlers who clutched the handles of the doors, ready to close them and seal my father inside.

The gravel crunched. There were no shouts; no signs of a struggle, just the regular sound of footsteps. I fought the urge to dart forward and look out at the driveway. Instead, I looked at the Varns. Their faces were blank and they seemed composed. The King, catching my eye, moved forward and came and stood beside me, sandwiching me between Kaspar and himself. Whether he thought I was going to try something or whether it was some act of solidarity, I didn't know.

The crunching stopped and was replaced by the echoing clatter of several people climbing the steps. I let go of Kaspar's hand. As soon as I did, Eaglen passed through the entrance, followed by Henry and Joanna. And a few paces behind was my father, each arm clasped by a vampire, but they needn't have bothered. He walked calmly in like he was strolling into his own home and let his eyes roll over the inhabitants of the entrance hall, the corners of his mouth downturned in disgust.

Something inside me erupted as his eyes settled on me; I broke out from between Kaspar and the King, my duty forgotten as I rushed towards him. He wrenched away from the two vampires grasping him and pulled me into his arms, clutching me to his chest, even as he stumbled back a few paces because I hit him with such a force.

'Violet,' he muttered, repeating it over and over into my hair as he pressed scratchy kisses onto my forehead, his beard just beginning to grow back, greyer than I remembered it. I buried my head in his chest as we both struggled for balance. Out of the corner of my eye, I could see the King placing a hand on Kaspar's chest when he took a step forward, his lips moving as he mumbled something to his son. I closed my eyes, shutting off the scene, inhaling the scent of my father's pale blue shirt. It smelt like home: of freshly washed clothes and burnt toast and the lavender perfume my mother always wore.

'I am capable of walking, you know. But that doesn't mean drop me, leech!'

I tore away from my father like he was a hot coal. I knew that voice: it was almost identical to my own, only slightly higher in pitch. I moved around my father.

'What the hell is she doing here?' I screeched, my jaw dropping to the floor where a girl with violet eyes was scrambling to her feet. Her skin was pale and gaunt, just like that of a vampire and there were dark purple circles under her eyes. A colourful orange and yellow scarf was wrapped around her head, tied in a knot at the front, and her eyebrows were very fair, like they had been bleached.

'Lily? Is that you?'

She straightened up, assisted by the vampire who carried her in and very dramatically rolled her eyes.

'No, Violet, I'm the Queen of England. Of course it's bloody me.'

I took a few hesitant steps forward and then pulled her into an embrace too, pulling her head onto my shoulder. 'You idiot,' I groaned. 'You stupid little girl. You shouldn't have come. You're ill!'

She pulled away as two other men were dragged flailing and kicking through the doors, which were closed with a resounding thump behind them. 'Not any more. I was given the all-clear two months ago.' I began to break into relieved stutters, but she cut me off. 'Of course, you wouldn't know that.' She turned and glared at the King, not even a hint of fear in her expression.

'Scum,' my father muttered, directing it towards the Varns, as the two men, one of whom I recognized as the Second Permanent Under Secretary, were let down beside him.

I froze. 'Don't say that,' I breathed. He shook his head, blank, and I realized I was speaking too softly for him to hear. *Guess that is what happens when you're around vampires.* 'Don't say that,' I repeated as my voice filled my mind.

Remember what you have to do, Girly, it said. *Remember you're a Heroine.*

I reached up and touched the locket around my neck, feeling the coolness on my skin.

My father's eyes met mine before he let them slide down to the pendant in the palm of my hand. The lines across his forehead deepened and he opened his mouth to speak, but I got there first.

'Don't you dare say that.' I let the locket fall back against the material of my shirt, beginning to back away. Then I turned and walked away from my father and my sister, towards Kaspar, whose face broke into relief as a small, triumphant, even proud smirk appeared on his lips. Maybe I was imagining it, but the corners of the King's mouth seemed to upturn too.

I slipped in between them both, allowing Kaspar's arm to wrap itself around my waist as I matched him, folding myself into his side.

My sister's hand flew to her mouth as she gasped and my father looked from me to Kaspar, stuttering over his words like he couldn't comprehend what he was seeing. But then with a thunderous roar, he surged forward, only just grabbed by three of the vampires.

'You promised!' he yelled, his chest heaving and his face

becoming bright red, almost purple. The vampires pulled him back and wrapped his arms behind his back until his hollers became questions and then pleads. Kaspar brought his hand down to mine and gripped it like he was trying to hold on whilst we were being torn apart. I couldn't help but feel he was worried I might rush forward again, but I didn't plan to. On the other side of the room, I saw Eaglen and Henry exchange glances, Henry's eyebrows raised. I flushed.

'You promised, didn't you? Violet? What the hell have they done to you?'

I didn't reply. *What is there to say?* But I was saved from doing so as the King moved forward, stopping just a few metres short of my father, who raised his chin as the King neared.

'What have you done to my daughter?' he demanded. 'What has your bloody Kingdom done to her? Tell me!'

The King sighed and a chill passed around the walls of the room like a wind. I shivered; so did Lily. 'More than you can ever imagine, Michael Lee,' he murmured, yet I could hear him as clear as a chime in the still air. He turned back to me with a face splintered with emotion that he seemed to try to be hiding. But his eyes were empty of life or feeling, as ever. 'She knows what you did,' he continued, looking back at my father and gesturing around the room. 'We all do.' My father's eyes widened then and for the first time, Lily looked afraid.

'Is this your revenge then, Your Majesty? Poisoning my daughter?'

'That was certainly not the preferred method of vengeance,' Eaglen said with the slightest hint of distaste, although he maintained a straight face. He came forward. 'I suppose you are familiar with what we call the King and Crown's Protection?'

'Of course.'

'You and your family are under it.' He cut off my father's surprised response with a wave of his hand. 'It can wait. I suggest we continue this conversation somewhere a little more comfortable and perhaps a little more rationally, I hope, for both your children's sakes.'

Neither of them objected and with a wave of the King's hand, my father was steered from the hall, his eyes staring straight ahead in a defiant effort not to look at me. He was followed by the two other men; the man who had carried Lily in went to take her arm but she pulled it out of his reach, recoiling from his touch like a spring. She strode forwards before he could attempt to grab her again and stopped just short of me, the lines across her brow deep. A slight blush tinged the apples of her cheeks like they had been pinched as she allowed her wide but bright eyes to pass across Kaspar, and then the rest of the Varns, who were dissipating and following in the wake of my father and the King.

'Why?' she demanded, turning her attention back to me, her face betraying her confusion and I realized with yet another sink in my stomach, her anger.

'It's complicated,' I muttered, extracting myself from Kaspar's hold and blushing myself.

'Really?' she said, dryly.

'Yes, it is,' Kaspar answered, his tone as cold as it had been when I first arrived. At my side I could feel his hands stuffed into his pockets to hide the fact they were clenched into fists and that he was flexing them.

Taken aback at being directly addressed by one of the vampires, Lily flustered for a moment. 'I wasn't talking to you, bloodsucker.'

'My God, there's two of them,' Cain chuckled; strolling

over with a grin on his face like this was a happy family reunion. 'Same eyes even,' he added, leaning forward and peering into her face. She didn't flinch but blushed as bright as the scarf wrapped around her head, which Cain was trying hard not to look at. If she noticed that his gaze flickered towards the short, almost grey tufts of hair that poked out from beneath the material around her ears, then she chose to ignore it.

'Feistiness must run in the family,' Kaspar said. Lily opened her mouth to reply, as did I, but we were interrupted when Valerian Crimson also joined us.

'I believe you are wanted, Miss Lee.' He took Lily's arm and gripped it tightly as she tried to pull it away. Cain, who was closest, didn't need prompting and wrenched her from his grip as I tried to place a lid on my anger.

'Don't touch my sister, Crimson. Don't even look at her,' I hissed through gritted teeth, but he wasn't even fazed. Bending his back slightly to bow, he spoke with all the false civility he was so skilled at using. 'Of course, My Lady.'

Lily, torn between looking at Cain's hand, which still gripped her, or Crimson's retreating back, didn't comment on the title he had used to address me, but her confused expression told me she had heard. I was glad. I didn't know where to begin explaining, and knowing that, I was anxious to join the King and Eaglen. I turned to Kaspar, who picked up on my anxiety.

'They're in the study. We'll join you in a moment.'

Cain abruptly let go of Lily's arm, almost as though he had forgotten he still grasped her and I led Lily towards the main corridor. She followed, silent with her lips pursed. It didn't seem as though she planned on talking and I stuffed my hands into my pockets, feeling the chill in the air from her distance.

'You look a lot better,' I prompted. She had gained weight around her legs, which disappeared behind a pale orange woollen dress that hugged the beginnings of curves. There was a permanent baby-pink tinge to her cheeks too, which were less chubby and swollen than I remembered them. But the scars of chemo were still there. Her eyebrows were not bleached, but nonexistent, drawn and filled in with light brown eyeliner. She still retained the puffy-eyed look of someone who was utterly drained as well.

She shrugged and I could see that she was fighting to not let her eyes roam over the splendour of the Varns' home, where paintings and marble and old-fashioned lamps lined the walls, and the floor was so polished and smooth you had to fight not to slide over it. 'I finished the chemo in September. I go back to school at the end of the month.'

'That's really great. I was worried about you,' I admitted.

She shrugged. 'You look worse. You look more tired than me and I have the excuse of the chemo.'

'I have been—'

'Shagging vampires all the time?' she cut in, her voice full of disdain. I froze in shock, first at hearing my little sister practically swear and secondly at what she was implying.

'I have not!'

She stopped and crossed her arms, blocking my way in the corridor as I tried to carry on. 'Dad said this might happen. He called it Stockholm syndrome. I didn't believe him because I didn't think you'd ever fall into bed with a murderer, but now I can see I was wrong.' She huffed and turned on her heel, marching down the corridor with her arms still folded. I darted after her, grabbing her arm and spinning her back around.

'You have no idea what's been going on, do you? None at all.'

'Try me,' she challenged.

I took a deep breath. 'Dad ordered the death of the Queen. Their mother,' I explained, gesturing back towards the entrance hall, trying to keep calm and make her understand.

'I know. Dad told me everything when I finished the chemo.'

'And that doesn't bother you? Not even one bit?'

She shook her head. 'Why should it? I never knew her, did I? Besides, they're vampires. Murderers. And I don't know what they've done to you, but you sound like you're defending what they do.'

'I'm not saying killing is right, but once you get to know them—'

'I'm not going to get to know them, Violet.'

Again she marched away, missing the entrance to the King's study. The ballet pumps she wore were too big and slipped off her feet every time she took a step, the sound echoing around the walls as a 'flip-flop'. I waited beside the door until she realized there was not a second pair of footsteps behind her. After a while, she hesitated and turned, blushing and hurrying back.

I knocked and the door swung open to reveal the King stood beside his desk, large drapes screening the light from the windows. My father was sitting on the high-backed wooden chair in front and the two other men were perched on the divan sofa a little further away. The vampires that had escorted them in were gathered around the edge, beside the floor-to-ceiling bookshelves, which Eaglen walked over to and pulled a large, red leather-bound book from. He looked up and acknowledged our presence as one of the manservants pulled a second chair up for Lily and offered me one, which I declined, preferring to stand as my stomach continued to clench. Setting the book down on the desk in front of my father, Eaglen opened the book, flicking through the pages until he was about a third of the way through.

'You are familiar with the Prophecy of the Heroines, I presume?' He pointed to the page he had stopped on.

My father did not look down, resolutely staring dead ahead at the heavy velvet drapes across the windows. 'Of course.'

'And again I will presume that you are aware that the first Heroine has been found. It is that in fact that triggered your attempt to get your daughter back today. But I wonder if the Prime Minister knows about this?' My father said nothing. 'Well, no matter. What concerns you is that the second Heroine has been found.'

Three guesses who, I thought dryly. But my father didn't need three guesses. He turned around straight away and looked at me.

'But she is human.'

'Dhampir, actually. But the Prophecy states that the second Heroine has 'no birth', indicating that—'

'Dhampir? What do you mean, dhampir?'

Silence fell. Eaglen shifted, closing the book with a soft thud. The Permanent Secretary glanced at the other man beside him.

'Half-blood,' Eaglen said slowly, as though lengthening each word would lessen the blow.

'I know what it is,' my father snarled, pushing himself out of the chair and rounding on me. 'But do you mean to say you *contain* vampire's blood?'

I said nothing. He didn't know why I was a dhampir. I didn't want him to know and I pleaded with my eyes to Eaglen, but it was the King who broke the silence.

'Her Lady Heroine had little choice in such a matter as

the situation was . . . problematic and unforeseen. But we can talk of such things when time is not so pressing.'

The door opened yet again and Kaspar and Cain slipped in; Kaspar stopped dead as his eyes glazed over me, then my father and onto Eaglen's worried expression.

'What the—'

'Was it him? Did he make you drink it? Is he why you're a dhampir?' my father demanded, glaring at Kaspar. I shook my head, feeling a little desperate and wishing that someone would change the subject as I tried to press my father's hand, which pointed at Kaspar, back down, flushing again.

'No, nothing like that. Look, it doesn't matter so much, just forget about it.'

'Forget about it? How can I forget that my own daughter has the blood of murderers in her veins?' He turned away, burying his face in his hands. 'No daughter of mine would do that! So who are you? Who are you?'

Cain launched himself forwards, only just grabbed in time by Kaspar. 'Stop it! It wasn't her fault! None of it was her fault. She was attacked and that blood saved her life and she's just found out she is a Heroine and all you can do is hound her for letting herself be poisoned by murderers, or whatever you call it. What kind of a family do you call yourself?'

The whole room was silent, shocked at Cain's sudden outburst. I waited for my father's response, my skin starting to crawl with a feeling I thought I had forgotten.

'Attacked?' my father breathed. 'When? Who?'

I didn't answer. Nobody did.

'It doesn't matter. It's no big deal. It was ages ago now.' I couldn't tell him who. He would try and kill Valerian Crimson for what his son had done, and it wouldn't be Crimson coming off worse.

'Doesn't matter? Of course it matters!'

'Everything is fine, there's no need to talk about it, okay?' I began, trying to salvage the situation.

'No, we are going to talk about this now—'

'No, we're not,' I corrected, seeing Eaglen mouthing for me to go. I didn't need any encouragement and I turned on my heel, leaving the occupants of the room in embarrassed silence. Kaspar reached out towards me but I recoiled, just as my sister had done earlier.

'I'm fine!' I snapped, leaving the room to mutters of 'My Lady'. I bolted upstairs, locking myself into the bathroom and scrubbing my hands and splashing my face with cold water until my cheeks turned red and my skin tingled.

When I was done, I slipped out onto the balcony outside Kaspar's room, sinking down against the banisters and listening to the voices and footsteps of the people who passed below.

The grounds were bare and empty now. The warm hues that had ringed the mansion earlier on in the autumn had descended to the lawns, dappling them with spots of muddy brown. It was still windy and I curled up in the corner of the balcony, tugging the short sleeves of the blouse down as far as they would go and folding my arms across my chest. The hairs across my arms stood up as a bitter breeze passed through, rustling the piles of leaves scattered across the ground like a child crumpling sweet wrappers.

'Are you trying to freeze yourself to death?'

Untangling myself from the material, I wrapped it around my shoulders. 'No.'

'Your father is being difficult,' Kaspar said, coming and sitting down beside me. 'Reminds me of someone, actually.' He gave me a knowing smile, but I didn't give him the satisfaction of responding. Instead, I stared at the blanket around my knees, shivering beneath it.

'Did he actually get that I'm a Heroine?'

'Yes, but in all honesty, he was more bothered about, well
. . .' He left the sentence hanging. I pulled my knees in
closer to my chest and rested my head on the blanket, which
was already becoming damp from the specks of rain continuing to fall. *He is only being protective,* I told myself. But the
tone he had used; the words he had chosen; the way he
had demanded *who?* still hurt.

But what did you expect? my voice asked. I had expected
him to be angry over Kaspar and over me turning, but I
hadn't expected what Ilta had done to come up. I hadn't
been prepared for that.

'Will he come to Athenea with us?' I muttered.

'Who? Your father? Probably,' Kaspar answered. 'It will
mean we can keep an eye on him.'

I shook my head. I knew that: it was common sense. 'I
meant Valerian Crimson.'

There was a pause which answered my question better
than any words. Resigned, I nodded into the blanket.

'But Athenea is huge. You won't even know he is
there,' Kaspar continued in a more hopeful tone. 'And he
wouldn't dare touch you, not now you're under the Sage's
protection.'

I didn't doubt that. But just his presence was too much.
All I wanted to do was forget about it, but every time he
appeared I felt as though I was the dirt crushed below his
boot, pushed further and further into the gravel, like I had
been just a day before.

I felt tears prick at my eyes and closed them, burying my
face in the folds of the rough material. 'Ilta tried to kill me.'
A spot burnt in the centre of my palm. 'He knew I was a
Heroine and he wanted to finish me off. I'm lucky he didn't
just get straight to it.'

Kaspar growled. 'Don't say that. He had no right to do that to you, Heroine or not.'

'There'll be more like him though,' I muttered.

'No, there won't. It will all work out, you'll see, Girly. It's not the end until everything is all right.'

I didn't answer, losing count of how many times I had heard that. After a while, the rain began to trickle down the back of my neck and into my shirt and I got up, handing the blanket back to Kaspar and deciding to head back in. Inside, the room was dark as the lamps weren't lit; neither was the sun shining in.

'Your father wants to see you, you know. He said he will listen,' Kaspar called, emerging from between the voiles surrounding the doors. 'It can't do any harm to try and make him understand. And you're the only one who can do that.'

'He doesn't have to understand, just agree to resign,' I pointed out, leaving the room for my own to change into something dry. When I reached my wardrobe and picked out a fresh shirt, I heard movement behind me. I turned to see Kaspar leaning against the frame of the doorway, his arms folded across the chest.

'But he won't agree, which is why we need you.'

At that moment there was a curt knock on the door and I jumped, startled. Kaspar went to open the door.

'Oh, it's *you*.'

'What are you doing here?' I heard a second voice say: my father's voice. A little piece of me groaned and I let my hair fall back around my face. Kaspar said nothing and my father continued, his voice becoming more irritated with every word. 'Where's Violet?'

I took a deep breath and stepped out, noticing the distance between my father and Kaspar right away, as well as the glares they were shooting each other. Kaspar went to leave but I raised my hand and told him to stay. My father's frown deepened.

'Why won't you agree to resign?' I demanded, crossing my arms across my chest. Kaspar perched himself on the windowsill, studying my face and then my father's. 'You're putting mum and Lily at risk too. It's not fair.'

'I don't see why I should resign,' he replied, mirroring my folded arms. I closed my eyes, willing myself to be patient. He would have to agree eventually, I knew, but I would prefer it to be sooner rather than later.

'Because what you did was wrong and you're too much of a risk—'

'Because I put the welfare of the people of this country before the life of one woman? Is that so wrong?!'

I opened my mouth to reply but it wasn't the sound of my voice that filled the room. Instead, I heard the springs of the bed being forced down and then the strangled cry of my father as a hand enclosed his neck.

'Kaspar, get off him!' I cried out, dashing around the bed and yanking at his hand. He didn't even seem to hear me as his eyes became black from the pupil out, like a dark fire consuming the forest and pluming smoke. He shook my father, whose face was becoming blotched and red as he stuttered and gasped for air. His eyes roamed across the room like he couldn't focus until they settled just to the left of me, pitiful and bloodshot.

'Kaspar! Let him go!'

To my surprise, he did, leaving my father to rock back on his heels and splutter. I wrapped my arm around him, helping him upright again.

'If she had signed that treaty, your kind would have run unchecked,' he forced through gritted teeth. 'People would have died. I stopped that.'

Kaspar surged forward again and I only just managed to dive in front of him, blocking his path.

'Enough! Dad, shut up, and Kaspar, get out!'

Without saying anything he left, leaving me alone with my father. I walked away from him to the window, looking out towards the grounds.

'Lily should go home if you come to Athenea with us. She needs to rest,' I sighed, forcing deep breaths into my lungs. 'In fact, why did she even come in the first place? It's not safe here.'

'We weren't expecting this.'

'That was naïve,' I snapped. He said nothing. I glanced at him out of the corner of my eye. He stood stock still, his face still a light shade of purple. His shirt was dishevelled, as was his greying hair. It was so unlike him – he was always so tidy. 'Just resign. They're not just threatening to kill *you* if the protection is removed. It's mum and Lily too. They hate you. I can't even believe how civilized they have been so far, because you don't deserve it.'

I heard a hiss as he forced his breath between his gritted teeth. 'Listen to yourself. What have you become? Don't you remember what you saw in Trafalgar Square?' I turned sharply back to the window. Of course I remembered. *I will never forget it.* 'Men torn apart worse than any animal is slaughtered. Families left behind; they rape women – women like you – and kill children. Humans are not just food. They're playthings. And you are telling me you want to join that, Violet?'

'Whether I want it or not is irrelevant. I'm a Heroine and I have no choice. But, as you ask, no, I don't mind turning.'

'Would you say the same thing if that Prince was not around?'

This time I didn't reply and stared at the blotched patches

of green through the windowpane, as the rain fell harder
and the colours of the forest became one even emerald
shade, matching Kaspar's eyes. My silence answered the
question.

'And what will you do when he drops you? When you
argue? When things go wrong? Who will you have?'

Each question broke a rib, puncturing my lungs and forcing
the air out in rasps. I'd asked myself those questions, of
course I had, but to hear them from another's mouth, to
hear them spoken with such cool contempt, triumphant yet
desperate contempt, brought each and every question and
every uncertainty to the surface with such a force I found
myself turning and screaming at my father.

'We're tied! We can't drop each other! Fate doesn't work
like that.' My voice was definite, but in the back of my mind
I felt the first pangs of doubt.

'You believe in that stuff?'

I recoiled. 'You don't?'

'I'm not sure what I believe anymore. But I do know that
I want the best for you and this isn't it.' I sunk down onto
the windowsill, watching as the rain pummelled harder and
harder against the glass, teardrops warping into cubes of hail
that streaked towards the earth, hitting it over and over.
'You're my daughter and I love you. All I want is for us to
be a family again. Is that so much to ask?' I didn't answer.
'Come home, Violet. I was thinking Lily could have another
few months off and you could defer your university place
until next September, and we could spend the spring travel-
ling. Somewhere hot, by the sea, Australia, maybe. Just
name what countries you want to see and we'll go, I
promise—'

'Stop.'

'A-and we could get you someone to speak to about . . .

about what has been done to you. You don't have to tell me who it is if you don't want to, but—'

'Stop.'

Thousands of beads leapt back off the swelling surface of the water in the fountain, lapping over the stone walls. The grass was flecked with white, like a frosty morning and the sky split open with a ferocious crack, the grounds of Varnley lit up by a flash of lightning.

'No, I'll tell you what's going to happen. Tomorrow night, I'm going to become a vampire. Then in two weeks time I'm going to go to Athenea and so are you. But before that, you, Lily and those other two men are going to go home and you are going to hand in your resignation from your position and the party. Eaglen will accompany you to ensure it is done. You leave early tomorrow.'

I left the window, passing his dumbfounded face, splitting into a temper like the sky.

'Is that it? I lost my son, I almost lost my youngest and now I shall lose my daughter?'

I paused at the door, gripping each side of the frame with my fingertips. 'Don't you know the Prophecy? "Destined to betray her kin." That's how it is.' Even I was surprised at the hollow tone of my voice. 'Now don't you have a letter of resignation to write?'

I didn't hang around to hear his reaction. It was cruel, it was cold-hearted, but I needed him to resign. I couldn't worry about my family's safety as well as everything else. And more importantly, I wanted him and Lily away when I turned. Far away.

'Fate truly does choose well.' My eyes, fixed on the floor, shot upwards to see Eaglen, his tiny, frail frame leaning, quite casually, against the wall of the corridor. The impish smile of a much younger man was perched on his lips. I narrowed my eyes and glanced back at the door of my room, swinging shut and sealing my father in.

'You heard all of that?' He bowed his head and raised it again in reply. 'Then will you do it? Go with him and ensure he resigns?'

He chortled. 'I am duty bound to do whatever you tell me to do, young Heroine. If you were to order me to throw myself from a cliff, I would do so.'

I bit my lip. *Right.* 'Well, that's good. Not the cliff part though. That's not good. Don't do that.'

He continued to chortle, shifting his weight from one foot to the other and tugging at his beard with an amused expression of someone in on a private joke. 'I suspect Athenea are going to find you quite . . . intriguing. But I will ensure that all you told your father will be done. Good afternoon, My Lady.' He bowed and still unused to such treatment, I stood for a few more seconds before realizing now was the polite moment to move away. But I had hardly made it to the top of the staircase when I stopped, cocking my head to one side.

'Eaglen, just one question.

'Did you know all along? That I was a Heroine, I mean.'

'Yes, My Lady.' *I definitely preferred Miss Lee to My Lady.* 'I had my suspicions from the moment I heard the young Prince had taken you. When I first encountered you at the dinner for the council members, those suspicions were confirmed.' I cast my mind back to that dinner, straining to remember my first introduction to Eaglen. *He had stared at me. Is that when . . .?*

'How did you know?' Silence. I waited, but he did not speak. I felt my palm clench, frustrated that yet again, I was being denied answers. 'Well, why didn't you say anything? None of this would have happened if you had.'

'In a game of chess, My Lady, one has to make certain moves at the right time in order to win.'

What sort of an answer is that? I had been imprisoned, almost raped, bitten and almost killed in the past few months. Somehow, it seemed there was a little more at stake than in a game of chess.

'Then at least tell me this. What's going to happen after these two weeks?'

'Why, My Lady, you, along with the entire court, will go to Athenea, where further decisions will be made,' he replied in a flat, unemotional tone. I whipped around to face him, the anger in my face and voice evident.

'You know what I mean,' I hissed. 'All I want are straight answers. Why won't you give them to me?'

He straightened up, drawing himself to his full height – he always stooped so I never realized his true size, which left me feeling considerably smaller.

'And neither, My Lady, does one know of the next move in a game of chess. Now excuse me, I must attend to your father and I believe His Majesty wishes to speak to you.' He pointed one of his crooked fingers towards the staircase and bowed, disappearing into my room. I scowled at the spot he had been standing in for a few seconds before someone behind me cleared their throat.

'Your Majesty!' I dropped into a curtsey as soon as I saw him, forgetting I didn't need to, just as he swept a hand behind his back and bowed.

'Lady Heroine, may we speak?' I nodded and he gestured towards the door to Kaspar's room, which was nearest. A little hesitant, I followed him in. He closed the door behind me and I watched as his eyes glided over the contents of the room – first the wrought-iron bed, which was untouched, not used for weeks – not since I slept in it. They moved to

the closed French doors; the voiles; the drapes and the falling
hail behind, hitting the balcony and producing a constant
drumming. From there they slid to the grate of the fireplace
and the cluttered mantle, strewn with paper and deodorant
cans; and just above that, they settled, hovering on the great
picture of himself in his younger days and his beautiful,
kind-hearted wife, her eyes staring at the bed she would
never again lie in.

How long is it since he has been in here? I wondered. His eyes
did not leave the painting, his Adam's apple rising as he
swallowed hard, his hand frozen on the doorknob.

'Your Majesty?' I began as tentatively as I could, thinking
that this was perhaps not the best place to talk.

He turned towards me, looking like he had only just realized I was there. 'Forgive me. I would suggest my study, but
it is presently in use by the Sage.'

The King released his hand from the door and returned to
his usual manner, moving to the centre of the room in one
brisk motion and, I noticed, turning away from the painting.

'I thought it time that I offered you an explanation for
my behaviour over the past few months.' *Damn right it's time.*
'But first, Kaspar tells me that you wish to turn tomorrow
night.' I nodded. 'And he asked permission to turn you. That
is your wish, correct?' Again I nodded. He nodded too, like
he was absorbing that information. 'I think it best that we
do not inform the rest of the household about your chosen
date. And perhaps, to also ensure your privacy, it would be
best for you both to retreat into here tomorrow evening.'
He nodded to himself and almost as an afterthought, added,
'Is this agreeable to you, My Lady?'

Again I just nodded. I couldn't do anything else; I didn't
trust my tongue as a knot of nerves squeezed its way through
my gut.

'That is settled then.' He took a step forward. 'He also asked my permission to court you.'

I seized up. Frozen, like a wide-eyed rabbit in headlights, I held my breath, waiting for his next sentence. I knew that if the King said no, that meant no, Heroine or not.

'My son is quite devoted to you, My Lady, quite devoted, and I have known that for some weeks now. I have no shame in admitting that it was therefore a great evil of me to try and prevent such an attachment from forming.'

I loosened the tiniest amount, but inside, I was begging him for a straight yes or no answer – the rest could come later. He, on the other hand, seemed intent on explaining himself first.

He clutched his hands behind his back, beginning to pace between his spot near the door and the bed. 'Rumours began circulating about the Heroines months ago, long before you came to us. Those that believed the Prophecy, myself included, knew that the time was coming and that the first Heroine would be found sometime in the next decade or so. Although I never expected it to be this early,' he added in an undertone, speaking to himself more than me. 'Long ago, in the time that the Prophecy was written, my wife had a most extraordinary experience—'

'I know,' I interrupted. 'She met Contanal.' He froze mid-pace, looking quite astounded. 'I read your wife's letter to Kaspar. It was an accident. It was how I found out about being tied,' I admitted, feeling sheepish and trying to make my voice sound apologetic.

'You know about that?'

'I know about it all. I know you knew the Prophecy was coming true and acted out of love for your family, and to protect me and the Kingdom. I understand now.'

His eyes couldn't find any one spot to settle as he absorbed that information and I watched in utter astonishment as something extraordinary happened: he held out his hand for me to shake.

'I lost my temper, My Lady. I punished you and Kaspar for events beyond your control. And for that I am deeply sorry.'

His hand never dropped in all the minutes that I allowed to pass, and I knew that his determination was how he showed his sincerity, because Kaspar did the same thing – he never gave up. So I reached forward, and I forgave him.

A gale whipped up, passing the windows which shook in such a violent way that I could see the frames vibrating and one of the French doors burst open, springing back on its hinges and slamming against the frame, letting the fierce wind in. I jumped and clutched my chest in surprise, breaking our handshake; the King's abruptly hunched shoulders relaxed and he pulled both doors shut, pulling the drapes straight again.

He sighed and he was back to his explanation. 'And then in the early hours of yesterday morning, we were alerted to the fact the borders between this dimension and the first had been reopened, quite out of the blue. Athenea utterly denied involvement, claiming that it had been the first Heroine. Yet just a few hours later, the guards notified us that two Sage had entered the three mile border around Varnley, and were headed towards Varns' Point. Immediately, I ordered the lighting of the beacons to call the council, but it had the reverse effect. Only minutes after the beacons were lit, I received a note.'

I averted my gaze as he pulled something from an inner pocket of his jacket – a crumpled piece of paper, which he passed to me. I took it, smoothing out the folds.

'Do you recognize the hand in which it is written?' I

watched as he retreated to lean against the bedpost, looking every bit the picture of his son. I blushed, realizing what I was thinking and quickly redirected my attention to the note.

It was crumpled, but scrawled across the centre of the sheet was a message, short and to the point:

Michael Lee struck bargain with hunters for Carmen's death. Lee girl knows. Pierre will confirm.

It was not signed and I didn't recognize the handwriting: it was scribbled and half-joined, like it had been written in a hurry. It was unsettling to know that I was holding the same piece of paper that whoever had betrayed me held. It was more unsettling that they had specifically mentioned that I knew. They must have anticipated what would happen to me once the King found out about my father's involvement, which meant somebody didn't want me around. I swallowed.

'No,' I answered, handing it back.

'Sadly, you are not the only one,' he sighed. 'It did occur when I first read it that it was a hoax, but the dates of when your father's party was elected into government and the time in which my wife visited Romania correlated. Pierre confirmed it within the hour and the rest I am sure neither of us wishes to voice.' Even in the relative gloom of the room, I could see his eyes were tinged with pink and as he caught me looking, I turned away, pretending I hadn't seen.

'But you are a Heroine, and it does not do to dwell upon that which has been. I told Kaspar that I have no objection to his courtship of you, although I recommend you keep it a private affair at least until December. I see that you have given Eaglen orders concerning your father, and I am most grateful that you intend to remove him from our company until we leave for Athenea.' He bowed, but stopped when he reached the door, turning back with the first true smile I had ever seen on his lips. 'Welcome to my Kingdom, Lady Heroine.'

Just twenty-four more hours of being human.

SIXTY-ONE

Violet

The cold wrapped itself around my skin, caressing my sides and shoulders like hands. Drops of rain bounced off the stone of the railing in front of me as I took shelter in the alcove beside the main entrance. Like tiny shards of shrapnel, they ricocheted in all directions, some hitting my shirt, flecked with damp; I caught others in my outstretched hand, turning it, watching, mesmerized, as the drops raced across the curvatures of my palm and fingers before eventually plummeting to the ground. Puddles were forming on the grass, reduced in patches to mud as the rain fell as hard as when it had started, six or seven hours before.

'In a relationship with a girl I would have been an idiot to let go yesterday. A girl who breathed life into this place. A girl who made me feel again. How natural.'

I wrapped my arms around my middle, imagining his arms around me, his touch, his breath . . .

I shivered, more from the temperature than anything else, but I savoured the feeling. I wanted to remember how the night air felt cold, and how my toes curled so they wouldn't touch the frosty stone, and how each drop of rain on my skin felt like it left an icy burn behind.

'Mine,' a voice sighed in my ear. 'All mine,' it repeated, as arms clad in a black shirt placed themselves just above my own arms, wrapped around my middle. His hair tickled my neck as he bowed his head, his lips finding a vein and kissing their way down it, hands not hesitating to find my breasts, pulling me closer as I cupped his hands with my own and took an involuntary step back into his chest.

'You like that, Girly?' he purred, closing his fists a little. I answered him with a sigh as the air in my lungs rushed out in one breath. He chuckled and his hands slid down, finding the hem of my shirt and pulling it up. I didn't have time to react and in a second, he was holding it, leaving me standing in my bra and jeans.

'What are you doing?' I crossed my arms over my chest, very aware that the double doors to the left were thrown wide open to the night. He didn't answer, but grabbed my hand and led me out towards the strip of light cast along the steps by the lamps in the entrance hall. I only just had time to kick my feet into the pair of dolly shoes I had placed aside. 'Are you crazy? Somebody will see!'

'Let them see,' he replied, leading me out onto the gravel. He was too strong to resist and my back-pedalling proved useless, especially as he entwined his fingers in my hair, pushing my now drenched fringe out of my eyes. 'Let them see how beautiful you are.'

I stretched out my free hand and pushed his own wet fringe out of his eyes, stifling a girlish giggle. 'You do know it's raining, right? And that it's freezing cold?' I could feel my jeans tightening as they became soaked through and streaks of water raced down my chest from the tips of my hair.

He looked up at the night sky, studying it with a bemused expression. 'Raining? I never would have guessed.' Drops of water landed on his face, running along his jaw and down his neck, which he wiped away with a brush of his own free hand. 'But not cold. Temperate.'

'Really?' I shivered as I said that, emphasising how cold it really was. 'I must feel like a hot poker then.'

'As hard to handle as a hot poker,' he muttered.

'Hey!' I placed a hand on his chest and shoved. He moved, but I knew that wasn't anything to do with my strength. I took a few steps back and reached down, scooping a handful of water up in my cupped hands from the fountain and throwing in his vague direction. Most of his shirt was already wet but it caught his sleeve, plastering it to his skin. In a comically slow way, he looked down at it, arching an eyebrow.

'Really, Girly?'

Before I could blink, he had darted forward and splashed me. It knocked the wind from my lungs as it hit me and I threw my arms around myself, thinking the glowing light and relative warmth of the entrance hall looked very appealing. He reached down to splash me again and I scarpered out of the way, around to the other side of the fountain. He rounded it one way and I dived the other, but he soon caught up with me, catching me by the waist.

'Kaspar, don't! I'll catch a cold or something!'

Should have thought about that before you splashed him, my voice commented.

'No, you won't. Turning will stop anything like that.'

I groaned, relaxing into his arms as he steered us away from the fountain. 'What if something goes wrong tomorrow night? What even happens when a human is turned?'

'I take some of your blood, and you take some of mine. It's simple. Nothing will go wrong.'

'Yes, but what if—'

He pressed a finger to my lips. 'If you were very old or very young, or seriously ill, then yes, it is likely that something could go wrong. But you're not. In fact, you're a dhampir, so there's even less chance. So stop worrying.'

I made a disgruntled noise through my pursed lips. 'What about after the blood bit then? How long does it take?'

'It takes a few days for your teeth to completely sharpen and it will be a while before you develop hunting skills, but almost everything transforms in a few hours. It's amazing to watch somebody pale like that.'

'You've turned somebody before?'

He nodded. It was reassuring to know that he knew what he was doing, but something else, jealousy perhaps, crept in.

'Who?'

He shook his head, like he was trying to remember. 'One of the maids here, not long after the war. Anne, I think her name was.'

Something in the pit of my stomach fell away. 'Do you mean Annie?' Yet again he nodded. His eyes tinged pink and I didn't have to ask to know what had happened. *Well, that explains a lot.* I felt another pang of jealousy, mixed with guilt too.

'If something were to go wrong though, would—'

'Father won't be far away, and he knows everything there is to know about turning.' Again, I didn't know whether to be reassured or concerned.

'Do you want to know something?' he said, clearly keen to change the subject as he entwined his fingers with mine. He didn't wait for an answer as he placed my hand over the spot on my chest where my heartbeat was the strongest. 'I can't wait until that heart stops beating.'

I rolled up onto my toes and planted a kiss on his lips. *I could wait, but if there is ever going to be a good reason to turn, it is for more of these moments.* I rested my head on his shoulder. He had his back to the mansion and I looked up at the place that had been my home for the past three months. I stared at it, wondering how such a large, empty, cold house could feel so *right*, even after everything that had happened.

And from the top floor, a face stared back: the King's. His expression was neither kind nor angry, just blank, just as I thought his heart had been for so long. But now I realized he suffered, more than any of us; and a floor below that, a second man looked on: my own father. I didn't need to study his face to know that it was full of hurt.

I pressed my bare midriff into Kaspar, hoping they wouldn't see and glad the darkness hid my flushed cheeks.

I won't let any feud between them come between Kaspar and I. I can't let it.

SIXTY-TWO

Violet

All traces of the storm had disappeared by the next morning. The sun streamed through my windows, voiles thrown open by Kaspar to wake me up before he left. He had gone to hunt, because he wanted to make sure he wasn't thirsty before he turned me.

Today is the day. Today, I become a vampire. Today, I seal it all.

The hairs on my arms stood on end. My legs slowly warmed as strips of light divided the sheets I was tucked beneath; moments before they had been frozen from his touch.

This is it.

The clock on the bedside table read a little after nine. When the hands reached half-past, my father and Lily would leave, escorted by Eaglen.

There is no going back.

It could be months before I saw Lily again. I hadn't even seen my mother.

Tonight is the night.

I slipped my feet from beneath the sheets, cursing how cold the floor was as I pulled one of the sheets with me, to cover my nakedness. When it occurred to me that no would see, I dropped it, letting it pool at my feet as I picked my way through the sprawled clothes that lay on the floor.

So much for not being able to forget.

The mirrors in my wardrobe reflected every inch of my form: haggard, drawn, the cold making me rosy-cheeked – not for much longer. The skin was taut over my bottom rib – it never used to be. My hips jutted out more than I liked and my knees looked scrawny. I was thin: too thin for a body that had once been rounded and curvy. My skin was torn and bruised from weeks of torment and caress under Kaspar's hand. My eyes were wide, always wide; always fearing what would come next.

'Is this what you want, Violet?' I whispered to my reflection, reaching out and touching my glass shoulder. 'Truly?'

My reflection did not answer, but stared back, lips only parting as mine did to sigh.

Truthfully, want was never a luxury you were permitted to have, my voice said, so clear in my mind that it could have come from a real person beside me.

'I know,' I replied, turning away and pulling a clean shirt down from the railing. When I had dressed, I attempted to pull a brush through my damp, tangled hair, but it only left it frizzier, so I gave up.

The entrance hall was still quiet when I reached the bottom of the stairs. The butlers stirred from their stone-like stature when I passed, bowing. A maid replaced the black roses in the vases with fresh white lilies, pressing the petals of the withering flowers between the pages of a heavy book she had placed upon the table.

Nothing was out of the ordinary. Nothing had changed. Nothing would change, but me.

In the kitchen, Cain greeted me with a grin, laughing and joking from behind a tumbler of flowing red liquid, which swirled from side to side, staining the glass pink. His eyes twinkled as he asked after my sister; dulled when I replied that she was leaving shortly.

The apple I picked from the bowl was as red as the blood he drank. I sank my teeth into it, wondering if this was how it felt to sink fangs into flesh – but no, skin would be softer. I swallowed a chunk of the apple, moist and sweet, forgetting to chew most of it.

The digital clock on the wall read 9.26 a.m. I contemplated returning to the entrance hall. *I should say goodbye. But how do I say goodbye when I only greeted them a day ago?*

Lyla's beaming face appeared in the doorway, chased by a cheering Fabian, who chuckled and grabbed her as they pulled closer and locked lips. I saw them only as figures against a bleary background. Felix and Charlie followed, not far behind, and bowed. It slowly percolated my skull that they lowered themselves for me. Declan, late; spread a newspaper across the counter, his fingers tracing the edge of each page, headlines and pictures and columns merging into one black-and-white whirl. I found myself walking away, reminded of my first morning at Varnley.

'But you choose to kill people instead.'

The metallic smell filled the corridor, seeming to stick to the carpets of the living room like smoke. It filled my throat, drained my saliva and left me propped against the back of the sofa, clutching my throat and gagging.

A few hours and I will lust for the stuff.

When my breathing eventually slowed, I moved off in a daze, not convinced I was even awake. My hand rested on the door out of the living room and I froze, wanting to stay, to just let them go; forget goodbye, because goodbye was too hard and I knew that tonight, I would betray them, particularly my father, in the ultimate way.

But it wasn't goodbye for good. It was goodbye to the Violet they knew, who ate and drank and got ill; the Violet who would die before she had seen a century pass; the Violet who they had loved and cared and fed and taught for the past eighteen years. *That's all.*

I took a deep breath and twisted my wrist to turn the handle, allowing the door to swing inwards. I stepped through, seeing Eaglen first, then my father and the other two men from the government, arms grasped by the guards. Lily stood close by. She saw me first; her face a picture of sadness and disappointment, only outshone by my father's face as he looked away and refused to meet my gaze.

'Dad?' I breathed. I felt tears prick the underside of my eyelids every time I blinked. He did not react. But Lily did. She broke away from the group, dodging one of the guards that moved forward to stop her.

'I want to speak to you before we go,' she said once she reached me. 'In private,' she added, glancing over her shoulder at Eaglen.

I nodded at him and the guards. 'We'll be two minutes.'

She led the way outside, ducking into the alcove I had sheltered under just the night before. With a slight blush, I realized my soaking shirt was still draped across the banisters, where Kaspar had left it the night before. I picked it up, squeezed out the water and laid it out flat in a patch of sun to dry.

'That's your shirt?' Lily asked. I nodded. 'How did it get there?'

I stared at the ground, refusing to say it in words.

'I didn't think you'd ever fall into bed with a murderer, but now I can see I was wrong.'

'I guess this is goodbye then,' I muttered to fill the silence.

'Yeah.'

'I'm sorry I didn't get to see you for longer.'

'Me too.'

'But it's not safe for you to come to Athenea. You and mum will be safe at home. You understand that, right?'

'Yeah.'

Again we fell into silence. I wanted to stare at my feet, scuffing against the stone, but instead I watched my little sister, burning her image onto my memory, like I had the cold the night before. I wanted to remember the healthy glow in her cheeks that hadn't been there for more than a year and the twinkle of her violet eyes and the way she didn't seem so short anymore.

'Violet?'

'Yeah?'

'Do you remember when you were doing your exams and you told me that you would read me some Shakespeare once you had finished studying?'

My lips twitched. I had promised her that whilst she was having one of her chemo sessions the previous May. 'You mean that time I really annoyed you by talking in Shakespearean language the whole day?'

'Yeah, then. But you never did read me any and when I was really bored in hospital, I decided to read *Romeo and Juliet* myself because I wanted to impress you when you came home and so I could get ahead with my English GCSE next year.'

I tried to smile. 'Did you like it?'

She scowled. 'No. Romeo and Juliet were naïve and blinded by lust.'

'Oh.'

'I hated it and I forgot all about it until last night, when that Cain guy let me into the library and I found a copy, it. And it reminded me of something Juliet had said that I thought I should tell you.'

'Really? What was that?' I asked as I looked over her shoulder towards the entrance hall, where I knew Eaglen would be eager to leave. *Maybe I'm even eager for them to leave.*

'It's quite famous. You probably know it.' She looked up at me, waiting until my eyes slid back to her before she carried on. *'Deny thy father and refuse thy name; or, if thou wilt not, be but sworn my love, and I'll no longer be a Capulet.'*

Her words hit me like a punch to the stomach. I gasped, stepping back, the badly hidden tears behind my eyelids leaking out. 'Lily!'

'I'm sorry for what's happened to you. I know a lot of it isn't your fault, but you did have a choice; you can't have gone hurtling towards all of this without being able to back out.' She began to step away, tears now seeping from her eyes. 'You're going to give up being human for that Prince guy, so let's face it, Violet. You're more of a Varn than you are a Lee now.'

From behind her, Eaglen emerged, my father not far behind, as two unmarked cars with tinted windows pulled up.

'My Lady,' Eaglen called out to me, bowing and getting into the front seat of the car that was furthest away. Lily walked around to the back seat, pausing and looking at me with tears streaming down her face before she ducked inside. Without even looking up, my father got into the other back seat of the same car as his two men were pushed into the car behind. The door slammed on my last glimpse of him as his human daughter and without any hesitation, they pulled away.

Nobody watched them leave except me. My gaze followed

the cars as they weaved along the gravel driveway, passing one of the gardeners who swept the fallen autumn leaves into a pile; then around the one edge of the forest until they delved into the cover of the trees, disappearing from view.

I sank against the banister, falling into the puddle my wet shirt had created and, from far up the hill, I heard the crackling of a fire as the beacon at Varns' Point was lit once more, filling the air with the stench of burning.

SIXTY-THREE

The sun was just beginning to set when Kaspar returned. The Thames Estuary glistened under the fading rays, becoming a glaring orange sheet. Just above that, a thin strip of puffy violet clouds hovered, marking the divide between sea and sky.

I knew that dwelling on the past made the future seem bleaker, but I couldn't help but think back to the time when I would never have considered standing here, time running out as the falling sun marked my minutes left as a human.

I felt sick just thinking about it. I had already rushed to the bathroom twice that afternoon and despite not eating anything since the apple, my stomach twisted and knotted, threatening to throw up what little was left in my gut.

'I prefer you in the rain,' Kaspar muttered in my ear, rubbing my shoulders in slow circles. The continuous motion helped to ease the tension in my muscles, so rigid and stiff that my fingers could not loosen themselves from where they gripped the stone banisters of Kaspar's balcony.

'Don't worry,' he continued. 'It will all be over before you know it.'

I nodded, unable to speak because I didn't trust myself to open my mouth in case my stomach betrayed me.

'Violet, it will be dark soon.' I nodded and didn't move. He tried to tug a little on my arm, but my knees just wouldn't bend so that I could take a step. However, it was enough for him to be able to prise my fingers away from the stone and half-carry me towards the door to his room.

He walked over to his bedside table, picking up a red velvet cloth and bringing it over to me. It remained rigid as he placed it flat in his palm, unfolding the corners of the cloth to reveal a small, ornamental dagger, encrusted with emeralds along the spine of the handle. The blade itself was wafer thin and looked horrifyingly sharp.

I must have seemed alarmed, because he pulled a reassuring smile. 'Diamond-encrusted blade. It's for me to cut a wound on my wrist with.' He frowned. 'It will give a clean cut, which will make it easier for you to drink from.'

'Right,' I breathed, suddenly feeling queasy.

He tugged at his bottom lip with a fang, looking me up and down. 'You don't have to do this, you know. Just say the word and we'll forget it.'

'No. I'll do it.' I tried to sound defiant, but it came out as more of a squeak. Lines appeared across his brow and he placed the knife aside, taking one of my hands in his own.

'Violet, I want you to know something. My blood might give you eternity, but I can't save you from the pain of living forever. As far as I'm concerned, you're worth living all those millennia for, but when people go their separate ways or pass away, going on is as horrendous as dying. Do you understand what I mean?'

I nodded, although the mounting dread in my chest

threatened to squeeze all the air out of my lungs. He lowered his eyes, picking up the knife again and wiping it clean with the cloth.

'Then don't worry about it. It won't trouble you for a long time yet.'

He clenched his free hand, bringing the knife to the inner part of his wrist, tracing a vein. Without so much as a wince, he dragged the blade across his skin, drawing blood from a long, deep wound.

I knew we had to act fast: he would heal quickly and if we didn't do it soon, I would lose my nerve. So I pushed my arm into his grasp and he pulled it up to his lips, inhaling the scent of my blood beneath my skin. Kissing my balled fist, a smirk curled the corners of his mouth as he unfurled my fingers.

Unable to watch, I looked away and stared at the portrait of the Queen – watching us, I was sure, as oil and in spirit – as he bit down. I gasped, gritting my teeth to try and stop tears from escaping. It wasn't as painful as when he had bitten my neck, but it still sent a shudder right through my body. He felt it and paused, lapping at the blood that flecked his bottom lip.

'Violet, are you truly sure about this?'

I nodded. 'I don't have any choice.'

He raised my wrist to his lips again as I took his hand in mine, bringing his blood to my own quivering lips, swallowing back a whimper. But just before he began to drink, he paused, breaking out into his characteristic smirk.

'I love you, Girly,' he said.

'And I love you, leech,' I replied.

Acknowledgements

I sincerely wish I could thank each and every single Wattpad fan of *Dinner With A Vampire*, but 16 million reads boils down to a lot of people, so I will have to settle for saying that you are all utterly and entirely kaspary. You catapulted this story into the spotlight on the wide expanse of the Internet, coached me in my grammar, made me laugh with your crazy comments and after a year of absence, stuck around and proved to be the loyalist fans a girl could ask for.

Much love and gratitude, Canse12.

A special thank you to Joanne (blazing_dreams4) for so much: acting as an informal PA, beta reading hundreds of thousands of words, creating some beautiful artwork to bring my world to life, and of course, introducing me to new and awesome bands. Edmund is eternally yours.

No acknowledgement section would be complete without thanking my long-suffering family and friends: my parents for (finally) recognizing that staying up all night to write and becoming devil's spawn the next day is acceptable because I'm an artist; my best friends Stefan and Becky for listening to endless writer-talk but somehow managing to withstand vampire-indoctrination; and to Chris, for soothing me through the times I was frustrated, stressed and worried.

Thanks to my editor, Amy, who came all the way down to Devon to help me cut a massive manuscript down into a shorter massive manuscript, and ultimately, create a better novel. Also, for introducing me to vanilla latte and helping me to never look at stickers on books the same way ever again.

Lastly, a massive thank you to my agent, Scott, for being crazy enough to take on a vampire book and being an awesome negotiator. Scrub, scrub.